PRAISE

THE FAN WHO KNEW TOO MUCH
A KIT PELHAM MYSTERY

"Laugh-out-loud-on-the-bus funny."
Ben Aaronovitch, author of the Rivers of London series

"A dark, funny look at fandom from someone who really knows."
Jenny Colgan, bestselling author of *Do You Remember the First Time?* and six *Doctor Who* novels

"I loved this funny, intriguing, moving, bonkers story. It's a world I recognise and a must read for any fan of science fiction."
Sophie Aldred, Ace in *Doctor Who*, 1987-1989

"This is a delight. Nev Fountain's genre savviness, his sardonic humour and his skill at storytelling come together in a perfect storm of crime-fiction fun."
Andrew Cartmel, author of the Vinyl Detective and Paperback Sleuth series

"Funny, acerbic, ingenious… a witty, twisty murder mystery."
Simon Guerrier, author of *David Whitaker in an Exciting Adventure with Television*

"Revels in sci-fi nerdism, spoofing it and extolling it simultaneously… a murder classic."
John Lawton, author of the Inspector Troy and Joe Wilderness series

"Nev Fountain is a very funny writer. *The Fan Who Knew Too Much* is a very funny book."
Simon Brett, author of the Mrs Pargeter, Fethering Village and The Decluttering mysteries

NEV FOUNTAIN

The FAN WHO KNEW Too MUCH

A Kit Pelham Mystery

TITAN BOOKS

The Fan Who Knew Too Much: a Kit Pelham Mystery
Print edition ISBN: 9781803365527
E-book edition ISBN: 9781803365565

Published by Titan Books
A division of Titan Publishing Group Ltd.
144 Southwark Street, London SE1 0UP

First edition: July 2024
10 9 8 7 6 5 4 3 2 1

A CIP catalogue record for this title is available from the British Library.

Printed and bound by CPI Group (UK) Ltd, Croydon CR0 4YY.

This book is dedicated to Ian 'If' Fountain.

"The play's the thing, wherein I'll catch the conscience of the King."

Hamlet, Act 2, Scene 2

Extract from the 'Vixens from the Void' Programme Guide, originally printed in 'Into the Void' Fanzine #1.

CORONATION. (Serial 1A)

Transmitted: 18 September 1986

Recorded: Studio: BBC Television Centre
16-17 May 1986
Location: Brighton Pavilion,
Brighton, 16-27 June 1986

Arkadia: Vanity Mycroft
Magaroth: Emilia Green
Medula: Tara Miles
Vizor: Roger Barker
Captain Talon: Patrick Finch
Tania: Suzy Lu
Velhellan: Jennifer McLaird
Elysia: Samantha Carbury
Excelsior: Maggie Styles
Costume Design: Joan Peverin
Stuntman: Duggie Fletcher
Production Design: Paula Marshall
Writer: Mervyn Stone
Script Editor: Mervyn Stone
Director: Leslie Driscoll
Producer: Nicholas Everett

Synopsis:

The female empire of VIXOS spans the whole galaxy, ruled by the VIXENS. The peace of the empire is shattered by the news of a tragic accident. The royal shuttle crashes in a barren area of space known as the VOIDLANDS. VIXOSSIA the PRIME MISTRESS of VIXOS is killed, along with half the royal family.

The sister of the PRIME MISTRESS is MAGAROTH, who was already ruling in her older sister's absence. When the news comes of the accident she is expected to step down in favour of ARKADIA, third in line to the throne, next to her mother and her older sister BYZANTIA (who also perished in the crash).

To the surprise of many, MAGAROTH refuses to step aside and assumes the role of PRIME MISTRESS, claiming that ARKADIA is too young and inexperienced to rule, and offering tutelage to ARKADIA in the royal palace.

CAPTAIN TALON, meanwhile, makes a journey to the VOIDLANDS to recover the royal ship, and becomes suspicious that the accident may not have been an accident at all...

Notes:

'Vixens from the Void' was pitched by producer Nicholas Everett and writer Mervyn Stone to the BBC to fill the hole left by the cancellation of 'Doctor Who'. They summarised it as 'Dallas' meets 'Dynasty'... but in space!

The BBC was particularly interested in the idea, as Head of Episodic Serials Hugo Treadway had recently issued a directive to include more female voices in BBC drama.

Treadway showed the proposal to his wife for approval, who hated it, and pointed out it was written by two men. Thankfully for 'Vixens from the Void' fans, Treadway dismissed her strong reservations as his wife's 'moody time-of-the-month stuff' and 'Vixens from the Void' was commissioned.

'Vixens from the Void' premiered on BBC1 on 18 September 1986. A party was held in BBC studio

8 to celebrate the new show, attended by the cast, production team and the Head of Episodic Serials with his new wife, former personal assistant, Selena Treadway, who became Head of Sitcom Development the following year.

The opening episode concerned the offstage death of a character and the other characters' reaction to that death. The soap opera 'EastEnders' did something similar a year before.

The first episode of the series, 'Coronation', was given a larger than usual budget with extra days for location filming, as it was decided that generic exterior shots could be taken and slotted into subsequent episodes. The same practice was undertaken for the first episode of series two, 'Assassins of Destiny - part two', and all subsequent series.

The climax of series one, 'Assassins of Destiny - part one', was largely filmed in the studio because the series budget had run out at that stage. If the story is watched as a compilation, it is interesting to note there is a point around the fifty-minute mark where everyone decides to go outside.

'Vixens from the Void' was an instant success, with nine million viewers tuning in regularly for the first series.

However, in recent years the programme has been marred by allegations made relating to its inception. Accusations were made by several woman writers claiming they had been asked to contribute to Hugo Treadway's 'female voices' initiative by pitching ideas for a new sci-fi programme in 1985. They were invited up to his office on the eighth floor, where they were confronted with a naked Treadway, a bottle of chilled

Dom Perignon and a sofa that folded out into a bed. These allegations have been reported to the Metropolitan Police's 'Operation Mulberry' department (set up in response to the '#metoo' movement) and are currently being investigated.

PART ONE

PROLOGUE

Brighton, 2022

Pillows were stapled to the walls and the ceiling. Even over the windows.

The shed looked like the inside of a padded cell.

The occupant of the shed certainly looked like a lunatic. He had a rambling untidy beard. His black hair was long and fell in a lank centre parting. His clothes were loose and shapeless, as if some unseen authority figure had confiscated his belt, shoelaces and any sharp objects he had about his person.

But the shed was not a lunatic asylum, and Wolf Tyler was not a lunatic. Not quite. Wolf Tyler was a podcaster.

Wolf took a huge slurp from his coffee, pulled his headphones over his ears and grinned at his Special Mystery Guest, who was sitting quietly by the desk.

"Okay," said Wolf. "So, we're about to go live any second. We're just going to chat for thirty minutes or so, about your life generally, and then after that we'll really get into the subject and talk for another hour."

The Special Mystery Guest asked why the interview would be an hour-and-a-half long. There really wasn't that much to tell.

Wolf cackled.

"Don't you worry about that. I once managed to talk for two hours about C-3PO's right leg. Believe me, the time will just fly by. Ready?"

The Special Mystery Guest nodded.

"Fantastic. Let's go for a take. I'll do an intro. Just keep quiet while I do that."

The air was filled with a bass-heavy hip-hop instrumental; *Star Wars* fans might have recognised Darth Vader's 'Imperial

March' buried in the mix, but it had been cut into shreds to stay out of the clutches of Disney's copyright lawyers.

Wolf yelled over the music. "Welcome one and all to the *Nerd Mentality* podcast! I am your host, Wolf Tyler, and remember, in space… no one can hear you meme!"

The music dipped into the background.

"I'm here with a SPECIAL MYSTERY GUEST for a special episode! Now, I know I promised I was going to give you my definitive list of Top Ten Klingon Foreheads, and we will definitely do that, I promise. But this week we are completely livestreaming this episode, because what I've got just won't wait for all that pre-recording bollocks… Me and my SPECIAL MYSTERY GUEST are clearing the schedules for a scoop!"

He pushed his chair away from the microphone and howled an '*awoooo*' into the air.

"And have we got a scoop! A NEW FACT! An actual bona-fido thirty-six carat NEW FACT from an actual classic science-fiction series!"

He howled again and grabbed another swig of coffee.

"Yes, I know, I can barely believe it too! It took a bit of arm-twisting but my SPECIAL MYSTERY GUEST is here to tell you about this major exclusive…"

Wolf paused, gulped and blinked furiously.

The Special Mystery Guest looked at Wolf impassively.

"Ha. Um. Where was I? Yes, let me repeat that one more time – an actual NEW FACT that isn't on any website, programme guide, Blu-Ray production note or reference book. They will ALL have to be re-written, so in your FACE all you super-nerds, you're just going to have to delete that Word file and start all over again! But first…"

He leaned into the microphone and his voice dropped an octave.

"Do you get sweaty testicles? I know I do… So why not buy The Loin King? That's the all-in-one pelvic freshening kit, which includes ball-balm deodorant, winnet wipes, fuzz trimmer and gentle alcohol-free aftershave that guarantees no nasty surprises in your downtown abbey…"

Wolf paused again. He had lost focus on the words in front of him. He shook his head, as if waking from a dream. "Woah…" He tried to continue, but his voice was slow, uneven like an old vinyl record that had warped in the sun.

"Iiiii… don't use anything else to keep the horrible hum off my… errr… happy-sacks… So… That… That's 'The Loin King', formerly known as 'Scrotey McScroteCase'…"

He never got the chance to finish his advertorial. He never got the opportunity to tell his listeners about the six different scents available for the ball-balm deodorant or let them know about the thirty per cent online discount at Loinking dot com with the offer code 'NERD', because the Special Mystery Guest grabbed a microphone stand and smashed it in Wolf's face.

Wolf screamed. "Ow, what the-fff—!"

He clawed at the recording desk, as if reflexively trying to keep the podcast going, but he was dazed, sluggish. The Special Mystery Guest whacked the stand into Wolf's head again. Wolf paddled his swivel chair backwards in a vain attempt to get away, but only succeeded in hitting a cable and toppling the chair – and Wolf – to the floor.

Wolf flailed his arms and legs and struggled to right himself, but he couldn't move.

"Yrrrrr!" growled Wolf. "Nrrr wyre yurrrr…"

The Special Mystery Guest straddled him, wrenched a pillow from the wall and pressed it down on Wolf's face. Wolf scrabbled at the pillow feebly but his arms couldn't reach. His elbows were immobile, pinned to the floor by the Special Mystery Guest's knees.

The seconds stretched to minutes, as Wolf's struggles and his muffled screams subsided and his arms flopped to his sides.

The Special Mystery Guest stood up, gasping with the effort and the sudden explosion of adrenalin.

The listening audience of the live *Nerd Mentality* podcast only heard one more thing – the crash of the shed door as the Special Mystery Guest left.

1

Whenever she took the train to Brighton station, Kit Pelham always looked up at the criss-cross of metal beams that formed the roof over the platforms and thought them rather beautiful, like the drydock station for the Starship Enterprise (*The Motion Picture*, 1979) or the docking bay for either Death Star (*Star Wars*, 1977 or *Return of the Jedi*, 1983).

As the train nosed into the platform and the doors hissed open, a tiny shiver of excitement rippled up her spine. When she emerged blinking in the sunlight, she liked to imagine she was disembarking from a space shuttle and stepping foot on an alien world.

Which, in a way, she was.

From 1986 to 1993, the production team of the BBC sci-fi TV series *Vixens from the Void* decamped to Brighton for location filming, and this tatty stretch of the English coastline officially became the planet Vixos, the hub of the Vixen empire.

Kit knew this fact, and many many *many* more facts besides, because she was a fan of *Vixens from the Void*.

Not your common-or-garden fan, oh no! Heaven forfend! Not anymore. She hadn't been *that* type of fan for a long time. She was no longer *that* type of fan who waited in long queues to get autographs, or *that* type of fan who bought merchandise on the day of release no matter how much of a rip-off it was. And *certainly* not *that* type of fan who followed celebrity guests into toilets during sci-fi conventions just for the thrill of urinating next to an actress who once played one third of a crab-creature in 1988.

No, she was a *Professional* Fan now.

As she'd tried to explain to her Uncle Geoff many times, the job of a *Professional* Fan could not be defined easily. Her roles were myriad: interviewer at conventions, columnist for cult magazines, talking head on behind-the-scenes documentaries, host of DVD commentaries, author of twelve little-read biographies about little-known TV celebrities (published by Crazy Badger press) and presenter of her own podcast called *The First Cult is the Deepest*.

And, of course, she wrote obituaries.

* * *

The passengers spilled out of the train and scurried for the exits. Kit was well ahead of them, her *Mandalorian* backpack (a freebie she got from a launch party) bouncing on her shoulders as she half-walked, half-jogged out of the station.

Most of the passengers drifted down towards the coast to the shops, bars, hotels and beaches, but Kit walked the other way, deeper into the interior. Into the unfashionable end of Brighton. Where her friends lived.

Despite the blazing summer sunshine, she was wearing heavy platform boots, a black frock coat in crushed velvet and a patterned waistcoat from which dangled a gold watch chain. A pink velvet 'newsboy' cap was on her head, perching precariously on a tangle of bright red hair, shorn at the sides and sweeping forward into an impressive fringe.

Kit's look was very important to her. She tried to find an image that she thought was very 1980s (her favourite period in Earth history) but also slightly eccentric – studious but cheeky, jaunty yet authoritative. A bit of Annie Lennox, a soupçon of Cyndi Lauper… In reality it didn't quite work. Every morning she looked in the mirror she was forced to admit she looked like every David Bowie that ever existed happening all at once.

Binfire said the frock coat and the waistcoat made her look like a Dickensian orphan who'd just come into a fortune from a mysterious benefactor. But what did *he* know?

Even though she looked like Ziggy Stardust playing the Man

Who Fell to Earth looking for his China Girl, no one gave her so much as a glance. Because this was Brighton, where trying to outweird each other was as much a pastime as getting bombarded by seagulls.

Kit walked with a spring in her step, despite the sad circumstances of her visit. It was always good to meet with friends, if only for a short time.

Especially for a short time.

It wasn't long before she could see the sign for Hanover Parade. Some wag had scraped a 'G' between the 'N' and 'O' of the word 'Hanover' – with good reason. The whole street looked like it was recovering from a heavy night. The terraces had long since seen better days; rusty microwaves, broken furniture and children's toys littered the front gardens, as if the houses had been eviscerated and their internal organs placed out in the open as a warning to others. Crisp packets frolicked around her boots and chased each other along the kerb.

No. 33 Hanover Parade was better kept than most, but with its dead lawn and crumbling garden wall, it still wasn't particularly inviting.

The chipped front door was ajar and Kit pushed it open. The interior did nothing to dispel the impression of a student house: letters piled on the mat, movie posters tacked to the walls and homemade bookshelves (planks wedged between piles of bricks) groaning with paperbacks, DVDS and Blu-Rays. She skirted around a tottering tower of *Akira* comics topped with volumes of *Cerebus the Aardvark* and ventured further inside.

The décor morphed from 'student flat' to 'serial killer's lair' as she went along a grim corridor, through an even grimmer kitchen, until finally she was bathed in light; a modern conservatory had been added to the house like lipstick on a leper.

The back garden was just as scrappy as the front. Parts of the lawn were either yellow or overgrown. There was an inflatable paddling pool half filled with muddy water and sprinkled with dead leaves like a giant cappuccino. The pool was placed in front of a rusty swing, hinting at long-past hijinks. Lightsabers were lying in the flower beds, their plastic beams and handles bleached almost white by the elements.

At the rear of the garden was some faded decking. In the left-hand corner was a shed with the words *NERD MENTALITY PODCAST STUDIO* burned into the frame above the door.

The shed where Wolf Tyler had been...

Kit didn't know what to expect, probably yellow slashes of police tape criss-crossing the door, but it looked just the same as on her last visit. She guessed the police had finished examining the crime scene and packed up and left.

Everything looked so... normal.

In the right corner of the garden there was a rusty barbecue, fizzing and hissing angrily. A round-faced, shaven-headed overweight man in his fifties was standing over it, wearing an apron with *MAY THE FORK BE WITH YOU* written across his belly. He was poking at a rack of burgers and sausages.

In the centre of the lawn a young woman in her early twenties was spread out like a starfish on a tie-dye rug. She was wearing sunglasses, but that was her only concession to the heat. Like Kit, she was in unseasonably warm clothes: black leggings, black skirt and black pullover.

That was odd for a start: Freya was a Brighton goth so she never exposed herself to the sun. She only took the job at Forbidden Planet on the condition she stayed in the basement with the graphic novels and never saw daylight.

Wolf's death must be hitting her hard.

When Kit slid back the screen door of the conservatory it made a *shunk*. The fat man in the apron looked up at the noise, smiled at her and waved his spatula. Freya levered herself up on one elbow and pulled her sunglasses off, revealing heavy black make-up in the style of Daryl Hannah from *Blade Runner* (1982). It looked like her sunglasses had left rings around her eyes like a joke telescope, and in the circumstances Kit couldn't help but smile. Luckily, Kit could pretend the grin meant 'nice to see you'.

"Hello Freya."

Freya was so delighted to see Kit she hurled the sunglasses into the flower bed, scrambled to her feet and gave Kit a big hug. Kit prayed that black make-up stayed attached to Freya's face and didn't transfer to her velvet coat.

"Thank you sooo much," she hissed in Kit's ear. "I am sooo grateful you wrote that obituary for Wolf in *StarCrash*. Thank you sooo much Kit."

"It was the least I could do."

This response satisfied Freya and she did more hugging. It also satisfied Kit, because it was factually accurate.

Freya Grant was Wolf''s 'widow'. Not that she and Wolf were married, but they had been going steady for a few years. They had shared a room, a collection of first-edition Marvel comics and a bong shaped like a Death Star.

"You came," she said. "I hoped you would."

"I told Binfire I would be along."

The tubby man waved his spatula. "Binfire makes a lot of stuff up. We couldn't be sure. I put some veggie sausages on just in case."

"I do *not* make stuff up, Robbie! You mutha frokker!"

Binfire (aka Ben Ferry) was standing on the roof of the conservatory, holding a pair of binoculars. He was a ragged looking man in his fifties with a lumpy, shaven head, mad bushy eyebrows and a flattened nose. He wore aviator sunglasses, cargo pants and a sleeveless T-shirt that showed off heavily tattooed arms, thin but threaded with muscle. He looked like a GI Joe action figure that a sadistic child had put in the microwave.

He also wore a disturbing-looking necklace.

Ten years ago at the Birmingham sci-fi convention 'Phasers Set to Brum', Kit saw this strange guy strutting around the sellers' tables wielding a Nerf gun and striking action poses. Kit, being Kit, couldn't help but stare at the string of ears threaded around the man's neck.

Binfire noticed her stare, and Binfire being Binfire, just looked her straight in the eye, grinned madly and said:

"You like my necklace, pilgrim?"

"Erm, very nice. I like the… ears."

Binfire had pulled the necklace away from his throat and thrust it into her line of sight so Kit could see the ears were made of rubber.

"Each one of these ears is a battle trophy. I fight Trekkies at conventions. I don't like Trekkies. Every fight I win, I take their Vulcan ears and add them to my collection." He pointed to a pair of large brown ears. "Look, I've even got a pair of Klingons."

"Why don't you like Trekkies?"

Binfire slapped his forehead. "Because Starfleet glorifies the neoliberal American industrial military complex." He shrugged. "*And* I'm a recovering alcoholic and I think all Federation starships look like bottle openers."

At that moment Kit knew she had to be friends with Binfire – there was no alternative. Through Binfire she met Robbie, and through Robbie she met Freya, and through Freya she met Wolf, and through Wolf she met Victor. And when Victor bought 33 Hanover Parade and her friends moved in together, she was happy to visit, as long as she didn't have to stay *too* long.

Binfire saluted and waved his binoculars. "I had eyeballs on you, pilgrim. I was watching you make your journey with my night-vision goggles."

Kit craned her head up. "It's not night time."

He patted the binoculars. "They've got a day setting."

"By 'day setting' you mean an 'off' switch?"

Binfire grinned. "Nothing gets past you, pilgrim."

He clambered halfway down the drainpipe and dropped the rest of the way onto the patio. He leapt up and aimed a few playful jabs in the vicinity of her solar plexus, causing Kit to flinch. Then he held out a palm, inviting a high-five. When Kit started to reciprocate, Binfire snatched his hand away and lunged forward, holding Kit's face by her cheeks and licking her nose.

Kit spluttered, screwing up her eyes. "Ewww! You are disgusting!"

Binfire put his hands on his hips. "That's my new post-Covid greeting. Now it's your turn to lick *my* face."

"I'm not licking your face! You'd be like one of those South American toads! I'll be hallucinating for months!"

Kit put up her hands to wipe her face and then stopped, realising it would mean her hands touching Binfire's saliva. She was paralysed with disgust until someone sidled up to her and pressed a handkerchief into her hand. "Here you go, mate."

"Thanks."

"Sorry Kit, I should have warned you about Binfire's new greeting."

The owner of the handkerchief was Victor, Robbie's boyfriend. He had a long, sort-of-handsome face with prominent cheekbones, and curly orange hair clung on to his scalp like a fuzzy crash helmet. His slender form was enveloped in a suit that looked slightly too big for him. He was younger than Binfire and Robbie, closer to Kit's age – Kit was nearly thirty.

She rubbed her face with the handkerchief and tried to return it to Victor, who held up his hands in surrender. "No thanks. I think we'd better burn it like we did his mattress."

Binfire huffed. "He always brings up the mattress."

"It was disgusting, mate."

'Mate' was Victor's well-worn term of affection. Kit suspected he used it a lot in the office when he didn't know the names of his colleagues.

"I was trying to grow a new form of life out of my sweat. And you destroyed my experiment."

"Damn right I did. Have you showered today? Because you did promise…"

"No way. I did *not* promise."

"I'm not getting in that shed with you if you haven't showered."

"Yeah, I frokkin' showered, alright?"

When Kit was at university, she observed that people thrown together in shared accommodation often fell into pseudo family groups. The inhabitants of 33 Hanover Parade were no different.

Victor was obviously the 'dad' and he self-consciously lived up to that role. He always wore a suit, even when he was at home. It was his statement, just like Kit's velvet outfit, and the statement was: *Yes, I live with these lunatics, but let's not forget I'm the one paying the mortgage on this house. I have a job, and a good one – I'm a senior administrator at a very prestigious hospital trust. Let's not forget that.*

It was no surprise to Kit that it was Robbie standing over the barbeque with the novelty apron, because Robbie was definitely the 'mum' of the family. He organised the laundry, the cleaning rotas, the food shops, and was always first to slip on the Marigolds and put his hands in the sink.

Nervous energy came off Robbie in waves, as if perpetually aware that his boyfriend was younger, better looking and had the ability to leave him at any moment. Kit often felt strong Joe Orton/Kenneth Halliwell vibes in the way Victor and Robbie quarrelled, and half-expected a middle-of-the-night phone call to tell her that Robbie had gone mad and caved Victor's head in with a hammer.

Perhaps I shouldn't be thinking these kinds of thoughts now. Not actually the right time to imagine another murder in 33 Hanover Parade.

Freya was the good daughter, an ineffectual dreamy soul who thought the best of everybody. Goth on the outside, hippie on the inside. Binfire was the unruly son, with the metaphorical catapult in his back pocket.

And Wolf?

What role had Wolf taken in this family unit?

Wolf was many things: the racist grandfather in the attic, the sinister uncle, the boyfriend the parents disapproved of. The one living in the house on sufferance because he was dating Freya.

The one who was difficult to like.

Kit had felt little surprise on hearing of Wolf's death. *It was just a matter of time.* That was what she thought when she'd heard the news. She was embarrassed at how little sadness she felt, but it was an incontrovertible fact: Wolf was a man who had measured success by how many people he pissed off on any given day.

Lost in dark thoughts, Kit was caught off-balance when Victor spoke.

"I guess now you're here we can start?"

"What? Oh yes, of course."

"Give her a chance, Victor." Robbie put his hands on his hips, watching his barbeque spit and snarl. "She's only just got in the door. Let her get a drink and a veggie sausage."

Victor gave a sideways glance at Kit. "Be honest, mate. Do you want a drink and a veggie sausage?"

"If I'm honest, I'd like to get straight on to recording the podcast."

"I knew you'd say that." He grinned at Robbie. "I knew she'd say that."

Robbie pulled a mirthless smirk. "Bully for you, Doctor Strange."

"Shall we start, then?"

Freya was waiting at the door of the shed.

"Sure, let's do it."

2

So. The shed.

Freya, Victor and Robbie went inside, but Kit hesitated. Binfire slapped her on the back.

"Don't worry about it, pilgrim. They took the body away weeks ago."

The place felt different somehow. Darker. As they squeezed round the table and stared at each other, Kit was uncomfortably reminded of a séance.

Freya put the earphones on her head and asked her guests for level. They dutifully talked nonsense into their microphones for a few seconds, then Freya activated the hip-hop-not-quite-Darth-Vader-Imperial-March theme tune and whispered sadly into the microphone.

"Hello everyone… Sooo glad to welcome you to the *Nerd Mentality* podcast. I'm Freya Grant, sitting in Wolf's chair, where he has sat so many times for this podcast. You probably know me, as I have been a guest on this show many, many times, but for those who don't, I was Wolf's lives-partner and soulmate."

She swallowed hard and fanned her face, as if trying to dry non-existent tears. Robbie leaned forward and gave a comforting pat on her elbow.

"It's been three weeks since Wolf's last fateful broadcast and I – we – have had hundreds of lovely emails sending their love and support. Sooo lovely. And also asking about the future of *Nerd Mentality*. Well, that's a decision for another day. For the moment it's just me, and I'm here to take this opportunity to commemorate the life and works of Owen 'Wolf' Tyler. Cult hero, podcaster extraordinaire and… the man I loved sooo much."

The guests made sympathetic noises.

"But before we begin…"

Freya picked up a piece of paper and started to read in a hollowed-out, tearful drone. "Do you get sweaty testicles? I know I do. So why not buy The Loin King? That's the all-in-one pelvic freshening kit, which includes ball-balming deodorant, winnet wipes, fuzz trimmer and gentle alcohol-free aftershave that guarantees no nasty surprises in your downtown abbey… I don't use anything else to keep the hum off my happy-sacks…"

Binfire surrendered to giggles, ending in a snort of amusement, his nose exploding with snot. He wiped it with the back of his hand, still sniggering.

Robbie harrumphed.

"I'm sorry, Freya, but do we have to do the advert? This is a respectful tribute edition for Wolf, after all."

Freya stopped, put the paper down and sighed. "They insisted. The sponsors were not happy that Wolf was slurring his words when he read out their advertisement last time."

Robbie was outraged. "He was being murdered! His murderer had spiked his coffee with ketamine and he was losing consciousness, for crying out loud! Then he got smothered with one of his own noise-cancelling pillows!"

"Yes, I did point that out. But they said that was the reason why they want us to repeat it. The say the fact he was being murdered while doing their advert brought negative connotations to the Loin King brand."

"I guess we should start again," said Victor.

"Don't worry," sighed Freya. "I'll go from the start of the advert. I'll edit it together."

Freya read the script again and everyone listened in tense silence with one wary eye on Binfire, in the knowledge that if anyone so much as tittered, they would have to do it all over again.

Finally the torture was over and Freya put the paper down.

"To start the tribute I've taken the opportunity to put together some montages of best bits, so we can be reminded, one more time, of Wolf's genius."

She pressed a key and the air trembled with Wolf's voice, played at an indecent level. Lots and lots of clips of him being a bit cheeky to interviewees, sharing gossip and honking with laughter with his guests about terrible superhero movies.

Kit was unimpressed. Not really what *she* would call a 'genius'.

More clips followed, more bits of interviews, crank calls to bemused celebrities from old TV shows, more gossip and in-jokes with his guests. The seconds stretched into minutes. Then came the chat. The anecdotes about Wolf being a great bloke, even though Kit knew he was nothing of the sort.

Kit soon found her mind wandering.

If a podcaster gets killed in the middle of a podcast and no one listens to it, does it really make a sound? And when goths mourn, how can we tell? Shouldn't Freya be wearing bright yellow trousers and a luminous kaftan?

* * *

"...thanks for your great obituary in *StarCrash*."

Kit suddenly realised Freya was talking to her.

"When you were writing it, did you find anything interesting about him that his fans wouldn't know about?"

Kit's mind was a blank. In her research she hadn't found anything about Wolf she didn't know already.

"Not... really. I... think we all know that with Wolf, what you saw was what you got."

Everyone nodded approvingly at this comment.

"Perhaps we'd better address all the speculation as to his murder," said Robbie in a portentous voice.

Freya winced. "Do we have to? It's *sooo* distasteful."

"Sadly, I think we do, Freya. It's getting pretty ugly out there. I've looked at the websites – they know who they are – and there've been a lot of silly rumours flying around fandom, and I think the police are getting a lot of calls from 'amateur sleuths'." He did the air quotes. "So I think it's only fair to them that we quash some of the wilder theories."

Robbie enumerated them on his fingers. "Hello listeners. Can I say to all of you out there, once and for all, that there is *no* evidence to the rumours that Wolf was choked to death by his priceless Boba Fett doll with the spring-loaded rocket that was removed from sale because it was a choking hazard."

Binfire sniggered in a way that suggested he was the one who started the rumour.

Robbie continued. "Neither is there *any* evidence that Wolf's murderer was a vengeful celebrity who got annoyed by one of his prank phone-calls and hired someone to kill him. Mentioning no names… And there is *absolutely* no evidence that he was killed by a rival podcaster, and *certainly* no evidence that he was murdered by anyone close to him."

Like many cult TV fans, Kit had a pedant monster. A tiny grumbling creature that sat on her shoulder and whispered things in her ear.

'Oho! Oft recited myth alert!' it would say to her. Or: 'Methinks I think you'll find that is nothing more than erroneous hearsay packaged as a truism.' Or even: 'You cannot leave this keyboard until you squish this King of Lies and salt the ground so that he or she never darkens this internet forum again.'

Now she had been elevated to 'professional fan' status, Kit was proud that she had caged the pedant monster. For example, when interviewing stars at conventions she never fact-checked them when they were recounting dusty anecdotes. As long as *she* knew the truth of events, there was no need to embarrass them on their faulty memories.

But occasionally, on rare occasions when her guard was down, the pedant monster broke free.

An occasion like now.

"That's not strictly true," said Kit.

Robbie looked at her, askance. "What?"

"When you said there's no evidence that he was killed by someone close to him, that's not strictly true."

"I don't get you."

"Binfire called me – he told me they took fingerprints and DNA swabs from all of you, to eliminate you from their enquiries."

"Yeah! It was frokking brilliant." Binfire was very chuffed. "We are so on file in a warehouse somewhere. They could clone us if they wanted to."

Kit continued. "He told me they only found your fingerprints and DNA."

"Well, obviously," said Victor. "We live here."

"I know that. I'm just saying that the evidence – such as it is – points to someone in this house."

"Are you serious?" spluttered Robbie. "Are you accusing one of us of murder?"

"Kit's just doing her pedantic thing, Robbie," said Victor. "Keep calm, mate."

"Keep calm?" Robbie's voice went up another octave. "She accuses one of us of murdering Wolf and you want me to keep calm?"

"I'm not accusing anyone. I don't believe any one of you killed Wolf – not for a second. I'm just saying it's inaccurate to say there's no evidence that someone close to him killed him."

Binfire leaned into the microphone and hissed in a sepulchral whisper, "Perhaps one of us *did* kill him…"

"Binfire, mate. Just stop," said Victor.

"Robbie, man, you were always moaning about you and Victor having the second-biggest bedroom in the house. If you killed him, you could move in and put Freya in the boxroom!"

There was a squeal from Robbie's chair as he stood up, quivering with indignation. "You take that back!"

"Sit down, Robbie," said Victor wearily.

"Not until he takes that back!"

Robbie jabbed his finger at Binfire, and Binfire gave a grin, sliding lower in his chair. Kit suddenly realised they were in the middle of the 'furious blonde woman yells at smug cat' meme.

"He's just provoking you, as usual. And it worked. As usual. He doesn't mean it."

Binfire was indignant. "Who says I don't mean it?"

"Don't say you mean it," sniffled Freya. "It's all too horrible to think about."

Victor leaned across the table, the harsh overhead light bathing his face in yellow and making him look like a zombie. He gave Binfire a cold, withering glance. "You know it doesn't make sense, Binfire, mate, so don't say it."

"Why doesn't it make sense?"

"Firstly, it's *my* house, and I gave Freya and Wolf that room myself, because I didn't want our room to look out onto the street. There's no way Robbie and I would want to move in there."

Robbie crossed his arms and sniffed. Obviously that was an argument for another day.

"And secondly, and most importantly… Wolf said over and over that he was with a SPECIAL MYSTERY GUEST. You heard the podcast – what there was of it. That's who killed him. I hardly think any of us qualifies as a special mystery guest, do you?'

"Oh yeah." Binfire looked disappointed.

"Precisely," sighed Victor, rolling his eyes. "We all appeared on his podcast hundreds of times. None of us are special, and we definitely don't qualify as mysterious. It has to be someone from outside."

"I hadn't thought of that. Sorry, Robbie – as you were."

Robbie sank slowly back into his seat. Calm descended.

"Fine," said Robbie stiffly. "I accept your apology."

"I think the stress of the last few weeks has taken its toll," said Victor. "It's only natural we get a little snippy."

"I've got another clips package to play," said Freya. "Shall I do that?"

"Seriously though, who would do it?" blurted Robbie. "I mean – who? Who would do such a terrible thing? Murder is bad enough, but murdering Wolf seems so much worse than your average murder."

"Why is it so much worse?" Kit couldn't help herself.

"Well… because he was such a colourful character, so full of life and into the dramatic."

"Huh."

"Huh?"

The pedant monster had broken free again. Kit was about to go down another unwise conversational cul-de-sac. She knew it, but again she couldn't help herself.

"If he wasn't so colourful… If he wasn't so 'into the dramatic', he would have just announced who his special mystery guest was and we would know who'd killed him." Kit scratched her forehead. "Actually, come to think of it, if he had announced the identity of the guest *straight away*, Wolf would probably still be alive."

"That's sooo unfair," said Freya.

"Actually, it's not," said Victor, surprisingly. "Wolf must have had an inkling that his guest was dangerous. Or at least not willing to share whatever secret they had with the world."

"We don't know that." Freya was now close to tears again.

"Exactly," said Robbie. "Thanks for the deduction, Mr Data, but they're just theories. They are all very well, but we don't know anything. Neither do the police it seems."

"Don't they?" Kit was intrigued.

"Victor has a policeman *friend*," snapped Robbie. "Don't you, Victor?"

"I know a lot of policemen, Robbie," said Victor wearily. "Policemen come into my hospital because that's part of their job."

"Of course! Part of their job." Robbie rolled his eyes.

This was obviously the vestigial tail of a very long argument between Robbie and Victor.

"Anyway, what did *he* say Victor?" sneered Robbie. "*Please enlighten us.*"

"He *said* they had no witnesses. And no good leads. From what he hears they're just trawling though the internet and making lists of people who said they hated Wolf. They could be doing that for months. Probably years."

None of them said anything after that. The futility of the investigation into Wolf's death was finally brought home to them.

That was the problem with murdering podcasters, Kit thought. *In many ways it was the perfect crime. There are thousands of podcasts out there where, if the host and his entire studio was napalmed and all that was left was a blackened corpse and the smell of burning polystyrene, there wouldn't be a jury in the land that would convict the perpetrator.*

"I'll play the clips package now," said Freya.

Freya played the clips package.

3

They emerged from the shed, blinking in the fading summer sun. Kit started to head back to the house, but Robbie grabbed her arm.

"Wait a second, Kit. We've got one thing left to do."

"What?"

"We're doing a ceremony. We're going to film it as an extra, for subscribers to Wolf's Patreon page."

"Come on, you guys," said Binfire. "Gather round."

Binfire had emerged from the house holding vodka bottles full of luminous blue liquid. Victor, Freya and Robbie joined him on the lawn, standing in a rough circle. Kit joined them.

"Here, have some Romulan Ale."

Victor and Robbie took a bottle each. Kit also took one and looked at it doubtfully. Robbie shook his head and grinned.

"I wouldn't drink it if I were you. It's fifty per cent vodka, fifty per cent mouthwash."

"Wait a second, guys," said Freya. She ran into the house and emerged carrying a digital camera. She pointed it at the little circle of friends.

"Wait… wait… Just… Okay, sooo… I'm recording. You can start."

Binfire held out his bottle to the camera. "The Vixenhood are here to pay tribute to our homie Wolf Tyler with some genuine Romulan Ale, purloined from Orion slave traders near the Neutral Zone." He cleared his throat. "Not that I'm a fan of *Star Trek*, but Wolf was, so you know, respect for his memory and all that…"

"Get on with it," snapped Robbie.

Binfire turned the bottle upside down and allowed the vodka-mouthwash to splatter onto the decking. "To Wolf Tyler, a comrade and friend, Vixphile and Jedi, Whovian and Trekker, Potterhead and Thronie, Browncoat and Lurker, a hoopy frood who really knew where his towel was."

He looked up in the sky and saluted. "I'm sure that, somewhere in the multiverse, there's a version of Wolf who isn't dead, and he's looking through a dimensional portal and smiling down at us right now."

The others all said "amen" and also poured their bottles onto the wooden decking, with rather too much vodka-mouthwash cascading over a wide area. Kit stepped back to rescue her boots from the splatter.

After a few awkward seconds, Freya's camera beeped, and she lowered it. "Got it. That was sooo fantastic."

"That was very moving," Kit said, not sounding moved at all.

Binfire held up a finger. "Ah-ah-ah! We're not finished yet, Captain Kit!"

He reached behind his back and pulled a gun out of his belt.

"What's that for?"

"It's part of the tribute."

Kit was unnerved. *Is this a cult? Have my friends become disciples in Wolf Tyler's coven in my absence? Have I been invited to a mass suicide?*

As usual, Binfire read her mind. "It's not a real gun, pilgrim." He broke it open and showed it to her. The gun was fatter, the barrel huge. Nestling inside was a massive cartridge. "It's a flare gun."

"Where on earth did you get that?"

"Got it off a pirate."

"A pirate?"

Binfire shrugged. "Video pirate. I got him some seventh-generation copies of 'Doctor Who and the Evil of the Daleks' episode seven and he owed me. We're gonna use it to shine a light for Wolf. Are we ready?"

Freya looked up. Dusk was spreading across the horizon and the sky was bruising into a deep purple.

"Yes, I think it's dark enough now. Let's go for it."

Binfire yelled, "We're going for it! Get ready!"

Freya activated the camera again and knelt down until she was level with Binfire. "Okay. We're rolling."

Binfire pushed his face into the lens of the camera and said, "Hi folks. We're still here paying tribute to Wolf. Now we're gonna use this flare to shine a light in the heavens as a beacon for his force ghost to come and find us."

He aimed it into the air. "Stand well back, everybody."

Freya walked backwards, training her camera on the skies. Kit, Victor and Robbie scuttled over to the far side of the decking by the barbeque.

Binfire fired the gun and the stillness was shattered by a deafening *crack*. A red light appeared and threaded through the blackness. Kit heard an "oooh" next to her ear. She looked at the source of the "oooh".

Freya gave a sheepish grin. "Sorry," she whispered. "I always 'oooh' at fireworks. Force of habit."

Binfire had his precious military binoculars in his hands and was training them on the sky. "Here it comes! Re-entry alert!"

"What?"

They watched as the ball of red light descended back to planet Earth like an escape pod from an exploding alien spaceship. It glided slowly down into the garden of 33 Hanover Parade, or to be more specific, the piece of decking where the gang had all just poured four bottles of vodka-mouthwash cocktail.

The decking erupted in a carpet of blue flame.

"Holy fuck!" gurgled Robbie, and staggered backwards, knocking over the barbeque and hurling smouldering hot coals along the decking. Before any of them had a chance to react, the fire spread along the splatter pattern of the Romulan Ale and started to grow, feeding on the elderly planking and roaring with gusto.

Kit turned to Robbie.

"Where's the fire extinguisher?"

"What?"

"Do you *have* a fire extinguisher?"

"Kitchen – I think!"

Kit and Robbie started sprinting for the house. Freya and Binfire had the same idea and they all collided at the back door. Kit entered the kitchen first and looked frantically round. "Where?"

Robbie pointed at a piece of plastic moulding above the fridge. "It *was* there!" he screamed.

"Well, where is it now?"

"I don't know!"

Freya was behind them. She suddenly screamed "Shit!" She looked up and yelled, "Wolf, you idiot!" She ran upstairs, still shouting, "Shitshitshit!" and soon they could hear the thud of her feet as she entered her bedroom.

"What the hell?" yelled Robbie. "What in the name of Thanos is she doing?"

Behind them, the glow from the garden was huge. Kit scarcely had the courage to turn back and see how big the fire was.

There was another sequence of thuds as Freya ran across the landing and back down the stairs. She was wearing a large backpack complete with long tube and nozzle.

"You remember! Last year's Halloween party?" she shouted.

"Oh Christ, yes!" Robbie clutched his head. "Wolf made it into a *Ghostbusters* proton pack!"

The fire had consumed the deck like an aperitif. Now it was gorging on the shed, which was little more than a golden column of flame stretching into the sky.

Freya pointed the nozzle, but the lever was on the fire extinguisher, and the fire extinguisher was behind her, immersed in gaffer tape and papier-mâché.

"Allow me," said Kit. She pulled the safety pin and pushed the lever. The nozzle erupted in a jet of grey gas which – of course – reminded Kit of the Dalek extermination effect from the Doctor Who movies (*Dr Who and the Daleks*, 1965, and *Daleks: Invasion Earth 2150 AD*, 1966).

Freya advanced towards the conflagration, dragging Kit along behind. The gas chased the flames around the wall of the shed, making swirling black shapes. The fire retreated but didn't seem any less angry.

"Out the way! Coming through!"

That was Binfire's voice.

Binfire and Robbie were behind them, struggling and wrestling with the half-filled swimming pool, holding it like it was a giant taco, trapping the water inside. They swung it back and forth and hurled the whole thing at the shed. It glided through the air like an old-fashioned flying saucer. The water hissed and didn't seem to have much of an impact, but the pool itself clung to the front of the shed, popping and shrivelling until it smothered the fire with a thick layer of melting plastic.

The motion sensitive lights came on, and from where she stood Kit could see the silhouette of Freya brandishing her fire extinguisher nozzle, framed by clouds of smoke and a shapeless monstrous mass of foul-smelling blue ectoplasm.

It was one of the best cosplays she'd ever seen.

* * *

It was a very pleasant evening. Everyone found the exploding shed hilarious in hindsight, even Robbie. Binfire had a Nerf-gun battle with Freya in the dusk, and no one minded when Victor got his acoustic guitar out. Kit even acceded to Robbie's advances and ate one of his Linda McCartney veggie burgers, on condition she could check the box and find out how many calories it contained.

Kit was startlingly thin, but she was acutely aware she wasn't *naturally* thin. Both her parents (now retired, living in a farmhouse in Dorset) were jolly ruddy-faced people shaped like Teletubbies, and the Pelham genes stalked Kit's sleepless nights like the ghost of Christmas future.

She *liked* being thin and had no desire to become the cliché of a bull-necked lesbian, so she monitored what she ate with a discipline bordering on mania. She knew there might be an eating disorder waiting inside her, preparing to claw itself out of her ribcage like an acid-blooded alien, but as far as she was concerned she would direct that particular flamethrower at that particular Xenomorph when she came to it.

And so, like a TV show where one of the principal characters suffered a shocking death at the end, the evening silently faded to black. Kit started to make a move. She rebuffed the gang's pleadings to stay in their spare room for the night.

"I've got a room in the Travelodge booked, so I can easily go to the train station in the morning."

She had booked a room in the Travelodge because she knew she would be exhausted by having to interact with so many people today. She had no desire to wake up in 33 Hanover Parade the next morning and sit through long meandering chats over breakfast or fend off calls to go to the pub for a lunchtime drink and endure more drawn-out goodbyes.

She was at the door shrugging on her velvet coat when Victor came up to her.

"Hey matey. Are you leaving straight away tomorrow morning?"

"That's my plan."

"Hum. I don't suppose you could hang around for a bit?"

"I'm not sure why I'd want to do that."

Victor lowered his voice. "Because I need talk to you… in private."

"Why do you want to do that?"

"Shhh!"

Kit lowered her voice. "Why do you…?"

"Because I think I know who murdered Wolf."

"Criminy."

For the past couple of days Kit had been experimenting with a new catchphrase; she had decided to say "criminy" to signify surprise.

"It's true."

"Criminy."

She wasn't sure the catchphrase was quite working, but she had decided to give it a few more days just to make sure.

"Do you want to know who killed Wolf?"

"Well, of course I do. But shouldn't you just tell the police?"

"You'll understand when I explain. Meet me at the Grind House on Ship Street tomorrow morning at eleven o'clock. Come alone."

He turned away.

"Make it nine o'clock," she said.

"What?"

"Make it nine o'clock."

"That's a bit early, matey."

"I want to get a morning train. I have a yoghurt in my fridge that expires tomorrow and I want to get home so I can eat it for lunch."

"I can buy you lunch."

"If you want to talk to me, I'll be there at nine o'clock. Otherwise I won't be there. Your choice."

4

The Grind House was part of a cluster of coffee shops at the top of Ship Street. It was ideal for a clandestine meeting because it was incredibly murky. It had sacks full of plastic coffee beans littered around the place, gloomy illumination provided by dangling light bulbs hanging inside glass jars, hard wooden chairs made from driftwood and tall partitions around the tables. There were plenty of dark corners to hide in.

Victor entered the shop to the sound of a jingling bell, and Kit waved from her particular dark corner. He slid in opposite her.

"Hi," he said.

"Hello," said Kit.

"Hello," said Binfire.

Victor looked at Binfire, who grinned at him.

"I said I wanted to see you in private," said Victor.

Kit blinked. "Oh. You meant private as in 'on my own'?"

"That's what private means."

"But it's Binfire. He's not really a person as such, are you, Binfire?"

"No," said Binfire. "I'm what you would call a force of nature."

"And I got the impression that you're about to tell me something about Wolf's death."

"Yes…"

"I'd feel better if Binfire's here. When things get tense my stammer comes back. He's my security blanket, because he's better at processing shocking information than me."

"Do you *really* want him to stay?"

"Yes."

43

"Okay. Fine."

"Brilliant!" said Binfire. "Can I have a cake?"

At that moment the waitress arrived. "Would you like to order?"

"Yes," said Victor. "I'll have a cappuccino. Kit?"

Kit wrestled with indecision. *Pick the most calorie-neutral option.*

"Coffee," she said at last. "Black."

"Binfire?"

Binfire grinned. "I like my coffee like I like the Millennium Falcon."

The waitress looked bemused.

"Flat white."

Victor sighed. "And can I have a millionaire shortbread for my lunatic friend with the ear necklace?"

"You got it."

The waitress left. Kit got straight to the point. "You said you knew why Wolf was killed."

"I do."

"But you've not told anyone yet?"

"No."

"Shouldn't you tell Freya?"

"It's not as simple as that, mate."

"Why?"

"It's a long story." Victor paused and took a deep breath. "Does the name Lily Sparkes mean anything to you?"

Kit blinked and uploaded the memory to her brain. "Of course it does. Lily Sparkes was an occasional extra in the original series of *Vixens from the Void*. And by 'extra', I mean she was one of a number of local girls brought in to bump up the numbers of Vixos warrior guards during location filming in Brighton."

Kit kept rattling off the facts like a robot. "She appeared as a Vixos warrior guard in the very first episode 'Coronation', and the second part of 'Assassins of 'Destiny' in season two. She was *also* seen briefly in various episodes throughout season one, because they re-used the location footage to make the studio-bound stories look more expensive. That shot of her running around the side of the palace was used in three other episodes: 'Quest to Danger', 'Prophecy of Armageddon' and 'The Doomsday Sequence'. Until about five years ago fandom didn't know her identity. As she wasn't a member of Equity her name wasn't even included on the credits. I tracked her down to interview her for my podcast."

Victor sipped his coffee. "I know you did, mate. It was amazing work. One of your best investigations."

Kit frowned. "Not really. It was very disappointing once I discovered she'd died. I did try to talk to her best friend, but she didn't want to talk, and I attempted to interview her parents, but they were very hostile, very strange people. I had to edit it down to practically nothing."

Victor smiled. "Nevertheless, it was an amazing piece of work. To track down a non-speaking extra, with no paper trail, no BBC documentation – just on what you could see on the footage. It was amazing."

Silence fell.

Binfire leaned in and hissed in Kit's ear. "I think you're meant to say, 'thank you for the compliment, Victor'."

"Oh," said Kit, surprised. "Thank you for the compliment, Victor. But it wasn't that hard. I'm a subscriber to the British newspaper archive. I just looked at the local newspapers printed at the time to find articles like 'Brighton Girl Becomes BBC TV Star' or 'Local Girl Gets Telly Break in Sci-Fi Show'. They always do it. Without fail."

"So they do. It's the articles you found about Lily Sparkes that started all this."

"Started what?"

"About a year ago, Wolf and I decided to write another book about *Vixens from the Void* – about location filming."

"There's not a lot to tell. There wasn't a lot of location filming."

"Yes, I'm aware of that, mate. Apart from a few days in Betchworth almost all of it was around here, in Brighton and in Pulborough chalk pit. So we decided that, if we were going to make the book worthwhile, we should really drill down on the background info, put in a lot of context about what was happening at the time, in the country in general and Brighton in particular."

"Sounds sensible."

"So we looked at the articles you found."

Victor pulled a folder out of his satchel and flapped it open. Inside were transparent sleeves containing newspaper articles from the *Brighton Argus*, all from the 1980s. He pointed at one. It was dated 2 July 1986.

POLICE APPEAL FOR PUBLIC'S HELP TO FIND MISSING 17-YEAR-OLD

Police say they are "increasingly concerned" about Lily Sparkes, a missing teen last seen three days ago. Officers are now appealing for the public's help.

The 17-year-old lives in Hove and works as a receptionist at the Hotel De La Mer in Brighton. She was last seen leaving the hotel at the end of her shift around midnight on 30 June. She did not arrive home. She was wearing her work clothes, a green jacket and skirt and a white shirt.

A police spokesperson said, "Lily's parents are very worried about her and want to make sure she is safe and well."

The piece was accompanied by a picture of Lily. It was obviously a school photo because it had that background that could only be described as 'queasy blue'. Lily wore dark eyeliner and pink cheeks that demonstrated a newcomer's enthusiasm for make-up. Her red hair was large and feathered and screamed 1980s, cresting over her head like Melanie Griffith in the beginning of *Working Girl*.

She looked painfully young and innocent. Kit wondered if that was a conscious strategy of local papers – to use school photos whatever the circumstance. Whether the child was missing, dead, on the run or arrested for shooting up a petrol station, the school photo was designed to prod the reader into feeling sadness for innocence lost.

Kit looked up and raised her eyebrows as if to say, 'so what?'

"You read that fast."

"I don't have to read it. She didn't 'disappear'. She ran off to America. She rang her parents and her best friend to tell them she was alright and she was in Hollywood trying to make it as an actress."

"Exactly."

"And she came back a year later because she didn't make it in Hollywood. The paper carried an update a few days after this article to say she had been located, she had rung her parents to tell them where she was, and she was safe and well. I don't understand what you're getting at."

"Okay," said Victor. "So how about this one?"

He slipped another plastic sleeve across the table containing another article. This one was dated 15 June 1987.

18-YEAR-OLD THOUGHT DEAD AFTER JUMPING OFF BRIGHTON PALACE PIER

A teenager is thought to have committed suicide after jumping off Brighton Pier last Saturday evening.

Lily Sparkes, 18, lived in Hove and was a receptionist at the Hotel De La Mer in Brighton.

Lily made headlines when she went missing for three days last February and police made an appeal for help to locate her whereabouts. It was later discovered that she had flown to America to pursue a career as an actress without informing her parents.

Lily had been bitten by the acting bug after featuring in the BBC television series *Vixens from the Void* in a small role. She returned to Brighton after a year to resume her job in the popular beachfront hotel.

Chief Superintendent Neil Stamp, from Sussex Police, said, "We believe that Lily jumped from the end of the pier in the early hours of Saturday. Someone has come forward to say they witnessed a woman falling into the water.

"A suicide note was discovered at the scene, in which she wrote about her intention to throw herself off the pier. Her friends have also told us that she had been very depressed recently. We are not treating this incident as suspicious.

"Police and coastguard searched for several hours in very difficult and dangerous weather but have been unable to locate Lily."

This piece was accompanied by the same school photo of Lily. Obviously *The Argus* had it on file.

Kit looked up. "I know all this. You still haven't got to a point yet."

"Okay, mate. Here goes. Here's my point." Victor leaned back and laced his fingers behind his head. "Isn't it a huge coincidence that Lily Sparkes runs away from home during one *Vixens from the Void* location shoot, and kills herself during ANOTHER *Vixens from the Void* location shoot?"

"I would say it's a complete coincidence. Wouldn't you?"

He gave a grim smile. "You have no imagination, mate."

"It's been said."

"So, Wolf and me, we got to theorising. We re-read these articles and this time we read *between* the lines."

He held up the first article.

"We looked at it this way. Here's this girl, young and impressionable, and she's working at the hotel where the *Vixens from the Void* production team is staying. She hears they need extras, so she auditions. She gets a tiny non-speaking part in the show, and she's having a ball. Perhaps she's encouraged by one of the production team that she might make it as a professional actress? But oh no! How can she even attempt to do that? She's got crazy control-freak parents! What can she do? She can't ask the person who told her she'd be a good actress for help because they've all moved on, back up to London. So she goes about it the only way she thinks might work. She runs away to America..."

Victor shrugged then continued. "So she goes, and she fails to make it in Hollywood, obviously, and she comes back home, humiliated. And, hey presto, the *Vixens from the Void* production team arrives back in Brighton one year later! Same place, same hotel. And there she is, just like last time, working on reception. This time she decides on a different strategy. She demands that the mysterious person who encouraged her gives her some proper help to become an actress."

He gave another shrug. "I dunno what that could be. Money to apply to an acting school? A place in London so she can escape her parents? Or a proper speaking part on telly?"

He held up the second article. "So perhaps it turns nasty. Perhaps this mysterious person doesn't want to be bothered by her. Or perhaps this mysterious person had an affair with Lily, or Lily knows something bad about this mysterious person. I'm sure the staff in the hotel get to see lots of guests in compromising positions almost every day. Anyway, Lily gets killed, and it's made to look like suicide."

"Frokk," said Binfire. "This is massive. And you and Wolf worked all that out just from reading two stories in a local paper?"

"Yes."

Kit folded her arms. "This is all nonsense. Guesswork. Wish fulfilment."

"Perhaps."

"No 'perhaps' about it. It's complete guesswork. You haven't got a shred of evidence, have you?"

Binfire looked at Kit, then back at Victor, like a bemused tennis spectator. "Have you?"

Victor held up his hands in mock surrender.

"Sorry mateys. I haven't. No."

Binfire made a *ffsss* noise and slumped lower in his seat, a dejected toddler being told there was no time for ice cream.

"You're right, Kit," said Victor. "We had no evidence. And I admit it. It sounds exactly like the kind of baseless conspiracy theory fan bollocks you find on some badly made website. Just like the stuff they're making up about Wolf's death right now."

His eyes started to shine. "We *knew* it was just a bit of fantasy when we came up with it, just me and Wolf getting a bit drunk of an evening and moving the facts around to create an exciting story." He leaned forward until he and Kit were almost nose-to-nose. "Until exactly one month ago, just one week before he was killed. That's when Wolf told me he had found the evidence. He said we were right all along. Someone who met Lily on location in 1986 killed her a year later, after filming wrapped in 1987. He said he knew for a fact that Lily had been murdered *and* he knew who did it."

"Who?" said Binfire.

"He wouldn't say."

"He wouldn't say?"

"The next thing I know, he's lying dead on the floor of his studio."

Binfire looked aghast. "He didn't even tell you?"

"No."

"That's frokking crazy."

"It's not, actually," said Kit primly. "If he found out an actual *new* fact about *Vixens from the Void*... Well, that would be gold dust. Knowing Wolf, he would want to keep it to himself just in case it leaked out before his big announcement. I would guess that's why he did the podcast live."

"So, you believe me, mate?" said Victor. "You believe that someone on the *Vixens from the Void* production team murdered Lily Sparkes and then murdered Wolf when he found out?"

"I don't *believe* anything..." Kit adjusted her cap into a slightly more rakish angle and pursed her lips. "But I *accept* that Wolf Tyler was murdered. That's a *fact*. And it is a *fact* he was murdered by this, this... Special Mystery Guest. Whoever it was. And it's a *fact* that he was killed just before he was about to reveal something important. So, I accept as *fact* that someone killed him to shut him up."

"Great! Finally." Victor exhaled.

"This now begs the obvious question: why are you telling *me* this?"

Victor sat up straight and stared at the table, as if trying to focus himself before responding.

"Okay. While me and Wolf were putting the book together and we were making up conspiracy theories about what happened to Lily Sparkes, and how she might have been murdered, we joked about how we could prove our hypothesis and thinking of ways we could find out who killed her. I said there was no way we could get all the suspects together, unless we organised a convention and invited them all, which probably would be a bit over the top, and Wolf stood up and laughed and said there was actually a much easier way to bring them together."

He paused for effect.

"Do a Blu-Ray documentary!"

"What kind of documentary?" asked Binfire.

Kit knew immediately what Victor meant and provided the answer. "He means a 'then and now' kind of documentary."

Binfire looked confused. "I don't buy Blu-Rays, so I don't know what a 'then and now' is."

"They're very popular. They're a documentary where they invite the surviving members of a production team to a place where they shot the series. They ask them about their memories of filming in the area, get them to walk around the place and remark about how it's changed, or how it's not changed, and maybe even re-enact a few scenes from the original show."

Victor pointed at Kit in approval. "Got it in one! Look, *Vixens* was filmed here in Brighton. We pitch a documentary for the forthcoming Blu-Ray to the BBC and get the original production team to come down here. Get them to stay in the exact same hotel they stayed in – the one where Lily worked, let's not forget – ask them a few questions, see how they react and then hopefully…"

"You do a Hamlet."

Victor's eyes widened in astonishment. "What do you mean?"

Kit frowned as if it was obvious. "You do a Hamlet. 'The play's the thing, wherein I'll catch the conscience of the King.' Hamlet re-enacted a murder scene to see if the murderer would give himself away. You want to recreate the events of Lily's 'murder'" – Kit put air quotes around the word 'murder' – "and see if any of the suspects react."

Victor nodded. "That's right, mate. That's exactly what I mean."

Kit thought about this. "And of course, even if the murderer *doesn't* reveal him or herself, one of the other guests might recall some tiny important detail from their time in Brighton – if their memories are prompted by the documentary – and that might lead to the identity of the murderer too."

"Exactly," said Victor. "I hadn't actually thought about it that way, but yes, I guess that could also happen."

"That sounds like a great idea!" said Binfire.

"Thanks mate!"

"No, it sounds like a terrible idea," said Kit.

"Why?" said Victor, looking hurt.

"Because those kinds of documentaries usually only have about two or three guests. If you want to investigate everybody who went on location filming to Brighton... you must be talking about two dozen people at least."

"Ah! No. That's where you're wrong, mate." Victor struggled to get a piece of paper out of his folder. "Wolf said it was someone who met her in '86. All we need to focus on are members of the production team who were there in '86 and '87. And guess what? There's only six of them!"

He pushed the piece of paper forward. Kit picked it up and scrutinised it. There were indeed just six names.

Vanity Mycroft (actress) 'Arkadia'
Roger Barker (actor) 'Vizor'
Patrick Finch (actor) 'Captain Talon'
Tara Miles (actress) 'Medula'
Duggie Fletcher (stuntman)
Joan Peverin (costume design)

Kit looked at the names, made some calculations in her head, and was surprised to realise that it was completely true. The two location shoots had different directors, different cameramen, different soundmen, a different lighting crew... Even the series producer, Nicholas Everett, who in normal circumstances made a point of being present at all film shoots, had been struck down with illness during the second Brighton filming and didn't attend.

Victor was right. The only personnel who visited Brighton those two times were the six names on the list.

She dropped the paper and pushed it back towards Victor. "So there's only six people. That's at least twice more than the usual number of guests. It's going to cost a fortune! Do you know what the budget for one of these Blu-Ray extras is?"

"No mate, but I bet you do."

"About fourteen thousand pounds. Maximum. And that has to include everything. Food, accommodation, filming permissions… There's no way you can hire six guests, put them up in a hotel, get a production crew together, hire an editing suite and do all that for fourteen thousand pounds."

"You let me worry about that. All you need to do is make the pitch to the BBC."

"Why me?"

"Because you've done it before. You've been on a Blu-Ray extra."

"I was only a talking head."

"But it still means you're known to the BBC. They'll trust you."

"But I've never done a documentary on this scale. There's no way—"

Victor reached out and put his hand over her knuckles. Kit shrivelled from the sudden contact and withdrew her hand.

"Do I have to spell it out, Kit? You're a *girl*. And you're *gay*. And you're *young*. Most *Vixens* fans who pitch these projects are fat old guys in their fifties."

"Like Robbie," said Binfire.

Victor smiled. "Yes, like Robbie. But don't tell him I said that. They don't want that type of fan in their shiny new Blu-Rays. They want *you*. You tick more BBC boxes than a… a… professional BBC box-ticker."

Binfire nodded. "He has a point."

Kit thought about it. "Fine," she said at last. "Fine."

"Brilliant. I can direct, you can do the interviews. Binfire can handle a camera."

"That's true," said Binfire. "I would be a great cameraman. I would frokkin' nail it. Can I have a drone?"

"Sure," grinned Victor.

He brought his fingers together to make a square. "I can swoop." He whirled his hands in the air. "I can do *extreme close-ups*." He brought his fingers right up to Kit's face, making her flinch.

Victor laughed. "And we can get Freya and Robbie to help."

"Are we going to tell them?"

"Well, we won't tell them why we're *really* doing this. They'll just get upset. They're both too emotional and they'll give the game away. All they need to know is we're making a documentary for a Blu-Ray. Which is true, isn't it? I'm sure they'd love to get involved."

"They would," Binfire agreed. "How big a drone can I get?"

Kit sighed. "This is all very well, but how long is this shoot going to be?"

"I'd say four or five days."

"Five days? You're talking accommodation and meals for six guests for four days? There's no way we can—"

"Let's just tell the BBC we've got a special deal on the hotel. Half price on accommodation and food. I'll fund the rest of it. I've got a lot of savings put away."

"But we'll be lying."

"What they don't know won't harm them. They'll be getting a really expensive-looking documentary with a huge cast of top-drawer guests for a tiny budget. It's a win-win for everybody."

Kit thought it sounded too good to be true. In her experience, if someone in a TV series said something like 'it's a win-win for everybody' in the pre-credits sequence, they were usually dead before the titles started.

5

Victor was right. *Of course* he was right. As soon as the pitch arrived in a BBC inbox with the name 'Kit Pelham' attached, they all but bit her hand off. They were delighted that a 'youthful female' voice was being added to their range of top-quality Blu-Ray extras.

In Kit's opinion, 'youthful' was stretching a point. She was nearly thirty, after all. But she was younger than most. Not being around when the original series was broadcast, she always felt like an outsider. When she joined the local Vixenhood fan group, she found a small group of middle-aged men who looked upon her like a fabulous beast, like a unicorn. Yes, they were friendly enough (very friendly, before they found out she was gay) and she enjoyed her time at the official video weekends and meetings, but she knew that when those get-togethers finished those fans would have smaller, less official get-togethers that she wasn't invited to.

She felt no actual *hostility* from them whatsoever, but she sensed they couldn't be bothered making the effort to incorporate a young woman into their cosy male clubs.

But that all changed in 2020.

During the 2010s the prospect of a remake of *Vixens from the Void* appeared occasionally, and then, Brigadoon-like, floated out of view just as quickly.

Lazarus Media and Hurley-Burley Studios both announced they were going to remake the series, in 2012 and 2015 respectively. But those announcements, like so many announcements in *Broadcast Magazine*, dribbled away to nothing.

The fans darkly talked about these fanfares in terms of 'tax write-offs' and 'publicity stunts'. Then, in 2018, a production company called Er... That's It went into the offices of the streaming giant Fliptop and said the inevitable words: "Think *Game of Thrones*... but in space!"

And the deal was done.

A very cynical fandom expected their patience was about to be tried again, but to their astonishment the announcement was followed up by starship designs, casting announcements and interviews with the new producer. Filming started in 2019, and in 2020 the new show was streamed on Fliptop. A continuation of the story fifty years later (incorporating fleeting cameos from a few aged-up classic series characters), but given a new, harder sci-fi edge. The costumes were less revealing, the cumbersome and rather comical Styrax robot monsters were given a CGI makeover, and the extra budget meant the oft-talked-about-but-never-seen indigenous race of dragons finally managed to make some on-screen appearances.

There was grumbling from die-hard fans who preferred catfights in Lycra to exploring 'hot-button issues' through the medium of science-fantasy, but to be honest...

...it wasn't half bad.

All of a sudden there was an influx of different types of fans, cool young things, hipsters, millennials and Gen Z-ers, and Kit didn't feel quite so alone. *Vixmag* appeared on the stands, a magazine devoted to the new series, and it was desperate for contributions from fans like Kit, so she became the pre-eminent pundit and go-to girl for convention interviews, vox pops and interviews on the BBC news channel.

However, not everyone was best pleased at her stratospheric rise. A certain older superfan, Graham Goldingay, made it clear in no uncertain terms that he did not approve, and claimed that, as Kit had not been alive to actually feel the static electricity and smell the warm dust on the cathode ray tubes in the back of an ancient analogue television broadcasting the original episodes across four hundred and eighty pixels, then Kit could never be thought of as a 'true' fan.

But more of him later.

* * *

And so the stage was set.

The Hotel De La Mer was booked for five days in February next year. The fact that Victor, Robbie, Freya and Binfire all lived locally meant they didn't need accommodation – thank goodness. It was only Kit who needed a hotel room.

Victor suggested that Kit could stay at 33 Hanover Parade too, but Kit was adamant that she wasn't staying in that filthy, noisy house. She didn't say that out loud, of course. She just argued that if she was staying in the hotel, she could observe their guests last thing at night and first thing in the morning, when their guard was down. Victor saw the logic of that argument.

Kit and Victor decided to hold a Zoom meeting and discuss tactics. Kit spent the hour before the meeting untidying her study, arranging the books on her shelf so they appeared higgledy-piggedly in an authentically disorganised way, and sat down fifteen minutes before the scheduled meeting so she could take enough time to frame her screen to include the best posters and adjust her hat to the right angle.

She took her dachshund, Milo, out of his basket. She thought his presence on her lap gave her a very intellectual impression, even though Milo's rumbling snores did force her to raise her voice on more than one occasion.

"Okay mate. Let's talk strategy. The next stage is inviting our six suspects," said Victor. "So, let's round them all up. It shouldn't be a problem."

"Really? You don't think it'll be a problem? We don't even know if they'll all agree to take part."

"Why not? Free hotel room, free food and booze, and a

chance to be in front of the camera... What's not to love?"

"It's not quite that straightforward. Joan Peverin is certain to take part. She does a lot of these. So does Roger Barker. But those are the only definite ones."

"Why are they the only definite ones?"

"You don't know these people like I do."

"That's why I need you, mate. What's the problem with the others?"

"Well... Vanity is notoriously fickle about these things. She has to be approached really carefully. If you find her in the wrong mood, she'll just say no."

"Okay."

"I haven't seen Duggie Fletcher do any interviews in years. He's completely disappeared. Tara Miles lives in Surrey. She's a yoga instructor, massage therapist and feng shui consultant. She's completely retired from acting and she's shown very little interest in going to conventions. She's barely done more than two events since the show finished."

"Oh."

"And as for Patrick Finch... Well..."

"Well, what?"

"He's the most difficult of all of them, obviously."

"Why is he the most difficult of all of them?"

"He's still got a *career*."

Patrick Finch had managed several almost-impossible transitions in his career: from policeman to bit-part actor to respected thespian to household TV name. For Patrick – a man certain to get a knighthood in the not-too-distant future – appearing in a Blu-Ray documentary about *Vixens from the Void* wasn't merely slumming it, it was sleeping under a bridge by the embankment in a pile of pigeon sick.

"I'll get them. Leave it to me, mate," said Victor.

"You keep saying that."

"I keep meaning it."

"What are you going to do?"

"I'm going to offer them such ridiculously stupid money that they would be raving mad to turn it down."

"You can't do that, Victor. BBC fees are standard. They'd go mental if you did that. Everyone would start asking for ridiculous fees. We'd be blacklisted until the heat death of the universe."

Victor considered this. "Then I'll offer sweeteners, off the books. Luncheon vouchers. Free air miles. A donation to their favourite charity. Anything they bloody want."

"Victor…"

"I'm serious, mate. A friend of ours is dead…"

A friend of yours, perhaps.

"…and it's our duty to find out which of those bastards did it."

Victor was typically a cool type, almost over-casual sometimes, happy to be everybody's mate. The fact he sounded so determined impressed Kit.

"You do what you feel you need to," she said. "I can't stop you. But if I get anyone from the BBC ringing me up, I will disavow all knowledge of what you're up to."

"Fair enough."

Kit thought for a moment. "Why don't we split up? Why don't you approach Roger Barker, Joan Peverin and Tara Miles? I suspect they'd be the ones most open to your form of bribery. I'll do Duggie Fletcher, Vanity Mycroft and Patrick Finch. I think they'll be the tricky ones."

"Brilliant. Great idea. Thanks Kit. You're an absolute star."

"The brightest one in the galaxy."

* * *

Kit's predictions proved to be true. Victor secured his list of guests quite easily. Roger Barker was first to say yes because he was always the first to say yes to anything. As far as Roger was concerned, if there was a free bar and a chance to chat up girls, he was definitely going to be there. Being paid was a bonus.

Joan Peverin was next to agree; she lived nearby in Worthing and was glad to get out of the house.

Tara Miles was initially a polite no, but Victor persisted. He did a little research into Tara's passions and dangled a huge donation to help the persecuted peoples of Tibet if she took part. After a few days' thought, she agreed.

That left Kit with her part of the list.

The difficult ones.

Duggie 'Don't Lean Against That Window' Fletcher was hard to track down. He seemed to have vanished off the face of the Earth, but Kit refused to admit defeat. She contacted the British Stunt Register, and through them she got hold of one of Duggie's old colleagues, a stuntman who doubled for Ian McShane on a few episodes of *Lovejoy* when he had to carry heavy antiques upstairs. He hadn't been in touch with Duggie for years, but he did have a very old mobile phone number that used to belong to him.

Kit sent a 'hello' text, outlining the job – and the fee – and waited. There was no reply for several days and she was ready to concede that the phone was definitely defunct, until a very simple message came back, with three simple words:

No thank you.

The words seemed very final. With a heavy heart, Kit pulled up her WhatsApp account and sent Victor a message.

Just had a definite 'no' from Duggie.
Sorry to fall at the first hurdle.

Twenty minutes later a little blue dot appeared on Kit's screen. A reply from Victor.

> **No worries, mate. I'm sure he'll change his mind. You carry on with Vanity and we'll come back to him. It will happen because justice is on our side. V.**

Kit thought Victor was being wildly optimistic, but she knew he was right. Time to move on to Vanity.

At least Kit could contact her directly. Kit once looked after Vanity for a few conventions. Vanity had taken a liking to her and dubbed Kit her 'little girlboy'. Kit had even been given the honour of having Vanity's phone number.

Her actual home phone number! Of her actual home!

Vanity's phone rang for a very long time.

A heavy accent came on the line. "Yees? Grayson residence?"

"Is Ms Mycroft there?"

"Vanity? Oh, she having a colon cleanse. Just a meenit…" The voice raised to a bellow. "Lady on phone. She want you."

There was a muffled altercation.

"Fuck's sake Magdalena! Take a fucking message!"

"I go. My mother she dead now. You say I can go to funeral, so I go."

"You can't leave me like this, you bitch!"

"Yes I can. Fuck you, old woman! Phone is on table! Get your skinny ass down here! Bye bye!"

There was a door slam, yelling and thumping of feet on stairs. Kit had a sinking feeling she had called at the wrong time.

Vanity came on the line.

"I've got liquid shit running down my leg. This had better be good."

"Miss Mycroft, it's Kit Pelham."

"Who?"

"From the conventions? I used to help you when you were a guest, carrying your photos and taking your money. You used to call me your 'little girlboy'?"

Vanity was frosty. "How did you get this number?"

"You gave it to me."

"Oh. So what the bloody hell do you want?"

"I'd like to offer you a job."

"Christ, I haven't got time for this…"

A long silence descended from the other end of the line, until she said, "You'd better come over."

* * *

Kit had seen the house once. After a cab ride from a London sci-fi convention, she'd watched Vanity drunkenly totter up some steps to a rather beautiful townhouse by the Chelsea embankment with a porch held up by Doric columns and white flowerboxes in every window that spewed out beautiful red geraniums.

Oh, to see the wonders within that palace…

And now, finally, she would.

She trotted up those same steps, pressed the big brass button and heard a tinny facsimile of the chimes of Big Ben reverberating through the house. After a very long time, almost to the point where Kit agonised about pressing the doorbell again, the door rattled open to reveal a plump young woman with a face like an elbow. She was dressed in an overcoat, black wool dress and leggings. Kit guessed she was Magdalena.

"Yis?"

"I'm here to see Ms Mycroft?"

"Okay. Whatever. Come in if you coming."

Kit entered a brilliant white hallway with a pale marble floor. A mirrored console table groaned under the weight of a huge bouquet of white flowers arranged in an earthenware pot.

As the woman turned to shout back into the interior of the house, Kit could see her hair was held fast by an elastic band, into a fist-shaped bun.

"HOI! SOMEONE HERE TO SEE YOU!"

Vanity's voice floated out: "Who is it?"

Magdalena looked back at Kit. "Who are you?"

"Kit Pelham. We talked on the—"

"SHE IS KIPPER LEMON!"

"What does she want?"

"As I said on the phone, I'm here to offer her a—"

"I DON' KNOW! I'M GOIN' NOW!"

"Fuck's sake, Magdalena! Show her into the bloody drawing room!"

"IS THORSDI! AFTERNOON OFF! YOU COME DOWN AN' SHOW HER INTO YOUR OWN BLOODY DRAWING ROOM!"

"Fuck you, you bitch!"

"FUCK YOU BACK IN YOUR WRINKLY ASS OLD WOMAN! HOPE YOU FALL DOWN THE STAIRS AND DIE FROM BREN INJURY! BYE BYE!"

The woman brushed past Kit and left through the front door, slamming it behind her.

Alone and left to fend for herself, Kit walked cautiously into the house, looking for the drawing room.

The walls were filled with photos of Vanity. There was the infamous nude over-the-shoulder photo taken by Lord Lichfield, another black-and-white shot in full Arkadia costume, pressing a penis-shaped ray gun between her breasts. That one had been taken by David Bailey. There was a framed Duran Duran album cover showing a huge Vanity in vampiric make-up towering over a moody picture of the boys playing their instruments. Simon Le Bon's autograph meandered across the bottom.

There were covers of *OK!* magazine, one depicting her first glitter-coated wedding to Jerry Dervish, record producer of many late-1980s hits, now the hugely dynamic CEO of Spinny Records and salmon farmer. The second cover showed her second, more sober wedding, this time to Tom Grayson, financier, property developer and now less dynamic heart-attack victim and dead person.

The corridor opened out into a large white space, bathed in sunshine from a massive skylight. There were fluffy white chairs and sofas arranged around a fluffy white rug, and a ball chair in the Eero Aarnio style with a white plastic carapace and a deep red velvet interior. A spiral staircase curled around a white piano.

I hope this is the drawing room.

Kit didn't feel brave enough to try the fluffy sofas or the chair; she was sure to make some kind of appalling stain. She stood awkwardly in the middle of the room and waited.

"Darling!"

Vanity glided down the staircase. Her hair was wrapped in a towel, and she was dressed in a silk kimono with two Chinese dragons crouching over each breast, eyeballing each other as if preparing for a territorial fight for the whole bosom.

"Haven't seen you in fumfty years. How the devil are you, darling?"

She lunged like a snake, pushing her head forward. Kit was ready for this. The first time Vanity did the traditional actor's greeting, she'd jumped back like she'd been scalded, but now she knew what to do. She stayed put and allowed their cheeks to brush together, while Vanity went 'mwah'.

"Have you been offered a drink?"

"Ah…"

"Of course you bloody haven't. I'm so sorry about Magdalena, darling. She's an utter cow, but it's nice to have someone around since the departure of my hubby, and she's the only maid I've had who doesn't lock herself in the bathroom for a cry."

She went to a bookshelf, to a statuette of a bronzed barbarian brandishing a spear, pushed open his loincloth and slid a cigarette out of his crotch. She lit it and poured herself a drink.

"Please sit down, darling, you're making a very expensive place look untidy."

Kit panicked. *Which chair?* She stepped back to survey her choices, bumped into the ball chair, staggered and nearly fell into it.

Vanity arched her eyebrow. "Yes, sit there, if you like. Tracey Emin made it for me. It's modelled on my vagina. If you look closely, she stitched the name of every man I've slept with into the folds. Quite a big job, but she managed it. I find the only way you can actually sit in the bloody thing is by crossing your legs and resting your head on my clitoris. Go on. Have a try."

Slowly, and with great trepidation, Kit clambered awkwardly inside the chair. She turned around, scooped her legs inside and leaned back until her head came into contact with a round velvet cushion fastened into the rear wall of the chair's interior.

"What do you think?"

"Ah…Very…"

"Hideously uncomfortable, isn't it? But I couldn't hurt the mad cow's feelings. It's the thought that counts. Now, why are you here, darling? Not that I'm not glad to see you."

"I rang you yesterday."

"About work! That's right. I remember. So, tell me all. I negotiate all my jobs now, because my agent retired. Or died. I'm not sure which." She waggled the glass in Kit's direction. "Go on. Fire away."

"Well, it's a *Vixens from the Void* documentary…"

"Oh." Vanity was obviously hoping Kit would say 'movie', or 'Netflix series'. She didn't bother to conceal her disappointment.

"But with a difference. We're filming it all in Brighton and we're going to re-enact scenes that you recorded on location."

Vanity just frowned, staring blankly at Kit's mouth, as if she was deaf and trying to lip-read the words. Unnerved, Kit pressed on.

"It's going to be a lot of fun."

"Really."

"Yes, we're even going to go back to the original hotel. The Hotel De La Mer. I've been told it's barely changed since the 1980s. We'll all be staying there."

Kit's words were drowned out by a long drawn out "Fuuucccckk. You're actually going back there? Jesus Christ! That place is cursed! Every time I go there something dreadful happens to me. It must be built on the remains of an actor's graveyard or something, because it's an utter hex."

She shook her head, dislodging her towel. "Sorry, darling, it's not for me. I'm not going back there, not for all the tea in China. It's just not worth the risk. Thanks for playing, darling, but I'm not going."

So that was it. Kit was worried this would happen. She'd caught Vanity at the wrong time. Now she had spoken and there was nothing she could do about it.

Or was there?

As she looked up in despair she rolled her eyes around the inside of the ball chair, along the names stitched in the wall. In the jumble of letters she could clearly make out a familiar name:

Douglas Fletcher.

"That's a shame," she said casually. "Because there are lots of other people going, and I'm sure they'd love to see you."

Vanity grunted, unconvinced. "You either don't know me very well, or you don't know them very well."

Kit unpeeled her body from the inside of the chair. "There'll be Roger Barker."

"Eek!"

"Joan Peverin."

"Gah!"

"Tara Miles."

"Yuk!"

"And Duggie 'Don't Lean Against That Window' Fletcher…"

Vanity's eyebrows sprang up on her forehead. Her cigarette hovered above the ashtray. "Duggie? Really? He's coming?"

Kit didn't like lying. She wasn't opposed to it in principle, but in her view the act of fibbing created problems. New fictions to keep track of. Stories to keep straight in one's head. She needed her whole brain to contain facts about cult television. She couldn't waste it with imaginary nonsense.

But this was an emergency.

"Yes, he'll be there," she squeaked.

Vanity stroked her chin thoughtfully, like a villain from an old 1920s silent movie.

"Duggie Fletcher? I hear he's a widower now… Do you know what – it would be nice to catch up on old times. Duggie was a lot of fun. He always was a bit of a boy. Who cares about actor's superstition, eh? It's just a lot of silly mumbo jumbo when all's said and done."

* * *

Kit fled Vanity's house in a blur of terror. Her hands were sweating so much she could barely slap her Oyster card on the reader. As the tube rumbled to the Embankment, her mind sprinted through the horrific possibilities if Vanity found out that she'd lied about Duggie. She could barely contemplate the repercussions.

She'll put conditions in all her convention appearances. She'll insist I'm banned from every con she attends!

It was a very grim-looking Professional Fan who left the train and trudged up the Embankment steps. She surfaced by

Hungerford Bridge and her phone chimed with relief. Just like Kit, it was thankful to be back in daylight, able to suck in information once more.

It was another text from Duggie 'Don't Lean Against That Window' Fletcher. Kit could scarcely believe what she was reading.

Perhaps Victor is right? Perhaps this is going to happen because justice is on our side?

This one said:

Change of plan. I'll be there. Please text details.

6

Kit Zoomed Victor to give him an update.

"I went to see Vanity, and I got her to agree to come."

"Oh, brilliant mate! Well done!"

"And I got a text from Duggie Fletcher. He's changed his mind. He's coming."

"Fantastic!"

"It was a bit quick, to be honest. One minute it was a 'no', the next Duggie texts to say 'change of plan' and he's coming…"

"That's because the gods are smiling on us, Kit. Five down, one to go. How goes Patrick Finch?"

"Badly, just as I predicted. The gods may be omnipotent, but their powers are nothing compared to a high-powered agent. I only have Patrick's agent's email, and she replied very quickly with a firm 'no'."

"Damn."

"I suspect the agent hasn't even bothered to tell Patrick about our offer. I find that's often the case with the bigger stars. But there's not much we can do about it."

"Shit."

"However…"

"What?"

Kit gave a grin. "As luck would have it, Patrick is touring in a play and it's coming my way, to Tunbridge Wells, next week."

"Oh my god!"

"I'm going to pop down and see if I can talk to him at the stage door."

Victor clapped his hands to his head. "Mate… That's brilliant. Just brilliant. I mean, that's amazing! What are the chances that

Patrick Finch comes to *your* hometown just at this very moment? They must be astronomical!"

He got up out of his chair and did a little happy dance. "Yes! Yesyesyes! This is really going to happen, isn't it? All the suspects together! This is karma, Kit! This is fate, mate!"

Kit could have pointed out that Patrick's play was touring pretty much every theatre in England, and the odds of Patrick coming to Tunbridge Wells were a lot less than astronomical, but she didn't. Victor looked so exuberant she couldn't bear to dampen his mood.

"It's as I've said all along, mate. We are being helped by the cosmos to do this."

"Victor."

"Yeah?"

"I've had a bit of time to think. And I've been thinking a bit more about the circumstances of Wolf's death."

Victor sat back down. "Oh yes? What about it?"

"It was something we discussed on the podcast, and it has been nagging me ever since. About *why* Wolf invited a murderer onto his podcast. It does seem a bit foolhardy."

"Well, foolhardy was Wolf's middle name."

"I guess…"

"He was like that. Well, speak soon. Bye, mate."

Victor was extending a finger to end the call when Kit continued: "But if we *assume* Wolf blackmailed Lily's murderer to go on his podcast, then the murderer would be arrested anyway. So how did the blackmail work? You see my point?"

Victor sat back in his chair and grinned. "Hey Kit, you know what? I've just thought of *another* really good point. How did Wolf blackmail this murderer to go on the podcast if the point of the podcast was to reveal the murderer as a murderer? How does that work?"

"That's *my* point!"

71

"What?"

"My point is the same as your point!"

"Well, it's such a good point it's worth saying twice. Do you have any thoughts?"

"No. Do you?"

"I dunno. Perhaps… Perhaps…"

He thought hard, casting his eyes to the ceiling.

"Okay mate. Picture this scenario. Perhaps Lily's murderer *told* Wolf that he or she *wanted* to give themselves up? That he or she was tired of keeping this dark secret and wanted to confess? You know, get it off their chest? And it was all a ruse so Wolf would keep his guard down so the murderer could drug him and kill him? I bet the murderer didn't even expect that Wolf was able to stay conscious enough to start the podcast. I bet the murderer wanted to finish him off long before."

He approved of his reasoning, nodding in agreement with himself. "That makes sense."

"Yes… That makes sense…"

"It must have happened that way, mate."

"Can you tell me *exactly* what Wolf said to you? When he told you he'd found out who killed Lily Sparkes. Did he talk to you over the phone, or face to face?"

"Erm… let me think. He called me, mate. That's right. I remember. I picked up a message on my phone for him to ring me, because he'd discovered something amazing. When I called him back, he was really breathless, excited. He reminded me about our conversation about Lily being murdered by someone during the *Vixens* location filming, and he told me to hold onto my hat, because it was all true. All of it. And he had proof."

"What did you say?"

"What do you think I said? I asked him who it was, and he said he was going to tell me 'all in good time'."

"He said that?'

"Yeah, pretty much. A week later, we find Wolf's body in the shed. We tried to revive him, but he was long gone."

"Have you still got that first message?"

"I think so. It's only short. It won't tell you anything."

"Indulge me. I'm a completist. I want to hear all the evidence. It makes no difference if I'm researching the production schedule for an old television show or investigating a murder, I'm going to have to do it in exactly the same way. It's the way I'm programmed."

"Okay mate, if you want it. Let me just check if this is the one…" He lifted the phone to his ear and listened to the message. "Yep. This is it." He tapped at the screen and a few seconds later Kit's phone went *ping*.

"Thanks."

Victor shook his head. "I just listened to it again. There's not much to it. It's really not going to help us."

"Probably not. Did you tell the police about Wolf's phone call?"

"Um… Actually, I didn't."

"Why not?"

"Well, to be honest, mate, I didn't think they'd be very interested in my theory. You must admit, you were pretty sceptical when I told you."

"I concede that point."

"I think they already had a huge list of suspects. They looked through Twitter and Facebook and they found a lot of people who utterly hated Wolf and talked about killing him for all sorts of reasons, like disrespecting *The Lord of the Rings*, and insulting William Shatner. Remember when he spoiled the end of *Avengers: Endgame*? There are a lot of videos on YouTube of guys threatening to smash him into bits with their Infinity Gauntlets."

Victor shrugged, embarrassed.

"Perhaps, if the police don't find anything – perhaps we can tell them about the message then? Or better still, if we find the murderer before them… Maybe we can even get a podcast out of it?"

Kit made a non-committal *hmm* noise and ended the call.

Maybe we can even get a podcast out of it?

That was how all this trouble started in the first place…

* * *

"Hey Vic, guess what? REMEMBER Lily Sparkes? Remember our little chat WHEN WE WONDERED what happened to her? Well, I'VE FOUND out! Woah, baby! Yeah, I know right? Wow. And I've got proof. I bet you're excited! HOO BABY! We need to talk ASAP. RIGHT NOW. Call me."

Victor was right. There wasn't much. It was just a few seconds of Wolf yelling into his phone.

Wolf was somewhere busy, somewhere outside. Where was he? In a shopping centre? No. There was another sound. Music. Singing. An off-tune guitar and an even-more off-tune voice. Someone was shredding 'Wonderwall' into tiny strips and throwing it like confetti into the faces of passers-by.

It sounded familiar to Kit, but she couldn't quite place it. Then, just before Wolf ended the call, the busker broke off and said, "Fank you, mate. You're a pukka gent."

That clinched it! She'd heard that catchphrase before.

In her quest to interview everyone involved in *Vixens from the Void*, Kit had travelled. A lot. Many of her subjects had been too baffled to work Zoom, or too frail to leave their homes, and so she had rattled up and down the country on trains for years and got to know most railway stations intimately.

She was sure of it. That was the definitely the hairy busker who annoyed commuters outside Crawley station.

But what was Wolf doing there?

Vixens from the Void had not filmed in Crawley, and there were very few things of note there for the committed fan. There was the yearly sci-fi/horror convention called 'Creepy Crawley', but that was about it.

Another mystery, she thought.

She wrote *Crawley* in her notebook.

* * *

Kit went to the Assembly Rooms. It was a large concrete brick of a building which, like most modern theatres, looked like it was designed to house nuclear weapons rather than touring productions of Agatha Christie.

She hung about the stage door, rubbing shoulders with cagoule-clad obsessives clutching autograph books. After about an hour, her prayers were answered and Patrick Finch emerged, hair slightly wet and with a tidemark of orange make-up on his neck.

Away from the cameras, Patrick always looked incredibly actory, almost *too* actory. He wore a purple velvet jacket, his paisley shirt was complemented by a paisley cravat, and a paisley handkerchief sprouted out of his top pocket. He was carrying a suit bag over his right arm and a bouquet of flowers in his left hand, and he had that funny half-and-half look on his face, concealing his discomfort with a veneer of charm.

He plunged into the crowd, pulling a pen from his pocket, grabbing proffered autograph books and scribbling on them, still balancing his suit bag on his arm.

"Hello! Yes! Lovely to see you! Glad you could make it! Oh, you are too kind!"

Kit waited. The autograph hunters got what they wanted and disappeared like wraiths. She was just about to approach Patrick when she heard a car horn; a shiny red Mercedes had drawn up on the opposite side of the street. The driver's tinted window glided down and an attractive middle-aged woman beckoned him to climb aboard.

Damn.

Patrick got in the passenger's side and Kit watched the car roar off down the street, her hopes disappearing with it. With an optimism she did not feel, she broke into a half-hearted jog after it, knowing deep down that Patrick was probably halfway round the one-way system and heading back to London. She loped down a couple of alleyways, straining to catch a glimpse of the car until a stitch started throbbing in her side and she bent over, hands on knees, sucking air into her lungs with great whooping gasps.

And then she saw the car. Parked only a few streets away, outside a rather nice restaurant called the The Mykonos.

Not for the first time, Kit had to concede that Victor had a point: *the gods were smiling on them*.

She entered, her eyes flitting around the restaurant. It was styled like a Greek taverna, with columns painted on the walls and plastic grapes tied to the beams. It was quiet and intimate, the perfect place for an after-show meal. Patrick was there in the corner, sitting opposite the woman, lounging with his arm on the vacant chair next to him.

With a wary eye on the waiter, who was serving a couple on the other side of the restaurant, Kit scooted over to them.

"Excuse me…"

They both turned. The woman was chewing on her starter, and she stared up at Kit with bovine curiosity.

"Sorry to interrupt your dinner, Mr Finch, I'd like to give you this." She held out a folded piece of paper. She could see the cogs turning in Patrick's brain, and she knew what he was thinking: *another autograph hunter who doesn't understand the concept of privacy*.

He took the paper with a slightly resigned air.

"Oh… kay." He rummaged in his pocket. "Fine. Who's it to?"

"You."

"I'm… not sure I follow."

"That's a job offer for you to take part in a Blu-Ray documentary about *Vixens from the Void*. We want to interview you and your fellow actors and get you to re-enact scenes from the original show."

He looked at the paper like he'd just been handed a dead rat. "A Blu-Ray documentary, you say? About *Vixens from the Void*?"

"That's right."

He broke into a delighted grin. "That sounds marvellous! That's just what I think I should be doing at this stage of my career! I would absolutely love to do it!"

The woman spluttered into her glass when he said this, sending a fine mist of retsina onto her breaded squid.

"Patrick!"

"Did you say re-enactments? My goodness, what fun! With costumes?"

Kit could scarcely believe her luck. "Yes. And laser guns."

"Well, of course! If there were no laser guns that would be a dealbreaker! Of course I'll be there!"

The woman stretched her hand across the table and tugged urgently on Patrick's cuff.

"Patrick, sweetheart, can we talk about this?"

Patrick looked at the women, then at Kit, then he laughed heartily, meshing his fingers together and kissing his knuckles to stop his guffaws. "I'm sorry my dear…" He patted Kit's arm. "My agent here has been ribbing me for this whole tour, saying it's a waste of time because I've been in telly for too long and I've forgotten how to act. I just thought I'd show her what this old thespian can still do!"

"Oh, Patrick!" His agent shook her head, smiling like an indulgent parent. "You completely fooled me. I actually thought you were completely serious."

"Well, that is the actor's art, Jennifer." He grinned.

"Bravo to you!" She applauded, holding her wrists together and delicately tapping the ends of her fingers. "Perhaps doing the tour wasn't a complete waste of time."

"So sorry, my dear," said Patrick to Kit. "I'm not interested in revisiting the past. The answer is a firm no."

There was a rubber plant slowly wilting in the corner, and Kit knew how it felt.

"Okay. Thank you for your time Mr Finch. I'm sorry to interrupt your meal."

She trudged out of the restaurant to the gentle strumming of a bouzouki and started to walk back home.

* * *

She was halfway home when her phone rang. An unknown number. She answered it.

"Hello, it's Patrick Finch here."

"Oh. Er…"

"I'll have to be quick. I'm ringing from the lavvy in the restaurant."

"How did you get my number?"

"It's on your proposal. I slipped it into my pocket when my agent wasn't looking. I'll do it. Your Brighton documentary. I'm in."

"But what about your agent?"

"What about her?"

"She just seemed… not keen?"

You sound like you're trying to dissuade Patrick Finch from doing it, Kit. Yes, it does sound like that, doesn't it? I would stop that if I were you, you idiot.

"Let me worry about her. I'll tell her I'll be taking that as my holiday week next year. Doing it in February is a bit odd, but she'll swallow it. This will be between us, okay? She must never know."

"It… You do know this will be released on a Blu-Ray box set as an extra?"

"My dear girl, my agent is not the kind of agent who scours Blu-Ray extras for her clients. I'm barely able to get her to go to the bloody theatre to watch me. I don't want a paper trail. If you must issue a contract, give it directly to me."

"Oh… kay…"

"Good. I'll see you in six months' time."

The call ended. Kit stood on the street staring at her phone for a very long time.

Curiouser and curiouser.

PART TWO

7

Brighton, 1987

A stiff breeze threaded its way through Lily Sparkes' hair as she stared down at the water. The suicide note in her fist flapped against her knuckles in agitation. She fastened it firmly to the rail of Brighton pier with sticky tape.

The weather seemed to be holding its breath, as if something huge was about to happen. What was the word for it?

Portentous.

Yes. Portentous. Lily liked that word. It turned up in *An Inspector Calls* when they did it for O Level. When they read it in class Mrs Creehan said she would have made a good Inspector Goole, and it caused the class to groan, because Mrs Creehan always said that about her, whatever play they were reading. Such a teacher's pet! It was a shame they didn't have time to put on a full production; she would have liked to point her finger at the hapless Birling family, the ones responsible for the death of that poor innocent girl.

Now she could do her own finger-pointing. A fantasy bloomed in her mind, standing by a crackling fire, leaning on the mantelpiece and glaring accusingly at a semi-circle of suspects. Her parents would be there. Vanity Mycroft, too. She'd be sorry – if she had any capacity for guilt. Tara Miles, Patrick Finch (Mr Two-Face himself) and of course poor Roger Barker. Poor, dumb, blissfully unaware Roger! And there would be others. What a scene it would be!

But no. You are responsible for your own fate. Lily knew that. She always knew it. That's why this momentous decision would be hers and hers alone. No guilt trips. No finger-pointing.

She glanced again at the turmoil beneath her, imagining how it would feel, leaping from the pier into the darkness. If you weren't killed instantly by colliding with the waves, the air would be crushed out of your body and replaced by water.

Then I would be silent. A non-speaking extra until the last moment of my life.

She shuddered, turned. And saw the figure coming out of the shadows.

8

It was six months until filming, but Kit was a great believer in preparation. She decided to review all the stuff she had about Lily. With a spasm of guilt, she remembered she'd lost interest after finding out Lily couldn't commit to an interview because she was inconveniently dead.

There wasn't a lot, just seven PDFs, but they were all there, just where she had left them, neatly collated in a file on her laptop. There were the two articles Victor had produced during their covert coffee-bar meeting. A third was Lily's obituary. A fourth was a report on the continuing search for her body. A fifth detailed her funeral. A sixth was an article about a concert at her old school, held in her memory to raise money for victims of depression. The seventh, and largest, was a two-page article titled 'Where is Lily?'.

She printed all the articles, to make notes and highlight passages. And she started with 'Where is Lily?'

About a year after Lily's death the local paper had printed the story, using the continuing absence of Lily's body as an excuse to present it as a lurid mystery. For a local newspaper hungry for readership, it was a perfect excuse to a) create a bit of excitement, b) ask an intriguing question that they never had to answer, and c) regurgitate the facts of her death in a way that required no extra actual journalism.

The only thing new thing in the article was a squeezed-in final paragraph, a cursory interview with a member of the Brighton Coastguard wearily explaining that bodies were often swept out to sea and it was not unknown for remains to be lost for weeks, months, even years.

Nevertheless, the article was useful as it recounted all the events of her suicide in great detail. There was a picture of an old man, sitting in his front garden, patting a large Alsatian. It had the caption 'Eyewitness: Arnold Tasker.'

Arnold was taking his evening constitutional with his dog Major when he saw Lily fall.

"I thought it was just a couple of kids larking about at first, so I was really shocked when I saw someone fall into the water. I was quite a way away, and it was dark, so I couldn't tell whether it was a man or a woman and I couldn't tell if they were alone or not.

"I went to the pier as fast as I could but they stopped me because I had Major with me. Dogs are not allowed on the pier, you see, except guide dogs. No one believed me when I got there. They found a note stuck to the railing the next morning."

There was a photograph of the note. It was a single lined piece of A5, ripped from an exercise book and inserted into a plastic sleeve to stop the ink running. There were strips of tape on the top and bottom where it had been fastened to the railing. In the top left-hand corner was a picture: Snoopy flying his kennel.

It read:

I'm sorry. I just can't cope with it all. I'm going to end it. Sorry. I don't want to live anymore.
Lily.

The handwriting was crude, childish and desperately sad. Kit felt her heart sink to the bottom of her ribcage.

Next she turned to 'Local School Performs Concert for Lily', an article dominated by two photos: one of the pupils holding musical instruments and dancing, and the other of two women, one in her thirties, plain, plump and smiling, the other younger, just out of her teens with big hair and lots of make-up.

The caption read: 'Mary Creehan, drama teacher (left) and Jackie Hillier, Lily's best friend (right)'.

The pupils at Brighton and Hove Girls School are going to perform a 'Concert for Lily' next week, to raise money for the Samaritans.

Lily Sparkes, an ex-pupil of the school, tragically took her own life last year, jumping from the end of Brighton pier. She left a suicide note that strongly suggested she was suffering from depression.

"Lily Sparkes was a bright, lovely girl who was very popular," said Headmistress Brenda Tate. "It was such a shock when we heard the news of her death. The staff and pupils thought it was a good idea to do something in her memory."

Lily's ex-drama teacher Mary Creehan no longer works at the school, but she has come all the way from Hampshire to help out with rehearsals.

"It was such a tragedy," Mary told us. "Lily was one of the most talented girls I'd ever taught, and I always had a hope that she would realise her dreams and go into acting. I was bereft. I felt her loss very personally.

"I hope that, in doing this, we might be able to help other young people feel there is hope, even in their darkest days."

Lily's best friend and ex-pupil Jackie Hillier has also returned to her old school to help out, printing flyers and assisting with publicity. "I wasn't a big drama fan when I was at school," she told us. "But I felt I owed it to Lily to volunteer for the concert. I hope Lily's looking down on me, and if she is, I hope she can see that I'm trying to help, and that will bring some kind of closure.

"I think it will all be worthwhile."

There was the date of the concert at the bottom, and the phone number of the school so people could book tickets. She read the last line again. 'I hope Lily's looking down on me, and if she is, I hope she can see that I'm trying to help, and that will bring some kind of closure.'

Kit was starting to feel much the same.

9

The Hanover Parade posse sorted out the bulk of the arrangements: the rental of the recording equipment, the permissions to film at the Royal Pavilion and, of course, the hiring of Binfire's beloved drone.

Once her usefulness in securing the guests was over, Kit's Zoom meetings with Victor became less frequent. Back in her little flat in Tunbridge Wells, away from the action, it was easy for her to feel detached from the whole thing. After a while it felt like a dream.

Did I agree to track down a murderer under the guise of recording a Blu-Ray documentary? No, that's just ridiculous. It can't have happened.

Just absurd.

It almost came as a shock when an envelope plopped onto her mat containing a train ticket to Brighton and the confirmation of a single room booking at the Hotel De La Mer.

She put Milo's squirming body in the loving arms of Mrs Lilywhite downstairs, carrying beds and dog bowls and toys and bags of dog biscuits up and down the narrow steps outside her flat as if in a daze. As she walked through the Pantiles to Tunbridge Wells train station, her backpack strapped to her shoulders and her little wheeled travel case rattling behind her on the flagstones, it still felt like she was moving around inside a bizarre holosuite program.

Even when she arrived in Brighton, it didn't feel real. It wasn't until she was standing in the lobby of the hotel that the reality of the situation finally started to descend.

The Hotel De La Mer was a very traditional-looking hotel. It didn't feel the need to curry favour with Brighton's cultural history by sticking up playbill posters, hanging fishing nets from the ceiling and putting antique fruit machines in the lobby. That kind of nonsense was for the newer hotels.

The place was tastefully decorated with muted oil paintings and animal heads protruding from the wood-panelled walls. The only concession to post-war culture was the American-style bar running along the back wall of the internal courtyard. The hotel seemed like an ideal base for BBC location filming in the 1980s because it was old fashioned, a bit run-down and slightly inefficient. Much like the BBC in the 1980s.

After a lengthy process that involved much tapping on an ancient computer keyboard, Kit was finally issued with a room key.

"Business or pleasure?"

She flashed a quick perfunctory smile at the receptionist, a sturdy-looking woman with a wild tangle of peroxide blonde hair.

"Ah. It's… actually business?"

I know I'm sounding surprised at the words coming out of my mouth, but I can't help it.

The receptionist gave Kit a knowing grin. "Well, I hope you have a pleasant stay. Your room is on the first floor. The lift is over there, breakfast is from seven until ten-thirty, except on Sundays, when it's eight until eleven. Would you like to book for the restaurant tonight?"

"I… um. Can I let you know?"

"No problem. We do get busy. Just to warn you."

"Thanks for the warning."

She got to her door without bumping into anyone she knew. That was a huge relief. No 'how was your journey?', or 'what time did you get here?' No small talk.

When she got inside her room it was an even greater relief. There was a bed, two bedside tables, two lamps, a desk in the corner and a door to the bathroom. It was wonderfully anonymous.

As she lay on the uninspiring beige bedcover and stared at the anaemic watercolours, her chest deflated with a huge sigh as the tension oozed out of her body.

It was just how she liked it.

10

She knew she couldn't put it off any longer. She had to go downstairs and wait for the arrival of their guests.

Lots of people. There'll be lots of people all in the same place. Okay. I'm ready. Just need to put my badge on.

She fixed a yellow smiley face to her lapel. Her 'panic' badge. If things got too much for her, she would twist it upside down. When Binfire saw the upside-down face, he was under orders to come to her aid, steering her away from people while inventing some kind of bullshit excuse – initially he came up with things like sudden pandemics or alien invasions, but after further discussion they agreed that he would tell her she needed to move her non-existent car from where it was illegally parked.

Even before Kit reached the bottom of the stairs, she knew that at least one of the guests had arrived, because there was a familiar voice barking over the hotel muzak.

"I'm not leaving them, darling. I'll wait."

Kit screwed up her courage, stepped out from the behind the forest of potted plants and into the radar of the star of *Vixens from the Void* (classic series).

Vanity was ready for her close-up. Her chestnut hair was lustrous and bounced playfully around her shoulders, and expensive make-up had been expertly applied to her face, sculpting her cheekbones until they were razor sharp. She was wearing a huge fur coat in dazzling white that made her look like she was being slowly devoured by a polar bear.

Kit steeled herself for small talk.

"Hello Vanity. I hope you had a pleasant trip."

"What do you care about my trip, darling. I'm here, aren't I?"

"Is there a problem?"

"No one's around to carry my bags and I really want to get to my room, darling."

"I'll keep an eye on them," muttered the receptionist.

"Of course you will, darling, I *trust* you…" Disdain dripped from her words.

The first paragraph of Vanity's obituary would inevitably include the phrase 'she didn't suffer fools gladly', which was a perfect anagram of 'complete and utter bitch'.

She turned to Kit. "Hotel staff are like seagulls. They just wait for their moment and pilfer anything that moves. And *she* wants me to leave all my bags unattended in the middle of reception? I wasn't born yesterday, you know."

Vanity Mycroft was, indeed, not born yesterday. Most of her was around sixty years old. Other parts, such as her breasts, forehead, jawline and teeth, were more recent additions.

The porter rushed in and started loading himself up with bags, Vanity coaching his progress like she was playing a giant game of human Jenga. She followed him to the lifts, still yelling as she disappeared.

"If you get to my room without dropping anything, come back here and this girl will give you a very handsome tip."

* * *

Kit found Roger Barker sitting at the bar. His jumper was threaded casually over his shoulders and his left brogue was planted on the foot rail, like he was a model posing in a cheesy old catalogue.

His carefully constructed tableau also featured once-blond-but-now-very-grey hair swept artfully across his forehead and a gold American Express card held between the knuckles of his left hand, which he tapped on the counter in an untidy rhythm.

He was attempting to chat up the barmaid, who was humouring his semi-sozzled nonsense with the air of a seasoned professional.

"It's nice to be back down in Brighton. I don't get down here as much as I should."

"Oh right."

"I have a yacht down here, moored in the marina down the road, would you believe? I never get a chance to sail the damn thing. So busy with telly work, theatre work, yada yada… You know. Barely have time to wipe my bum."

"Aha."

"Do you know the first time I was here?"

"No."

"It was 1983. I was over at the Theatre Royal starring in a farce."

"Oh really?"

"*Run for Your Wife*. Have you heard of it?"

"Can't say I have."

"It's a farce."

"Okay."

"Do you know what a farce is?"

"Sort of."

"It's a play where there's lots of *hilarious* misunderstandings. It's very hard to perform. Takes a lot of skill from the actors." He tapped the side of his nose. "Got to be at the top of your game."

"Oh."

The barmaid's response clearly wasn't enthusiastic enough for Roger. He popped his lip out. Then he held his whisky glass aloft, as if proposing a toast. "It's part of a noble English theatrical tradition. Like Shakespeare."

"Really."

"I don't know what you youngsters would call a farce nowadays. I guess you'd call it a sex comedy." He waggled his eyebrows. "Does that shock you?"

"No."

"No, you don't look the type. I bet it takes a lot to shock you."

"You're right."

"Thought so. Actually, you remind me of my second wife."

"Oh really?"

"Not my *real* second wife. She was a bitch." He guffawed. "I'm talking about the one who played my second wife in the *play*. She didn't get shocked easily either. She was very attractive too. Pretty face. Good body. Nice boobs. A lot like you."

"Ahaha."

Vanity had returned to take the stage and wrest the spotlight from her co-star. She vaulted onto the stool next to Roger and smiled at the barmaid. "Don't worry about Roger, darling. He's mostly harmless."

Irritated, Roger turned to face Vanity. The barmaid exhaled with relief.

Vanity pushed her face to Roger's cheek and did her 'mwah' greeting.

"Roger, darling."

"Vanity."

"You look well."

"You too. You haven't changed a bit."

"You too, darling."

"You must have a picture in the attic. Or a captive plastic surgeon in the basement."

"I keep him in *your* basement, darling. He hides behind unsold copies of your autobiography."

Roger's autobiography, *Barking Up the Right Tree,* had sold less than Vanity's autobiography, *Vixen to Fly*. Truth to tell, sales of both were tiny, but the difference between a few thousand and a few thousand and twelve was a valuable weapon in their eternal battle of one-upmanship.

Vanity waved her hand imperiously at the barmaid. "Have you heard of a Hanky Panky, darling?"

The barmaid smiled uncomprehendingly. "Is that a farce?"

"No, it's a cocktail. Never mind. I'll take a Daiquiri. Can you manage that?"

"Coming right up."

"She's paying." She waved a hand imperiously at Kit, who had yet to find the courage to sit down.

Vanity turned back to Roger. "Has anyone else arrived?"

"Yes. Joan Peverin is over there – on that banquette by the rubber plant."

He pointed at a woman, sitting primly and reading a Hilary Mantel. She was in her late seventies, and was very thin, almost skeletal. Like a tiny vampire.

"She's looking well. How is the old girl?"

Roger shrugged. "How should I know?"

"You've not even said hello?" Her eyes rolled back in her head. "God. Typical Roger. If she's older than seventeen you can't be bothered giving her the time of day. Have you *ever* in your life talked to an elderly woman – other than your mother?"

"I'm talking to *you*, aren't I?" he snarled. "Anyway, I don't see you going over there to have a chat with the old dear."

"I've just ordered myself a drink."

"Yeah, right. Same old Vanity. No interest in talking to anyone if they don't have a penis."

"I'm talking to *you*, aren't I?"

Having exchanged jabs, they settled companionably into their positions at the bar. Neither of them made any move towards Joan. They sipped their drinks in unison, sharing horror stories about conventions, moaning about the lack of parts for the more mature thespian, feasting on each other's failure.

After a while, Kit realised she had been rendered invisible. She thought about slipping away, but remembered the drinks still had to be paid for. She blurted out: "I hope you had a pleasant journey, Roger."

Roger stopped telling a not-very-amusing anecdote about a

disastrous meeting of the 'Sons of the Severed Ankle' celebrity fraternity club and looked at Kit with a *who the hell are you?* expression.

Kit was used to this. "I'm Kit Pelham. We have met before." *Only about a hundred times.* "I'm the co-producer of the documentary. And I'll be interviewing you."

Roger's expression snapped into 'boyish charm' mode. "Oh right, oh, you're going to be my interrogator, are you? Light in the face and thumbscrews for me, eh?"

"Haha. Not at all."

"Well, ask me any questions, anything you like, anyone will tell you my life is an open book."

"I thought your books got pulped," snipped Vanity.

Roger ignored her. "So do your worst, little lady. And yes, thanks, I did have a good journey. Straight down the M1 and then straight down the M23. Jag was running like a charm. Might even pop down to the marina and have a look at the old yacht."

"Great. And your room is to your liking?"

"It's fine. I'm assuming I've got your permission to break into the minibar?"

"Of course," said Kit, hoping that Victor's bank balance would survive.

"Nice one."

He downed his glass in one and started to push his bottom off the barstool. "Well – I might see you all downstairs for dinner, unless I nip out for a curry. If I do, I'll keep the receipt for expenses." He blew a kiss at Vanity. "If you get lonely in the middle of the night, dear, you know where to find me."

"Thanks for the warning. I'll find my own entertainment, if that's all the same to you."

"Ah yes," chuckled Roger. "I heard Duggie Fletcher was joining us. Good old Duggie." He caught Kit's eye and a filthy grin spread across his face. "Duggie was our stunt guy. A *real* stunt guy. A real expert when it came to stunts…" He raised his empty glass for another toast. "And by 'stunt' I mean—"

"There's no need to spell it out, Roger," Vanity snapped. "Kit is a fan, darling, and the fans know everything about us… and more."

"Ha!" He winked at Kit. "If you know so much about me, perhaps I should interrogate *you*."

"Hahaha."

Roger looked around. "Where's the lift?"

"Where it was last time. Just over there, between the grandfather clock and the painting of George the Fourth."

"So it is. God, this place hasn't changed a bit."

11

At that moment Tara Miles bounced into the bar, swigging from a Waitrose cup-for-life and swinging her luggage, a large sports bag that had *PINK* written on it in fat capital letters.

Tara looked like a walking, talking and jogging cliché of a health-conscious GILF. Kit had kept an eye on Tara's Facebook page over the years, and in the photos she posted she was always in a yoga pose or sitting Buddha-like in meditation. Her body was lean and fit, and her handsome angular face, toasted by the sun from countless Mediterranean spiritual retreats, was as brown as the mahogany walls that lined the hotel.

She wore a grey zip-up hoodie over a baggy T-shirt, leggings that stopped just below the knee and trainers that were so white they hurt the eyes. Her short hair, cropped close to the scalp, had been allowed to fade to its natural grey.

Tara turned back to the reception area and made a 'come on' gesture at someone just out of view. She waited for a moment, and when she didn't get the response she wanted, she beckoned again more wildly, stretching her face into a wide inviting expression, all eyes and smiles, as if tempting a stray dog into the house.

She was joined by someone Kit didn't recognise; another handsome woman in her late fifties, walking slowly and reluctantly into the open space of the bar.

This woman was tall, with a long neck and a frizz of dark hair that was half tucked under a bright paisley headband. She was wearing a patterned Laura Ashley skirt, burgundy suede boots, a daffodil-yellow shirt buttoned up to the neck and a patterned waistcoat that gave her a slightly gypsy look.

The woman looked around nervously, as if preparing to be attacked by an unseen assailant at any moment.

Tara noticed Roger and Vanity and then waved frantically. "Hiya!"

Tara put the strap of her bag into the bottom two fingers of her soy-latte hand, freeing up the other hand so she could link arms with the woman. She half escorted, half dragged the woman to join them at the bar. The woman looked like she would rather be anywhere else, but Tara's elbow held her fast.

"Hi guys, long time no see!"

"Indeed, long time no see," said Vanity.

"Yes," grunted Roger.

She waggled the fingers on her free hand. "So tempted to hug! I'm a natural hugger. But what with Covid, you've always got that thought in the back of your head saying, oooh, maybe not, eh?"

Vanity and Roger, who had both dismissed the lockdown from their minds the moment it ended, glanced at each other and shared a mental shrug.

"But what the heck!" Tara dropped her bag and performed the most delicate of hugs on them both, tapping their shoulders gently with the flat of one hand and her coffee cup. Then she laced her arm back around the woman's elbow, cutting off her escape.

"So how are you both? Do you know, I wasn't sure about coming, what with all the bad memories of the show. All that toxic misogyny. It wasn't something I felt I really needed back in my life. Because I have spent *decades* cleansing myself of all forms of negativity."

"Me too," said Roger, chortling into his refilled glass.

"But now I'm here, strange to say, I'm really quite excited!"

"Great!" Roger gave a thumbs-up.

"It's going to be so much fun, darling," said Vanity. "We have so much to catch up on."

"I know! Gosh, where to start?"

Kit stepped forward. "I hope you had a pleasant journey." She waited for the predictable confusion to set in Tara's eyes before saying: "Kit Pelham. Co-producer of the documentary."

Tara blew Kit a kiss. "Lovely to meet you, and yes, I did have a pleasant journey, really lovely. I met Dorothy here on the train, and we had a lovely chat on the way, reminiscing about old times."

"Pleased to meet you, Dorothy."

Dorothy gave an unconvincing smile.

Kit smiled back.

And then Kit realised who Dorothy was.

"Oh!" said Kit. "Oh! Very pleased to meet you... Dorothy!"

"Thanks."

While the pleasantries were being exchanged, Roger's and Vanity's eyes were darting at Dorothy. Roger and Vanity were alike in more ways than they cared to admit, and one of those ways was their brutal disregard for anyone who wasn't them. Kit could see that neither of them had worked out who Dorothy was.

"I mean, just being in this hotel again!" said Tara. "It's so vivid!"

"Tell me about it," said Roger.

"It hasn't changed a bit, has it, Dorothy?" Kit said. "I mean, from the *last time* you were here."

"No," said Dorothy.

"It must bring the memories flooding back from all the filming."

"Yes," agreed Dorothy.

Kit didn't know what to do. *I can't just step in and tell them, can I? Because it would be utterly crass*.

And Tara had no intention of helping. She was in the wonderful position of acting cool and progressive while at the same time savouring the ignorance of everyone else. She could virtue-signal to her heart's content because neither Roger or Vanity were interested in virtue nor signals.

Tara is going to put this situation through her juicer, squeeze it dry and drink it like a smoothie.

"Yes. It does bring back memories, doesn't it, Dorothy?" said Tara. "The hotel hasn't changed a bit, not since those crazy days."

"No. No it hasn't."

Vanity gave the woman another quizzical look, then turned back to Tara.

"Yes. We were just saying how it's not changed, weren't we Roger?"

"Yes," nodded Roger. "I don't think they've so much as replaced a door handle since we were here last."

"It's like déjà vu," said Dorothy.

Vanity guffawed. "Talking about déjà vu, Tara darling, I entered the hotel just half an hour ago, and guess what's the first thing I see when I come through the door?"

"Ooh, I haven't a clue."

"Just Roger sitting right here, drinking himself senseless, chatting up a girl behind the bar!"

She threw back her head and laughed. So did Tara.

"That's exactly what I saw the first time I arrived here in 1986!" said Tara.

"Never change. Darling!"

"Same old Roger," said Dorothy.

This time it was Roger who threw Dorothy a quizzical glance. Then he grinned smugly. "What can I say? Men like me, we search for conquest. And if you have the requisite charm to get what you want, then there's no stopping us. Boys like me and Duggie Fletcher have to sow our wild oats."

"Haha. I think those days are long behind me," said Dorothy.

Roger was on the verge of getting it, but Vanity was a fraction faster. She fought to keep the astonishment off her face. Then she wrestled her features into an approximation of delight.

"Duuu…arling! How lovely to see you after all this time."

Roger's eyes widened. The penny dropped.

"Duggie?"

Tara slipped back into the conversation. "Actually, Roger, once someone has transitioned you're not supposed to use their deadname."

"It's alright, Tara, it's fine." Dorothy was slightly irritated by her new self-appointed gatekeeper. "I needed a while to adjust to my new identity, it's only fair that I let others have that time too."

"Quite right, quite right," said Tara, nodding vigorously. "Absolutely. You're so wise."

"If you'll excuse me, chaps," said Dorothy. "I'm going to go to my room."

"I'll come with you," said Tara. "I'll help you carry your bags."

"No, it's really fine. I can do it myself. I'm going to have a lie down. It's been quite an *exhausting day*." She gave a pointed stare at Tara.

"Will you be joining us for dinner?" said Kit.

"Unlikely," said Dorothy. "I'll probably take it in my room. I am very tired. Nice to see you guys."

And then she was gone.

Tara watched Dorothy go and then turned back to the others. "Isn't she marvellous? I met her on the Brighton train and recognised her *instantly*. We had such a lovely long chat. She's so brave. Such an inspiration."

She's talking about Dorothy like she's dying from cancer.

"Well… I think I'm going to find my room now." She picked up her bag and threaded it down her arm. "Bye everyone."

She started to leave, stopped and turned. "Do you know, I think this is going to be a really positive experience for everyone? Up until this moment, I thought my wellness reboot in Cancún was the apex of my soul journey, but I can feel we're on the verge of something even bigger, right here in Brighton. Yes, I think we'll experience something truly amazing this week. I can just sense that we're all going to get in touch with our true selves."

And with that, she was gone.

Vanity and Roger watched her go.

Vanity pushed herself off her barstool. "If anyone wants me, I'll be drinking in my room."

12

Kit didn't feel like attending the welcome dinner that night. She already felt worn out by the whole greeting-the-guests thing and couldn't bear the thought of more socialising. Besides, she never trusted calorie counts on hotel menus. There were too many variables. Let Victor play the host.

She was outside her room, fumbling in her pockets for the keycard, when she heard scuffling inside.

She froze. She pressed her ear against the door.

Another noise. A clatter of objects on a hard surface. Definitely someone there.

It's just a mistake, she thought. *They've double-booked my room by accident.*

I hope.

She cleared her throat and said loudly, "Well, goodnight everybody. I'm going to turn in now. Now what's my room number? Oh yes, room *forty-four*. *That's it*. Well, goodbye everybody, again. Off to bed…"

She made a huge fuss of rattling the key card in the reader, to give any burglar time to escape out the window.

She pushed it open…

And Binfire was sitting cross-legged in the middle of her floor, playing a board game.

"Shit the bed!"

Binfire barely looked up. "'Shit the bed'? Great new catchphrase. Much better than 'Criminy'."

"You scared the life out of me!"

"You should expect the unexpected at all times."

Kit leaned against the wall and clutched her chest. "How do

you expect the unexpected?"

"You take lots of crazy shit, so you can get yourself into a state of being where *everything* is unexpected, then you can train your brain to get used to expecting it." He put his finger to his lips. "Don't worry," he whispered. "No one saw me."

"No one saw you do what?"

He tapped the side of his nose. "Exactly."

He got up, walked over to the window and pressed his head up against the glass.

"You've got a nice room here. I like it. I bet if I lean out of this window far enough, I could see Vanity Mycroft naked."

Kit sighed. "That would be incredibly stupid."

"Yeah, you're right." He sniffed. "Why would I risk my neck to see Vanity in the nuddy when I've got a perfectly good drone?"

"How did you get into my room?"

Binfire held up a piece of square plastic. "Credit card. You wedge it in the door jamb and hey presto. Now I've got Apple Pay it's the only thing I use my credit card for."

"Did you break in just to play a board game?"

"This is no ordinary board game. This is a map of the hotel."

"It's a Cluedo board," said Kit.

He rolled his eyes. "It *was* a Cluedo board, but *now* it's the hotel."

Kit looked at the board. The words 'study', 'billiard room' and 'conservatory' had been whited out and replaced with 'Vanity's room', 'Tara's room', 'Joan's room', etc.

There were facsimiles of women wearing cloaks and thigh-boots on the board. Kit recognised them immediately as *Vixens from the Void* action figures from the 1990s, made by Braxtons models.

Binfire held them up, one at a time. "Arkadia as Vanity Mycroft. She goes in there… Medula as Tara Miles in there… Vizor as Roger Barker… Patrick Finch as Captain Talon."

He rummaged in his bag. "I've got Duggie Fletcher in here somewhere."

"It's *Dorothy* Fletcher now."

"What?"

"She's transitioned. Duggie is now Dorothy."

"Oh." He thought for a second. "That's cool. That makes a lot of sense."

Kit looked confused. "What do you mean 'that makes a lot of sense'?"

Binfire shrugged. "Well, when he was on *Vixens*, he wore a lot of women's clothes."

"That was his *job*, Binfire," sighed Kit. "He was a stuntman and he had to dress up as a woman because they didn't have a female stuntman."

"Yeah, I *know* that, pilgrim." Binfire shook his head at Kit's stupidity. "But you look at all the behind-the-scenes stuff they filmed, you can see he stayed in the costumes *way* more than he needed to. Even when he was doing the interviews they recorded *way* after. No one else is in costume but him."

"Huh." Kit thought about it. "I think you have a point."

"Anyway, luckily enough I don't have to re-customise." He produced a doll from his rucksack. "As you can see, I used a normal Arkadia figure, but if you look closely, I've put a tiny plaster-cast on the arm from the time Duggie broke his humerus doing a stunt."

"Very creative."

"And this is Joan Peverin."

He held up another figure. It did indeed look exactly like Joan Peverin.

Despite herself, Kit was impressed. "This is really accurate. How did you make this?"

"I got a Ben Kenobi doll, painted his robes black, then got a Senator Palpatine figure, painted the hair white, popped his head off and stuck it on the Kenobi."

Kit took it and turned it around in her hands. "Isn't this a Ben Kenobi figure from original Kenner range, from the 1970s?"

"Yep."

"Isn't it really rare and valuable? Doesn't Robbie collect these?"

Binfire snatched it back and put it on the board. "Once he finds out we're solving a murder he'll understand. And if he doesn't, I'll pay him back with the reward money."

"Reward money? What reward money?"

But Binfire's butterfly brain had already fluttered on. He was arranging the figures, delicately twisting them slightly until they all faced inwards. He stared at them approvingly, hands on hips. Then he grinned and raised his index finger in a 'eureka' pose.

"The final touch."

He unzipped the front pocket on his rucksack, produced an action figure and waggled it in the air. Kit recognised it as a Vixos guard. Binfire placed it on the board, right in the middle, on the stairwell that he had re-christened 'Brighton Pier'.

"This little lady is Lily Sparkes."

Kit bent down and examined the figurine. There were two tiny yellow spots of paint on the body – one on each breast.

"I painted on those gold disc things she had over her nipples in series two. Just to make it distinctively her."

"You've put an awful lot of effort into this, haven't you?"

"Well, you've got to do it right."

"How is this going to help us, Doctor Watson?"

"*This* is how we war-game our investigation. Look." He pointed at all the figures in turn. "All our suspects start an equal distance away from our victim, right? Every time we discover a piece of evidence that points to a motive or an opportunity, we move the figure one square nearer to the centre. The one who gets to Brighton Pier first is the winner, or to put it another way, the murderer."

Kit wasn't entirely comfortable about the idea of Lily's death being made the subject of a board game, but she didn't have the heart to squish Binfire's enthusiasm. She patted him on the shoulder. "Good work."

"Thanks."

"Can I start?"

"Be my guest."

Kit picked up the Vizor/Roger Barker action figure and moved it one space forward.

"Motive one. Roger Barker likes to chat up young women. I now know – from a chat with our guests in the bar – that he chatted up a young woman working in this very hotel in 1986. Perhaps that woman he chatted up was Lily Sparkes?"

"Yes! That's good!" Binfire looked at the board with childish glee. "Now we're cooking with frokking gas!"

There was a knock at the door. Binfire dived to the ground, rolled over to the door and pressed his ear against it.

"Who goes there? Friend or foe."

"It's me, mateys," said Victor.

Kit opened the door and there was Victor, grinning like a Cheshire cat. He was immaculately dressed in black cargo pants, black jacket, black polo-neck shirt and expensive trainers. "How do I look? Do I look like a director?"

Binfire folded his arms. "You look like a Sith lord."

Victor shrugged. "Same difference."

"Are Robbie and Freya here?" Kit asked.

He shook his head. "Not yet. They're coming for the welcome dinner tonight. Robbie's very excited. He's not met Patrick Finch before." He frowned. "Have you seen Patrick? I've not seen him about. Everyone else is here."

"I'm sure he'll be here."

"Well, everyone else is here."

"You said."

"He did say he'd be here, didn't he?"

"We exchanged emails," lied Kit. "He's coming."

He insisted on no paper trail. I have nothing. I called the number he left on my mobile and it went straight to voicemail. I can't even email his agent because he doesn't want her to know. I'm a bit buggered on that score.

"Okay, fine. If you say so." He pushed his hands into the pockets of his black cargo pants and paced the room. "Hey. Have you seen what Duggie's done to himself?"

"You mean, what *Dorothy*'s done to *her*self," said Kit, cocking a disapproving eyebrow.

"Whatever."

"And I think you should keep your personal pronouns straight if you want to avoid an incident. I think you meant to say, 'have you become aware that Dorothy has transitioned to the gender she identifies with?' or something like that."

"I know that, mate." Victor snapped. "I spend eighty per cent of my waking hours on social media, so I think I know how to talk about trans people in polite company, thank you very much. You don't have to police my phraseology when we're on our own. She might have mentioned it in the email she sent you."

"She probably thought it was none of my business. And she'd be right. I don't know why you're so bothered about it."

"I'm not! I just wondered if this changes things."

"Why would it?"

"I don't know."

Binfire had managed to distract himself. He was inspecting the teabags by the kettle, reading the words on the packets, opening up the sachets, smelling the contents and grimacing. "It might change things for the better."

"What?"

"Didn't you want to ask Duggie to do that stunt again?

Climb up that tree pretending to be Vanity like he did in the first ever episode?"

"I was hoping he – she – would be persuaded."

"Well, if he – she does, she'll look a lot more like Vanity now than she did then."

Victor stroked his chin. "That is a good point." He noticed Binfire's presentation laid out on the coffee table. "What's this? Are you playing Dungeons and Dragons?"

"No," said Kit. "Binfire is going to war-game the investigation."

Victor examined the board game.

"We move the pieces when we find the clues," explained Kit. "You see, I've moved Roger one space, because I have reason to suspect he chatted up Lily Sparkes when he was here in 1986."

"Really? For sure?"

"He chatted up a girl behind the bar. I'll have to check it out to make sure."

"Well, if it's not for definite…"

To Kit's irritation, Victor moved Roger/Vizor back to his starting space. "Let's wait until we get something concrete. Still, this is impressive, Binfire. I like it. Good work."

"Thanks. So what's the plan tomorrow?"

"The plan," said Kit, "is *Hamlet*. As the quote goes, 'the play's the thing, wherein we'll catch the conscience of the King'."

Binfire grunted and pulled a face.

"We keep our eyes and ears open," said Victor. "When Kit interviews them, we see how they react to the questions."

"We can do better than that," Kit said. She snatched a piece of paper from the desk and held it under Victor's nose. "I got Freya to make up the schedule. Can you see what I've done?"

Victor's eyes skimmed over the piece of paper.

SCHEDULE FOR 'BACK TO BRIGHTON' DOCUMENTARY.

MONDAY

10 a.m. Vanity Mycroft, Roger Barker, Patrick Finch, Joan Peverin, Tara Miles and Dorothy Fletcher to meet at hotel reception. Transport will take guests to Royal Pavilion.

11 a.m. Roger Barker interview.
11.30 a.m. Joan Peverin interview.
12 p.m. Tara Miles interview.

1-2 p.m. LUNCH.

2-4 p.m. Costumes to be tried on at the Pavilion.

4.30 p.m. Wrap.

TUESDAY

10 a.m. Vanity Mycroft, Roger Barker, Patrick Finch, Joan Peverin, Tara Miles and Dorothy Fletcher to meet at hotel reception. Transport will take all guests to Royal Pavilion.

11 a.m. Vanity Mycroft interview.
11.30 a.m. Dorothy Fletcher interview.
12 p.m. Patrick Finch interview.

1-2 p.m. LUNCH.

2 p.m. Transport to Brighton beach.
3-5 p.m. Recording of "Back to Brighton Beach".

5.30 p.m. Wrap.

WEDNESDAY

9 a.m. Vanity Mycroft, Roger Barker, Patrick Finch, Joan Peverin, Tara Miles and Dorothy Fletcher to meet at hotel reception. Transport to take guests to Royal Pavilion.

9.30 a.m. Costume and make-up.

10 a.m. Recording of 'CORONATION' episode. Scene 2.

12–1 p.m. LUNCH.

1 p.m. Recording of 'CORONATION' episode. Scene 6.

4 p.m. Wrap.

THURSDAY

9 a.m. Vanity Mycroft, Roger Barker, Patrick Finch, and Joan Peverin to meet at hotel reception. Transport to take guests to Pulborough chalk pit.

10 a.m. Costume and make-up.

11.00 a.m. Recording of 'ASSASSINS OF DESTINY' episode 2. Scenes 13, 14.

1–2 p.m. LUNCH.

2–4 p.m. Recording of 'ASSASSINS OF DESTINY' episode 2. Scene 17.

5 p.m. Wrap.

Victor frowned. "I don't see… Wait, hang on. All the guests are being called to the interview sessions on both mornings."

"Exactly."

"What do you mean 'exactly'? You're getting them out of bed for no reason!"

"Yes. And there is a very good reason why I'm doing it for no reason."

Victor spread his hands to say 'what?'

"Don't you see? If they sit in and watch all the interviews, we can also see how *they* react to what is being said."

"Brilliant," said Binfire. "That's frokking brilliant work."

Victor looked troubled. "But what do we tell them when we drag half of them out to the Brighton Pavilion tomorrow morning just to drink tea?"

"Well, we are paying them for all the days, aren't we? I mean, *you* are paying them."

"Yes…" Victor clenched his jaw. "Yes. Yes, you're right. You're dead right. They're being paid very well for their time. And if anyone has any problems, we can tell them to suck it up."

There was a sudden *thud* on the door.

"What was that?" said Victor. "Are you expecting anybody?"

"No."

A muffled voice floated into the room. "You! In there! Girlboy! Come on out."

"That's Vanity!" hissed Kit.

Victor went pale. "Shit."

They looked at each other, frozen with terror.

"What should we do?" whispered Victor.

"Why are you asking me?" whispered Kit.

There was another *thud* on the door, followed by two more.

"Shields are holding, Captain," muttered Binfire.

"I'll have to open the door."

"Don't pretend you're not in there," she yelled. "I can hear you whispering."

"Shit," hissed Victor again.

There was more hammering. Much, much louder. The door started to shudder.

"Shields down to thirty per cent, Captain," said Binfire, grimly.

Kit made a decision. "You two get in the bathroom. Take your game with you."

Victor and Binfire folded up the board, grabbed the action figures and scuttled into the bathroom.

When she was sure she was alone, Kit opened the door.

Vanity peered into the room. "Who else is here?"

"No one."

"You were talking to someone."

"On a Zoom call."

Vanity made a *pff* noise as if such matters were beneath her.

"I'm just letting you know I'm going *home*."

"Did you forget something?"

"No, darling. I'm going home. I'm not coming back."

"I don't understand."

"I don't believe you fulfilled the requirements that were conditional on my attendance."

"Requirements?"

The smile on Vanity's face was wide, but the eyes were like flints.

"Yes, darling. Requirements."

"I'm sorry, I don't know what you…" Then Kit realised. "Is this about Dug— Dorothy Fletcher?"

Vanity's face stretched into a smile that showed off every one of her bleached fangs, threw back her head and hurled a quick mirthless laugh into the rustic chandelier. "Ha! Of course not, darling! Why, that would be utterly *ridiculous*."

Her right eyebrow cocked up like the hammer of a shotgun. "That sounds like the utter *height* of shallowness. Why, simply saying such a thing *out loud* demonstrates how ridiculous that would be. It sounds absurd, not to say something that could be construed

115

to be prejudicial against the trans community – who are *lovely*, by the way – so to say *anything* of that nature would be slanderous in the extreme, and if anything like that were to be said, on Twitter or anywhere else, I would be extremely active in pursuing damages."

She pointed down the corridor, in the vague direction of her room.

"No, darling. I'm talking about there not being a basket of fruit in my room. I *always* stipulate that there be a basket of fruit in my room."

"I–I can always get room service to—"

"Too late, darling. It has to be *waiting* for me. That's my point. That's my stipulation. I always stipulate that. I'm checking out after the dinner. Make sure my bill is settled on my departure, there's a dear."

With that final riposte, she turned on her heels, fur coat whirling around her, and tottered down the corridor.

Kit closed the door. There was a dead silence, broken only by the sound of a toilet flushing and two muffled voices.

"Jesus, Binfire. Did you have to go *now*?"

"Burrito from the Taco Bell. You know they always go straight through me."

"She's gone," Kit called. "You can come out now."

Victor popped his head out of the bathroom, his face sagging in disbelief.

"Is she leaving? Did she say she was leaving?"

"Yes, she said she was leaving."

"Because of a bloody basket of fruit?"

"Hardly."

"But you said you *knew her*. You must have known about her stipulation. Why didn't you put a basket of fruit in her room?"

"Because I've seen her use the 'basket of fruit' technique before!" She shook her head wearily. "It's her safe phrase. If she wants to leave, she complains about the basket of fruit." She sighed. "If you actually *put* a basket of fruit in her room, she gets offended and says it's a waste of money because you should *know* the only fruit she eats are the bits she finds stuck to the inside of cocktail glasses. It's a no-win situation."

"So it's actually about Duggie Fletcher being Dorothy?"

Kit fought to keep the sarcasm out of her voice. "I would say so. Wouldn't you?"

"Fuck it." Victor walked moodily back into the bedroom. "You should have prepared for this kind of eventuality." He looked directly at Kit as if to say *this is all your fault*.

"How could I prepare for *this* kind of eventuality?"

"Don't worry, Vic," said Binfire, stepping in as an unlikely peacemaker. "We can still question the suspects we have. We've got a five-out-of-six chance we have the murderer in this hotel. Them's good odds in my book."

Victor's phone rang and he answered it.

"Hi. Yes. We're coming down. I… No, we don't. Kit said she'd had an email. Okay."

He ended the call.

"That was Robbie. He's just ringing to tell me the guests are all assembling to go to dinner." He threw another hard expression at Kit. "And he says that Patrick Finch still hasn't checked in."

Binfire was happily reassembling his doctored Cluedo game. "Whoops. Well, we've still got a two-thirds chance of having a murderer in the hotel. Them's okay odds in my book."

"You definitely had a confirmation email from Patrick's agent?"

Victor's eyes bored into hers. Kit's face felt very warm. She knew that bright spots of pink were appearing on her face.

"I… Of course."

"Your face is changing colour," said Binfire. "Uh-oh."

"I think you'd better show me that confirmation email," said Victor.

13

"He wasn't happy, was he?"

"Do you think?"

Binfire and Kit were outside the Hotel De La Mer. Dusk had swallowed up the day and they were standing in a pool of light thrown out by the faux-Victorian lamps that decorated the entrance. Binfire was sucking on his lightsabre-shaped vape and kicking mindlessly at the kerb. Kit was standing, staring at nothing, trying to calm down.

They were outside because Kit needed some air. There had been an *altercation* because she had been forced to admit she had no confirmation email. Victor had yelled at her.

"What the hell were you thinking, mate?" he had screamed. "No confirmation? Nothing in writing? I thought you were the practical one!"

Kit's stammer had crawled its way into her mouth and sat on her lips.

"P-Patrick said he w-would be here."

"And you believed him? Actors lie, Kit! That's what they do! That's their job!" He had held his arms in the air, mimicking an emoji shrug. "All this money I've spent organising this, and you had one job! Just get Patrick Finch, Vanity Mycroft and Duggie Fletcher here to Brighton in one piece! *One job!*"

Kit had wanted to point out that her one job was by far the most difficult, but her mouth had completely lost the capacity to function.

She had twisted her 'panic' badge upside down. Binfire had been watching the exchange intently. When he saw the inverted smiley face, he had sprung out of his chair and said:

"That reminds me, Kit. I think your car is badly parked. I think we'd better go and move it."

Victor had clapped his hands to his head and glared at Binfire. "What are you talking about? She doesn't even drive! Jesus! You two are just as bad as each other! I should never have involved either of you!"

He had wrenched the door open with unnecessary force.

"I'd better go and meet my guests for dinner. What there is of them. Thanks for nothing, Kit."

And he had stalked moodily from the room.

Kit had to escape. Claustrophobia had gripped her by the neck and squeezed her windpipe.

"I n-need to…"

"No worries," Binfire had said. "Let's get the frokk out of here."

Without another word they had dashed outside, hoping to avoid bumping into… well, anybody, really.

And here they were.

"I've never seen him so mad," mused Binfire.

"Me n-neither."

"He must have spent a lot of money."

"Oh yes."

"He'll forgive you. Eventually."

"M-maybe. He was pretty cross. He was so committed to this project. He really thought he could find Wolf's m-m-murderer."

Her eyes darted in all directions. She felt cornered by events.

"I think I'll take a little w-walk. Do you want to come?"

"Nah," he said. "I think I'll carry on with the investigation. While our suspects are filling their faces, I'll break into their rooms with my magic credit card and see what I can find."

Binfire ran off. Kit was left alone.

She walked into Brighton along the seafront, past the string of hotels and restaurants. She danced nimbly around a shrieking, cackling group of women wearing corsets, fishnets, sparkly deely-boppers and angel wings.

Ordinarily she would feel a little self-conscious about walking around cities, but not here. Brighton, and her spiritual sister Blackpool, were the pre-marriage piss-up capitals of the UK – ergo they were the cosplay capitals of the UK. Of course, there were other places for committed oddballs to feel safe, carnivals and festivals and conventions that popped up around the country, and they were bright and exciting while they lasted, but they always flamed out by the end of the weekend. There was nothing to beat a major seaside town if you fancied wearing something a little outré any time of the year.

Another group staggered past her, also wearing corsets, fishnets, sparkly deely-boppers and angel wings. This time they were all men.

Brighton, she thought. *The city of a million dirty weekends. The city where countless guilty secrets are forged during innumerable stag nights and hen parties. This is the perfect town to commit a murder*.

She didn't know where she was going, but it seemed her feet knew anyway.

They took her to Brighton Pier.

At first, all she could see was collections of multi-coloured lights stretching out to the sea, like all the lighthouses along the south coast had decided to get together and have a disco.

Then, as she got nearer, she could see tiny black shapes milling around the entrance. It was off-season but it was still busy. She walked in under the clock, past the fish-and-chip stalls and the takeaways, past the ice-cream shop with the replica of a cow, past the gypsy-style wagon advertising tarot readings and then on into the amusement park.

Everything was incredibly loud. The classic scary shriek from the Horror House. The bellowing of classic pop songs.

The delighted screams of people being tossed around on the rides. They hurt her ears and forced her to walk faster, past the rollercoasters and the roundabouts and the bumper cars.

She ended up at the Wild River ride, where fake plastic logs ploughed into churning water, over and over again, to the delight of the damp occupants. This was right at the end of the pier. She was always surprised that she was able to get all the way to the end. The first time she came here she expected a web of protective barriers and warnings and clear plastic screens, but there was nothing. Obviously it was up to drunken revellers to manage their own safety.

She leaned on the railings, staring into the black rippling ocean swirling like an oil-slick around the legs of the pier. Unbidden, the ripples morphed into Lily's face. The Lily from her school photo, the smiling innocent cherub, scrubbed clean of cares and disappointments.

She remembered only too well what it was like to be seventeen, and even though the pressures piled on her as a teenager were probably very different to the ones experienced by Lily, she felt a vicarious shudder of terror on Lily's behalf.

So many emotions. So many dreams. So many doubts.

What was going through Lily's mind in her last moments on Earth?

Was she despairing about her life, or in fear of losing it?

Did she fall or was she pushed?

"I thought I recognised you."

She turned, and there was a pretty, sturdy-looking middle-aged woman standing behind her, swathed in a huge Puffa jacket.

The woman continued, "Your name rang a bell when I saw it, but when I saw your face it clicked. I'm good at faces. You have to be, in my job."

"I'm sorry. Do we…?"

The woman tugged the zip on her Puffa jacket to reveal the top of a white shirt and dark green jacket. There was a name badge on the lapel and she pulled it up so Kit could read it. It said *Jackie Hillier – Hotel Manager*.

"I signed you in to the hotel this afternoon."

"Oh. So you did."

"You looked very upset when you ran out with your friend. Are you alright?"

"I'm fine. Just a little disagreement with another friend."

"Okay. If you're sure you're okay."

"Yes. I think so. Just one of those things."

Jackie Hillier – Hotel Manager leaned on the railings and looked down into the water. Her topknot sagged forward and gave her an extra fringe.

"It's quite a drop, isn't it?"

"Yes," agreed Kit.

"I often wonder how likely it would be, you know, surviving… if you fell from a drop like this. Lots of people do, you know."

"Really."

"Yep."

"Sorry, have we met?"

"You mean apart from when I checked you in this morning?"

"Yes."

"No. We haven't met."

"Right, but…"

"I looked you up on the internet and read your website. I thought I recognised you from your photo."

Jackie Hillier! Of course! Kit was normally so good with faces. She consoled herself that thirty-five years was a long time and there was little resemblance between the woman in front of her and the grainy photo of the girl in the newspaper article. Lily's best friend had grown in all directions – the waiflike teenager had become round and matronly, but the smile was the same. Kit should have worked it out from the smile.

"I'm sorry. I should have realised. You were Lily's best friend."

Jackie nodded. "Correction: I *am* Lily's best friend."

Of course she is. Stupid of me. When someone dies you don't stop being their friend.

Jackie looked into the dark waters. The wind made her frizzy blonde hair jump around her forehead. "Do you still want to talk about Lily?"

Kit couldn't believe her luck.

"Seriously? I thought you didn't want to talk."

"Well, that was then and this is now. Do you mind if we get something to eat? I'm starved."

"Sure. Do you want to go back to the hotel?"

"God no. I would never eat in that dump. I know a place. A vegan café. They do amazing marmalade flapjacks. That okay?"

"Sounds yummy."

They walked off the pier, away from the lights, the shrieks and the twisted gravelly acoustics of Madonna singing 'Holiday'. They walked along the beachfront towards the café.

It was getting cold, and Jackie looped her arm around Kit's. Kit wasn't prepared for the physical contact, but the weight of Jackie's arm around hers felt very comforting.

As they walked along the seafront, Kit couldn't help but throw sideways glances at the windows of the restaurants and bars, glancing at their reflections to see what they looked like. They looked like a married couple, out for a stroll, enjoying the sea air before turning in for the night.

Kit liked it.

14

The café was small, barely bigger than Kit's hotel room, with a serving hatch at the back showing the kitchen, and four plain wooden tables in the dining area. 'Rustic' art adorned the walls – huge crude masks in bright colours and pictures of vivid swirling landscapes that were a definite nod to van Gogh.

They went to the counter and Jackie ordered the marmalade flapjacks and chatted to the café owner. Jackie's eyes were fixed on the large hippy-like lady behind the counter as she recounted titbits of gossip, and Kit took the opportunity to furtively examine Jackie's profile. She watched the tiny downy hairs on her nose as they glowed in the electric glare of the café lights. She watched her heavy pink lipstick stretch and crack as it was forced to keep up with the words coming out of her mouth.

Her eyes travelled down Jackie's neck, resting on the part where her throat met the crisp white cotton of her shirt, and she glimpsed a triangular shape pulsing on her clavicle. She realised it was a tiny part of a tattoo, winking in and out of vision as her neck muscles flexed and pulsed.

What was it? The wing of a bird? The tail of a snake?

She couldn't be sure.

"Are you okay?"

The question came from Jackie, and it was directed at her. Jackie was looking at her now. She had been served their flapjacks and was holding two small plates.

"Sorry," Kit fumbled for words. "I was miles away."

"Let's find a seat."

The marmalade flapjacks were indeed delicious. The calories

were clearly labelled with little paper flags, so Kit ate hers with a clear conscience.

* * *

Jackie was a very no-nonsense type of woman – Kit assumed she had to be, to work in a busy hotel – and she didn't waste time with small talk.

"So you still want to know about Lily?"

"Definitely. Is that okay?"

"You rang me up and asked me if I wanted to talk about Lily for a thing you were doing?"

"That's right."

"A podcast."

"That's right. Of course, I understand why you didn't want to talk to me. Painful memories and all that."

"Oh, it wasn't that. It was Lily's parents. They were real pains in the arse. Sorry to say that, but they were. When Lily… decided to… do what she did… they saw it as proof of all they said about the temptations of showbiz. All that sinfulness in Hollywood. I didn't want to be interviewed, because I just knew what I said would get back to them, and if I even hinted that Lily's… decision… was in any way their fault, I'd never hear the end of it. Knowing them, they probably would have taken ads out in the newspaper or picketed my house or something deranged. If they dragged the hotel into it, I could have lost my job."

"Oh."

"Still, they're both dead, so sod them. I can say what I like now."

She looked like she instantly regretted her sharp words. "But, to be fair to both of them, they had bloody reporters sniffing around from time to time, trying to get a quote to pad out their newspapers, using Lily to sell a bit of sensationalist crap about something like…" – she put her hands in the air, curling her long pink fingernails into air quotes – "'The Curse of Brighton Pier' or somesuch bollocks to splash over a couple of pages instead of having to write about actual news for a change."

"Horrible."

"That's journalists for you. Utter bastards" She smiled. "Sorry, I'm being a bit rude. You're a sort of journalist yourself, aren't you?"

"Oh no." Kit frowned, thinking. "Well… In the spirit of full disclosure, I *do* write for magazines, but they're the kind with hobbits and spaceships on the front. I definitely don't work for *newspapers*. I'm not *that* kind of journalist. Oh no. As I said on the phone…"

"You said it's just because Lily was in *Vixens from the Void*, right?"

"That's right."

Jackie stared out of the window and didn't speak for what seemed an age. It was obvious she was casting her mind back all those years. Back to her long-departed friend.

Finally, she said, "She was only on the telly for a few seconds. She didn't even say anything. All she did was stand at the back and hold a silver hairdryer. I can't believe anyone would be interested."

"You'll be surprised. Funnily enough, I'm down here making a documentary about filming *Vixens from the Void* in Brighton. You could be in it if you like."

Jackie's coffee cup stopped just before she reached her mouth. She pursed her lips. "I don't want to be on camera."

"Of course not." Kit realised she had pushed too far. Her mind scrambled onto other possibilities. "But it would be nice to have your input for the documentary. Whatever you like. If you don't want to be on camera, I can just record your voice. If you don't want either, I can just put quotes from you on the screen."

She thought about it. "Yeah, I don't think I wanna be seen. Perhaps you can just record my voice?"

"Okay."

"Will you do it now?"

Kit looked around at the café. Apart from the two of them, there was just one other person drinking coffee in the corner.

"Yes. I could do that. If the background noise becomes too intrusive, do you mind if we try to record you again back in my hotel room?"

"No problem."

Kit brought out her phone, clicked on voice memos and placed it between them. "So, Jackie Hillier, we're here in Brighton, it's 2022, what can you tell me about Lily Sparkes?"

Jackie blew air out from her cheeks. "Well, what can I tell you? Lily was a fun girl. She was really clever. Spunky. Always ready for a laugh." She pulled a face. "When her bloody parents let her. Yeah. She…"

Her voice cracked and she looked away. She blinked a few embryonic tears from her eyes and turned back.

"She was my best friend, and more. She was like my guardian angel. Every time I was tempted to do something stupid, or…" She smiled. "…I wanted to sleep with someone I shouldn't, she'd be there talking me round. Perhaps all that Bible bashing her folks forced her to do did some good. She had more common sense in her little finger than all my other friends had in their whole bodies."

"You'd say she was a sensible person."

"Oh yeah. Sensible was her middle name."

"But she ran away to America and didn't tell anyone?"

Jackie frowned. "Yeah, she *did* do that, that's true. She did do *that*. But you've got to understand – Lily was driven to it. Her parents were totally mental. They were crazy Jesus creeps. Just mad, the both of them. They didn't even have a telly. Lily had to come over to my house to see herself on *Vixens from the Void*."

Jackie went, "Huh," and had another sip of coffee.

"They didn't even want her to work in the hotel, you know – and it's a nice hotel, you can see that, can't you?!"

"Absolutely."

"But they thought it was a place where 'people go to fornicate' and all that bollocks – so they didn't like that, wanted her to work in a library or a nunnery or something like that. But it was the best-paid job Lily could get after she left school, and they didn't believe in supporting her on the dole, so they had to accept the logic of her working there. But there was *no way* they would have let her go to acting school. They would have locked her in the cellar before they let her do anything like that. When she ran away – yeah, I was a bit shocked, but I wasn't *surprised*, know what I mean? I mean, if she really wanted to become an actress what else could she do?"

Kit nodded sympathetically.

Looks like Victor guessed right.

"Did she talk to you about her time filming the show?"

"Oh god!" Jackie leaned forward in her chair and gave a full-throated cackle. "Haha! Did she ever! She talked about nothing else! My god, did she talk about it until it was coming out of my ears! 'You'll never guess what Patrick Finch did,' and 'oh that old lady Emilia Whatsherface is such a scream.' She never stopped going on about how great they all were, and what great mates she was with them."

"Did she not ask any of them how she could become an actress?"

Jackie looked surprised. "Of course she did. One of them, I can't remember her name. She was the one who told her to go to America."

"Really? Which actress?"

"Sorry, it's on the tip of my tongue. I didn't really watch the series, but I caught it now and then. When I did, she was all dressed in black leather like a dominatrix."

"You mean Tara Miles?"

Jackie snapped her fingers. "Yeah! That was her name. Lily said to me that that was her advice to her. 'That's what she said to me, Jax,' she said. 'She said go to Hollywood. You learn nothing from those bloody acting schools, it's all men wearing tights and pretending to be trees. You learn by getting out there, going straight to where the action's happening. That's what you want to do, Lily, go to Hollywood. That's what she told me last night, Jax.'"

"That's really interesting."

"Is it? I guess so."

"So did she like Hollywood?"

"Yeah. Yeah, I think so. She used to ring me all the time from America. In secret, of course. Her mum and dad would have had an eppy if they knew we were talking. She told me all the things she was doing. All the parties she went to, all the auditions she went for and didn't get. She was disappointed that it didn't work out, obviously, and she was depressed about being back here." She waved her hand about the café. "I mean, wouldn't you?"

"Not really. I like Brighton. I'd quite like to move down here."

"Lots of people do. It's fun. But it's not Hollywood, is it? I think I would be depressed if I went to Hollywood for a year and I was back working in the same hotel and all I had to show for it was a tan and a boob job."

"A boob job?"

She laughed and held her hands out in front of her, fingers splayed. "Yeah, that was funny. Lily came back with great big bazingas! She said she wasn't going to get anywhere in Hollywood with the boobs she had. I thought it was a bit over the top myself, but I didn't take the piss. As I said, she was a bit depressed. Obviously she was, otherwise she wouldn't have done what she did…"

Her eyes misted over again. "I wish I'd helped her a bit more. If I'd just known how she really felt."

Kit switched the phone off. "I know I don't know you at all, but to me you look like a good friend. I'm sure you did everything you could to make her feel better about herself."

Jackie grabbed a paper napkin and blew her nose. "Thank you."

"And thank you for talking about her. You've really given me a nice flavour of what Lily was like."

Jackie chuckled with obvious relief. "Is that it? If you just want me to talk about how fun Lily was, I could go on all night."

"Well, it's getting late and I *do* have a busy day tomorrow… But I would love to talk some more about her later. If that's okay with you."

"I'd like that."

Jackie leaned over, put her hand over Kit's and squeezed it. Her skin felt incredibly warm. "I'll tell you what I've got, sweetheart. You know those phone calls me and Lily had? I recorded them so I could play them back, because… Well, I missed her, obviously. Anyway, long story short, I've got tapes of all of them. Old cassette tapes. I got 'em all in a big carry-case. All filed by date and time."

She sighed. "Here's a stupid thing, though. I've got all these tapes, but my ghetto blaster died twenty years ago, so I've got nothing to play them on. Don't make the machines anymore, do they? Or they do and they cost about the same as a Porsche. I mean, it's a shame, but what kind of loony spends that kind of money on a cassette player?"

Kit gave a little smile. *Oh, you'd be surprised.*

She fished in her pocket and tugged out her beloved Sony Walkman, bought on eBay for almost a hundred pounds.

"Would this help?"

Jackie's face was a mixture of disbelief and delight. "Oh my shitting hell! I can't believe it! What are the chances?"

"Indeed," smiled Kit. "What are the chances? I can come over and we can both listen to them."

"God, I can finally listen to them. I haven't listened to these tapes for – what? Oh yeah, twenty years." She laughed. "Definitely! You come over, listen to them – hell, you can use them for your documentary if you like!"

As they walked back to the hotel, Kit's mind was buzzing.

I'm walking arm in arm with a woman who makes her own recordings and files them in date order.

I think I'm in love.

* * *

"I'll say goodnight, then," said Jackie when they got back to the hotel. "I live over near the marina, so it's a bit of a walk."

To Kit's surprise, Jackie rushed forward and enveloped her in a bear hug, squeezing the breath from her body. "Thanks for the loan of your Walkman. And thanks for talking about Lily," she said. "Thank you so much."

"It's me who should be thanking you." Kit's voice was muffled from being imbedded in Jackie's Puffa jacket, and the smell of polyester and nylon was suddenly inside her nostrils, like she was being slowly suffocated inside a sleeping bag.

Jackie released her from her embrace. "It's just nice to chat about Lily as a person. With someone who doesn't see her as a victim."

Kit shuddered. It could have been a shudder from the brisk sea breeze, but she suspected it was a twinge of guilt.

I do see her as a victim. We all do. That's why we're doing this.

"Anyway, see you later." Jackie started to walk away from the light spilling from the hotel windows. Her body was almost swallowed by the darkness when she turned.

"I do sometimes wonder if she might still be alive."

"Really?"

"They never did find Lily's body."

"Yes, I read about that."

"I go to the pier sometimes, on her birthday, or on the day she... disappeared... and wait for her to pop up from nowhere. Or sometimes when the landline rings – nobody uses landlines anymore, do they? So when I pick up the receiver, I half expect it's going to be her, and she's going to let me know that she's alright, and she got washed up somewhere down the coast, and she just ran away again, like when she went to America."

Jackie was talking quickly now, the words tumbling out of her mouth.

"But sometimes I try not to think about that, because in a way it's worse, you know? Lily being still alive and not bothering to keep in touch. Anyway, here's me talking shit. See you later."

And then she was gone.

15

Kit entered the hotel with a skip in her step and a new sense of purpose.

So what if we don't have all the guests? We've got tapes and we've got some of the suspects. I'm sure I can work out who murdered Lily. I can do this. I can do a Poirot.

She entered the lobby, and the first thing she heard was Vanity's laughter boomeranging around the bar. She walked cautiously to the archway and looked through. Robbie, Vanity, Tara, Joan and Roger were all spread out on the low sofas. Dorothy had found the courage to leave her room and was perched on the back of a chair, talking to Freya.

Someone was holding court in the middle, gesticulating wildly. Vanity was at his right elbow, practically resting her head on his lap.

"So the officer said to me, I'll let you off the parking ticket if you take over from my sergeant!"

More uproarious laughter. This time Vanity was joined by Roger Barker at his left elbow.

It was Patrick Finch. He had arrived, complete with his cravat, handkerchief and velvet jacket.

"That reminds me of a funny thing that happened to me when I was touring," said Roger. "It was *Run for Your Wife*. Oh, the press loved it! I got incredible reviews everywhere we went. *The Yorkshire Evening Post* said—"

"I'm sure they did! How wonderful for you!" chuckled Patrick, expertly cutting through Roger's CV. "We actors have such precarious lives, it's so nice when we get some appreciation of our work."

"Absolutely!" trilled Vanity. "That's why I was so gratified when I got those fabulous notices for Lady Bracknell in *The Importance of Being Earnest* last year."

Patrick patted her knee. "I saw you were touring in *The Stage*. I was so sad that I missed it. I'm sure you were marvellous."

Vanity's face glowed with pleasure. She directed her eyes and teeth towards Patrick and put them on full beam. Just for a split second her gaze flicked up, catching Kit's, and she gave a brief nod of approval at her 'little girlboy'.

The tension flooded out of Kit's body and she sagged against the wall.

"He got here, finally."

Victor was suddenly at her side, swigging from a bottle of beer.

"Apparently there was a snarl-up on the M25 and he got stuck in traffic."

"Right."

"And now Patrick's here, I think Vanity's going to stay too."

"Hah. Do you think? From the way she's acting, Patrick is going to need a restraining order."

Victor cackled. "Look, I just want to apologise, mate. I'm sorry I doubted you when you said you'd got Patrick."

"It was a logical assumption. He didn't look like he was turning up."

"But I overreacted. Perhaps we can put this past us and get on with our investigation. Friends again?"

"Of course."

Victor exhaled with obvious relief. "Great. Come with me."

He skipped up the stairwell and Kit followed. When he got to the top of the gallery, he looked down at the bar.

"Here we are, Kit. We've done it. You and me. We've got them all together under one roof."

"We have."

She peered over. The hotel bar was in an internal courtyard, set in the well of a series of galleries leading to the rooms. She could see everyone below, all their guests sitting together on sofas, chatting, laughing and drinking. It was framed so perfectly, like the climax of an Agatha Christie play.

Victor made the shape of a gun with his hand and cocked his finger, pointing in turn to the six guests below.

"Roger Barker. Patrick Finch. Joan Peverin. Tara Miles. Vanity Mycroft. And Dorothy Fletcher. One of those people sitting on those sofas is a murderer."

"Perhaps."

He gave Kit a puzzled look.

"No perhaps about it. Our investigation starts tomorrow."

16

Kit was too wired to go to bed. There was no way she was going to get to sleep after the heart-pummelling events of the past few hours and the new facts swilling around her brain.

She opened her laptop, accessed the hotel's Wi-Fi and accessed the Fliptop streaming platform.

Kit felt an urge to watch Lily's scenes. She couldn't put the feeling into words, but listening to Jackie talk about Lily made Kit feel like she *already* knew her. It was like experiencing a sort of déjà vu, like she'd already known everything about Lily before Jackie had even started talking.

She knew it didn't make any sense, but the feeling was there and she wanted to keep it going, to feel close to Lily. And there was only way Kit knew how to do it: through the medium of a trashy old science-fiction television show from the 1980s.

She clicked on series one, episode one, 'Coronation', and fast-forwarded past the credits (clips of women running, jiggling and pointing their space laser guns) and the first scene (a surprisingly good model shot of the royal space shuttle crashing onto the surface of an asteroid) until she got to scene two – an exterior scene that took place outside the palace of Vixos (aka the Royal Pavilion).

Arkadia (Vanity Mycroft) and Medula (Tara Miles) were crouching in what passed for undergrowth. They were holding laser rifles.

"Did you see it?" said Medula, her head twitching back and forth, her severe black wig flapping in the breeze.

"Over there, I think," replied Arkadia. "There was movement in the bushes."

Medula gave Arkadia a doubtful look and holstered her laser rifle.

"If this is just another one of your jokes…"

"On my honour."

"Well, if it's on *your* honour it's definitely not here. I'm going back."

"I'm telling you—"

"If I know my Gruntarks it'll be long gone by now."

Medula holstered her rifle and turned back to the palace.

Arkadia ran to a tree and started to climb it. There was a quick cut, and 'Arkadia' was climbing up the tree like an expert. Kit knew that it wasn't Vanity; from the triceps bulging in her arms it was obvious she'd been replaced, and Duggie Fletcher was showing his versatility by playing the gruntark *and* Arkadia in the same scene.

'Arkadia' called out from the top of the tree (Vanity's pre-recorded voice), "I bet I can see it from up here!"

Medula looked up at the tree, aghast. "Come down from there, you stupid Zarkrod! You'll do yourself some real damage!"

Then Duggie was there again, shuffling into shot as the gruntark (wearing an armadillo costume sprayed purple and with a horn attached to its head). It sort-of-attacked her, flailing at her with big rubber claws. Tara screamed gamely and helped the illusion by grabbing the claws and practically pulling the gruntark on top of her.

'Arkadia' jumped from the tree, landed, and rolled across the grass. There was another quick cut as Duggie was removed and Vanity Mycroft reinstated. Vanity stood up, gracefully shook her hair out, levelled her weapon and fired.

A ray blast wobbled out of her gun at an arthritic pace and struck the monster. A tiny explosion flared on the monster's carapace and it cried in pain (another pre-recorded sound, very likely the sound of a braying donkey slowed down and played backwards if Jack 'Special Sounds' Speedwell had anything to do with it).

Medula struggled out from under the now-empty gruntark costume and dusted herself down.

"I told you it hadn't gone." Arkadia sounded triumphant.

"Don't be smug. I hope you haven't charred the flesh. Mother does like them rare."

Then Vizor (Roger Barker) entered the garden. He was wearing loose flowing robes and a circlet around his forehead, a bit like a Roman senator. He was flanked by two young women. There, standing by his right shoulder, in a tangerine Lycra top with a sparkly cloak, holding a laser gun and wearing a helmet in the style of a Roman centurion, was Lily Sparkes.

Kit paused the episode and stared at Lily. To her surprise, she found her hand reaching for the screen and giving Lily's tiny, pixelated face a stroke. Even submerged under layers of extremely 1980s make-up, Lily shone with so much energy it made Kit feel so incredibly sad.

Lily didn't have much of a role. She was just required to stand there and look tough, but the contrast between her and the girl who played the other soldier was stark. The extra who wasn't Lily looked disinterested with what was going on. She couldn't hide the boredom of TV filming from her face. Lily, on the other hand, had an intense expression. She *was* a palace guard in the very hub of power in the galaxy. Her eyes were narrowed, her jaw jutting forward grimly. She looked like she was ready to spring into action, ever alert for any threats from within or without the palace.

And she was very pretty. Not just with the glow that always came with youth; she had beautiful cheekbones, intelligent eyes and a wide mouth that Kit *knew* she could turn into a dazzling smile if she wanted to.

Kit pressed play and allowed the scene to play out. Vizor unfroze, saluting.

"My mistresses."

Medula scowled. "How dare you interrupt us during our recreation period, Vizor!"

Vizor fell to his knees. "A thousand apologies! I mean no disrespect."

"Men have been liquidated for less."

Arkadia chortled. "We should get the guards to decapitate him, sister. His head would look good on the sanctum wall next to the gruntark."

"Spare me, my mistresses. I humbly regret my intrusion, but I bear important news that cannot wait. Prepare yourselves. The royal shuttle has crashed in the Voidlands."

"Crashed? What do you mean crashed?"

"Apparently it collided with an asteroid."

Vanity did some acting. She gasped and put her hand to her mouth.

"Mother? Is everyone alright?"

"We lost contact moments before impact. Alas, we live in dark times."

Medula frowned. "Is anyone doing anything useful? Like going there?"

"Mistress Magaroth has ordered an immediate rescue mission led by Major Karn."

Arkadia smiled. "Karn's good."

"Yes, but he's a male," Medula snapped back. "This is too important to be left to a man. I'm going to lead it myself."

Vizor kept on cringing near the floor. "What should I do, my mistress?"

"Get off your knees, for a start. Go and tell the chef he's getting a fresh carcass for the banquet."

Vizor looked horrified. He pointed a quivering finger at himself. Medula rolled her eyes. "Not you, you idiot! The gruntark!"

With evident relief, Vizor got to his feet, bowing profusely. He entered the palace, followed by the guards.

Kit watched them depart; she watched Lily until the last fold of her cloak disappeared from view, then she flipped on to the next shot that was filmed on location.

This time they were on one of the balconies of the Pavilion, one of its domes beautifully silhouetted against the sky. (Leslie Driscoll wasn't the best director in the world, but he did have his moments.)

Medula was leaning on the edge of the balcony, lost in her dark thoughts. Behind her, the double doors opened and Captain Talon (Patrick Finch) loomed behind her, looking very young and dashing.

And there was Lily again, escorting Captain Talon. The other guard had been replaced, but Lily had remained. Presumably the director saw Lily's star power too. Medula gave Captain Talon a series of sinister orders, explaining to the audience how evil and duplicitous she was, and Captain Talon – her willing henchman – saluted and left, accompanied by the warrior guards.

What was that?

Kit had watched these scenes dozens of times before – probably hundreds of times – but she hadn't noticed that before. She skipped back thirty seconds and watched it again.

Yes! She hadn't imagined it.

When Patrick Finch turned to leave, he walked through the doors first and the guards then turned to follow him. But as he passed Lily, Patrick glanced at her and gave a slight smile.

There was *definitely* a look that passed between them!

Kit raced through the other location scenes that were seeded in through series one, looking for other bits of Lily, but there was nothing as satisfying as the first two scenes, just clips of her standing in doorways and that one of her running around a corner that they used *far* too often.

Kit decided to move on to series two, the filming that took place one year later, after Lily had run away to America and returned home in failure.

Kit joined the story halfway through series two, during the episode 'Assassins of Destiny'. Prime Mistress Arkadia was leading a taskforce into the Voidlands. This taskforce included Captain Talon, Vizor and a squad of guards.

The Vixos spaceship (a forced perspective shot of a model) had landed on the desolate planet Chevron (Pulborough chalk pit). Arkadia and Captain Talon were standing by an airlock door in front of a ramp (the only part of the spaceship that was full-size).

"Is this the place?" asked Arkadia.

"It matched the co-ordinates supplied by Mistress Medula."

"I do wonder if this isn't a pack of lies, and she isn't just getting me out of the way so she can depose me in my absence."

Eight extras dressed as warrior guards charged out of the airlock and stomped down into the quarry, forming two lines. Captain Talon addressed the troops. And there was Lily again, right at the start of the line. It was unmistakeably her, but she looked a lot more 'Hollywood', just like Jackie said. Her complexion was tanned and her bosoms had ballooned to twice their original size.

Apart from Lily, she couldn't spot any of the teenage extras from series one. Good. That ruled out one of her theories: that it might have been some jealous rivalry between Lily and another girl that had been carried over to the second shoot. It looked like it was just Lily who had been retained as an extra for the following year – and with good reason. She was the only one who could act in 1986, and it looked like she was the only one who was still able to act in 1987.

Of all the girls standing to attention, only Lily looked as though she was listening. When Patrick said the line, "I trust the Prime Mistress's faith in you is not misplaced," only she provided a widening of the eyes and a slight shake of the head. She also pushed her shoulders back, so her new cleavage shot forward and the camera fought to keep it in focus.

Kit examined Patrick Finch to see if any more looks were exchanged between them, but there were none. He sailed right past her. If anything, he gave more of his attention to the other girls in line.

An acting choice? Or was there a bit of awkwardness between them?

Vizor emerged from the spaceship, grumbling and patting his robes. "This planetoid is filthy! There is dust in every fold of my cloak. This place will bury us all."

Captain Talon sidled up beside him and hissed in his ear, "Be careful what you wish for, Lord Vizor."

There was a cut to Arkadia struggling up the side of the chalk pit, followed by her guards. It was a high-angle shot, looking down on the actors.

The young women in Lycra struggled into the frame, one by one, and when Lily came into view the camera seemed to 'accidentally' focus on her bosoms. Kit knew this bit of the episode very well, and she couldn't deny that during her turbulent teenage years she found herself playing this bit once, twice or even three times before she dropped off to sleep.

She knew she was staring at them even now, and she felt a twinge of guilt that she was ogling a dead girl, but in truth it was difficult for anyone to take their eyes off them. The surgeons had done a good job, and they didn't have that immovable 'plastic' look. They moved independently of her body, as good natural bosoms were meant to do, up and down and side to side. The costume department had even added bejewelled pasties where her nipples met the Lycra.

No wonder the BBC got complaints!

Kit found her fingers were back on the keyboard, hovering over the button that propelled the episode back thirty seconds. Then she decided against it. She let the scene carry on to the dramatic cliff-hanger, when the Styrax robot appeared on the horizon, then switched the laptop off and went to bed.

17

MONDAY

10 a.m. Vanity Mycroft, Roger Barker, Patrick Finch, Joan Peverin, Tara Miles and Dorothy Fletcher to meet at hotel reception. Transport will take guests to Royal Pavilion.

11 a.m. Roger Barker interview.
11.30 a.m. Joan Peverin interview.
12 p.m. Tara Miles interview.

1–2 p.m. LUNCH.

2–4 p.m. Costumes to be tried on at the Pavilion.

4.30 p.m. Wrap.

When Kit left her room she heard a babble of voices in the courtyard below. Lots of female voices.

She looked down and saw a group of teenage girls standing in a ragged line leading out into the beer garden. There was a ripple of excitement in the air, as if they were waiting for… what? Was this some kind of school trip? To a hotel?

She winced. *So many of them…*

Instinctively her fingers moved to her panic badge, ready to turn it upside-down if needed. She started to descend the stairs, the swell of chatter growing in her ears and threatening to engulf her.

It was only when she reached the bottom of the stairs that she saw they were queueing up in front of a trestle table draped with a tablecloth with the word *AUDITIONS* printed across it. Robbie and Freya were sitting behind it, handing out pieces of paper.

Kit sidled past the girls, holding her breath, trying not to inhale the clouds of cheap perfume. She made her way to the front of the queue.

Freya saw her and waved. "Hi Kit! How's it going?"

"Great."

Freya handed a piece of paper to the girl at the front of the queue.

"How many is that?" asked Robbie.

"She was number… thirty-five."

Robbie raised his eyebrows and pursed his lips in a silent whistle. "Thirty-five. Amazing!" He smiled. "We've had such a good response from our advert in the paper. It's going to be difficult to choose just eight."

"Are you alright?" said Freya to Kit. "You look a bit out of it."

"I'm a bit nonplussed, to be honest. I had no idea we were going to have auditions."

"Well of course," said Robbie stoutly. "How on earth did you think we were going to recreate the scene on Chevron with the squad of Vixos warrior guards?"

"I just thought we'd cheat a bit."

"Cheat?" Robbie stiffened in his seat. "There'll be no half measures on my watch. We're going to do everything the production team did in 1986 and 1987."

Freya added, "It's all part of making the whole thing authentic. Isn't it great?"

"Well, yes. I mean, I take it your extras are not getting paid 1980s wages?"

Freya tittered. "That would be silly."

"We're offering sixty quid a day."

"Eight extras at sixty pounds each? For both days? That's…"

"Nine hundred and sixty pounds," said Freya.

"Wow."

"Yep," said Robbie.

"Plus we're getting Joan Peverin to create the costumes for them."

"What? How much is that going to cost?"

"Well, that's classified infor—"

"A thousand pounds," said Freya.

Robbie shot her a look.

"Goodness."

"Yeah, that's what she said."

"Does Victor know about this?"

"Victor insisted," snapped Robbie. "We sat down together to plan it, and he said that I, as *director* of those scenes, should have all the resources I need to make all the re-enactments as authentic as possible."

"Gosh."

Robbie eyed her suspiciously. "Is that a problem?"

"Not at all. It sounds fantastic. I can't wait to see how it turns out."

Freya giggled. "It's going to be sooo amazing."

Robbie put his hand over the side of his mouth and spoke in an ostentatious whisper. "It will be amazing, if any of these lovely ladies can act. I think we can make a start by weeding out the chubby ones."

"Oh, Robbie." Freya rolled her eyes. "You can't say things like that."

"If we're going to be authentically 1986, then I can definitely say things like that."

"Okay," said Kit. "Have a good day."

Freya gave a dazzling smile. "We will *definitely* have a good day! I'm squeeing already! Are you excited? I'm sooo excited."

"I'm sooo excited," said Kit, aping Freya's speech patterns. But Freya hadn't noticed. She had just decided to be sad.

"I wish my darling Wolf were here," she whispered mournfully. "He would have so loved to see this."

Kit looked around at the young girls showing off their legs and cleavage. She remembered all the lascivious comments Wolf used to make on the podcast about *Doctor Who* companions and Orion slave girls and Seven of Nine from *Star Trek* and the Lady Cylon out of *Battlestar Galactica*, all of which he made while Freya was sitting within earshot.

"Yes," she said softly. "I'm sure he would have loved to see this."

"I'll see you after lunch. I'm coming to the Pavilion to help Joan with the lady's costume fittings." She tittered. "Look at me saying 'Joan' without even using her surname. Like we're old mates! Can you imagine helping the actual *Vixens* costume designer to put the actual actors in their actual costumes? If I could travel back in time and tell the younger me what I was doing, she'd never believe me!"

"I'm sure she wouldn't. See you later."

18

The hubbub was making Kit's head hurt, so she slipped into the restaurant, where the shrieking and giggling was reduced to background noise, replaced by the civilised *clink* of cutlery and the gentle *thud* as the toasting machine vomited out an almost-brown slice of bread.

Sighing with relief, she tucked herself behind a huge fern and waited for the optimal moment: the point where the breakfast buffet would be empty and she could grab a coffee and a bowl of muesli without performing the 'dance of the buffet' with another guest.

She heard two familiar voices on the other side of the fern.

"Christ, look at them. Bloody hell, takes you back, doesn't it?"

"It does."

It was Patrick Finch and Roger Barker. She cautiously peered through the undergrowth and saw they were having breakfast together. Patrick was in a burgundy jacket, dark cavalry twill trousers and two-tone brogues. As usual, a cravat was peeking out of the collar of his crisp white shirt and a paisley handkerchief flopped out of his pocket in a bid to be slightly more actory than every other actor who had ever lived.

Roger was decked out as he always was – as if he was on the way to play cricket – in cream chinos, white shirt and jumper.

Roger was staring at the queue of young women waiting for their audition. His eyes were bulging like the fried eggs on his plate. He was masticating furiously, stabbing bits of sausage and mushroom with his fork and stuffing them randomly into his mouth.

"Well, this is the life. Yes siree."

"Oh yes?" Patrick was sipping his coffee. He looked lost in thought.

"Bit of sea air, free food and booze, and all the crumpet you can eat!" Roger nodded vigorously in the direction of the hopefuls, just in case he didn't get the double meaning of 'crumpet'.

Patrick gave an absent-minded chuckle. "Oh! Haha. I see what you mean. Shame we can only look."

Roger cackled. "Speak for yourself, mate. I've still got my mojo. I've got my boyish charm and my little blue pills. I'm sorted."

Patrick winced. "Watch it, Roger. Times have changed. You can't just take a young girl up to your hotel room, let her spend the night and let her out the door the next morning with a slap on the bum."

Roger gave an uncomprehending glance. "Why not?"

"You know why not. Operation Mulberry for a start."

Kit knew very well what Operation Mulberry was. It had been in the papers for months. It was a response to the #metoo movement, an investigation conducted by the Metropolitan Police targeting powerful individuals in the media who abused their positions to harass young women. Most of the investigations concerned incidents that occurred in the 1970s, 1980s and 1990s.

As someone once wrote, 'the past is another country', she thought. *The past in this instance being a mixture of Italy and Afghanistan, where women should be grateful to have their bottoms pinched and end up in a world of trouble if they dared open their mouths to complain.*

If Roger was worried about Operation Mulberry, he didn't show it. He shrugged like a little boy and allowed a big shit-eating grin to crawl across his face.

At that moment a rather tall girl in knee-length boots, a crop-top and a denim skirt that stopped just below the crotch clattered across the foyer, right past the heads of the two men.

"Oh my god…" sighed Roger. "Look at that the size of that one! You have to be a minimum height to go on that ride, eh?"

Patrick prodded the handle on his coffee cup and pushed it around in a circle. "She's young enough to be your granddaughter."

"I don't have any granddaughters. None of my wives stayed around long enough."

"You surprise me. Perhaps, in this day and age, it might be safer if you tried chatting up ladies a little older? The ones who expect a bit more from a relationship than a lolly and a packet of crisps? If you can chat up the more mature type of lady, of course."

"Of course I can. I have infallible techniques for all ages, types and nationalities. Even the Scots, and you know what chippy bastards they can be."

"Fiver says you can't chat up a woman over twenty-five."

"What? You're on. Just watch me."

Now the bet had been accepted, Patrick looked embarrassed he'd even brought it up. He had another slurp of his coffee and stared at the young women, lost in thought.

He watched as the aspiring actors took their little coloured sheets and clumped across on their unsuitable footwear to a long row of chairs facing the restaurant. Some of them sat like men, crossing their long brown legs and resting their ankles on their knees, so their tiny skirts gaped open and showed what little of their modesty was left. Embarrassed, he averted his eyes.

"Seriously, Roger," he said at last. "Aren't you concerned about Operation Mulberry? I mean, after all that happened back in the 1980s?"

"Of course I am. But you can't worry about those things. If it happens, it happens. I might live in dread of a knock on the door from PC Plod, unlike you, but at least I had fun."

He grinned and gave a huge wink.

Patrick shook his head. "I don't think any of us are really safe. You know how this stuff works. Ninety-five per cent of the men who get caught are predatory sods who deserve everything they get."

"Like me, you mean."

"I didn't say that… Well, yes, I did. You are a randy little shit."

"Guilty as charged."

"But there's always one or two who get brought down by nudge-nudge-wink-wink innuendo, and they're usually high-profile celebrities who get their reputations dragged through the mud before they get exonerated."

"Like you, you mean."

"Well, I'm not arguing with that…"

19

Roger and Patrick finished their breakfast and headed out into the lobby.

Roger's head was still bobbing, eyes travelling from one girl to the other. Assessing his chances.

Kit hurled a black coffee down her throat and followed them into the lobby. Victor was waiting by the entrance, standing by a pile of metal boxes and dressed in his 'director gear'.

"Morning." He nodded into the courtyard. "It's all happening, isn't it?"

"It certainly is. I didn't know we were holding auditions."

"Didn't I tell you?"

"No."

"Oh well. We're holding auditions. Now you know."

"Thank you for telling me." Kit's sarcasm could have dissolved rock. "Are you paying the hotel for the use of their rooms?"

"Of course."

"How much?"

"Only two hundred quid."

"Two hundred? And you're paying a thousand for Joan to make new costumes, and nearly a thousand for extras? Are you mad? Victor, this is becoming ridiculous…"

"Look." Victor cast his eyes right and left and lowered his voice to a whisper. "Robbie and I haven't been in the best of places recently. He wanted to get married, did you know that?"

"No. I didn't know that."

"I didn't want to get married. I didn't want things to change. Well, you know Robbie, he just took that as me wanting to keep my options open."

"I'm not sure what you're getting at."

"I want to make him happy, and making him feel like a proper *Vixens from the Void* director is the best way I know."

They were interrupted by a piercing whistle from the courtyard, like a football referee had just spotted a foul. They turned to see Robbie standing on a chair, holding a clipboard.

"Okay everyone – little bit of hush, please? Can everyone with blue sheets of paper go through to the 'Max Miller' room? Red and yellow sheets can wait in the 'Nellie Banks' room."

Coats were snatched from chairs and bags were grabbed from tables. The excited chatter dwindled into a low murmur as the courtyard slowly drained of teenagers. Robbie strode after them, gripping his iPad. Freya scuttled behind.

"Look how happy he is," whispered Victor.

"It's costing you a fortune."

"It would have cost more to pay for a wedding and a honeymoon." He shrugged. "And look at it this way. All this is going to be great for our investigation. Imagine our suspects' faces when they see our team of Vixos warrior guards in full costume. That will certainly prompt a few memories!"

Kit looked at Roger's expression as he leered over the gaggle of teens.

It will prompt more than that.

Victor took her silence for condemnation. "It's fine. Trust me. Let's talk about this later. I have to drive over to the Pavilion and help Binfire set everything up. I'll get him to bring the minibus over to you as soon as I get there. You'll be okay to get everyone there?"

"Of course."

He gave an insincere smile. "Just make sure you don't lose Patrick again, okay?"

"I didn't—"

But he was out of the doors before she could protest.

20

"Excuse me, are you Kit Pelham?"

Kit turned. A girl with purple hair dressed in a dark green trouser suit was smiling at her.

"Yes."

"I've got a message for you, from our hotel manager, Jackie Hillier?"

"Oh!"

"Yes, she's looking for you. She's got something that you might be interested in?"

The girl had a habit, imported from Australian soap operas, of giving every sentence an upward inflection, so everything became a question.

As if on cue, Jackie appeared from the restaurant. She bustled up to them, slightly out of breath. Her face was as pink as her shiny lipstick.

I wonder if that's why I'm so fascinated by her, Kit thought. *Her hair and make-up are straight out of the 1980s.*

No. It's not just that. Definitely not just that.

Kit couldn't help but notice that an extra button had come undone on her shirt, and a bit more of her tattoo was on display. She could now see the triangle was at the end of something long and tapered, like a claw, or a tail.

"Finally! I've been looking for you everywhere."

Jackie caught her breath, looking around at the bustling courtyard, her face a mixture of amazement and amusement. "So this is all down to you, is it?"

Kit looked embarrassed. "I'm afraid so."

"This is even more of a fuss than when they came down here

to make the actual telly show."

"I'm sure it is."

"It's a lot of effort for a… what, a Blu-Ray extra?"

Kit cleared her throat in embarrassment. "Well, you have to understand, most *Vixens from the Void* fans own the episodes already – quite a few times over. They've already got the script books, the edited video, the un-edited video, the DVD with the terrible cover, the DVD with the nice cover, the DVD special edition, the DVD special edition with the collectible keyring… And they can also watch them whenever they like because they subscribe to BritBox and Fliptop. If we want them to buy the episodes all over again on Blu-Ray, we've got to give them an extra-special something."

"Well, it certainly looks extra special from here. Anyway, here you go!"

Jackie proffered a small Jiffy bag. From the weight and shape of it, Kit knew what was inside.

"Thanks."

As Kit took the package, Jackie's thumb brushed against her wrist. A shudder of excitement spread through her and her body gave a little shake like a dog coming in from a rainstorm.

"Thanks again."

"I knock off at six. Perhaps we could listen to the other tapes tonight?"

"Definitely."

Jackie lowered her voice. "That's a date then."

And with those words, she trotted back to her station, joining the purple-haired girl behind the reception desk.

Kit ripped off the end of the Jiffy bag and slid the contents into her hand. Sure enough, it was a battered C90 tape with childish writing on the side.

Phone conversation with Lily. 12/9/86
8.42 a.m.

On the part of the card insert normally reserved for track listings, it said:

If lost please return to:
Jacqueline Hillier
293 Argyle Crescent
Brighton BN1 4QA

It was wrapped in a note. Jackie Hillier's handwriting hadn't changed a lot in thirty years.

Something to listen to when you have the chance!
And there's plenty more where this came from!
Love
J xxx

Kit felt the hairs on her neck prickle. Was it because the investigation was finally producing evidence, or was it because Jackie signed the note with three kisses and a 'love'?

She reached behind and patted her backpack. She felt the comforting bulk of her Sony Walkman in the side pocket.

Something to listen to on the journey.

21

Patrick leapt to his feet as he spotted Joan Peverin tottering at the top of the stairwell and hurried to assist her.

Joan was in her usual ensemble of black trousers, white button-down shirt and red boots, but she had swathed herself in a massive coat, a quilted multicoloured patchwork affair that looked like it had been snipped out of an antique bedspread. A rainbow of bracelets clattered and glided up and down her arms.

He took Joan's arm and helped her wobble down the stairs, one step at a time.

"Allow me," he said.

"Oh my goodness. *Such* a gentleman." Joan's voice was high and scratchy, as if it had been recorded on a wax cylinder.

Vanity appeared behind them, saw her opportunity and rushed down the stairs to intercept, slipping her arm around Patrick's other elbow.

"Oh yes. Such a gentleman," Vanity echoed.

Once again, Vanity was dressed for both summer and winter, her body submerged in her huge white fur coat and her eyes submerged behind huge sunglasses.

Trapped by Joan's sluggish gait, they went down the stairs three abreast.

"This reminds me of the big walk down we did when I played Miss Hannigan in *Annie*. I was *sensational*. I do love musicals, don't you?"

"Oh yes. Love them."

"I hear there's a revival coming to the West End. I'm sure only those represented by top-drawer agents will be seen. I wonder if...?"

"Excuse me. You're him, aren't you?"

They had reached the bottom of the stairs. The voice had come from a short, stout brunette girl in a crop-top with a scooped neckline, a short demin skirt and white stilettos.

Patrick gratefully unfastened himself from Vanity's arm and guided Joan to a sofa in the lobby. "Yes, I am. I am indeed him."

A tall blonde girl – the one who was the subject of Roger's fascination at breakfast – joined her. She nudged her sidekick in the ribs. "Sorry about her. You're Patrick Finch, that's what she's trying to say."

"I know that," the brunette snapped. "My mum loves you."

Patrick grinned. "Oh. I get a lot of mums."

The brunette looked embarrassed.

"She doesn't mean anything by it," said the blonde one. "It's just a fact. My little sister loves you too. And me. You're really good as Wistful."

"Thank you."

"I'm Sandra," said the tall blonde one. "She's Bethany."

Patrick bowed his head. "Pleased to meet you, Sandra, Bethany."

Bethany raised her hand and waggled her fingers, like she was answering a question in a classroom. "Could we get a selfie?"

Sandra looked askance at her friend. "Beth! He's obviously busy."

Patrick gave his full twinkly smile at them, showing off his immaculately capped teeth. "Of course you can!"

Patrick allowed himself to be manoeuvred into position between Sandra and Bethany, and each girl in turn pushed their bodies against him and held their phones out to get a photo.

As this ritual of the selfie took place, Joan Peverin looked on with frank bemusement, and Vanity, who had been put in the awkward position of 'actress who had not been recognised', simmered in silence, a plastic grin pinned to her face.

Sandra and Bethany checked their phones to make sure they had decent photos. Satisfied, they turned back to Patrick.

"Thanks so much," said Bethany. "My mum's gonna flip out when I send this."

"Thank you, *Patrick*," added Sandra, using his name slowly and with great purpose. "We really appreciate it."

"It's my pleasure," twinkled Patrick. "Who knows? Perhaps we might be working together?"

Sandra looked mystified for a second. Then she aimed a sparkly fingernail in the direction of the head of the queue. "Are you gonna be in this?"

Patrick nodded and winked.

She turned to Bethany and they gripped each other's elbows. "Fukkk…innn' hell! We have sooo got to get a part!"

"We sooo do!"

As if an instantaneous telepathic message jumped between them, they both yanked down their tops to release extra boob.

"We're gonna be your leading ladies, Pat!"

"Bet on it!"

Patrick chuckled and waved. "I believe it!"

Patrick went back to his seat next to Roger, who pushed an elbow into Patrick's ribs and muttered a few words. Kit couldn't hear what Roger said, but she had a shrewd idea the message was something along the lines of 'you're in there'.

22

Dorothy was next to arrive. She was wearing another floaty skirt, but the yellow shirt and colourful gypsy-style waistcoat had been discarded in favour of a charcoal polo-neck sweater.

She flashed a wintry smile to the others and sat by herself on the sofa on the other side of the doorway. In case she left the others in any doubt as to her unwillingness to mingle, she placed her large leather shoulder bag on her knees like a closed drawbridge and took out a book to read, holding it directly in front of her face.

Tara appeared moments later, carrying her *PINK* sports bag. If Kit didn't know better, she would guess that Tara had been waiting to ambush Dorothy.

She made a beeline for Dorothy and sat next to her. As soon as Tara plonked herself down, Dorothy held her book tighter and uncrossed and crossed her legs, so her left foot was in the air and pointing away from Tara.

"Morning."

"Morning."

"Did you sleep well?"

"Yes. Fine."

"I found it difficult myself. But I always do in strange beds. I can only cope with a certain amount of ambient noise when I meditate, and I couldn't bring my white noise machine with me. Too bulky."

"Aha. Right."

"You are so beautiful."

The compliment came out of nowhere. Dorothy was so taken off-guard she let the book fall to her lap.

"Oh. Thank you."

"Yes you are. Very beautiful. And you know where that beauty comes from? Courage. Courage to be you."

"Right."

"That's the courage I'm talking about."

"Oh."

"The only courage there is."

"Really? The only courage?" Dorothy's northern accent peeped out and showed itself. It was salted with irritation.

"Oh yes."

"What about the courage of climbing the side of a tall building? Or throwing yourself out of a moving car or hurling yourself sixty feet out of a window into a pile of boxes? Because I did that too."

"No. That's not courage."

"I think it is."

"No."

"No, it *really* is."

"We both know what courage is. *We know.*"

As if to emphasise how well they both knew, Tara's hand glided across and fastened itself to Dorothy's knee. Dorothy stared at the hand, and then raised her head. She caught Kit's eye and looked imploringly at her.

The expression said *help me escape from this lunatic.*

Kit's phone pinged. It was a message from Binfire. She took a breath, stepped into the middle of the foyer and clapped her hands.

"Hi everybody. The minibus is here!"

Vanity looked askance at Joan. "Did she just say… *minibus*?"

Joan either didn't register the horror in Vanity's voice or chose to ignore it. "How novel!"

* * *

The guests exited the hotel to find a shiny minibus waiting for them. Patrick, Vanity and Roger took one look at it and dashed for their cars, promising to meet the others at the Pavilion.

That left Joan, Dorothy and Tara. Binfire leapt out of the driver's side and struck a pose, hands on hips.

"Ladies of the Vixen empire. If you would like to board this imperial shuttle bound for the planet of Vixos, then we will be there in no time, thanks to these state-of-the-art warp engines. Please keep your arms inside the carriage at all times."

Joan entered the minibus like she was boarding the *Queen Mary* on its maiden voyage. Dorothy followed. Kit, thinking on her feet, dashed in behind and sat next to her.

Tara entered seconds later and pouted when she saw the seat next to Dorothy was occupied. She settled for a seat at the front. Dorothy threw her head back and sighed with relief. Kit felt a warm glow inside her chest, just below her panic badge.

Binfire saluted his passengers, slid the door shut, and off they went.

Once the minibus left the hotel and turned onto the seafront, Kit slotted the cassette into her Walkman, put the earphones on and pressed play. After a few moments of hiss there were the familiar pops and clunks that told her someone had been fiddling with the buttons on an old cassette recorder.

The conversation started mid-sentence. The decision to record must have been taken at the last minute.

"*...how's life out there?*" That was Jackie's voice. Higher, trembling with insecurity, the voice of a little girl.

"*Really good. The weather's good. I've managed to find a shop that sells teabags so obviously that's good news.*"

It was strange, but Kit had never heard Lily Sparkes speak before. It was a bit of a surprise. She was expecting Lily to be full of life, but also earthy, like Nancy from *Oliver Twist*. There was Estuary English in there, but only a trickle. She sounded like any well-spoken public schoolgirl, no different to the girls Kit went to school with, the ones with designer clothes, who drove to school in their own cars and went out with boys whose parents owned villas in Spain.

Jackie laughed at the teabags reference.

"*Well, you're missing nothing back here. Same old, same old. Someone tried to smuggle a dog into one of the rooms and it shat on the floor. That's about as exciting as it gets.*"

"*Sounds amazing. My Hollywood friends are so interested in my dog poo hotel stories. They keep on at me all the time to tell another one.*"

"*Sure they are. How's the acting? How's that going?*"

"*I've got a good feeling about my next audition. It's for* Dallas."

"*Wow. What do you have to do?*"

"*Serve some coffee to JR. That's about it. Oh, and I've got a* Dukes of Hazzard *audition.*"

"*Well yee-hah!*"

"*Yee-hah indeed. I'm auditioning for a woman who breaks down on the side of the road and the Duke boys come to my aid.*"

"*Nice work if you can get it.*"

The conversation chugged on in a desultory way for a few more minutes. Every time Jackie mentioned Brighton and the hotel, Kit could hear Lily switch off. She wasn't interested. And once the 'wow' factor subsided, Jackie didn't sound very excited to hear a list of Lily's failed auditions.

"*Well,*" said Jackie at last. "*I'd better go. I think my breakfast is ready.*"

"*It's okay, I think my breakfast is ready too.*"

"*Bye then.*"

"*Bye.*"

"*Love you.*"

That was when Jackie's voice cracked. The emotions bubbled over like a cauldron and Kit could hear the tears start to flow.

Lily's response was simple and kind and heartfelt, but the emotion was not reciprocated.

"Love you too."

Then there was a clatter as Lily abruptly put the phone down. And the cassette resumed its empty hiss.

23

Barely five minutes into the journey the onion-shaped minarets of the Royal Pavilion came into view over the more traditional English skyline. The domes looked crazy and exotic and utterly out of place, like a tattoo of a flaming skull on the wizened bicep of a pensioner.

Binfire parked outside the Pavilion, pulled open the door and gave another low bow as Dorothy, Joan, Tara and Kit disembarked.

"Welcome to the planet Vixos, ladies. Remember, if you own any men, they must be chipped and registered or they will have to be castrated."

Vanity, Roger and Patrick were already standing outside the main entrance like a coachload of tourists in front of an exotic foreign hotel. They were chatting to a woman in her fifties. Kit presumed – from what Victor told her via email – that she was Dr Alexandra Loske, the Pavilion's curator.

The woman oozed academia; her long dark hair was feathered with grey, and she wore a grey jacket and black culottes. A silk scarf was draped around her neck.

As Kit approached, she could gradually decipher what Roger was saying to the doctor.

"…brains *and* beauty? That's quite a combination."

Dr Loske laughed awkwardly. "Aha. Well… That's very…?" She turned gratefully to Kit. "Hello, you must be Kit Pelham."

The doctor had a faint German accent. *Just when you thought she couldn't possibly be more of a stereotypical art historian.*

"I am," said Kit. "Thank you for having us."

"Haha! Thank *you*! Now the Pavilion is a trust and only

partially funded by the local authority, we need all the sponsorship we can get. Your donation is very generous and very welcome."

Very generous? How much had Victor agreed to pay?

"Um, well... I'm glad we're very generous. Getting the chance to film in this beautiful place is cheap at twice the price!"

Dr Loske laughed. "I may hold you to that!" She turned to the waiting group. "Hello, I'm the curator of the Pavilion, Alexandra Loske, and I would love to show you around the place, but I gather you've all been here before, or should I say you've been to the planet Vixos before..."

There was a ripple of polite laughter.

"...and I know you're on a tight schedule, so let's get started." She indicated the black-clad teenager standing awkwardly by the doors. "This is Marie, she'll stay with you during the day."

Marie gave a little wave.

"She'll be on hand if there's anything you need. I'll be just upstairs in my office if anything happens that's above her pay grade."

Dr Loske led them into the Pavilion. Roger trotted alongside her. "Amazing building."

"It is."

"Quite amazing."

"Yes."

"So do you live in Brighton?"

"No. I commute."

"Really."

"I'm responsible for curating several museums. I stay in a hotel when I'm down here."

"Aha. Hotel! Us too!"

"Snap."

"So, what's a nice girl like you doing in a place like this?"

Dr Loske gave him an askance look. "I beg your pardon?"

"How did you end up here?"

"Doing my job?"

"Aha, yes. But what makes a nice girl like you do a job like this?"

She glanced at him like he was a lunatic. "A love of antiquities, would you believe? I happen to have a doctorate in art history. Hence the 'Doctor' part of my name?"

"Oh right, so you're not a doctor of *medicine*. Haha. Shame. I was hoping you could have a look at my back. It's been playing up lately."

"I'm obviously not that kind of doctor."

"Are you sure you wouldn't want to check it? I'm sure you'd be glad to see the back of me!"

He chortled at his excruciating joke.

Dorothy and Kit were walking behind them. Dorothy was listening to their conversation, her mouth open in astonishment.

"What is that idiot doing?" she murmured.

"It's part of a bet," said Kit.

"What bet?"

"Patrick bet Roger he wasn't able to chat up anyone over twenty-five."

"Really? I'd take that bet in a heartbeat." The northern twang crept back into Dorothy's voice. Kit remembered she sounded a lot more Mancunian when she was Duggie. "Everyone knows Roger has a *type*."

A sardonic grin spread across her face, and Kit realised it was the first time since she got here that she had seen Dorothy smile.

Meanwhile Roger was in up to his neck in cringe, and still merrily plunging his spade into the soil.

"Well, I'm just telling you now, even in a building as lovely as this, your beauty has not gone unnoticed."

"I'll take that as a win." The sarcasm in Dr Loske's voice was so thick it could have been used to lacquer the ornamental Chinese cabinets they were passing.

"I'm glad you love antiques. I approve."

"Really."

"Actually, I'm a bit of a collector of antiquities myself."

"I can tell from your chat-up lines."

24

No matter how many times Kit visited the Royal Pavilion (and she became quite a regular visitor when she realised she could just buy a ticket and walk around an actual *Vixens from the Void* set) she was never quite prepared for what lay inside.

It was like someone had set off a fusion bomb and fused every fusion restaurant together. There were murals and stained-glass windows and faux bamboo and every kind of colour thrown together in an orgy of sensory overload. There were columns shaped like palm trees and chandeliers shaped like lilies. And dragons. Lots and lots of dragons. Big ones, small ones, angry ones and silly ones. Dragons curling around palm-tree-shaped columns and dragons holding up lily-shaped chandeliers.

In her Big Brain of Useless Facts, Kit knew there were so many dragons in the décor (a fine example of the British cultural insanity of the period) that the *Vixens* script editor was forced to write them into the script.

"Let me show you where you're filming today."

Dr Loske led them through the doors and they *ooh*'d and *aah*'d their way through corridors until they entered a room covered in golds and reds.

"The music room," she said with evident pride, flourishing her hand like a magician.

"Wow," said everyone else.

It was a large space, dominated by deep red womb-like walls and a massive pipe organ at the far end. Huge chandeliers shaped like lotus blossoms hung from the domed ceiling, glowing with their own soft light. And, of course, there were dragons. They snaked up and down curtains, around pillars and played with each other on the carpet.

"I think this will be a very useful place for the sound balance on your interviews, because this room was designed for acoustic perfection. King George the Fourth loved music and sang and played the piano. He hosted many concerts in here, and even got an orchestra to perform in honour of the Italian composer Rossini when he visited here. You know him?" She hummed a few bars of *The Marriage of Figaro*.

Apart from two high-backed ornamental chairs perched on a dais, the only furniture in the room belonged to Victor's production team: six folding chairs arranged in a row, some lights and a camera on a tripod. Set against the riot of golds and reds and dragons, the items looked comically prosaic, like a Kinder Surprise nestling in a collection of Fabergé eggs.

Dr Loske continued: "Interestingly, only a few months after you finished filming in 1987, we had the great storm that lashed southern England. Hurricane force winds. One of the huge stone balls on the roof crashed through the ceiling into this very room and landed precisely... there."

She pointed to the middle of the room. Patrick walked to the spot where she indicated and looked up at the ceiling.

"Huh. Do you know something? I think this is exactly where you stood." He pointed at Vanity.

Vanity's face twitched in confusion. "What's that, darling?"

"You stood here, back in 1987, when you did that speech about going to fight the Styrax." He clicked his fingers. "It is. It's the very spot where you stood."

"If you say so, darling."

"Makes you think, doesn't it?"

Roger guffawed. "Think what? That God has great aim, but his timing's lousy?"

"I was thinking that perhaps fate is a funny thing," said Patrick, with an edge to his voice. "Especially when you're an actor. If that ball had fallen while we were here, and just missed you, we'd instantly think this place was bad luck, because by nature we're a superstitious lot…"

He raised his voice slightly, going into full monologue mode.

"…but can you blame us for being superstitious? We're being constantly thrown into odd places and forced to mix with all kinds of strange types. It's only natural that things happen to us. Much more than would happen in almost any another profession. We get swindled by producers and agents, we get blackmailed. We get put on horses we can't ride, forced to drive cars we've never driven, told to pretend to drown in lakes no one's swam in. Things happen to us. All the time. People – good and bad – gravitate to us. Through no fault of our own, it happens all the time, doesn't it?"

While he was talking, Patrick was looking around at everyone there, focussing on them in turn, one by one. Then he looked at Kit. The look metastasised into an icy stare, eyes cold and unblinking. Even when he finished talking, he still stared at her. Then he blinked and smiled.

This day has taken an odd turn, thought Kit.

Tara started wandering around the room, arms held tightly to her chest as if she felt chilled. "There's certainly an energy around this building. I wonder what the feng shui looks like? Perhaps if I have time I can do a bagua map."

Dr Loske walked to the centre of the room. "Of course, you're not the only ones to film here. The Pavilion has played host to some big productions. We had Harry Styles here a few years ago, and back in the 1960s we played host to a major film starring Barbra Streisand."

"*On a Clear Day You Can See Forever*." Dorothy automatically supplied the name. "I watched it just last week. It was my wife's favourite film. It was so weird to watch Barbra Streisand emoting in the very same place where I dressed up as a giant armadillo."

"I love Ms Streisand too," twittered Joan. "I have all her albums. I love her so much. She's definitely one of the good Jews."

The silence that descended was total. Joan smiled sweetly, either blissfully unaware she had created the sudden chill in the air or delighted that she had caused it.

Dr Loske broke the silence.

"Now I'll show you to the Adelaide Suite."

She led them upstairs and into one of the smaller rooms. It was covered in yellow wallpaper displaying eye-watering geometric patterns and containing black tables and deep red velvet chairs.

A breakfast bar ran across one side of the room, laden with trays of sandwiches, a tea urn and a coffee machine. Daylight streamed in from a row of French doors leading to a private balcony with a heavy stone balustrade.

Kit recognised the balcony immediately; it was the one where the *Vixens from the Void* production team filmed the scenes she had been watching only that previous night. She knew with absolute certainty that if she walked out onto the balcony and looked down, she would see the same tree that 'Arkadia' (aka Duggie Fletcher) climbed in that very first episode.

Dr Loske gestured around her. "These are the Adelaide rooms. This one used to be the Pavilion's café before it relocated, so luckily we still have catering facilities, such as the bar area. This room will be locked, so you can leave your bags here and make yourself comfortable. There's tea and coffee and sandwiches. Please help yourselves."

Tara took a brief, disdainful look at the sandwiches and walked to the end of the bar that was next to a power socket. She pulled out parts of a machine from her bag, which she erected with the ruthless precision of a squaddie stripping a rifle. When the machine was finished it looked a lot like a *Vixens* prop, a mini space-cannon, silver with a squat black muzzle.

Vanity couldn't resist. She sidled up to Tara and looked over her shoulder.

"Are you planning on disintegrating us all, darling?"

Tara smiled and pulled out a bag of celery. "It's my celery juicer. I'm on a gluten-free, grain-free, sugar-free, dairy-free, no-carb diet at the moment." She gestured to the tray of sandwiches. "I can't eat any of this, obviously."

"Well anticipated, darling. This is actually one of the more healthy spreads. You would not believe what they serve us at conventions."

"That's part of the reason why I don't go to them."

"There are areas in the north who think a Greggs pasty and a packet of crisps is a meal. I normally survive on a diet of fags and black coffee. I'll probably do that this week."

"Oh my god, dear, that's incredibly unhealthy." She considered for a moment. 'Would you like some of my celery juice?"

"Darling, I would *love* to try it!"

Tara inserted some celery sticks and the machine crunched its way through them. She proffered a tiny plastic cup to Vanity, who sniffed and swallowed.

"What do you think?"

"Not bad, darling. Could use some vodka."

Tara failed to suppress a grin. She glanced at Vanity's fur coat. It was obvious she was fighting the urge to comment. It wasn't a long struggle. "That's real fur, isn't it?"

"Can't pull the fur over your eyes, my darling. It is indeed real."

"I see."

"Not going to judge me, darling? Because I've been judged by experts."

"No, I'm not *judging* you but… what poor creature had to die so you could get to wear that?"

Vanity gave a savage grin. "My grandmother."

This time Tara laughed, very loudly.

* * *

Dorothy and Kit scuttled over to the other end of the bar and helped themselves to beverages. Next to the urn was a coffee machine, complete with a basket of little plastic pods.

"Ooh, proper coffee!" grinned Dorothy.

"Can't beat proper coffee," said Kit. "I insisted Victor get a machine. "I've seen the horror of conventions with jars of freeze-dried granules."

"God yes. Can't stand that stuff. It's like soluble gravel. Well, well done you for insisting on the good coffee. I'm almost glad I came!"

"I'm glad you're here."

They popped in their pods, pressed buttons, pulled levers and watched the nozzles gurgle thick black liquid into toy-sized cups. It was a deeply satisfying experience.

Once she had collected her coffee, Dorothy moved to the doors and stepped out onto the balcony. She leaned on the stone balustrade and looked out onto the sculpted Pavilion gardens. Kit joined her.

The gardens were largely deserted. High summer would boast girls in crop-tops lying in the laps of boys in sleeveless T-shirts, but for now, on this chilly February morning, the garden had been abandoned. All Kit could see was a few joggers and an angry tramp fighting an even angrier seagull for a discarded slice of pizza.

They stayed there, not speaking, listening to the shouts of 'fuck' and the furious squawking.

"My wife just loved that film," Dorothy sighed. "She was so buzzed when I got to film here at the Pavilion. I remember buying her postcards of Barbra in the gift shop to mail home."

She turned to Kit. "Thank you for what you did, back in the minibus."

"Don't mention it." Kit's eyes darted back to Tara for a split second. "I could see things were getting a bit… you know."

"Tiresome?"

"I wouldn't exactly say that."

"*You* can't say that. I bloody can." She sighed. "Tara means well, she always has, bless her, but it is so exhausting when people just want to talk to you about one thing. Being defined by just that... it's just... It's a bit suffocating. That's all."

She shrugged helplessly.

"I get that," said Kit. "When I came out as gay, my mum and dad spent the first two years buying me T-shirts saying things like 'I'm gay and happy with it' and 'out and proud'. And I *was* gay and happy with it, but I didn't want to keep telling people via the power of my clothing. I didn't do slogans on T-shirts before, and I certainly didn't do them after."

Dorothy nodded furiously, her earrings bouncing along her jawline. "Exactly. You can't *blame* them, can you? But you end up getting reduced to being an 'it'. I mean, I'm still me. I may look different and have a different name, but I'm still the same person. Older, a *tiny* bit wiser..."

She winked and held up her hand, and held up her thumb and index finger until they were about a centimetre apart.

"But I'm still me. I mean, for fuck's sake! Vanity and Tara. I don't know if you know this, but I had an occasional thing going with both of them, back in the day."

Kit did indeed know that.

"Now look at them. Vanity won't look me in the eye, and Tara – she's treating me like I've just cured world hunger. And they're not the first. Or the worst."

"Is that why you didn't want to come?" asked Kit.

She sighed. "Well... Pretty much, yes. When Liz died a few years ago – my wife – well, I didn't really let her know. About how I always felt I had been born in the wrong body. I'd been leaving things trundling on to spare her feelings, so when she went, I was finally free to think about transitioning. I could cope with the guilt trip from friends and family. I mean, slap 'em on.

But I couldn't take their *kindness*. And their *sympathy*… It was like being bereaved *twice*."

"So what made you decide to come after all?"

"Ah. Oh. I can't say. I can't really go into that…"

She put the coffee cup on the balustrade, stretched out her arms and glided along the balcony, singing as she moved, singing just as Barbra Streisand once sang in the grounds of the Pavilion, about looking out on a clear day, and being able to see forever.

Then she stopped. She went rigid. Her nostrils flared and her lip quivered, as if she'd suddenly entered 'fight or flight' mode. Her eyes were wide and afraid, training her gaze laser-like on *something* below them in the gardens.

Kit peered over her shoulder. It wasn't hard to see what – or who – she saw on this clear day. The figure was enormous, a huge round splat of a man, waddling with murderous intent from the refreshment kiosk towards them.

The man was in a constant battle with gravity. His stomach was fighting to make a break for it, trying to wrestle open the buttons on his shirt, and a big unruly beard was dangling from his chin, pulling his face down. He was wearing a horrible brown suit.

Kit recognised him. Of course she did. It was Graham Goldingay, 'superfan', self-entitled narcissist and *Vixens from the Void* puritan. There was always trouble when he was around.

He didn't look up, so he wasn't aware he was being watched. He continued remorselessly until he passed underneath them, lurching into the Pavilion.

What was he doing here?

Much as Kit was outraged by the unexpected arrival of Graham Goldingay on the scene, it was nothing compared to Dorothy's horrified response.

She looked like she had seen Death himself.

25

After a couple of wrong turns, Kit found her way back to the music room. Victor was sitting in the ornamental chair like a king. Binfire was fastening wires to the floor, bits of black tape attached to his forehead, forcing his eyebrows up into an expression of permanent surprise.

"Hey pilgrim," said Binfire. "Look at me. I'm an alien-of-the-week on *Next Gen*. Help us, Picard, our planet is dying!"

Kit fought to keep her voice calm and casual. "Hi there. I just saw Graham Goldingay in the gardens."

"Oh."

"He's just walked into the building. He's *in* the building."

"Eek."

Victor widened his eyes and allowed his mouth to drop open, like he was going through the motions of acting surprised.

"You know he's here, don't you?"

"Well, yes."

"My god."

"I was going to tell you, mate."

"When?"

"Calm down, Kit. I know you and Graham aren't exactly friends."

"The way you say it is like it's some kind of feud between us. *I* don't have the problem. *He's* the overbearing monster."

"He's just here in an advisory capacity."

"What, like we don't know enough about *Vixens from the Void*?"

"It's good to have a second opinion."

"You know he's going to take over."

"No, he's not. He's not going to do that."

"*You* can't vouch for his actions. Because *he* can't vouch for his actions. He's a massive man-baby with no impulse control. You know the phrase 'like a bull in a china shop'? Well, bulls have an equivalent phrase. They say, 'Like Graham Goldingay attached to any project.'"

Victor laid his hand on Kit's shoulder. Kit was too angry to flinch.

"He's not going to take over, mate. I will stop him. Because he will listen to me. He's got a stake in this project too. "

"What do you mean?"

"Oh."

"'He's got a stake in his project too'?"

"Ahaha."

"What do you mean 'ahaha'?"

Victor ran his fingers through his short curly hair. "Well, now seems to be as good a time as any to tell you…"

Kit's jaw dropped. "Oh no. You didn't."

"Not *all* the extra funds came from me."

"You did! You idiot!"

"Kit – it was tens of thousands of pounds! What was I supposed to do? Spend all my life savings?"

"Yes! Because that's what you *told* me you were going to do!"

Victor flapped his hands as if to say 'details, details'.

"He's got leverage now! He'll really throw his weight around, and that's a lot of weight to throw around! What happens if he tells anyone he's involved? He's already persona non grata with the BBC since that business in Cornwall!"

"He won't tell anyone."

"He'll destroy us! I don't know what you're thinking, getting him involved!"

"Listen, it wasn't just the money. I didn't think I had any choice."

"Of course you had a choice!"

"Look… He heard about the documentary and wanted to be a part of it. He kept badgering me…"

"You could have just said no."

"Then he said we would never get Duggie Fletcher for the documentary without his help."

"What?"

"That's what he said. He said Duggie – I mean Dorothy – would never do this in a million years. And *at the time*, you'd just told me that Duggie had given you a flat 'no'. So I told Graham that if he could get Duggie to say yes, then he could be part of the project. I gave Graham a chance to put his money where his mouth is, and he came through."

"Victor, I could have tried to—"

"Did Duggie – Dorothy – suddenly come back to you with a 'yes'?"

"Well…"

"Did he?"

Kit sighed. "Yes."

"Then there you have it. As far as I'm concerned, Dorothy is only here because of Graham, and that means he's just as important to what we're doing as you and me. And Binfire."

Even though Binfire was hidden from view, taping down cables on the edge of the floor, a hand appeared and gave a thumbs-up.

"Fine," snapped Kit. "But mark my words – this is going to end in tears."

Binfire was crawling along the floor with a screwdriver in his mouth, intentionally evoking Sylvester Stallone from the *Rambo* films. He wriggled over to Kit's boot, rolled over onto his back and plucked the screwdriver from his mouth.

"Anyway, pilgrim – correct me if I'm wrong, but he was continuity advisor in the classic *Vixens* back in the day, so what's the problem?"

Kit threw her hands up. "What's the problem? They only made

Graham 'continuity advisor' because he was such a pain in the backside on set! He was always hanging around during the studio filming and on every location shoot, making a nuisance of himself, buttonholing the script editor, and loitering around the dressing rooms when the cast were changing! So to keep him busy they gave him a chair and a notebook and a folder in the production office to stick his suggestions in, all of which they chucked in the bin."

Binfire's "Oh" floated up from the floor.

"Does that answer your question?"

"Yeah. I guess."

"Good."

"Oh wait. I've got another one. Given that you just said Graham was hanging around *every* location shoot, wouldn't that mean he was here in 1986 *and* 1987? Wouldn't that make him a suspect too?"

Victor and Kit looked at each other.

"Shit." Victor's face was pale. "I hadn't thought of that."

"Me neither."

"He's not on the official BBC documentation."

"No. Of course. It was a made-up job, so it wouldn't be on the paperwork."

"Shit," said Victor again.

"No, wait." Kit flapped her hands frantically. "Let's think logically. The '86 location shoot happened before *Vixens from the Void* was broadcast."

"Of course! You can't be a fan of a TV series that hasn't happened yet, can you?"

"Exactly."

They both sighed. Their shoulders dropped in unison.

Binfire retrieved the screwdriver from his mouth.

"Yep. Unless he read about it being made in the trade press and came to see the filming to see what the new show is like. Lots of people do that."

Kit folded her arms. "Shit."

26

Kit stalked out of the room – and ran straight into Graham Goldingay.

"Greetings to you, Kit Pelham."

"Hello Graham."

He loomed over her, blocking her exit. She could hear his stentorian breathing. She could see the hairs up his nose vibrate as he sucked in great gobfuls of air in wheezy asthmatic gulps.

"I'm glad you're here, Kit Pelham."

"Oh really?"

"I read your article on the creation of the Styrax in *StarCrash* magazine last month."

"And what did you—"

"I wanted to make you aware that you made a number of factual omissions."

"I don't think I did."

"You did not include the fact that the Styrax were invented as an emergency stopgap because they couldn't get the rights to the Daleks."

"Graham, that's utter nonsense."

"Mervyn Stone said that was the case in an interview at Convix 14. And as he was creator of the Styrax, that really is the last word on the matter."

"It was a joke! He was making a joke. He was asked why the Styrax seemed so similar to the Daleks, and he made a joke about not getting the rights to the Daleks. That's what it was. A joke. He said a joke."

"I don't think he would joke about such things."

"Yes, he would. He does little else. Ask him."

"I do ask him. He doesn't respond to my emails."

"Well, what a surprise."

Graham stopped talking for five seconds. Then he said: "I told Victor I did not approve of you doing the interviews for this Blu-Ray documentary."

"And what did he say?"

"He said he would take my opinion under advisement."

"Good."

"So, as he agrees with me, you should step aside and let me do the interviews."

"No, he doesn't agree with you."

"He said he would take my opinion under advisement."

"That means he's telling you to fuck off."

"No it doesn't."

"Yes, it does."

"I have given Victor a great deal of money to help make this documentary happen, so my opinion—"

"And Victor has *sold* this documentary to the BBC on the understanding that I present it. So my opinion counts more."

Stalemate. Graham didn't move. Didn't speak. He just stared impassively.

Kit decided to break the silence. "I need to go now. Can you get out of my way?"

Graham considered this. He raised one enormous tree-trunk-sized leg and moved it one foot to the left. Then the next one joined it, allowing a tiny gap for Kit to squeeze through.

Kit started to walk away, then turned. "Anyway. Why would he get *you* to present the documentary? You're hardly a proper *Vixens from the Void* fan, are you?"

Graham's eyes narrowed until they became tiny black marbles, and a low rumble started deep inside his throat. "I am far more of a fan than you," he snarled. "Not only are you not fit to touch my original props, but you are also not fit to touch the glass cases my original props are kept in."

"But you didn't even attend the first *ever* location filming, did you? That's what this documentary is all about, and you weren't even there. That must reaaally get to you."

For a second – just a second – Graham looked like he was about to explode. His pudgy hands flexed into fists. Then he growled, "I have an unrivalled collection of memorabilia from that time: documentation, off-set photos, behind-the-scenes photos, location rushes, costumes and props. If you and Victor wish to access my vaults, you would do well not to cast doubt upon my fan authenticity."

If he'd been there, he would have said so, she thought. *There's no way he would pass up an opportunity to boast.*

Okay, we've still got just six suspects. At least that's something.

As she hurried away, Graham called after her. "You should consider including an addendum in *StarCrash* magazine, pointing out your factual omission about the origins of the Styrax."

She swivelled on her heel and grinned coldly at him.

"I'll take your opinion under advisement."

27

Kit ran up to the Adelaide Suite, but the guests were already surging back along the corridor. She tried to catch Dorothy's eye as they went past, but Dorothy pointedly stared at the tapestries, the ornamental furniture and the ceilings, looking everywhere but in Kit's direction.

She admitted defeat and followed them back the way she had come into the music room.

The six director's chairs had been placed along the far side of the music room and the guests took one each, sitting in a row like gameshow contestants.

Graham Goldingay had also taken his allotted place, squatting on a stool in the corner, observing the proceedings with a toad-like gaze. Vanity and Roger cast quizzical looks in his direction, but none made any comment. Dorothy sat bolt upright, staring fixedly at the dais and the ornamental chairs, as if the merest glance in Graham's direction might turn her to stone.

Even though Kit was not good in public situations, firing a series of questions at celebrities in front of an audience at sci-fi conventions – or in this case under the cold gaze of a camera – held no terrors for her. She often thought about the contradiction and concluded that the sheer adrenalin rush of extracting facts about a TV show she loved stripped her anxieties away and allowed her to keep her nerve.

Roger was first to be interviewed. He strutted across to the high-backed ornamental chair and sat in it approvingly. "Hey, I like this. It reminds me of the throne I had when I played King Rat in *Dick Whittington*."

"Just give us a minute, Roger, we've got to mike you up." Kit leaned over Roger and clipped a radio microphone onto his collar, slipping the cord down his shirt.

"Brrr! Bit cold," said Roger, nodding and winking at Kit. "You could have warmed it up for me."

As she fed the wire down his chest, Roger's hand grabbed hold of her wrist and forced her palm onto his nipple. It happened so fast she didn't know how to react.

"Steady, my girl," Roger winked. "You don't want me to make a complaint about you molesting me."

Kit withdrew her hand like it had been scalded on a hot stove. She looked around but nobody had noticed. What to do?

What could she do? Stop the whole recording over something Roger would dismiss as a joke? Or carry on like nothing had happened?

She realised with a spike of fury that she had been put into the position of women across the ages, forced to choose between making waves and not rocking the boat. Of course she had to do the latter.

Was there any choice?

She blinked angrily, calmed herself, and called over to Victor, "Are–are we ready?"

Victor glanced over to the camera, where Binfire was standing by.

"You ready, Binfire?"

"When you are."

Kit took her place in the interviewer's chair and put her interviewer's notes on her lap. Victor hopped away from the throne and joined Binfire by the camera tripod. "Great. Let's go. Is everyone else okay?"

Vanity was staring at the schedule. "Darling, there seems to be some kind of mistake. It says here that the people being interviewed today are Roger, Joan and Tara."

"Yeeeess. That's correct."

"Can you explain why I am sitting here, and not in my hotel bed ordering room service?"

Victor's mouth flapped open. The bravado seeped out of his body. He knew the words he had to say, but they wouldn't reach his lips. The only sound that came out was a tiny gurgle.

"We're trying something a bit different," said Kit smoothly, throwing herself on the grenade. "We're conducting the interviews with everyone present, so it will refresh your own memories. When it comes to your turn, you can add to them or just correct each other's stories."

The schedule in Vanity's hand got shredded, as her long red fingernails punctured the paper.

"So I got up this morning, got dressed, blow-dried my hair, put all my make-up on to *sit here* all day? What. The. Actual. *Fuck??* I've never heard anything so ridiculous in all my life!"

There was an uncomfortable silence.

Joan slapped her knees. "Well, I think it's a splendid idea! I'm sure the memories will all flow better because we're all here together. It's like those bits on those DVDs where we all watch it and talk and everyone gets a chance to chip in. They're such a help in coaxing things out of my addled old brain. I definitely approve."

"I agree with Joan," said Tara. "I think being interviewed in isolation feels like an interrogation. It evokes negative energy."

"Of course it would," snapped Vanity.

"Pooling our memories feels far more spiritual. Like my shared meditation classes."

"You're all bonkers," Vanity snapped. "We're *artistes*, darling. We shouldn't be dragged out of our beds for nothing."

Patrick chuckled. "I *think* you and I are *actors*, darling. And as actors, that's pretty much our life. I've lost count of the times I've been dragged somewhere to do nothing all day. As long as we're paid and get fed and watered, we should be glad of it. That's just being professional." He grinned. "It sounds fun. Think of today as a rehearsal for your performance tomorrow."

"Yes, Vanity," smirked Roger. "I'm *very* professional, just like Patrick here, so I will turn up tomorrow. I'm sad to think that you would have such *unprofessional* thoughts."

"Fine, if that's what we all agree," muttered Vanity, trying to back down with good grace and failing. "I just think we should have had more notice, that's all."

"I got the schedule pushed under my door last night," said Roger, barely able to keep the joy out of his voice. "Didn't you get one? If you had *read* it and had a *problem* you could have raised it yesterday."

That ended the matter. Vanity obviously nurtured hopes that Patrick would go back to the National Theatre and recommend her for Lady Macbeth and magically restart her career. There was no way she'd dare take the risk of giving Patrick the impression she was *unprofessional*.

Victor broke the silence.

"Is everyone okay now?"

There was a chorus of yeses.

"Good. Binfire?"

"We're rolling."

Kit shuffled the notes on her lap.

"So, Roger... Do you remember filming in Brighton?"

Roger switched himself on like a light bulb. "Well, you know what they say – if you remember Brighton, you were never there." He chortled. "But seriously... yes, I remember it very well. It was a lot of fun. Filming in here was incredible." He gestured around him. "As you can see, all this architecture around us, it really gave the feeling you were acting inside a piece of history." He studied the opulent surroundings and gave another chuckle. "I think – to be honest – we were all scared of breaking something!"

Kit smiled politely. "Are there any stories you recall from that time?"

Roger tapped his nose and smirked. "Well, I'd tell you, but then I'd have to kill you."

Kit asked a stream of routine questions. *What was Brighton like then? Did he prefer filming in the studio or on location? Did he think he would still be discussing* Vixens from the Void *all these years later?* She knew the retelling of old anecdotes would relax Roger, allow him to put his guard down. Finally, she seized her moment. "The extras they brought in. The local girls. Did you get on well with them?"

Roger didn't even blink. "The extras? Oh yeah. They were very nice kids. It was really nice to have them around."

"Was there any particular girl you remember? Any particular one that made an impression on you?"

If Roger was worried about the way the questions were going, he certainly didn't show it. He tapped his chin and frowned. "Not really. We didn't really mix with them outside of the filming schedule. We said goodbye at the end of the day and went back to the hotel."

Kit nodded and looked back at her clipboard. On the very edges of her peripheral vision, she could see the expressions on the other guests' faces – disbelief from Patrick and Dorothy, amusement from Vanity and Tara, Joan frowning with confusion.

She went back to the rest of her questions. *Did you find the costume hot? What was your favourite story from* Vixens from the Void?

* * *

Joan was next in the hotseat. She stood up with some difficulty, gripped her cane and limped stiffly to the dais.

"You ready?" asked Victor.

"Absolutely," she snapped. "I am always ready."

187

"Okay. Rolling. Kit, when you're ready."

Kit made a show of examining her notes. "So, Joan, as costume designer, what did you think when you heard you were filming in Brighton?'

"Well, I was delighted. I spent a lot of time down here, in one's decadent youth. After I left the WRAC."

"The WRAC?"

Joan looked miffed at Kit's ignorance. "The Women's Royal Auxiliary Corps. I was a sergeant, would you believe!"

She exhaled deeply. "I left the army in '75 and decided to follow my other passion. The theatre. I took a course at Wimbledon, and then I came down here and became resident designer of the old Queens Theatre in the late 1970s." She shrugged. "It's gone now, like so many other smaller local theatres. That was before one moved into the televisual world."

She smiled almost apologetically, as if she was ashamed of betraying the theatre. "So I did know Brighton very well and loved it while I was here. That's why I retired to Worthing."

"Joan, what were the challenges of a costume designer, of filming on location?"

"Oh! So many challenges. One had to be prepared for all eventualities." Her millimetre-thin eyebrows waggled earnestly. "It's always difficult when one is out in 'the field' as it were. My military training put me in good stead to meet challenges. And this was particularly challenging."

"How so?"

"Because, as you've already mentioned, we needed a large number of costumes for the girls. In his infinite wisdom, dear Leslie, our director, insisted on only auditioning extras once we had reached Brighton."

She held up her arms in a helpless gesture. Her bracelets descended past her wrists and collided at the elbow with a deafening clatter. Victor winced and pulled the cans off his ears.

"Utter madness! The whole of the first day involved measuring up these young girls once they had been cast and finding *anything* that would fit. Boots, gloves. Fortunately their torsos were encased in a stretchy fabric. But one had literally *minutes* to spend on each extra. One wished one had more time to prepare, but one had to accept the hand that one was dealt."

"That must have been quite scary."

"Oh yes! To make matters worse, as the girls were not 'from the business', they hadn't the first clue about caring for their costumes. They were eating their meals without serviettes, sitting on damp chairs… It was utterly nerve-wracking to witness. If there was a wardrobe malfunction, I couldn't just nip back into the BBC costume department in London."

"Did you have many wardrobe malfunctions on set?"

"Quite a few." A long arthritic finger extended from her fist and tapped her chin. "I remember during our *second* time on location we completely ran out of spare costumes."

"Oh no! How appalling."

"Appalling is the word. We just were filming the very last scene in the quarry, and would you believe it? There was *another* incident. One of our young lady extras completely ruined the top half of her costume with her… décolletage…" She splayed her fingers and held her hands out in front of her, using the universal sign-language for 'bosoms'.

"Without spare costumes to hand, I had to perform immediate repairs to sort it. *Very* disappointing. Particularly as the young lady in question had filmed with us the previous year, so she should have known better. She *should* have taken precautions. One had to improvise extremely quickly to keep the filming schedule on track. Not a perfect solution, I'm afraid, but it had to do."

"Oh dear."

"Oh dear indeed." Joan gripped her stick until her knuckles

were bone-white and waggled it at the camera. "Frankly, I could have killed the little bitch."

Silence filled the room.

Kit cleared her throat and steered the interview onto other well-trodden topics. *What inspired the design of the costumes? How about the other costumes you made for the series?* Kit was barely listening to the answers; she knew them off by heart anyway. Her mind was buzzing because had just found another connection between Lily and one of their suspects.

Did it mean anything?

She wasn't sure. But it was one more fact to add to the others.

28

Now it was Tara Miles's turn. She trotted to the elaborate chair, moving with the easy grace of a woman who tied herself in knots on a yoga mat three times a day, twirled and sat with the poise of a ballerina. Then she tucked her feet under her knees and assumed the lotus position.

Someone – who was definitely Vanity – muttered, "Show off".

"What do you remember about being here in Brighton?"

"Ahhh. My main recollection is…" She gave a long sigh. "It was overwhelmingly spiritual."

"I see."

"I used to take long walks on the beach at night after filming. I found it very hypnotic. Of course, my consciousness hadn't been fully awakened at that time – I hadn't yet learned how to activate my vagus nerve – so I didn't know then that the sound of waves on the shore activates the parasympathetic nervous system, reduces stress and creates empathy."

"Really."

"Yes, and I needed that positivity at the time. It was very fraught. Lots of negative energy swirling around the filming. I had to shut myself off from everybody."

There was a faint "Hah!" from Vanity.

"So why was it so fraught?"

"Where do I start? We didn't have enough time to do all the things we had to. The scenes on the balcony were very difficult. Even though we did them really early in the morning, there were still people in the park making a racket. The runners had to keep running downstairs waving wads of pound notes to pay off the tramps."

There was a ripple of laughter from the other guests, and an "Oh yes!" from Patrick. It was obvious Tara's comments had awakened some memories.

This idea of having other guests present in these interviews really is a good one, Kit thought. *We must keep doing it for the other not-investigating-a-murder documentaries.*

"Any other problems with the shoot?"

"Erm… I can't think…"

"How about the extras? The supporting artistes? Did they help or hinder?"

"Ah. Hum. Well, as has been already said by Joan, they were not trained actors. They were lovely girls, absolutely. All of them. So enthusiastic and bubbly, it was such a lot of fun, so much energy and they really pitched in to make it work, but there was inevitably a lack of discipline just because they didn't know what was required of them. There was a lot of chatter on set, a lot of wandering in the eyeline when trying for a take. It added extra pressure on top of all the others."

"But you did your bit to help them out."

"Well, we did what we could."

"Didn't you become a mentor to one of them?"

Tara's face twisted in confusion. "Really? I'm not sure what you… I don't think…"

"I heard that you took one of them under your wing. I was told that you gave her advice how to become an actor. You told her not to bother with going to drama school and go straight to Hollywood."

"I… did… yes."

"That's so generous of you, that you took time out of your day to help a young aspiring actress with some good advice. There must have been a temptation to pull up the ladder after you."

There was another Vanity-flavoured cackle from the row of director's chairs. Even through her walnut-brown tan, Kit could see Tara's cheeks flushing with embarrassment.

"Well, pulling up the ladder, that's not a good attitude of course. One must always help everyone you meet because that energy gets reflected back…

"That's what any life coach would tell you."

29

The interviews were done for the day, and all that remained was for Vanity, Roger, Tara and Patrick to try on their new costumes.

Binfire nipped over to the hotel where the costumes were stored, put them in his minibus and shuttled them – and Freya – to the Pavilion, where they set up boys' and girls' dressing rooms in the Adelaide Suite.

His task accomplished, Binfire joined Victor and Kit in the music room, helping them fold up the equipment and pack it into the big silver boxes.

"Wow. That was good, mate! Really good," chirped Victor. "I think we got a lot out of them today." He grinned. "In more ways than one."

Kit nodded. "Did anyone notice any interesting responses from the guests? I was focusing on the interview."

"Deffo-nately," said Binfire. "Body language was off the scale. They were twitching like they were faulty androids. Gonna go through it, compile a breakdown, and deliver a report."

Victor closed his case with a satisfying *thunk*. "All in all, this has been a good first day for collecting evidence."

"You don't know the half of it."

Kit fished out the cassette box from her pocket and waggled it. "Guess what this is."

"What's that?"

"This happens to be a phone conversation between Lily Sparkes and her best friend. While she was looking for acting jobs in America."

"What?" Victor leapt forward and grabbed it. "What the hell? Where did you get this?"

"From Lily's best friend Jackie. She still works at the hotel. She's got loads more. Dozens of them. A whole carry-case full of tapes, she says."

"My god…" He stared at the little plastic case, turning it over and over, almost with reverence. "Have you listened to it?"

"Well, luckily for you I do have my Walkman to hand. So yes, I have played it."

Victor's eyes were blazing.

"And?"

"Well, having teased you with this amazing find, I'm sad to say there's not much to it. Just small talk, really. But there could be something on the other cassettes. Jackie leant me this one. I'm sure she'd let me go through the others. She can't listen to them herself, as she hasn't got a cassette player. We're going to arrange a meet-up and do it properly."

"Well done, Kit." Victor was still staring at the cassette case. "Can I hear it?"

"Sure."

Kit dipped into her pocket again and produced her Walkman, trussed up in a tangle of headphones. She took the case from Victor, flipped it open, extracted the cassette and popped it into the Walkman. Victor watched her perform this ritual with hypnotised fascination. When she handed it to him, she noticed his hands were shaking.

He put the headphones on and pressed play. Expressions travelled across his face: wonder, confusion, intense concentration and delight. Incredibly, a single tear ambled down his cheek.

Five minutes later the recording was over and he pulled the earphones off his head. He handed the Walkman back to Kit. "I see what you mean. There's not a lot to it."

"No."

"But you're right, there's no telling what's on the other tapes. We have to go through them all."

Binfire picked up the equipment and waddled off, the boxes clacking and clattering around his knees. He got to the door, turned and yelled, "How long are you going to be?"

"Shouldn't be long, mate. Our guests are just trying on the costumes for size. An hour at most?"

"Wilco." He saluted and left.

Victor watched him clank out, and winked at Kit, nodding at the cassette in Kit's hand. "That is an amazing find, mate. This is all going well. This is all going really well."

As if on cue, Victor's phone shuddered in his hand, announcing the arrival of a text. He looked at the message and went pale.

"We have to get upstairs now. Freya just sent me this."

He pointed his phone screen at Kit.

One word:

help

30

Victor was first to the stairs, his trainers clumping on the exotic carpets. Kit followed hot on his heels.

When they entered the yellow room of the Adelaide Suite, the one that had been designated as the girls' dressing room, they were greeted by a tableau that would rival any Leonardo da Vinci painting.

Vanity, Tara and Joan were standing, lounging and perching around the room, watching the scene unfolding in front of them with a mixture of mild exasperation and bored indifference. A clothes rack now filled the far wall. Graham Goldingay was in front of it, blocking access. He was holding a clothes bag.

"This is not acceptable. I was not consulted on this."

Freya was trying to dodge around Graham, but it was like trying to climb over a mountain.

"What's going on?" said Victor.

Freya waved her hands helplessly. "He won't let us try on the new costumes."

"What? Why?"

"He doesn't *like* them."

Graham jabbed a meaty finger in Victor's direction. "Victor. You said we were doing re-enactments of scenes from the original series."

"We are!"

"But these are not the original costumes!"

"Well no. Obviously."

"They're not even *remotely similar* to the original costumes!"

He unzipped the bag with some dramatic heft and pulled out the offending costume, like it was Exhibit A in the case for the prosecution. It was comprised of a severe high-necked leather tunic like a biker jacket, though more fitted at the waist, with epaulettes and insignia down the arms and chest. It was a mix of plum red and dark grey, with yellow highlights. There were also leather trousers in the same colours. Kit thought it looked very stylish.

In his other hand he held the headwear disdainfully between thumb and forefinger. Instead of the Roman legionnaire-style helmet from the 1980s, it was a smooth and shiny skullcap affair, with a tiny ridge cresting in the centre and forming a cheeky 'V' in the middle of the forehead. Again, Kit thought it looked very stylish.

"These are an abomination. They are as terrible as…" His brain rummaged for the worst insult he could find. "…as terrible as the costumes they're using for the *new* series!"

Vanity sighed and spread her arms to the heavens. "If he's going to stand there like a troll on a bridge, can we go back to the hotel? I need a bloody drink."

Victor ignored her – a dangerous hobby at the best of times, but he was too angry to realise what he'd done. "Come on, Graham, those are great costumes, made by the original costume designer from the original series. That's a *good* thing."

The look on Graham's huge face suggested that it was several hyperspace jumps from being a good thing.

"You can't seriously expect us to go and dig out those old costumes from the 1980s."

"Actually, that is precisely what I'm saying. What's the point otherwise. That's why I have brought the original costumes here at *considerable* expense."

He gestured to a pile of orange rags laid on a corner table.

So that's what the smell was.

"No, Graham…"

"There's no point doing it in these costumes. It would look completely different."

Victor clapped his hands to his head and pushed his fingers into his ginger curls. "That's the whole point of the documentary, Graham. Then and now. Pointing out the differences. Ringing the changes."

"I do not see the point changing anything."

Joan was perching against a table, listening to the words spewing from his mouth with a kind of haughty indifference. She had decided she'd had enough. She levered herself into a vertical position, went over to the sad pile of Lycra and lifted one up with obvious distaste.

"Look, young man, you don't know what you're talking about. Tch. Like most men, in my experience. You obviously don't understand the situation. These costumes are old and well past their use-by date. Moreover, they were designed to be worn by *girls*. You can't expect these ladies, these legends..." She waved her stick at Tara and Vanity. "...these *grand dames* of television, to humiliate themselves by stuffing their bodies back into Spandex at their age!"

Tara and Vanity exchanged a quick glance. Kit knew immediately what the glance meant. Despite both of them teetering on the threshold of their sixties, both women had figures that would make many thirty-year-old women jealous. They managed this feat through a mixture of healthy eating and vigorous exercise on the part of Tara, and very unhealthy dieting and vigorous sex on the part of Vanity. Tara and Vanity obviously couldn't decide whether they should be flattered that Joan was defending their dignity or offended at the insinuation that they wouldn't be able to fill their old costumes with the same degree of allure.

"Of course I expect them to wear them," snapped Graham. "They are actors. They will do what they are paid to do. I cannot in all good conscience let these other costumes be used in my documentary. It will be a disservice to the fans."

"*Your* documentary?" squeaked Victor.

"What fans?" said Freya. "I'm a fan and I think they look cool."

Graham glared at her as if to say, *do I have to spell it out to you little girl? You are not a real fan.*

"I told you," muttered Kit to herself. "I told you he'd take over, but you wouldn't listen."

Kit could bear it no longer. She felt the energy draining out of her and pooling inside her big boots. She peeled herself away from the wall, slid out of the room and slumped into a chair in the corridor. She plunged her head into her hands and forced her breathing to slow down a few notches below hyper-ventilation.

Calm. Calm.

She looked up – and there was Dorothy, leaning against a banister, arms crossed tightly against her body, staring at an ornamental skylight.

Kit remembered she still had responsibilities; this was partly her project, after all.

"Hi. Are you alright?"

"So many people ask me if I'm alright today."

"Well, are you?"

She laughed. "Now I come to think of it – not really."

"Hum."

"What?"

"I mean. I was going to… Did you want a different place to change?"

Dorothy shot Kit a look of disappointment. "Don't you be like them, Kit! Vanity is fine changing with me, and Tara wouldn't dream of me changing anywhere else. *They're* fine. *I'm* fine. We're *all* fine. Everything's *fine*. Life can sort itself out without someone holding a clipboard and telling people how to behave, you know. You don't have to cluck around me like a hysterical chicken."

"I'm sorry. But, I guess it *is* my job to make sure everyone's happy here."

Dorothy sighed.

"I'm sorry. You're right. It was an honest question. I get it. I'm just a little on edge."

"Is this to do with Graham?"

Dorothy didn't respond.

"I'm sorry, but I do get the impression there's something going on here. Has he got some kind of hold on you?"

She thought about this. Then she shook her head.

"I really can't tell you. It would just make things worse. If I said anything he would just go and... do something..."

"Like what? You can tell me."

"You don't—"

Dorothy's sentence was sliced off at the end, as an ear-piercing scream shredded the air.

31

Kit ran back into the girls' dressing room, Dorothy on her heels. It only took a split-second for them to piece together what had caused the scream.

Graham was outside the French windows, near the balustrade. His right arm was rigid and outstretched, one of the suit bags dangling from his meaty fist.

It was obvious that he had decided to show his disdain for the new costumes by throwing one of them over the side of the balcony.

It was equally obvious that Joan Peverin had taken exception to Graham's gesture by unsheathing a swordstick hidden inside her cane and pressing the tip of it against his jowls, hence the ear-splitting scream from Freya.

Graham was keeping very still. Only his eyes were moving, bulging and straining in their sockets to keep track of the blade threatening to penetrate his carotid artery.

Vanity and Tara were watching through the window with the half amused, half horrified expressions of actresses who knew they were watching a potential murder but hey, it could get *very* boring on a film set, and at least something interesting was happening.

Freya had her fist pushed deep into her mouth. Victor's voice was oscillating between saying, "Fuck," softly, and then saying, "I think you should please just stop," loudly, and then saying, "Fuck," quietly again.

Kit saw that Dorothy was edging around to the other side of the room, heading for the French window on the far right. She looked like she was going to enter the balcony, come up behind Joan and tackle her.

Once a stunt person, always a stunt person.

Joan's eyes didn't flicker from Graham's face for an instant.

"There's no need for that, Dorothy dear," trilled Joan. "No one is going to get hurt. Unless this young man decides he has a deathwish."

Dorothy backed away.

"Now, young man," said Joan sweetly. "I would advise you, if you want to keep that massive head on your shoulders, to put that bag back on the rack, leave this room and disappear."

She lowered the swordstick. Just a few millimetres, but Graham felt the pressure ease.

Slowly and awkwardly, like a robot from an old sci-fi series made with a very limited budget, he lumbered back inside and carefully hung the suit bag back on the rack. Then, without looking behind him, he lurched out of the room.

Kit watched Graham's monstrous shape disappear down the corridor.

Once she lost sight of him, Kit felt a huge weight lift from her shoulders. She knew it wouldn't be the last she saw of Graham, but she allowed herself to enjoy the moment.

Victor was still hovering in front of Joan, his arms stretched out like he was trying to calm a spooked horse. "Um... Joan... I'm not an expert in the law, but I'm not sure it's legal to carry around a weapon like that."

Joan slid her swordstick back into her cane and smiled at him sweetly.

"What weapon, dear?"

She strode passed him briskly, not a trace of a limp or arthritic gait, and pulled a couple of bags off the rack.

"Now, ladies. Shall we see how these costumes look on you?"

Tara, Vanity and Dorothy grabbed their bags with enthusiasm, unzipping them and pulling out the costumes like nine-year-olds on their way to a birthday party. Dorothy held her outfit cautiously against her body.

Vanity put her hand to her mouth. "Darling, that is so you! That is so going to suit your figure! You will look amazing!"

"Really?"

"Oh cross my heart, darling! If you climb up that tree, just like you did before, everyone is going to swear blind it's me! No one's going to believe it's not me, would they Tara?"

"Oh, absolutely." Tara nodded furiously.

Dorothy glowed with the compliment. A huge smile crept onto to her face.

"Thank you!"

Was that a tiny tear trying to escape from Dorothy's left eye?

How ironic that it was Vanity who had finally managed to get Dorothy to feel like she belonged. The uber-bitch herself, known for tearing down everyone around her. It was quite a thing to behold. Kit felt a slight wetness in her eye, too.

The incident between Joan and Graham had been forgotten. The moment had passed. Kit, Victor and Freya had been rendered invisible once more.

There was a clatter of footsteps in the hall and Dr Alexandra Loske appeared, with Marie in tow.

"We heard a scream. Is everything alright?" she gasped.

"Couldn't be better, dear," trilled Joan.

"Oh thank god." She planted a hand on her chest. "When we heard the scream, we thought another stone ball had been dislodged."

32

Kit, Freya and Victor convened on the landing at the top of the stairs, which was entirely decorated in an oriental style. They were surrounded by stunning wallpaper, an amazing skylight and a beautiful balustrade with railings shaped like bamboo, as if they were in the most exclusive Chinese restaurant ever. They were unable to appreciate it as they were still trying to comprehend the insanity of the last twenty minutes.

Freya exhaled. "*Oh my god!* I can't believe what just *happened*! I witnessed it and I still can't believe it."

"Me neither." Victor sagged with relief. "Fucking Graham. He's just a… bloody Graham."

"I told you he would be trouble," said Kit.

"We *all* knew Graham would be some kind of trouble, Kit," snapped Victor. "The issue is *how* much trouble he would be. Thanks to Joan, I think we've got him back in line."

"*If* he doesn't go to the police and get Joan arrested for assault and carrying an offensive weapon."

Victor glared at her. "He won't do that, mate. He'd never scupper this project for petty revenge."

Freya nodded. "Victor's right. He won't do that. I bet he's already forgotten about it. He is incredibly thick-skinned."

"Thick-skinned. Ha. Very handy, when you're being poked by a three-foot length of razor-sharp steel."

"Kit, just… lay off! It's bad enough dealing with our sus—" He glanced at Freya. "—our *guests* without you doing your Marvin the Paranoid Android act."

Kit was stung, and it showed on her face. Victor realised he'd gone too far. His hands emerged from his pockets and he performed his traditional 'calm down everybody' gesture.

"Look it's fine, mate. No harm done. We had a situation and it's resolved itself. Let's just get to the end of today and everything will be fine."

As if on cue there was *another* scream. This one was from the boys' dressing room. It was quieter and a bit muffled, but it was unmistakably a cry from Patrick Finch.

"Oh no," whimpered Freya. "I can't take much more."

33

When Kit, Victor and Freya entered the boys' dressing room, it was obvious that Patrick was in trouble. He had put on his new costume and was sitting awkwardly on a chair, his legs splayed. His hands were clasped to his head. His face had passed red and was heading to purple.

"What's happened?" said Victor.

Patrick gave a stoical smile. "I seem to be stuck."

Roger waved his arms helplessly. As he was in a glorified toga, the effect was rather comical. "The poor bugger can't get his helmet to come off, if you'll pardon the expression."

Victor, Freya and Kit looked at the two men in surprise, then at each other, then back again. "What?"

"It won't come off. It's attached to his hair."

Kit waited for Freya to take charge, but she just stood there, chewing a black fingernail. She looked at Victor, but he just shrugged helplessly.

Okay, so it's down to me then.

She stepped forward and examined the helmet. She noted that Joan Peverin had also subtly redesigned it. It was a still a classic pickelhaube design favoured by German Kaisers, but instead of a spike or an eagle on the top, a dragon was etched into the metal, clinging to his head. The dragon didn't look like it wanted to go anywhere.

She lifted the peak slightly and peered at the gap between the inside of the helmet and Patrick's head. Patrick winced.

"Sorry."

"It's okay."

He didn't sound okay, but he was putting a brave face on it.

Kit took an envelope off the floor and pushed it under the gap. It slid in for about half an inch.

She wiggled it about. Patrick let loose a tiny, "Owww".

"I'm really sorry."

This time Patrick didn't answer.

"Can you feel anything?" said Freya.

"There seems to be something sticky inside the helmet."

"That doesn't sound right," said Victor, trying to sound authoritative.

Kit wiggled the envelope backwards and forwards, trying to ignore Patrick's tiny whimpers.

"There's a strip of something running around the bottom of the helmet. It's attached itself to Patrick's hair."

"Well – what can we do?"

"I don't know." She directed her next comment to Patrick. "We could run a pair of scissors around the inside and cut you out."

"Ha ha. I'm not sure that's a good idea. I'm doing a telly right after this, and if there's any chance I turn up with chunks of my ear missing they would not be happy."

Freya piped up. "I'll go and get Joan."

Victor grunted. "Yeah, she can use her big sword."

Patrick looked alarmed. "Sword?"

"Don't worry about it."

Freya scuttled away. Kit put the envelope in her pocket and picked up a knitting needle from Joan's make-up box. She inserted it under the helmet, levered it off as far as she dared – ignoring Patrick's whimpers – and put her phone torch on, shining it into the gap.

"There's not a lot of hair snagged. Not really."

"Really?" said Patrick testily. "It feels like a *lot*."

"I bet it does," said Roger.

"Huh." Kit came to a decision. She raised her voice and waved at the doorway. "Oh, hi Joan! Glad you could come. We've got a problem here."

Patrick looked across hopefully, but Joan wasn't there. Taking advantage of the distraction, Kit wrenched the helmet off his head with one swift tug. It was accompanied by hideous tearing noise, like the sound of someone pulling apart two strips of Velcro.

Victor made an involuntarily yelp, Kit went, "*Eee*," and Roger went, "Woah!", but the only one who didn't make a sound was Patrick, who was too surprised to scream. He realised, several seconds after the event, that he had experienced a sudden burst of pain, and allowed himself to process it.

"Pheewww…" He pushed out a large shuddering breath. "Bloody hell."

Kit looked inside the helmet. Sure enough, there was a transparent strip of tape that ran around the inside. It was covered in a tangle of Patrick's grey hair.

"There you go, that's the culprit." She showed Patrick, who frowned.

"Yes, I saw it when I put it on. I thought it was just padding, to keep it comfy. I didn't realise…"

He turned to the mirror, moving his head this way and that, examining it in a way that reminded Kit of Doctor Who examining his face after he'd just regenerated.

"Well, I think you're right. No harm done. No bald patches." He flashed a smile at Kit. "No missing ears. Thank you, Kit."

"That's okay," said Kit, blushing. "I'm sorry this has happened. I have no idea how it got in there."

Joan finally arrived, her face pinched with concern. She looked suspiciously around the room as if expecting an ambush.

"What's amiss?" she snapped. "I had a garbled report from that young lady who looks like a panda. She said Patrick's head was stuck somewhere?"

"It's alright, I fixed it." Kit showed the helmet to Joan, who peered inside with utter incredulity. "His head got stuck to this tape."

Joan picked at a corner of the sticky stuff and blinked furiously. "Is this some kind of joke?"

"What?"

"This is tit tape!"

Everyone looked confused.

"Tit tape. Booby tape. Cleavage tape. It's a double-sided tape, designed to secure the edges of a strapless dress to a lady's cleavage. Often used in the theatre—"

"I know what tit tape is," snapped Patrick. "What on earth is it doing in my hat?"

"I haven't the faintest idea. I have some right here." Joan went to her 'box of tricks', a clear plastic case filled with scissors and needles and cotton reels, and started looking through it methodically. It didn't take long; the case looked very organised.

"It's gone!"

Patrick joined her at the case. "What do you mean gone?"

"I mean gone! I had some right in here, a reel of tit tape in this box. I saw it just this morning, and now it's gone!"

Patrick peered into the case himself and did a bit of token rummaging. "No, I can't see it. It's not here alright."

Roger had picked up Patrick's helmet and was taking his turn to peer into it. "Hmm. Very strange. I've seen some pranks in my time in the theatre, when I did *Run for Your Wife*." He chortled. "In fact, I was behind most of them. But I never saw anything like this."

Victor plucked the helmet from Roger's grasp and turned it around in his hands, his face grim. "I've worked out what's happened. Do you get what's happened here?"

"Not really," shrugged Roger.

"It's sabotage." He looked meaningfully at Kit.

"What?"

"Check yours," said Victor to Roger.

Roger picked up his own headgear, a rather fetching skullcap design. He poked a finger inside.

"It's been done to my hat, too! Sticky tape all around the inside."

"Sabotage," repeated Victor. "And there's only one suspect."

"What. You think… Graham?"

"Who else? He doesn't like the costumes, does he? We all just heard him say he didn't like the costumes. This is the kind of petty stunt he would pull!"

"He did it awfully quickly."

"The costumes have been sitting here in these rooms for an hour. He had plenty of time to examine them, hate the look of them, and do this."

It still didn't make any sense to Kit. "He could have ruined the costumes if he didn't like them… But try and do a mischief to Patrick Finch and Roger Barker, stars of *Vixens from the Void*? What would that achieve?"

"Who knows what goes through his fat head, mate? Perhaps it's just some way to put pressure on us to use the old costumes."

"That's a bit too bizarre. Even for Graham."

"Huh. If you look up bizarre in the dictionary, you'll see his picture spread across two pages."

"You think that walrus of a man did this? To my costumes?" Joan sounded like she was ready to kill someone.

Victor hefted the helmet in his hand like a basketball. "This is the final straw. I'm going to have it out with him once and for all. He's not going to do anything like this again. I'll see you all later."

He stalked out, carrying the helmet under his arm.

As he reached the door he bumped into Dr Loske and Marie, who were hurrying into the room.

"We heard another scream," she gasped. "Stone ball?"

"No," said Victor.

"Thank god again," she sighed with relief. "I know it's not happened in thirty-five years, but you never know, do you?"

* * *

Kit left the dressing room and helped Binfire pack away the equipment and take it to the minibus. As they got there, they found Joan, Tara and Dorothy sitting in the back, waiting to be ferried back to the hotel.

Binfire swung into the driver's seat and Kit climbed into the back. She barely sat down before the minibus rumbled into life. Kit reached into her pockets to find Jackie's cassette for a re-listen – and found the envelope she'd picked up from the dressing room. The one she'd inserted into the gap between Patrick's head and his helmet.

The envelope was unsealed, the flap tucked inside. On impulse, she untucked the flap and pulled out a letter. She unfolded it and read:

DEAR

FOLLOW THE ENCLOSED INSTRUCTIONS.

DO NOT IGNORE THIS MESSAGE. I KNOW ABOUT WHAT HAPPENED WITH LILY. THIS IS NOT AN IDLE THREAT. I KNOW YOU DON'T WANT YOUR NAME ALONGSIDE THE WORD 'POLICE' AS A HEADLINE IN THE NEWSPAPERS.

FROM

AN ADMIRER

The words zoomed crazily towards her like a fancy camera trick. Her eyes absorbed the typeface, blacker than any shade of black she'd ever seen before.

There were no other bits of paper in the envelope. The 'enclosed instructions' were not enclosed.

It must have fallen out of someone's pocket when they were trying on their costumes.

But whose pocket? Patrick? Roger? The corner that would have contained the name of the addressee had been torn off.

Kit suddenly realised she'd forgotten to breathe. She was holding the air in her lungs and she let it out with a shuddering gasp.

"Are you okay?" said Dorothy, leaning across the aisle. "You look a bit pale."

"Yes, I'm fine," smiled Kit, pushing the paper quickly back into the envelope. "Just realised I'd forgotten something on my 'to do' list."

34

The camera equipment had been stored in 33 Hanover Parade, the minibus parked and the memory cards extracted from the camera and stowed in a safe place in Victor's room. The first day of filming was officially over.

In the shabby living room, Victor, Robbie, Freya and Binfire were in high spirits, drinking and chatting and laughing, toasting their success and swapping stories of the day. Kit elected to sit in the corner and smile, but not join in. Her batteries were low, and she felt frustrated. She was desperate to show them the letter, but she couldn't say anything in front of Freya and Robbie.

"She did what?" gaped Robbie.

"She held a sword to Graham Goldingay's neck," giggled Freya.

"Seriously?"

Freya held up a hand. "I swear on the Nordic war god, Tyr." She gave a weary smile. "Oh my. I feel sooo sad again. Wolf would have so loved to have been here to see that sword on Graham's throat. The utter anarchy of the situation…"

Robbie nodded. "He would have whipped out his phone, recorded it and put it on his YouTube channel. Absolute guarantee."

"What did you say to Graham when you found him?" Kit wanted to know.

"Ah… Change of plan, mate." Victor took another swig and wiped his mouth. "I *did* start off looking for him. I was pretty mad, as you saw. Then, after I ran around the Pavilion for a while, I calmed down a bit. I reconsidered. I reappraised the situation."

"You 'reappraised the situation'?"

"Yeah, I reappraised the fact that Graham was supplying all the props and the Vixos spaceship for the scene re-enactments, and I thought it wasn't worth me having a go at him and him taking his ball away."

"Yes, hardly worth it," said Robbie acidly. "After all, if you can't commit a few acts of sabotage and vandalism and get away with it, what can you do?"

"Your sarcasm is noted, Robbie dear," said Victor, blowing him a kiss.

Kit was uneasy about letting Graham off so lightly, but it wasn't her call.

She nursed her glass of water and didn't say anything. Finally, she could bear it no longer.

"Okay you lot, see you tomorrow."

She made her goodbyes, grabbed her velvet coat and plunged into the night.

35

She walked along the moonlit backstreets of Brighton, the clump of her heavy boots ricocheting off the houses. They sounded terrifyingly loud.

The streets were deserted. She saw only the odd solitary figure walking to a pub or getting an Uber. She couldn't help but tense up, even when passing a person who showed no interest in her. If they so much as glanced at her, just appraising her appearance, her clothes, her hat… Her heartbeat accelerated wildly.

When walking alone at night, she often found it a good psychological boost if she walked while deep in conversation with her mobile. There didn't have to be anyone at the other end, she just needed to act confident, plugged into a discussion instead of silently wandering in the dark like a potential victim.

She decided to ring Victor. He answered quickly and she could hear the amiable burble of the others in the background.

"Hi."

"Hi mate." Victor had to raise his voice slightly. She heard him tell the others that it was her on the phone, and the burble decreased slightly.

"Look, I know we didn't get a chance to talk through our findings today, what with the unpacking and all. I've got something pretty amazing to show you. Perhaps we could meet first thing to compare notes?"

"No, I don't think that's really necessary, mate," he said. "We've got a lot to do tomorrow. I think we should touch base and discuss when we've got time to meet."

"Okay. Well, I have something I need to show you and Binfire. So I want to do it over breakfast at the hotel."

"Go all the way there?"

"Well you're going to be there anyway, aren't you?"

"We'd have to start really early if we have a discussion before we go to the Pavilion."

"Victor! This is important!"

"Okay, if that's what you want, mate. We'll be there."

And he hung up.

Relief washed over her when she saw the lights of the hotel.

When she walked in, she noted with a pang of disappointment that the purple-haired girl was still on duty. Jackie was nowhere to be seen. She went up to the desk.

"Excuse me, is Jackie Hillier still here?"

The purple-haired girl looked confused and harassed. "She finished for the day. I think she's gone home?"

I wonder what happened to our date?

Kit had a sinking feeling that she had been stood up.

The purple-haired girl was surrounded by huge men in tuxedos. She looked tiny. The men weren't acting threatening, not intentionally, but they were drunk and very loud. Some of them were lolling over the chairs. One was facing the wall, singing a Robbie Williams song to a stag's head.

The purple-haired girl was talking to the chief drunk, who was leaning heavily on the counter. "I'm sorry, sir."

"Greg. My name is Greg, love. Greg Greggy Greg."

"I can't let you into the bar, Greg, it's policy?"

"But we're residents," slurred Greg. "We've paid and everything."

"When you booked, we did not know you were a stag do? We don't accept stag parties?"

"That's bloody sexist."

"We don't accept hen nights either?"

"Look…" Greg was interrupted by a cheer from the men around him as one of their number collapsed into a plant pot.

"When we booked as a party of eight, we did it in good faith, no one said on the phone that we couldn't—"

"That was a mistake on the part of the hotel. The website does state very clearly."

"Bloody websites. I never read the small print."

"You are upsetting the other residents. I am going to have to get security to ask you to leave?"

A burly man with a crewcut and earring stood silently in the entrance to the bar, his hands cupping his crotch like he was preparing to defend a free kick. He was dressed in an apron, as if he'd been pulled off other hotel duties to deal with the emergency. He looked very calm, but ready to deal with anything unpleasant.

Greg made an *ugh* noise, like an eight-year-old being called in for his dinner.

The purple-haired girl smiled. "Can I suggest you go and sample the delights that Brighton has to offer and return *quietly* when you need to go to bed? The doors are unlocked until midnight."

"Midnight? What kind of stag night ends at midnight?"

"They get unlocked at five-thirty."

The man sighed and staggered to the main doors. "C'mon everyone. Let's find another pub. We're on the clock now."

There was a ragged cheer from the group, and they all half staggered, half fell out of the door.

Blissful silence descended. The purple-haired girl caught Kit's eye, and they both sighed with relief.

Kit had fully intended to go straight to her room, but she saw that three of their guests – Tara, Roger and Patrick – were in the bar. She walked in and perched on a nearby barstool.

She could tell the three of them were chatting about the day, discussing memories that had stayed long dormant and now bubbled to the surface. There was an occasional burst of laughter and Tara said, "My god! I'd completely forgotten about that!"

Roger and Patrick were splayed out on the sofa, still in the clothes they wore for the interviews. Tara had changed for dinner and was now wearing flared trousers, a smart red blazer and a T-shirt with *Namaste* printed on it in a Hindi script.

Kit was ready to sit there for a while, take the odd sip of her orange juice and spy on them like a birdwatcher, but to her surprise Tara turned, caught her eye and beckoned her over.

Kit did a *who me?* gesture and Tara nodded.

She slipped off her stool. Roger and Patrick stopped manspreading and gave Kit room to sit down.

"Hi," said Tara.

"Were your ears burning?" said Patrick. "We were just talking about you. We were just saying what a fantastic job you did today."

"Oh! Thanks."

"Very skilled and professional, I thought."

Roger raised his pint and made a silent toast to show he agreed with the sentiment.

"Yes, you were really good," added Tara. "I felt very at ease with you."

"Well, thank you again. I do try."

"Can I ask you something?"

"Sure."

Roger rolled his eyes at Tara. "It's fine Tara. You don't have to worry about it."

Tara continued. "Can I ask you for a small favour?"

"Er… You can ask."

"It's about the end of my interview."

"What about it?"

"It's not worth it, Tara," added Patrick. "Water under the bridge. Forget about it."

"Believe it or not, Kit, back in the 1980s, I was not always a beacon of positive energy. We all go on life journeys, and my journey has been longer and bumpier than most. When I was young, I was very much like a lot of other young actresses. I was just interested in moving on up and pushing others down on my way up to the top."

"You're being really harsh on yourself," muttered Patrick. "You were nicer than most."

Tara held up a hand to silence Patrick. "Maybe I was, maybe I wasn't. But I have to make peace with my past. It's important to me. So, when I gave the advice to… that young girl—"

"Lily Sparkes," Kit supplied the name. It was the first time the name Lily Sparkes had been spoken in the vicinity of the suspects.

Did Patrick just flinch when I said her name?

"—Lily Sparkes, yes. When I gave advice to Lily to go to Hollywood it was… not given in good faith. I was not trying to be a good Samaritan. It was actually a bit of an in-joke between the members of the cast. We used to try to give extras who wanted to be actors the worst advice we could possibly think of."

"Right."

Tara blushed. "It was funny at the time. If you wanted to start an acting career, the *best* thing to do is some amateur dramatics, then try for drama school. The *worst* thing you can do is run off to Hollywood. Go there without any qualifications or an agent? You'd just get chewed up and spat out…"

She leaned over and placed an immaculately manicured hand on Kit's knee.

"You have to believe me, Kit. I didn't think in my wildest imaginings that she would follow my advice. She seemed such a level-headed girl."

Just what Jackie said about Lily. Down to earth. Practical.

"You know. I do sometimes think about that girl. I hate to think I did anything that led to whatever happened."

She made a sad smile. "So you see, it's really not an example of me as my best person, so I am a bit hesitant to see it preserved for prosperity on a documentary."

"I quite understand," said Kit. "Consider it removed. I will personally make sure it doesn't make the edit."

"Thank you. Thank you so much."

"And for the record," Kit added, "I don't think you did anything wrong. I heard there were other factors in her decision to go to America. Her parents were incredibly controlling people, so I think she must have wanted to get as far away from them as possible anyway."

Tara fanned her face with her hand, waving away potential tears. "You don't know how much those words mean to me! That is such real relief to know."

"What's such a relief to know?" It was familiar nicotine-stained voice. "Has Buddha returned from cloud city and signed up for your yoga classes?"

Vanity had entered the bar. She was immersed in a big floppy hat and a 1960s-style Afghan coat lined with extremely synthetic orange fur.

"It's just a little matter between me and Kit."

"She's getting a bit of her interview excised. The bit about her telling Lily Sparkes to go to Hollywood," said Roger.

Tara's face darkened. Her eyes scorched Roger's face.

"What?" Roger shrugged. "Is it a secret?"

"No," said Tara, through gritted teeth. "*It wasn't.*"

Vanity perched on the back of the sofa. "Well, I'm not surprised you're ashamed, darling. It *was* a shameful thing to do. Telling that poor innocent naive girl to travel all the way to Hollywood? What *were* you thinking?"

"What?" Tara's normally serene voice escalated into a shriek. "I saw you do that to *dozens* of extras! I saw you do it to at least two girls who were on the actual *same shoot* in Brighton."

"Yes, but I would never have done it to *that* girl, would I?"

It was obvious to Kit that by making Dorothy feel included, Vanity had accomplished her single good deed for the day, and she was enjoying compensating for it by slipping back into bitch mode.

She drawled, enunciating each word with infuriating superiority. "I could *see* the little popsie was vulnerable and impressionable. I could see it in her eyes, darling. That's why I would *never* have done anything to upset her delicate little psyche."

"Except trying to get her sacked," said Patrick acidly.

"What?"

"You tried to have her sacked."

"Darling, I don't think I—"

"Don't deny it, Vanity. The first shoot? I saw you arguing with the hotel manager. I saw you pointing at Lily Sparkes and insisting she should be fired. I heard the hotel manager saying it was an honest mistake on her part and he couldn't in all conscience fire someone for that. I saw you point a finger at him and tell him he would regret it."

Kit could see obvious confusion on Vanity's face. Somehow, she had contrived to get herself into a position where Patrick – the person she was moving heaven and earth to ingratiate herself with – was glaring at her with hostility and disappointment.

Her mouth opened and closed several times.

Eventually she said, "I... don't remember."

"No, I guess you don't," said Patrick coldly. "I believe you." He stood up and nodded to Roger. "Are you coming?"

Roger scrambled to his feet and pulled his coat on.

"We're going for a boys' night on the town," said Patrick. "Don't you ladies wait up for us."

They walked out into the lobby.

Tara looked at her watch and leapt up. "Oh gosh! I'm having dinner with Joan in the hotel restaurant. I should have been at the table five minutes ago. I bet she's very punctual."

She got up, started to walk away, and turned, chewing her lip. "Do either of you ladies want to join us? I'm sure they could give us a bigger table."

"I have plans," snapped Vanity.

Kit made a show of thinking about it. "Thank you for offering," she said at last, "but I'm a bit tired. I think I'll get something in my room and have an early night."

"No problem," smiled Tara. "And thank you for obliging me over my small favour."

And then she was gone.

Kit was left alone with Vanity.

An awkward silence fell like a shroud. Kit tried to break the ice by flipping a polite smile in Vanity's direction.

"What are you smirking at?" she snarled.

Kit practically ran from the bar.

36

Kit ran up the stairs two at a time. She felt a palpable, physical relief when she saw the door to her room at the end of the landing.

And there was Jackie Hillier, waiting right outside. She was wearing jeans, a chunky sweater and her ever-present Puffa jacket. The fact that this was the first time Kit had seen her *not* in her hotel uniform filled her with an irrational excitement, like finally meeting a friend out of school.

Jackie saw her, smiled, waved and held up a tiny red suitcase like she was a chancellor announcing a budget. Kit accelerated to meet her.

"Hi."

"Hi."

"You're not wearing your name tag."

"I'm going incognito." She smiled. "I hope you don't mind. I went home and changed. Do you mind?"

"Of course not."

Kit fumbled with her card key, dropping it twice, and they tumbled into the room with giddy excitement.

Jackie put the tiny suitcase on the bed, which turned out – obviously – to be a cassette carry-case, covered in red faux leather and decorated with stickers.

She opened it up. "Voila."

The case was full of C90 cassettes. One row had labels handwritten in pink felt tip: Nik Kershaw, Howard Jones, the Cure, Ultravox and many others, all from the 1980s.

Exactly like my own tape collection.

The other two rows simply had *Phone conversation with*

Lily written on them, with dates and times, just like the one that nestled in Kit's pocket.

Jackie pulled a tape out. She held the cassette box tightly, rubbing her thumb over the cracked case like it was a diary full of priceless memories. Then she handed it to Kit.

"Can I do this one first? It's when she called me on my birthday."

Kit produced her Walkman, plucked the tape from the box, slotted it inside and offered it to Jackie.

She took the Walkman with exaggerated reverence and giggled. "I haven't used one of these things for years. It's a classic."

She pressed play and her eyes misted over, listening to her friend speak to her from across the years.

"Bloody hell."

Kit patted the bed and gestured for Jackie to sit down and listen in comfort. Then she busied about her room, looking for things that she could tidy up. There wasn't a lot, but she managed to waste a few minutes sorting out her pens and throwing out the dead ones. She realised she hadn't had any dinner, but luckily she had a Tupperware tub full of energy bars on the desk, and she helped herself to one.

Out of the corner of her eye she watched Jackie reach the end of one tape, pull the cassette box over to her and slot in another.

Kit didn't mind. *Let her listen to every single one of them. Let her fill her boots. She's been utterly invaluable so far. If she hadn't told me about Tara's terrible advice to go to Hollywood, I wouldn't have heard about Vanity trying to sack Lily. That's two motives to murder Lily for the price of one.*

And Kit liked having company. She liked glancing at Jackie's socked feet, her toes twitching as she reached parts of the recordings that really excited her.

After a while Jackie pulled off the headphones and said, "Sorry, the voices are going a bit drowsy. I think the batteries are getting a bit low."

"No problem." Kit dived for her suitcase, found the sleeve full of spare batteries and performed emergency maintenance. "There you go."

"Actually, I think it's time I took a break for tonight. Yeah, it's exciting, but it does get a bit repetitive after a while. I'd better leave you in peace."

"You're not disturbing me. Honestly."

"Promise?"

"Promise."

"Okay. Can I have a glass of water?"

"Sure." Kit poured her a glass from the jug which Jackie took gratefully. The glass was cold and the ends of Jackie's fingers were warm. The contrast made Kit's insides flutter.

Jackie took a sip, then drew her knees up to her chest and hugged them. "Anyway, how's it going with your documentary?"

"Good. Really good. Lots of good footage today."

"Mags couldn't believe the girls that turned up. Me neither. Huh. If only I was twenty years younger…"

Kit didn't know what to say to that.

Why? Did you want to audition with them, or did you want to snog them?

"Do you want to ask me any more questions?"

Are you gay, Jackie? That's my first question. Can you answer me that?

"Actually, there was one question I thought up."

"Fire away."

"It just came up today. You said that Lily got on very well with the actors."

"She did, yeah."

"A little bird told me that one of them tried to get her fired."

226

Jackie looked a little surprised. "What? Oh yeah. So she did. But that happens. Guests get angry for stupid reasons all the time."

"But it must have been a shock for Lily – why did she want her fired?"

"To be honest, Kit, I don't know. Scott was the manager then, and he was very tight-lipped about disciplinary stuff. He never gossiped. I think Lily was going to tell me, but the following day Vanity was as nice as pie to her. Couldn't be nicer. I think all was forgiven and forgotten."

"What was she like when she came back the following year? Was Vanity nice to Lily?"

"So Lily said, yeah. As I say, nothing came of it. I think. All best friends together."

"Hmm."

"Is that all? Did you want to tape me saying that?"

"No, it's fine. As you say, it's gossip. Probably not worth putting on the documentary."

"Yeah. So… is that everything?"

Kit's notebook was on the desk, and she flipped it open, the bookmark causing it to flop open at the last page she'd written on. In the middle of questions marks and notes, there was just one big word.

CRAWLEY

"Does Crawley mean anything to you?"

"How do you mean?"

"I don't know."

"You don't know?"

"Haven't a clue. You must think me a complete scatterbrain."

"I would never think that."

"I was making notes on Lily, and I've just written down *Crawley*, and I can't remember why."

227

A white lie. That's all. It's fine.

"Nope. Sorry. Doesn't ring any bells."

"She hasn't got relatives in Crawley?"

"She hasn't got any relatives. Not anymore. None I know about."

"Oh. Okay."

"Sorry."

"It's probably nothing."

"Yeah."

Jackie put her chin on her fist, deep in thought. Then her face lit up.

"Hang on, let me do something. I can just put a keyword search in my phone and see if there's any addresses I've got with 'Crawley' in them."

She tapped on her phone. "Oh," she said, surprise in her face. "There is one address in here. I completely forgot about her."

"Who is it?"

"Our old drama teacher, Mrs Creehan. She moved to Crawley after Lily died. She came back to help us with the concert. We were in the paper."

"Yes, I saw the article."

"Did you? I looked a right mess in the photo."

"No, you looked very nice."

"Those were the days! Did you want the address? If she's still alive I'm sure she'd love to talk to you about Lily. She got on really well with her. Lily was her prize pupil."

"Yes, please. I'll just get a pen."

"We can use AirDrop. Let me take your number and we can share our phones."

"Okay."

Is she after my number?

Kit did as she was told. After a few seconds her phone pinged and told her that Jackie wanted to share a contact. Would she accept? She did. There was another ping and *Mrs Creehan* appeared on her screen.

"Thanks."

"Don't mention it."

Jackie got up and stood facing Kit. She saw the edge of the tattoo on Jackie's neck, but the sweater was too high-necked to allow her to see any more of the picture.

"I'd better go. I need to get my dinner."

"Wait – please stay. I'll get room service. What would you like?"

"Oh. Um… Grilled haloumi wrap? I'll pay."

"No, I'll take care of it."

"I couldn't."

"I'm here on business. I can put it on expenses."

Kit rang down and order two haloumi wraps. "There. You have to stay now. You're trapped."

She grinned. "Looks like I am."

She held out her glass of water. "Cheers."

Kit grabbed her glass and they clinked. "It's bad luck to toast with water, you know."

"Is it?"

"If you believe that stuff. Which I don't."

"Ooh. Brave girl!"

It seemed very natural to be with Jackie. The fact there was twenty years' difference in their ages didn't seem to matter.

"So, do you live in Brighton?"

"Along near the marina. Not *in* the marina, mind. I don't get paid that much. I rent a flat. It's not much, but it's enough for me and the landlord's nice. How about you?"

"I've got a flat in Tunbridge Wells."

"Oh, I hear it's *really* nice there."

"It is."

"Your parents live there?"

"They used to. They retired and moved down to Dorset."

"Now that is *really* nice down there. I bet your parents are really lovely."

"Oh yes. Really lovely. Most of the time. A right pair of jolly round nerds. Actually, it was them who got me into *Vixens from the Void*."

"You're joking!"

"Oh yes. They were huge fans. Completely obsessed with it. I was actually born the day they broadcast the very last episode."

She looked at her. "No!"

"Twenty-eighth of January 1993. They missed the final episode, and it was a whole year until they managed to see it repeated it on BBC2, but by then they'd been spoilered by their friends."

"Spoilered?"

"They got told the ending. They blamed me. They said it jokingly, but I knew they meant it. Sometimes I think I only got into *Vixens from the Void* to please them, and to assuage my guilt."

"Wow," she said. "That's deep." She stared at Kit as if examining her for the first time. "You're very smart," she said. "I like your waistcoat. When I saw you in the lobby the first thing I thought was: I like her waistcoat."

"Thanks."

Kit considered what she would do now. Say nothing? She spent a lot of time saying nothing to her friends. Mainly because she had so few of them and didn't want to lose them by acting like a self-pitying wet blanket. Binfire knew, no one else did.

Probably time to change that. What the hell.

"When I was a teenager, I did wear waistcoats a lot. Mainly because a lot of my music heroes wore them in the 1980s. And lot of cult characters wore them too. Doctor Who, Giles from *Buffy the Vampire Slayer*, Frodo. Here's a confession for you. When I got too thin and my engagement ring didn't stay on anymore, I used to keep it in my pocket, right here, on the end of my watch chain, just like Frodo kept the one ring."

Jackie made an *awww* expression. Her mouth shrivelled into a tiny rosebud. "That's so sweet."

Kit said, "Then I started to think they were silly. A bit of an affectation. Who'd want to sweat in the summer under two layers of cloth when everything can fit in your trouser pocket? So I stopped wearing them for a while."

Then Kit gripped her courage and forced herself to carry on. "Then my fiancée… She left me, and I had a breakdown."

The word 'she' hung there. Jackie didn't react.

"I didn't want to see anyone. I was almost catatonic. I couldn't leave the house."

"Oh, poor darling."

Jackie started to struggle off the bed. Kit knew what she was going to do; she was going to give her a big motherly hug. But she didn't want that. Kit waved her to sit still. "It's fine. I'm okay now, truly. Have you ever heard of a thundershirt?"

She shook her head.

"When our relationship was in trouble, we thought one of the reasons might be that we didn't have kids. We talked about adopting, but I couldn't cope with the responsibility. So we got a dog, and being responsible people we avoided pet shops and puppy farms and we got a rescue. Little Milo, a dachshund-terrier cross. It was utterly lovely, a darling little thing, but before it got to us it had a bad life. It was utterly terrified of everything, shaking at the prospect of going anywhere, so we took advice and we got a thundershirt. It's like a fitted doggy coat, nice and tight, so the dog feels contained and held wherever it goes. And it worked."

She smiled. "I mean, it worked for the dog. The dog didn't work for the relationship. If anything, Milo irritated her more than me. But that's a long story." She tapped her waistcoat and buttoned it up. "Long story short, this is my thundershirt."

"Well, thank you. Thank you for sharing."

"You're welcome."

"Can I use your loo?"

"It's not mine, it's the hotel's."

"You're renting it."

"Then you have my permission."

She hopped off the bed and disappeared into the toilet. Then there was a knock at the door.

"Room service!"

Kit hopped to the door and grabbed the food, thanking the porter and giving him a tip. When she returned, Jackie was standing by the desk. Her demeanour had changed. She was standing bolt-upright, combative.

Her face was cold, thunderous.

I'd only been gone a few seconds!

"You've been keeping something from me. How could you?"

Kit deposited the tray on the bed, and held her hands up. "Now, I kind of did say I was gay. I'm sorry if I made you uncomfortable—"

"I know you're gay! I didn't float in here on a barge! You're gay, I'm gay, we're both gay! This is Brighton. Ninety per cent of people who live here are queer! I'm not angry about that! I'm angry about what's in the bathroom!"

"What about the bathroom?"

"Do you want to look? Shall we look?"

With sinking heart, Kit went over to the bathroom. She slowly pushed open the door. She had a sick feeling that she knew what she was going to see.

Inside the walk-in shower was Binfire's board game, all set up. All the figures were clearly labelled, including the figure of Lily Sparkes in the middle.

On the shower wall was a conspiracy theorist's wet dream. Photos of the guests were stuck up with Blu-tack. Red string was attached to each photo, forming what looked like a cat's cradle of paranoia. The lines connected to each other and fed the photo in the centre: the painfully innocent school photo of Lily Sparkes.

Post-it notes were stuck up around the photos, covered in Binfire's distinctive scrawl.

> ROGER: Did he chat up L?
> TARA: Told L to go to Hollywood.
> JOAN: Angry that L ruined costume?

It looked utterly crazy.

Binfire, you frokking FROKKING bastard.

"It's for a novel I'm writing." Kit didn't sound very convincing.

"No it's not."

"No. It's not."

"You think Lily was murdered? My friend was murdered?"

"It's just a theory," said Kit lamely.

"But you're still using *me*, aren't you?"

"No."

"You're probing me for information about my friend, just like those reporters who came sniffing round. You told me it was for a documentary! Tell me that's not *you* using *me*! Fuck you!"

"B-But w-we're making a documentary! I'm not lying! Cross my heart! We're definitely making a documentary! We've got cameras and guests and costumes. The investigation is… It's just a side-line."

"Like me, you mean?"

And that was the moment Kit knew she had lost.

"Am I a side-line?"

"I didn't mmm-mean it like that."

Jackie gathered up her cassettes and walked stiffly to the door. "Thanks for the use of your Walkman, Kit. It was really nice to hear her again. And in return I will tell you something that will help your investigation. Lily is dead. One hundred per cent dead. She committed suicide because she was tired of being in a world where everyone was really shitty to her."

She opened the door. "You can have my haloumi wrap. I'm not hungry."

The slam shook the windows and reverberated through Kit's soul.

37

Kit didn't move for a long time, but when she did move, she did a very Kit thing.

The chart in the bathroom is incomplete. I can't leave it like that.

She walked like a zombie to the desk, pulled out the Post-it notes and wrote in her tidy little handwriting:

> PATRICK: Is he being blackmailed over L? Why?
> ROGER: Is he being blackmailed over L? Why?
> VANITY: Tried to get L fired. Why?

She stuck them up and stared, listening to the voices inside her head. The voices told Kit to leave it, stay in the room and not try to patch things up with Jackie.

I can't fix things like people. It's too exhausting.

But she realised those voices came from fear and habit and leave-it-Kit-it's-much-too-painful.

She forced her legs to move towards the door. Left foot. Right foot. Left foot. By the time she had left the room, she was flying down the gallery like the devils of hell were after her.

She reached the lobby. No Jackie. The purple-haired girl was behind the bar. *What did Jackie call her? Mary?* No. She couldn't be sure. She wasn't listening. She never listened when it mattered.

Read her badge, you idiot.

"Hi, Mags. Have you seen Jackie anywhere?"

"No, she's not in today?"

"She *is* here, she was with me. She just left in a hurry. I wonder if she came through here?"

"No. Sorry."

"Oh."

Mags heard the desolation in Kit's voice.

"If she was going to leave, she'd probably leave by the staff entrance. It's on the other side of the hotel, I'm afraid."

"Okay."

Kit shuffled over to an armchair, fell into it, and let her face drop into her hands.

You tried and you failed. What other outcome did you expect? Back to bed you go.

I just want to stay here for a while. It's cool and quiet.

Inside the dark prison of her fingers Kit could see nothing, but she was dimly aware there was someone else in the lobby besides her and Mags. There was a voice she recognised, but it was different. It used to be slurred and belligerent but now it was tight with worry.

"We just came back, and he definitely came back with us."

"I don't know how I can help."

"Well, he can't have got far. We literally just walked through that door, crossed the lobby and went to the bar."

Kit pulled her head out of her hands. She was right; it was Greg the stag-do man. He still looked dishevelled but had sobered up considerably. His fellow stag-warriors were sitting quietly in the bar taking turns to fall asleep.

"He was just here."

Mags looked left and right.

"Perhaps he's in the toilets?"

"We've checked the toilets."

"His room?"

"Nope."

Greg noticed Kit watching them, and he flashed her a quick tired smile.

"I've lost the groom."

"Oh."

"Not good form for the best man."

"No."

"He's got to be at St Georges in the morning. Steff is going to lose her shit."

He wandered away to join his brethren in the bar.

Mags shrugged at Kit. "Looks like it's the night for disappearances!"

A chill crept inside Kit's waistcoat and gripped her heart. "I've got an idea where he is. I'll just go and get him back."

She ran to the bottom of the stairs, paused, looked back and said: "If I can."

38

Kit should have known. If she'd joined the dots earlier that evening, she could have predicted that, when humiliated, a certain someone would retaliate by indulging in predatory sex or nihilistic drunkenness. Or both.

Kit knocked quietly, then when she got no response, hammered until her knuckles started singing.

"*Vanity!*"

Finally, there was movement, and a protracted bout of rattling as Vanity attempted to work out how to open the door. It swung open with some force and Vanity stood there, leaning heavily on the frame.

"Not today, thank you, darling."

She attempted to close it, but Kit pushed past her and into the room.

Vanity staggered but used the wall to steady herself. "What the bloody hell do you think you're doing, barging in here?"

"Testing a theory."

Sitting in a chair at the corner of the bed was a man half-wearing a tuxedo. His lager-stained shirt was hanging on to his muscled frame by a few buttons. He was barely conscious, his glassy eyes wandering around the room with a detached interest. Two sparkly devil horns protruded from his head and an 'L' plate hung around his neck.

Vanity sashayed past him and pulled out a bottle from an ice bucket. "Well, if you're staying, you might as well have a drink."

"I don't want a drink."

"Suit yourself."

Vanity put two glasses out on the desk and tipped the bottle over them, sloshing champagne over the glasses, the desk and the carpet.

"Vanity… VANITY!"

Vanity spun round, a glass in each hand, spraying more champagne in a wide circle.

"Yes, darling?"

She pushed one of the glasses into the man's hand. He took it, too drunk to resist or understand why he'd been given it. He stared at it like it was a mysterious artefact.

"What's he doing here?"

"He followed me home. Can I keep him?"

"No, you can't keep him! This man has to go back to his friends. They're waiting for him downstairs."

"But darling, look at him! He's got an 'L' plate around his neck! If that's not a challenge I don't know what is."

"He's getting married in the morning."

"Well ding-dong. He's going up *my* aisle tonight, darling."

She groped for her phone on the coffee table, thumbed a few buttons and it started to play 'Baby One More Time'. Vanity started flailing around, her arms flopping like rubber bands. She grabbed Kit by the wrists and tried to force her into a jive, but Kit was not in the mood to become a co-conspirator.

She pulled away. "I think you should just put the music off and get to bed."

"Oh do you?" drawled Vanity. "Oh do you indeed? Well, here is my counter-offer." She blew a long crude raspberry. "If you don't want to dance with me, I'm afraid I'm going to ask you to leave."

"I'm not leaving."

"But I insist." She suddenly started screaming. "Help! Help! Call the police! There's a lesbian in my bedroom! Help! Call the dyke squad!"

Kit pedalled back to the doorway. Vanity grabbed the man's hand and tried to pull him to his feet.

"Come on, darling – dance!"

There are a lot of drawbacks having a hotel with an internal courtyard; sound travels *very* easily. On the upside, though, sound travels very easily.

Kit went to the other side of the gallery, leaned over the balustrade and shouted down to the stag-nighters in the bar.

"Hoi! You lot! I've got your groom!"

* * *

The stag-do posse arrived in their tuxedos, stormed Vanity's room and extracted the groom like a crack team of 007s. A few of them loitered outside, hoping that Vanity would drag them in instead, but Kit gave them a frosty look and slammed the door in their faces.

"You're no fun," grumbled Vanity.

She slumped on the bed, unwittingly assuming the pose of Titian's *Venus of Urbino*.

"Leave me alone. Go 'way."

"Why are you upset?"

"Why do you think? I told you. This place is cursed, darling. It fucks me up every time."

"It only fucks you up if you let it."

"Thanks for that, darling. Put it on a poster and I'll hang it in my loo."

"What happened here? Is this why you tried to get Lily fired?"

Vanity gave a long groan. "Go away. Want to go to sleep."

"Tell me and I'll go away. I'll even get you ready for bed before I go."

A long silence. Kit got the feeling that Vanity was assessing how drunk she was, and how tight her leather trousers were.

Finally, she emitted a huge shuddering sigh and surrendered. "She was a silly cow with a big mouth. Silly silly cow."

"Big mouth?"

"Oh god. It was such a ridiculous thing. When we did the

location filming, I went down to Brighton with a model friend I once knew."

"A friend?"

"A friend. With benefits. Darling, you get the picture."

She rolled across the bed until she was on her back, staring at the ceiling. "Unbeknownst to me, a few days later, Jerry, my husband at the time, comes down to Brighton for a surprise visit…"

Vanity's first husband. Jerry Dervish. Record producer of many late-1980s hits. Then hugely successful CEO of Spinny Records.

"…and that girl only said to my *fucking husband* darling, that 'Mr and Mrs Mycroft' had stepped out for the day and would be back later! I mean, Jesus fuck! I thought these people were given training! Anyway, Jerry wasn't the type of man who was into extra-marital arrangements. He went back to London without a word and divorced me within the year. And then, after several debauched years, most of them occurring while I was in the show, I settled down and threw my lot in with Tom…"

Vanity paused. Kit heard another long-drawn-out sigh.

"You really loved Jerry. You were a fucking fool, weren't you?"

There were a few seconds of confusion before Kit realised that Vanity wasn't talking to her. Vanity was talking to a younger version of herself.

Another pause, and then:

"Still, she's dead now, so sod her."

"Jesus…" said Kit softly.

Vanity heard her exclamation.

"I didn't ask for your judgement, 'girlboy'. But… I… I didn't mean that. I am… sad… that she is dead." She spat out each word as if they were fighting to stay in her throat.

"Fuck it. I was mad as hell, and I did try to get her sacked. But did she lose her job? No. Because I didn't pursue it. Because I bloody knew it was all my fault, darling. I was taking stupid risks because I thought I had a right to do it. And it was just a matter of time before some silly bitch working in some shitty hotel said something and it all would go tits up. If it wasn't her, it would have been someone else. Because I knew, deep down, that I would have carried on behind Jerry's back until he found out. So I was angry because I knew… It was my fault and my fault alone."

Kit was getting angrier and angrier on Lily's behalf. "So? Did you *apologise*? Did you tell her it was *your* fault, not hers?"

"Not as such. Nothing was said. We were friendly, yes, I think we were friendly. As I say, I spent the next six years playing the field. I was too busy convincing myself I was happy to even register her existence, let along stay angry at her. Believe me, darling."

"I believe you."

Kit wished she could believe her, but she had seen Vanity at sci-fi conventions, how she worked the crowds of autograph hunters and the panel audiences. She knew Vanity was very good at telling people what they wanted to hear.

Kit leaned over her prone form, undid Vanity's belt and the top button of her flies, and edged Vanity's trousers over her hips.

"Come on then, Mycroft. Hitch your bum up. Skin a rabbit…"

39

After she put Vanity to bed, Kit trudged back to her room. Her legs were so heavy she felt like she was walking through a black hole. She felt utterly drained, body and soul.

She strained to build up a head of fury at Binfire's stupidity, but she just didn't have the heart to do it.

I should be angry at Binfire, but wasn't I doing to Jackie just what Vanity did to her first husband? I was going to carry on playing games, hiding the truth, until it inevitably came out, sooner or later. Even if Binfire hadn't turned my bathroom into a scene from Silence of the Lambs, *I still left my bloody notebook on the desk.*

I was just asking to be found out, wasn't I?

And if that didn't expose me, what would happen if we actually caught Lily's killer? Jackie would have definitely found out then.

Me and Vanity. We're just the same.

The thought sent a shudder through her body, from her feet right up to the top of her head.

There was one last nasty surprise waiting for when she got to her room – a silhouette of a large man on the upper gallery.

Graham Goldingay, hands on the balustrade, was looking down on the bar like Henry the Eighth surveying his subjects.

He turned and walked back into a room. *His* hotel room.

So he's back. Great. The end to a perfect day.

She was tired and angry and she couldn't stop herself. She charged up the steps and hammered on his door. It opened. Graham had already slipped into an ornate shiny dressing gown, tied onto his huge body with a thick red belt. He looked like an expensive Easter egg.

"Kit Pelham," said Graham in his characteristic monotone. "And what can I do for you?"

"You can stop sabotaging Joan's costumes for a start," she snapped. "I don't know what you're thinking. You're being stupid and childish."

"I have been stupid and childish many times," drawled Graham. "As I am very wealthy, I have given myself permission to be stupid and childish. But I have not sabotaged any costumes. Say that again and you will be hearing from my lawyers."

"Fine." Kit sensed Graham was telling the truth, but she didn't want to give him the satisfaction. "Fine. Just watch it, that's all."

Graham stood there, staring at her. Expressionless.

Every fibre of her being screamed at her to leave, but she forced herself to hold his gaze.

"What hold have you got over Dorothy Fletcher?"

Graham blinked. "Hold?"

"You know what I mean. You've got something on her."

"If I told you then you would know."

"That's the idea."

"If you knew then I wouldn't have any hold over Dorothy Fletcher, would I?"

Incredibly, for the first time since she knew him, a slow smile oozed across his features.

"Goodnight, Kit Pelham."

The door was slammed in her face.

40

10 a.m. Vanity Mycroft, Roger Barker, Patrick Finch, Joan Peverin, Tara Miles and Dorothy Fletcher to meet at hotel reception. Transport will take all guests to Brighton Pavilion.

11 a.m. Vanity Mycroft interview.
11.30 a.m. Dorothy Fletcher interview.
12 p.m. Patrick Finch interview.

1-2 p.m. LUNCH.

2 p.m. Transport to Brighton beach.
3-5 p.m. Recording of "Back to Brighton Beach".

5:30 pm Wrap.

* * *

It was eight o'clock in the morning and the restaurant was quiet. The only other person Kit knew was Tara Miles. From her damp and tangled hair she guessed Tara had taken advantage of the hotel's tiny pool.

Kit found a little table as far away from Tara as she could, sat down and perused the menu.

"Howdy, pilgrim."

Binfire sat on the chair opposite and gave her his best mad grin.

"I tried out my drone yesterday. It's frokking amazing."

"Good for you."

"It's going to be so good for spying on the suspects."

He formed a camera lens with his fingers and held it up to his eye.

"You know, hovering outside windows. Tracking them wherever they go."

"Great. That means you won't have to break into any more hotel rooms."

"Well, let's not go mad."

"You broke into my room yesterday. You set up your war room."

"Yeah. I did."

"I took someone to my room, and they opened the bathroom door. And they saw it."

"What?" Binfire's eyes bulged out of their sockets. "You *never* have people in your hotel rooms! You don't even let the cleaners in!"

"Well, I did last night."

"Who was it?"

"Jackie Hillier. Lily Sparkes' friend. The one with the cassette tapes."

"Oh right. Oh." Then he said, "Oh." again. Then he said, "OH! The lesbian."

"How do you know that?"

Binfire helped himself to a slice of toast. "Because it's frokkin' obvious? Oh! OH!"

"Oh?"

"Oh."

"Why 'oh'?"

"Because I'm seeing Mags with the purple hair on reception…"

"You are?"

"Yep."

"How do I not know that?"

"Because you always focus like a laser beam on one thing and ignore everything else under your nose. So, I'm very good friends with Mags and she just told me that Jackie didn't come into work this morning. She was due in at six. She called in sick."

"Oh."

"Oh."

"Oh."

"Did you upset her?"

"*You* upset her! You turned my bathroom into the lair of the Zodiac killer!"

Binfire took another bite and chomped energetically. "She'll come round. They always do. I was once with a girl and I really upset her by…" His chomping slowed to a stop. "Yeah… Maybe I shouldn't tell that story anymore."

Victor walked into the restaurant, still in his director's outfit: black cargo pants, black polo-neck and black jacket. He joined them at the table, pulling up a chair.

"Okay, I'm here," he said unnecessarily, casting a quick wary glance at Tara. Fortunately for them, Tara had put earbuds on and seemed to be in a state of meditation. "Shall we pool our suspicions and synchronise our suspects? Anything to report from the examinations of their body language?"

Binfire leaned in close, his voice low. "It's actually kinesics. I've read up on it."

"Bully for you. What did you see?"

"Here is my report. Observation one: when Kit interviewed Tara and asked the question about how she gave advice to Lily to go to America, Vanity harrumphed."

"She harrumphed?" Victor sounded intrigued.

"Yep."

"She harrumphed? How did she harrumph?"

"Well, it was more like a 'hah', but it was silent, so she didn't interrupt the filming. It was like this." He opened his mouth and pushed the air out of his lungs. "She obviously thought Tara was not telling the whole truth. Observation two: when Roger said he didn't have any contact with the extras, everyone was grinning. *Everyone*. Like they all knew he *did* have contact with the extras."

"Can you stop there just a second, Binfire?" Kit said.

Binfire looked hurt. "I haven't finished my report."

"No, it sounds great, but a few things happened yesterday that I think might supersede your analysis."

She told them about Tara's confession about her 'good advice'. Then she told them about Vanity and her attempt to sack Lily. Then she showed them the letter. They read it with mouths open. Kit could see bits of moist toast crumbs nestling on Binfire's tongue.

"Shit," breathed Victor. "Where did you find this?"

"On the floor of the boys' dressing room."

"That's a blackmail note," said Binfire.

"Nothing gets past you, Binfire," sighed Victor.

Binfire turned the note upside down, examining every inch of it. "You see here? The blackmailer has been really clever, by not cutting letters out of a newspaper. That means there's no newspaper with gaps in it lying about to discover."

He waggled it in Victor's face, making the edges flap. "It's been printed with a normal common-or-garden printer. Now all we need to do is find the printer responsible and we've got your blackmailer."

"Good luck with that."

Kit plucked the note from Binfire's hands and examined it. "Do you think Wolf sent this note?"

Victor frowned. "Yes! Could be…"

"It fits in with our theory that Wolf was blackmailing Lily's killer. If only we had the other bit of paper with the instructions on it. It's odd, though…"

"What?"

"This phrase here." She read from the letter: "'I know you don't want your name alongside the word *police* as a headline in the newspapers.' It's a bit coy, isn't it? You'd think Wolf would be a bit more direct."

Victor took the note and stared at it. "Wouldn't it make sense to make the note ambiguous, in case it fell into the wrong hands?"

Binfire nodded. "Like ours."

"But we come back again to *how* and *why* Wolf blackmailed the killer," muttered Kit. "Why would he be so coy when he was going to announce the identity of the killer on his bloody podcast anyway? And why did he think he could threaten a murderer like this and not worry about the murderer murdering him?"

They fell into silence.

Victor spoke first, frustration in his voice. "So now we've got an amazing piece of evidence, but we don't know who it's from and we don't know who it's to."

"Yes."

"Damn."

"Frokk it."

"Well, this is still the biggest discovery yet, Kit. Well done. When you interview Patrick today, you really need to focus on questions about Lily."

"I'm already talking about the female extras in all the other interviews. It's starting to look like I'm obsessed with those girls."

"I'm sure you'll do it really subtly, mate."

"Thanks."

He tucked the letter back into the envelope and handed it to Kit. "Here. You keep it with you. It might help you prep."

He looked at the notes he'd made on a paper napkin. "Vanity tried to fire Lily. Tara messed with Lily's head and told her to go to Hollywood. Joan blamed Lily for ruining one of her costumes and she seems crazy enough to do something about it. And either Patrick or Roger were being blackmailed over something that happened with Lily, possibly her death, possibly something else…"

His eyes widened helplessly. "We have motives for *every* suspect on this list, apart from Dorothy. This is *incredible*. You know, I thought we'd manage to get something out of one or two of them. But *five*? I thought we'd be able to narrow it down by now."

He sighed, pushing the napkin into an empty cup.

A waitress arrived, holding a notepad. She gave them all a conspiratorial wink.

"I trust you slept well?"

"I did, thank you."

Binfire looked up at the waitress. "I didn't sleep well, I slept really bad," said Binfire.

Kit rolled her eyes. "But you didn't stay at the hotel, did you?"

"Of course I didn't." Then Binfire realised. "Oh right! I thought you were just making conversation."

Kit tapped her forehead. "Sorry about him, he's a bit…"

Binfire nodded "…telepathic."

"Would you like to order from the menu, or would you like to avail yourself of our breakfast buffet?"

"I'd like the eggs on avocado toast, please."

Two hundred and seventy calories.

"Right. Tea? Coffee?"

"I'll have a black coffee," said Kit, quickly.

"Fruit juice is on the table." She scribbled on her notepad, and turned to Binfire and Victor.

"I'll have a coffee," said Binfire. "Like the Millennium Falcon. Flat white."

"I'm fine," said Victor. "Him and me, we're not staying in the hotel."

"You still can have breakfast," she said. "You can just pay at the desk."

"Okay. I'll just have an orange juice."

"You can pour one from the buffet." She winked again. "I won't tell."

"Okay, thanks."

Victor went to get his orange juice. Binfire looked at his phone.

Kit thought about Jackie. She knew that rescuing their embryonic friendship was hopeless, so she was moping, running through the few times they were together, absorbing everything about her, the looks she gave, the words she said... Then she remembered something Jackie said when they parted outside the hotel two nights ago.

Victor returned with his orange juice and sat down.

"Perhaps Lily is still alive," said Kit.

Victor gave her a suspicious look.

"What?"

"You heard what I said."

"I did. It just sounded a bit mad coming from you. What have you done with the real Kit?"

"Hey! A new theory!" said Binfire. "I'm up for it. What's your evidence, Poirot?"

"Well, they never did find the body."

"That's true," said Binfire.

Victor leaned in. He perched his elbows on the table. "But you saw the clips from the local news, Kit. They explained all that. There are strong currents around Brighton. It's quite common for bodies to float miles out to sea."

"Good point," said Binfire. "Moriarty here has a point."

"Yes, but those bodies do get found *eventually*. It's not common to *never* find a body at all."

"Good point. One point to Poirot. Fifteen all."

"They had loads of theories. It could have been caught by a shipwreck, or snagged by discarded fishing net, or if it was out there long enough, picked clean by fish and her bones were just scattered on the seabed..."

Victor sipped his orange juice. "And her being still alive doesn't make any sense. I mean, what, she faked her own death?

She wrote her suicide note, jumped off the pier in front of witnesses and managed to swim back to shore? Why risk doing something that crazy? Why didn't she just leave her clothes on the beach like everyone else?"

"Moriarty has the advantage," said Binfire. "Forty–fifteen."

Kit pouted. "I know. I know it makes no sense. I just had a feeling, that's all…"

"Women's intuition?"

"God no. I just felt that she's still here, that some part of her is around me, watching me…"

Victor shuddered. "You're starting to spook me."

"I'm starting to spook myself."

"This is so not like you, Kit."

"I know."

"Kit… Has it occurred to you, that your thinking has gone a bit… well… like your head is a bit too deep inside *Vixens from the Void*?"

"What do you mean?"

"I mean you're thinking a bit like a *Vixens from the Void* scriptwriter. In the first-ever episode of *Vixens* the shuttle crashes and supposedly kills half the royal family, right? But they go to the asteroid and they don't find any bodies. They assumed they'd been vaporised."

Kit nodded reluctantly. She was well ahead of him.

"But in… what is it? Series four?"

"Yes. Series four."

"At the start of series four, Byzantia is found safe and well, and held captive by the Styrax. Because that's how the show works."

"That's true," agreed Binfire. "That's the law of sci-fi and fantasy. Nobody is really dead. Especially if there's no body. If a body isn't found, ergo the character is still alive."

Kit felt she was being patronised. "Yes, thanks, both of you. I do know how science-fiction works. But people *do* turn up alive after they can't find a body. They do it *in real life*. They do it *all* the time. They *do actually* fake their own deaths."

Victor sighed. "It's easy to get seduced by a compelling storyline. But remember the other storyline? Vixxosia, the mother of Arkadia and Medula and Byzantia? She was missing presumed dead… and that's how she stayed in the show. Just dead."

Victor almost sounded sad about it. "We never even met her, did we? Gone in the first-ever scene…" He made a *pouff* gesture with his hands. "Just an off-screen presence and a portrait hanging in the palace. Gone right at the start, stayed dead and gone forever. I think it's far more likely that Lily is gone forever. Don't you?"

"It was just a thought. I was just spitballing."

"Everyone has a right to spitball," said Binfire.

"I'm not saying she can't spitball." He glanced at the time on his phone. "But we are on a schedule here, we can't get distracted."

"Of course. You're right. I know the facts as well as anybody. Lily was seen by witnesses jumping into the water. I've seen the statistics. It's a pretty risky thing to do. And doing it at night? You would have to be mad, stupid or suicidal to do it."

"Right."

"Yep," nodded Binfire. "Unless the person who jumped off the pier happened to be a stunt person."

Victor stared at Binfire, then he groaned, pulled his napkin out of the cup, smoothed it out and made a note by Dorothy's name.

"Sod it. Just sod it. They all did it. All six of them. Why not?"

41

Day two started in much the same way as day one. Everyone gathered in the hotel lobby at ten o'clock, just as before. Vanity, Roger and Patrick made their own way to the Pavilion, and Binfire drove the minibus containing Kit, Tara, Dorothy and Joan.

This time Tara and Dorothy sat together and chatted amiably about how lovely Brighton looked in the morning. Tara had stopped acting like Dorothy was the second coming of Jesus – much to Dorothy's obvious relief.

When they arrived at the Pavilion, Dr Loske greeted them as before. As they walked through the building, Dr Loske kept nervously eyeing the ceiling, obviously spooked by the screams from yesterday.

"Are you alright?" said Kit.

"Talking about the past has made me paranoid. I'm half expecting a huge object to descend on us at any moment."

"Not likely, though. Is it?"

"Very unlikely. But I do get strange premonitions of disaster sometimes."

"That was probably Roger Barker's chat-up routine. You don't get more disastrous than that."

She laughed and lowered her voice. "Is he for real?"

"He's the type of man who grew up at a certain time and has a certain amount of power, so he's never had to adjust his behaviour. He had to be dragged kicking and screaming into the twenty-first century."

Dr Loske grinned. "Speaking as an academic, he's positively progressive. There are professors I know who are still waiting to be dragged into the nineteenth century."

Once again, Dr Loske showed them into the Adelaide room and disappeared. The guests settled down, ready to be interviewed. Kit joined Victor and Binfire in the music room. She sat on one of the guests' chairs and watched them set up the camera.

"You won't need me this afternoon, will you?" said Kit casually.

Victor frowned. "Well, no. We'll just be filming our guests walking down the seafront, pointing at things they remember. Why?"

"I'm going to take off."

"Where are you going?"

Binfire was waggling a light. "She's going to pursue her lady love and throw herself at her feet and beg forgiveness."

"What?"

Kit explained what happened the previous evening, how Jackie discovered Binfire's situation room and stormed off into the night.

Victor looked concerned. "So she knows we're investigating? Shit. Do you think she'll tell anyone?"

"I doubt it," said Kit defensively. "Who's she going to tell? The police? The hotel? Our guests? I don't think so. She's made it very clear to me she hates all the attention over Lily's death. Telling anybody would make it worse."

"She might even end up helping us," said Binfire. "Lily was her best friend, after all."

"Maybe." Victor frowned. "Perhaps it would be a good idea to get her onside. She has got all those tapes. They'd be good to have a listen to."

"I'll ask her when I see her," Kit lied.

"Right, I think we're ready," said Victor. "Anyone want to inform our guests that they can come down?"

"I'll go," said Kit.

She was halfway up the stairs when she felt a hand fall on her shoulder. She flinched, turned, then sighed with relief.

"Binfire!"

Binfire's eyes darted right and left. "Look, pilgrim, I want to help you. When you're dealing with your ex—"

"She's not my ex."

"Yeah, but all women are potential exes at heart. Take it from one who knows. I don't think you should go in unarmed, know what I mean?"

"No."

"You need something to hand. Geddit?"

"I really don't."

"You don't have to frokking attack her, just look like you mean business. So, between you and me, I've given you a little insurance."

"I have no idea what you're talking about."

"That's good. You keep saying that, and we'll both be laughing."

He pulled his right bottom eyelid down and winked with his left.

"Just between us."

And then he clumped back into the music room, whistling tunelessly. Kit stared after him, none the wiser.

42

Vanity was first in the chair. It felt rather anticlimactic after her drunken confession last night. Kit didn't try to ask any questions pertaining to Lily, or Lily's part in the destruction of Vanity's first marriage, for the very good reason she didn't need to. She already had all the information she needed. Vanity's chat became a typical anodyne interview about how everything was *marvellous*, and the hotel was *marvellous*, and how yes, it was a *such* a tense shoot, but it was so much *fun*…

Then came Dorothy. She was in good spirits today, relaxed and smiling. She sat down, fanning out her skirt so it floated gently onto her knees.

"Can I ask how you got into stunt work?"

"I was an extra for a while, I think everyone knows that, taking the odd job here and there. Then I decided to expand my range, make myself a bit more commercial, so I took a course in stage fighting. I got a *lot* more work after that. I was touring non-stop. Every Shakespeare company needs someone in the cast who knows how to swing a sword, so I was always in demand. And when the directors I was working with in the theatre moved to telly, they took me with them. One of those directors happened to be Leslie Driscoll, who, as you know, directed the very first episode of *Vixens*."

"And you stayed on *Vixens* for the entire run."

"Yep. I loved those costumes. Just loved them. As you can see, I love dressing up…"

She gestured to her own ensemble. She was back in her flowing skirt, yellow shirt and gypsy waistcoat.

"Nothing boosts the ego more than a spangly cape, big boots

and Spandex. I think I preferred being Vanity Mycroft to being the giant armadillo!"

There was a titter behind Kit from the guests, but not a mocking one. It was a supportive laugh. Dorothy was enjoying being herself in front of the camera, and there was no denying it, it was lovely to see.

"Now, the stunt you did for that very first scene, where you climbed up the tree and fell out of it. Did you train for that too? Because that's not sword-fighting."

"Yes, that's right. Once directors started asking 'can you fall off this building?', or 'can you jump out of this car while it's moving?' I joined Mayhem! a company that specialised in that kind of thing, and they trained me up."

"Leaping out of cars? Falling off buildings?"

"Yep."

"Was the Brighton shoot a difficult job for you?"

"Not really. Falling out of a tree onto a mattress – no bother. The armadillo costume was the worst part. Very sweaty. I think it was summer, wasn't it?"

Kit nodded. "June."

"That's right."

"But if they did ask you to do something more dangerous, would you have been prepared?"

She shrugged. "It depends what it is."

"I don't know… How about leaping off Brighton Pier?"

Dorothy's expression didn't flicker.

"Could you have done that?"

She looked like she was seriously considering the question. "No."

"Why not?"

"Too many variables. The tide. The depth of the water. Weather conditions… But there's the most important reason of all."

"What's that?"

"I'm afraid of heights."

There was a ripple of laughter.

"Seriously?"

"It's true, luv. I get vertigo. I never got into this business to throw myself off buildings. I got into this business to act, and maybe do the odd sword fight. If anyone asks me to climb anything taller than a tree, it's a flat 'no' from me."

Kit laughed. Then she went on to her other questions. *Did you study the way Vanity and Tara walked so you could look more convincing in the long shots? Did you think the show would be so much of a success that you would be talking about it thirty-five years later?*

While she was asking questions, her mind was working.

That was an awfully convenient response. Was it too convenient?

Kit brought the interview to a natural end, and the other five guests erupted into spontaneous applause.

Dorothy's face twisted in confusion. She didn't know how to take it at first, she was always on the alert for gestures that forced her into the role of victim. But then she could hear the thumping in her chest and saw her hands trembling and she realised how much the simple act of just *sitting* there and talking on camera – as herself – had taken so much out of her.

She decided to take the appreciation in the spirit it was offered. She smiled at everyone, waved, curtseyed, raised her head…

And then the joy drained from her face. She was staring off-set and Kit followed her gaze.

Graham Goldingay was back, sitting in his chair in the corner of the room.

Glaring straight at Dorothy.

43

Now for the final interview. Patrick Finch. The legend of the theatre. The man who'd never been interviewed before for a Vixens from the Void *documentary, DVD or Blu-Ray. Even when they made that goofy documentary for BBC2 to celebrate twenty-five years of* Vixens, *he declined to be available.*

Vanity wouldn't like anyone to say it out loud, thought Kit. *But let's be brutal: he's star of this show.*

He mounted the podium and sat down. He crossed his legs, undid his velvet jacket, smoothed his cravat, tickled his handkerchief until it sat better in his pocket and placed his hands elegantly on his lap. Not for the first time, Kit was struck by how Patrick was the most actory actor in all of actordom.

"So, Patrick, what were you doing before you turned to acting?"

"Oh. Well, I left school at sixteen and went straight to Hendon as a police cadet. Became a full copper at eighteen. After a couple of years I got tired of it. It wasn't a particularly good time to be a copper as it was during the miners' strike. We didn't feel particularly loved by the community at large – to say the least! I left at the end of '84 and, like Dorothy, I signed on as an extra."

He smiled a little ruefully. "I was very lucky. Very very lucky. In my first month as an extra I got a job as a spear-carrier on a *Play for Today*. The director liked me, and the next thing I knew, I had an agent and a photo in *Spotlight*. That all happened in six short months."

Kit was very good at reacting as if she'd never heard *Vixens* anecdotes before. At the words 'six short months', she raised her eyebrows, shook her head disbelievingly and gave a well-rehearsed, "Wow."

"A lot of people assume *Vixens* was your first speaking role, but it wasn't, was it?"

Patrick gave a long-suffering smile. "That's a little bit of an urban legend. I had small parts in *Memory Lane* and *Coronation Street*, just walk-ons – and for both of them I played a policeman, would you believe! There's irony for you!"

A titter from the others.

"But yes, when I got cast as Captain Talon in early '86, that *was* the first time I had been cast as a regular character in a television series. So it meant a great deal to me."

"Filming in Brighton must have felt very daunting."

"Not in some ways. We'd already done the studio filming, so we had already 'bonded' as a cast."

His delivery of 'bonded' was flavoured with sarcasm, and there was another ripple of amusement from the other guests.

"What were your memories of filming in Brighton?"

He exhaled. "Ooh. God. Fun. It was fun. I enjoyed filming in the Pavilion. I mean, why wouldn't you?" He gestured to the chandelier above their heads. "It's so utterly beautiful. But for me personally, it was really nice to film by the sea. On location you can spend weeks stuck inside stately homes wearing heavy frock coats and have nowhere to go but the catering van, but here you could knock off, walk down to the beach, buy some candyfloss, go along the pier. It was like being on holiday."

Kit trotted out more questions. *Was it difficult filming in public? Did you have any idea the show was going to be such a success? Do you get asked about* Vixens *a lot when you're performing at the National Theatre?*

Then she moved gently on to other matters.

"And did you enjoy filming with the extras? How were they?"

"How do you mean?"

That threw her. It was the first time an interviewee had queried a question.

"How were they to work with?"

"They were fine."

"Fine?"

"Yes."

"How so?"

"They were absolutely fine. Next question."

Was there a hint of hostility creeping into Patrick's voice?

"Erm, that's good. So no problems with them."

"Why would there be?"

"It's just that Joan and Tara said…"

"You seem very interested in talking about the extras."

"I… they were part of the shoot."

"Yes, they were, but they were *extras*. They were background artistes. And you seem almost obsessed with them."

There was definite hostility from Patrick. His face was cold.

"It seems to me that, during these interviews, all your questions lead to them. Isn't that odd?"

"I s-see your point…" Kit's stammer was making an unwelcome return. "B-but I th-ink the fans would—"

"In fact, it always seems to lead back to one extra in particular. Which seems really odd, always nudging interviews about a big television show towards one fragile suicidal teenage girl."

His eyes were as cold as diamonds. "Speaking as an ex-copper, I would find that line of questioning rather provocative. Perhaps I should ask for a lawyer?"

This time, Kit wasn't able to say anything. Her tongue was lying in a coma inside her mouth.

"So in the absence of my own counsel, young lady, if you so much as insinuate that I had *anything* to with the death of Lily Sparkes, if you so much as *suggest* I killed her, or if you even use my name *in the same breath* as hers, then my team of very expensive lawyers will sue you for slander, and they will rip you into tiny pieces in court, and destroy you so completely you'll be just like Lily, in the sense that, no matter how hard they search, they will *never* find your fucking body…"

And then he slumped low in the chair and sighed. "Fuck it," he said at last. "I killed her, didn't I? That's what I did. I bloody killed Lily. I'm going to the hotel to pack my things, then I'm going to the police station to confess."

And with that he got up, stepped off the dais and walked slowly and stiffly out of the room.

Everyone listened to the dying *clump-clump* of his shoes on the carpet, paralysed with shock. It wasn't until the footsteps drifted into silence that Victor, Kit and Binfire charged for the door.

44

They tumbled out of the main entrance of the Pavilion, only to watch helplessly as Patrick slid into the driver's side of his shiny E-Type Jaguar.

"Wait!" yelled Victor. "Patrick, mate!"

Patrick ignored them. He slammed the door, and seconds later, the engine rumbled into life.

Victor rushed forward and flailed his arms uselessly, but the car was already nosing out of the car park.

Binfire scrabbled at the handle as it roared past then started to run after the car in that choppy, arm-pumping style he'd borrowed from Tom Cruise in the *Mission: Impossible* franchise, but it was to no avail. The car sped out the North Gate, and as it passed Kit could see Patrick's silhouette. Grim-faced. Eyes fixed on the road.

"What the hell just happened?" gasped Victor, watching the back of the car disappear. "What – the – hell – just – *happened?*"

Binfire jogged back to them, his face flushed with exertion. He stood with his hands on his knees, waiting for his breathing to slow. Then he straightened up and grinned. "Gents, we just got ourselves a frokking confession."

"I don't believe it."

"I know. Amazing, eh? We did it."

"No, I don't believe *him*."

"Don't believe what?"

"I don't believe Patrick's our murderer, mate."

Binfire pointed a shaking finger in the direction of Patrick's exit. "What? Pilgrim – he just *said* it. Right there. Case closed. We've done it, guys."

"No, it can't be. It's too easy."

Binfire threw his head back and slapped both palms on his forehead. "Listen to yourself, pilgrim – you just gave Kit the lecture at breakfast. It's not like telly. You don't have to have a confrontation with the villain on top of some high building. Sometimes some dude cracks under a bit of pressure and we get to go home early."

"No, there's something else going on."

"Remember what Freud said. 'Sometimes a vape pen is just a vape pen.'"

"This is not over, mate."

"Talk to him, Kit. Tell him he's being a complete orc."

Kit was silent.

"Kit?'

Binfire stared wildly at both of them, first at Kit and then at Victor. "Christ guys… we got a *confession*!"

Kit tried to speak, but she was still suffering PTSD from the interview.

"W–Wu–wu…"

"You answer in your own time," said Binfire. "In your own time."

"W–w… Wu–Wolf."

"Wolf?"

"W–what about W–Wolf?" said Kit.

"What about him?"

Kit folded her arms and focussed very hard on a small piece of ground in front of her. "P–Patrick just c–confessed that he killed Lily. He didn't say anything about W–Wolf."

"Yeah, but that goes without saying…"

"G–goes without saying? Goes without saying?!" If one thing got Kit's blood up, it was assumptions. Many a time she'd come across appalling inaccuracies on IMDB because some lazy individual assumed that, just because two actors had the same name, they were the same actor.

Enraged, her stammer evaporated like morning dew. "We are assuming that Lily's and Wolf's deaths are linked. But what if they aren't? What if Wolf was wrong when he said he had evidence of Lily's murderer? What if Wolf's special podcast wasn't about Lily at all? What if Patrick killed Lily, but wouldn't know Wolf from a hole in the ground?"

"The point," breathed Binfire. "The *point*... is... that we have a *confession*."

"No. The *point* is we don't know anything. We don't know what Patrick is saying to the police. We have to find out what he's confessing *to*. We have to find out if he claims responsibility for both their deaths. Otherwise we're not finished here."

"What do you suggest, mate?" asked Victor.

"Let's keep going until we know what's going on," said Kit. "I'm not needed this afternoon. I'll go to the police station right now. In the meantime, you two carry on, go filming on the beach like we planned. I'll report back."

Victor nodded. "That sounds like a plan. What say you, Binfire, mate?"

"Yeah, sure." Binfire was sulky. "I guess that makes sense."

"Ask for Sergeant Royce," said Victor. "He comes in the hospital sometimes. I know him. He might talk to you."

"Thanks."

* * *

They found the music room deserted, so they headed upstairs to the Adelaide Suite.

Roger, Vanity, Joan, Dorothy and Tara had done what all people who work in television do in the absence of further instructions: go to lunch. They were sitting around a table talking in low voices and looking shellshocked. Tara was nibbling nervously on a cheese sandwich, the non-dairy, gluten-free parts of her diet forgotten for the moment.

Vanity's voice was loudest. "What the bloody hell was that all about? What's got into him?"

Victor and Binfire were about to step into the room when Kit stood in front of them, blocking their path, her finger to her lips. She held her palm out in front of her and tapped her ear.

Wait. Listen.

Joan was bemused. "Did Patrick say something about killing someone?"

"He did indeed," Roger muttered, his expression dark and thoughtful.

"That was crazy." Dorothy looked grim. "Why did he say that? It was a completely tasteless thing to say. Lily committed suicide."

"Oh, we're talking about that one?" said Joan. "The one who jumped off the pier?"

"Yes, we're talking about that one," sighed Vanity.

Joan sniffed. "Just checking, dear."

Vanity continued. "He's gone mad. I bet they're all raving mad in the National Theatre. It was built in the 1970s, wasn't it? I bet it's completely stuffed with asbestos and lead."

"I've seen this kind of thing before." Tara spoke in an ominous whisper. "I went on this serenity retreat in Morocco once – which I might add was the most stressful week of my life. You've no idea how competitive people get when it comes to meditation…"

"Get to the point, if you have one," snapped Vanity.

Tara flashed a tight smile at Vanity and continued. "The point was, this yogi, he got us all to purge ourselves of our negative thoughts, and in the middle of a meditation one man jumps up and starts screaming that he killed his wife. He hadn't, of course, he'd cared for her for years, and she'd just died of multiple sclerosis, but the simple fact the yogi told him to get rid of his guilt caused him to short-circuit and realise he blamed himself for her death."

"And you think Patrick's blown a fuse?" Roger sounded scornful.

"Well… yes! You know I felt a twinge of guilt about the way I behaved to Lily. I said so. Perhaps Patrick felt some kind of residual guilt too?"

Roger sniffed. "I can't see it myself."

"I'm not surprised, darling," snapped Vanity. "Any residual guilt poured out of you a long time ago."

"I don't think he's guilty over nothing. I reckon he did do something."

Dorothy rolled her eyes. "Please, Roger. No. There's bad taste and there's bad taste."

"Hear me out. He was going on about Operation Mulberry at breakfast yesterday morning. Talking about waiting for the police to knock on his door. The poor old sod obviously has something to hide…"

"You'd better be careful what you say. There is a thing called slander," said Tara, cautiously.

"I'm just saying what happened. He said, 'Aren't you worried about the police arresting you?' 'Aren't you concerned about certain young ladies coming forward after all these years?' You know, the usual stuff."

"'The usual stuff'," scoffed Vanity. "God. It's obvious he was just curious about why you haven't been arrested by now, darling. God knows, I haven't the foggiest idea why you're still wandering around free when they got that MP just for slapping his secretary on the backside and calling her 'toots'."

"He sounded like there was something on his mind, that's all." He took a bite out of a ham sandwich. "And while we're talking about it, Patrick was right when he said what he said about the questions they're asking. They're weird. The questions. They're all about the girls…"

In the corridor outside, the three friends pulled panicked

expressions and stared at each other.

"...and they all end up about Lily Sparkes. I think it's very suspicious. Far too many questions about her."

"Well, obviously you'd think there were too many," retorted Vanity. "Given you shagged her."

Roger was stung. "Maybe I did. So what? At least I didn't try to get her sacked, did I?"

Vanity's eyes flashed. "But the girl didn't get sacked, did she?" She waggled a finger under his chin and he slapped it away. "And you *definitely* screwed her, and most likely caused her irreparable psychological damage."

"He shagged her too!" Roger pointed at Dorothy, who arched her eyebrows and placed her hand on her clavicle in a comical *who me?* gesture.

"'He'?" Vanity rolled her eyes. "Get your pronouns straight, Roger, or you'll have even less of a career than you do now."

"Haha! But that's the bloody point, isn't it?" Roger snarled, still pointing at Dorothy. "Duggie's got a get-out-of-jail-free card now, because he's grown himself a pair of tits and got his dead wife's sling-backs out of the wardrobe."

Dorothy's face contorted with disgust. "Jesus... You are such an utter—"

But Roger didn't stop. His blood was up. "I bet the police won't be knocking on *your* door for shagging her – because if they do, they'll have the woke squad down on PC Plod like a metric tonne of bricks."

"Oh fuck off, Roger," Dorothy's accent thickened into a northern drawl. "They won't be knocking on *my* door because *I* was a gentleman who gave girls a good time and I was bloody good at it. And I didn't coerce them or make promises I couldn't keep, or make them feel worthless by keeping a tally on the back of my bloody script, with subcategories of hair colour, size of bust and the noises they made during sex."

Kit had heard enough. It was all very interesting, but it was getting dangerously close to a full fistfight. She turned to the Victor and Binfire, gave an ironic thumbs up and they walked through the door.

"Hi everyone. Sorry we disappeared but…"

Five pairs of eyes turned in their direction and everyone started talking at once.

"Is Patrick alright?"

"Where is he?"

"Is he in trouble?"

Victor said, "Well, we saw him drive off. So we're guessing… he went to the police station…"

"Yes," Dorothy sighed. "But is he in *trouble*?"

"I'm going over there now, to see if he needs anything," said Kit. "I'm sure we can sort it out."

"I'd call for the men in white coats," quipped Roger.

Victor clapped his hands. "In the meantime, shall we have our lunch and go and record our memories of Brighton beach?"

Roger's mouth was about to dock with a triangular sandwich. It stopped just before entry.

"What? Patrick just admitted to murder and ran off to the police, and you want us to walk along the beach wearing 'Kiss Me Quick' hats like nothing's happened?"

"Er… yes. We do *need* to finish the documentary. That's what we're here for."

"I don't bloody think so. I'm in shock. Look, my hands are shaking."

Roger held out the hand with the sandwich in it and wiggled it, dropping crumbs on the table.

"Darling! What are you saying?"

It was Vanity. She pointed an exquisitely manicured finger at Roger. "I sincerely hope you're not saying you're backing out of filming, just because Patrick's left us? That's hardly *professional* is it?"

"No. I didn't say that."

"I think you just did. I think you said exactly that. We stick to the *schedule*, darling. Didn't you *read* your schedule when it was pushed under your door this morning? *I* did…"

"Oh, fuck off," snapped Roger, but he knew he was beaten.

Vanity stood up and stretched her arms wide. She was obviously enjoying herself. Kit suspected – no, she *knew* – that Vanity had resented ingratiating herself with Patrick, because she hated being controlled by anyone. With Patrick gone she was free to indulge herself. She was once more in her element, reinventing herself wholesale as the heart and soul of the project.

"I'm sure whatever cell he's currently languishing in, Patrick's deepest wish is that the show goes on. Because after all, that's what he would want, because that's the *professional* thing to do."

Feeling suitably cowed, the others fell silent and munched their sandwiches. Kit knew that they would all go meekly to the beach and eat ice creams and get filmed building sandcastles.

Because that was the *professional* thing to do.

45

As Kit walked to the police station, she thought about Patrick's confession and just how weird it was. She was glad that Victor had agreed to continue the investigation, because she had severe doubts about Patrick's guilt. Of all the six suspects, she considered Patrick to be the least likely murderer – of Wolf, anyway.

He's one of the most well-known faces in the country. Could he risk walking into Hanover Parade, go up to 33, enter the house, kill Wolf and walk out again without anybody recognising him? And he must be very rich. If he wanted to kill Wolf, couldn't he just hire somebody to do him in?

It didn't make sense.

The police station was only a ten-minute walk away. It was a large ugly building, blocks of concrete punctuated with big windows, and it looked a lot like the anonymous hotels Kit found herself in whenever she travelled across the country.

She went to reception and smiled at the desk sergeant, a young woman with a severe buzzcut that didn't quite suit her.

"Can I help?"

"Yes, I'm looking for Patrick Finch. I gather he's here?"

The desk sergeant pulled out a cockeyed grin. Her eyes narrowed. "Patrick Finch?"

"Yes."

"Inspector Wistful?"

Kit sighed. "Yes."

"He's not real, you know."

"I know that."

"I mean, god, I'd *love* him to work here, because he solves more cases in a month than we do in a year, but he's not real."

Kit did her best withering glance, but it didn't seem to travel through the bullet-proof glass.

"I know he's not real. And I'm not a raving loony."

"I wouldn't say that."

"Okay."

"Because we're not allowed to say that. I call you a raving loony, the IOPC would be down here before I finished saying 'raving'."

"Mr Finch is doing some filming here in Brighton with my production team."

"Really?" The desk sergeant was impressed. "Right here in Brighton?"

"Yes. And he said he was coming here, to the police station."

"Why?"

Kit had considered her answer to this during her walk. She had decided to keep things vague.

"To be honest, I'm not sure why. I think he said something about someone keying his car? Anyway, he said he was coming here about an hour ago, and our filming is getting behind schedule, so I thought…"

The desk sergeant shook her head. "Sorry. Everyone comes through me to get in here, and I've not seen Inspector Wistful come in. And I would know if I had. He'd need to do selfies with half the station, with me first in the queue…"

"Okay. Damnit."

"If you leave your contact details, if he comes in I can mention you're looking for him.."

"Great."

"*After* I get my selfie, of course…"

* * *

Kit left, wondering what to do next. She half expected that Patrick Finch wasn't telling the truth about coming to the police station, but the satisfaction of being proved right didn't do her any good, did it?

She walked back to the hotel and knocked on Patrick's door. No answer. She asked at the desk and Mags said she hadn't seen him.

He could be anywhere. What kind of state of mind was Patrick in?

Unwelcome images flashed in her head, her imagination churning out grim concepts for her delectation: Patrick driving his car into the side of a bridge; Patrick stepping into heavy traffic; Patrick following Lily's example and jumping off the end of Brighton Pier.

Well, what could she do now?

Nothing. She could wait at the hotel, wander around Brighton aimlessly on the off chance of finding him, or she could go and do the thing she dreaded more than tracking down a killer.

Go and make up with Jackie.

She was just about to pull up Google Maps to plan a route to the marina when her phone rang. The screen said *Mrs Creehan*. Kit didn't recognise the name until she remembered the contact details given to her by Jackie. It was Lily's drama teacher. The one who lived in Crawley.

"Hello?"

"Hello? Did you contact me?" An old-lady voice. Words thrown out sharply, as if aware that time was short.

"Yes, I did."

"Hello?"

"Hello?"

There was a long silence.

"Sorry, I had it going through my earbuds in my pocket. I listen to murder podcasts while I eat my lunch. I've got you on speakerphone now."

"Right."

"You left a message for me? You said you wanted to talk to me about Lily Sparkes?"

"That's right. Can we talk later? It's just that I'm a bit busy at the moment."

"I am very busy too."

"Oh."

"I help out in Oxfam most days. They rely on me. I'm the only one who knows how to work the till."

"Okay."

"But I am free this afternoon."

"Right. Yes. Yes, of course. I'm afraid I'm in Brighton at the moment."

"I know Brighton very well. If you take a train, you can be here in an hour."

"Great. I'll head to the station."

"I'll wait in for you."

The tone of her voice indicated that Mrs Creehan was doing Kit a huge favour.

Kit went straight to the train station, her ever-trusty backpack clinging to her shoulders. She managed to dash onto the platform and catch a train just before the doors closed.

As she sank down into a seat covered in an eye-watering pattern, she prepared herself to talk to Mary. Perhaps this distraction was a positive thing? Perhaps what awaited her in Crawley was the key to the whole case? It certainly helped Wolf Tyler make a major discovery.

The one that led to his death.

Among the many neuroses that jostled for space inside Kit's slender body was a dissociative disorder; not the best thing for coping with relationships, but it was proving surprisingly useful when investigating murders. She had already put Jackie's fury with her in a little box and filed it in the back of her brain, and now she stuffed Patrick's confession and disappearance into another, similar little box and slid it right next to the first one using an imaginary fork-lift truck, just like the end of *Raiders of the Lost Ark* (1981).

She was now completely focused on talking to Mary.

She checked the National Rail app on her phone. It was going to be half an hour on the train, and with any luck she would be back in time to greet Victor and the others the moment they finished filming along the seafront.

She sent a text to Binfire and Victor.

**No sign of Patrick. Not at Pol
station. Will keep looking. K.**

After a few seconds she received two thumbs-up emojis.

* * *

When she arrived in Crawley, she heard a familiar tuneless strum, and a terrible voice that was pinning '(I Can't Get No) Satisfaction' to the floor and waiting for it to bang the canvas and surrender.

It was the hairy old busker, tapping his foot like Sisyphus putting out an eternal cigarette. He was waggling his head and winking madly at the passers-by. Just to confirm her theory, she stopped at his battered fedora and dropped a five-pound note onto the little pile of coins.

"Fank you, miss," he croaked. "You're a pukka gent."

That settled it. She was right. Wolf had definitely been here.

Mary Creehan's Home – Flat 77, Phoenix Place – was only half a mile away. Ten minutes later she was there, a huge sigh erupting from her lips as she stared up at a monstrous block of flats, jutting into the sky like the headstone of a giant.

Mary Creehan's flat was a very big number, and she had a nasty premonition it was on the top floor. She pressed the buzzer and got no response. She stood there awkwardly for ten minutes, pressing the buzzer, watching the cars roar past, sometimes making pit stops in the huge Tesco on the main road.

Finally, a breathless man in Lycra carrying a bicycle arrived and opened the door. Kit slipped in behind him with a brief apologetic grin and made a pointy gesture up to the top floor.

Flat 77 was definitely on the highest floor. She trudged to the lift, stared blankly at the *OUT OF ORDER* sign on the door, went to the stairwell and put a foot on the first step.

46

When she finally got to the top, she leaned on the banister outside Flat 77, fighting for breath. Was it her imagination or was her backpack heavier than usual?

The door to Flat 77 was gleaming white, the only door in the building that had seen a fresh coat of paint in the last decade. There were pink and purple fuchsias erupting from two hanging baskets dangling either side and a welcome mat lay at the bottom, decorated with smiling hedgehogs. Mary had managed to carve out a tiny bit of country cottage in the middle of a concrete dystopia.

Kit knocked, and after much rattling and unfastening of chains, the door opened a crack and Kit could see a tiny sliver of a person in the gap.

"Mrs Creehan?"

"Yes?"

"I'm Kit Pelham."

The door slammed shut, and for a moment Kit thought Mary had changed her mind, that she'd been given the brush-off, but then there was more rattling and unfastening. The door opened wider and revealed more of Mary.

Like Jackie Hillier, it was difficult to connect the person standing in the doorway with the blurred black-and-white photo in the *Brighton Argus*. Mary was a plump woman in her seventies with a wide pleasant face topped with short dark-brown hair pushed from her forehead by a pink headband. She wore funky pink glasses, a pink mohair sweater, pink flared trousers and pink sandals. She reminded Kit of the kind of furry toy that teenage girls obsessively collected and filled their bedrooms with.

"Well done for finding the place. My friends try to visit me, they ring up to say they're here, and they just disappear, doomed to wander the corridors. Phoenix Place is like the Bermuda Triangle."

There was no hallway, so Kit stepped straight from outside into the sitting room. The interior was as clean and well-maintained as the exterior.

The furniture was very 1960s retro, though Kit suspected that Mrs Creehan had bought it all when new. Potted plants were perched on every surface, providing splashes of colour, which was desperately needed as the cream walls were bare. There was just one large mirror on one wall and a few theatrical posters hung on the others. They were for shows Kit didn't recognise, presumably school productions.

"Would you like a cup of tea? I bet you would after climbing all those steps."

Kit considered asking if she had black coffee but decided against it.

Let's not make things complicated.

"Yes please."

Mary scampered away, pushing through a bead curtain. It clacked and clattered, sashaying from side to side and giving Kit brief glimpses of the kitchen.

"You have a nice flat, Mrs Creehan."

"Thank you. You can call me Mary."

Kit always took a while to settle in a stranger's house. She stood awkwardly, listening to the gentle hiss of the kettle and the tinkle of teaspoons hitting a tray.

Mary re-emerged with a tray of tea things. "Here we are. The only biscuits I've got are digestives, I'm afraid."

"That's fine. Thank you."

Kit remained standing, staring out of the main window. The whole of Crawley was laid out before her like an oil painting. She could see tiny brushstrokes of mobile phone masts in the distance, and little dabs of children playing in a park far below.

"You have an amazing view."

"Thank you. There are some drawbacks to living this high, but they all pale into insignificance compared to the sight that greets me in the morning when I open my curtains."

Mary put the tray on a low coffee table and looked expectantly at Kit to join her. Kit surrendered and they both sat down on sturdy green chairs.

Kit sipped her tea, and even nibbled the edge of a digestive. *It's wise to be polite*, she thought. *And, after all, digestives are one of the better biscuits. Only seventy-one calories.*

"So, you wanted to talk about Lily."

"For our *Vixens from the Void* documentary. Yes. That's right. For a Blu-Ray. It's all about the filming in Brighton, and as part of that we're getting a few people to talk about Lily. After all, she was part of the filming and we can't speak to her anymore."

"That makes sense. Lily had such a good time doing that show. I recorded it and kept it, and we watched her bits so many times. I think the cassette is still on top of my television if you want to see it."

"I do have my own recording, so thanks, but I'm fine." Kit smiled. "I'm sorry to bother you."

"It's no trouble at all."

"I'm sure you get bothered all the time."

"Not really, it's nice to have visitors. My son sometimes comes to visit, but he doesn't stop long. That's sons for you."

"I gather a colleague of mine came to see you last year. He probably asked you all the same questions I'm about to ask you now."

She looked confused.

"No... I don't think so."

"Owen Tyler? Called himself 'Wolf'. Skinny guy? Baggy clothes? Long dark hair? Looked like an evil hippy?"

She laughed. "I'd certainly remember someone like that. No, I haven't talked to anyone about Lily since... Well, since that awful time she took her own life."

"Okay." Kit just about managed to keep the disappointment out of her voice. "I guess I was mistaken."

"So what would you like to know?"

Kit reached into her jacket pocket and pulled out her phone. "First, before I start, would it be okay if I recorded this? So I don't have to take notes."

"Just like those the police interrogations in *Line of Duty*!" Mary emitted a girlish giggle. "I have the right to be interviewed by a teacher of a senior rank or above, you know! No, I don't mind at all."

Kit put her phone on the coffee table and pulled out a notebook from her backpack and put it on her lap. There was nothing written in it, she was just giving the impression that this was simply a run-of-the-mill interview.

She pressed record.

"Okay, this is me, Kit Pelham, interviewing Mary Creehan about her ex-pupil, Lily Sparkes, who had a non-speaking part on the first two series of *Vixens from the Void*. First off, Mary, can I ask – was Lily a good actress?"

"Oh yes." Mary purred with the memory. "One of the most promising pupils I ever taught. I always gave her the best parts in all our school plays, because I knew she could handle anything I threw at her. And, I hasten to add, I was teaching at a girls' school, so the girls were performing male parts as well as female parts. She was Big Daddy in *Cat on a Hot Tin Roof*, Macbeth in *Macbeth* – of course – and Tony in *West Side Story*. It was a joy to teach her. A complete joy."

Sadness crept into her voice. "When she left school, we kept in touch. I told her she should audition for drama schools, or at least get some experience in amateur dramatics. But of course… I don't know if you knew this, her parents were very controlling and they frowned on that kind of thing. They had no interest in that 'sinful nonsense', as they put it. They wanted her to get a proper job."

"How did she get involved with the filming?"

Mary put a finger to her lips. "Well, let me see… I think she saw an advertisement in the local paper. That's right. She already knew the television people were going to stay at her hotel, and when she saw the advert, she thought… Well she thought it was destiny."

"And then what happened? Did she tell you?"

"Oh yes! She recounted it to me in great detail. They had a little room set aside on the ground floor to take the names of the young girls who were interested – there weren't that many who turned up, she said, and that surprised her – and when she brought the coffee and biscuits in for them, she said, 'As a matter of fact, I'd like to audition for you while I'm here!' And they were surprised, and they laughed, and they told her she'd be perfect, and it all went on from there."

"I see." Kit pretended to glance at her notes. "So the first filming session – that was for two weeks."

"If you say so."

"Did Lily tell you any stories from the filming? Any stories about how she got on with the actors?"

"Nothing specific, really. Not really. She said it was very busy, and there wasn't a lot of time to chat."

"Right."

Mary must have caught the mild disappointment in Kit's voice because she hastily said, "But of course, they all went back to the hotel after filming, and she got to know them a lot better."

"Anyone in particular?"

"Well, not really. She said everyone was very nice. The ladies in the cast were a bit off with her, but I was a young actress once, before I became a teacher." She winked. "That goes with the territory, doesn't it? She liked them, but she did find them all a bit tiresome at times. I think she much preferred the men. Unsurprisingly for a teenage girl! She liked that actor with the blond hair. The one who used to pop up in the odd sitcom."

"Roger Barker."

"Yes. She talked about him a lot. Oh, and she said the stuntman was very funny – always cracking jokes and making everyone laugh."

"Did she mention Patrick Finch?"

"'Inspector Wistful', you mean?" Mary grinned. "She did mention him. Well only the first time she did the filming. Not during the second."

"That's very perceptive of you."

"As a teacher you learn how to read the subtle signs. Even when you're teaching a lot of girls, you always know who's fallen out with who, just from the way they change the subject. But I am overstating things for dramatic effect, as usual. Yes, she liked some more than others, but she liked them all."

"Even Vanity Mycroft?"

"Who is that? I'm sorry. The name doesn't ring a bell. Wait… was she the woman who was in *Memory Lane* for ages?"

"That's right. She was one of the stars of *Vixens*. She tried to get Lily fired."

"Oh yes, she did tell me about that. You mean the business with her husband and the 'extra-marital friend'?" She nodded knowingly. "You're saying that Lily might have held a grudge. Oh no. Lily was mortified about what happened. She blamed herself. She was so grateful the lady didn't pursue it further."

She poured the teapot into two cups decorated with robins.

"Yes, she really enjoyed it. I think it really whetted her appetite to do some more."

"Hence her running off to Hollywood."

Mary gave her a sharp look. "Yes. That put the cat among the pigeons and no mistake."

"Did she tell you she was going to do that?"

"Absolutely not. If she'd shared her intentions, I would have definitely advised against it." Mary stared out of the window, where a flock of starlings were making short work of a dangling coconut shell. "I might not have spent a lot of my professional life as an actress, but even I know that jetting off to America just like that is the height of folly. That way lies all sorts of madness. Lots of lowlifes out there willing to take advantage of a young girl who doesn't know the ropes."

"And when she came back home, she went back to work at the hotel."

"Yes."

"Then *Vixens from the Void* came back to Brighton, one year later."

"That's right."

"Was she excited? Did she enjoy it as much as the first time?"

"I… don't think so. She seemed… jaded. Yes, that's the word. Jaded. She was weary. I think she felt her life wasn't going anywhere, it was just getting complicated and more difficult."

"How so?"

"Well… Um…" Mary started to flounder. "Her parents… obviously… They weren't best pleased, as you might expect. Lily didn't think she could get away from them again."

She frowned. "Is all this really relevant to your documentary? It's not really something I want to talk about."

"No, you're right. It's not relevant. I'm getting way off topic." Kit hastily changed course. "Did she keep any souvenirs of her time filming *Vixens from the Void*? Anything she showed you?"

Mary chewed her lip. "I've no idea. Apart from taping it off the television, like I did. Oh. I think she took some photos. I have no idea who's got them now. I'm guessing her parents would have destroyed them."

She stood up. "That's all I can remember. If you want to see any memorabilia I have from my teaching days, I'm sure I can find a few programmes and posters that feature Lily. But if you're only interested in Lily's work in *Vixens from the Void*…"

"You'd be surprised. I use all sorts of background information when I put things together. Can I see them?"

"Of course. I'd be delighted so show you. I have a suitcase on my wardrobe."

She disappeared through a door, adjacent to the bead curtain, and after some thuds and crashes she returned with a big squashy leather suitcase. She dragged it across the floor and it left a thick line of dark brown soil in its wake.

"Erm… is that dirt?" said Kit, pointing at the trail.

Mary looked down at the pile of dirt and grew flustered. "Oh my. That's not the right suitcase. I've got confused again, haven't I? Sorry…"

She dragged it back again and slammed the door shut.

Kit waited until she heard more thuds and sprang up to look around the flat, inspecting every inch. There was something odd about the place she couldn't put her finger on. For some strange reason Vanity's Chelsea house swam around inside her head and she couldn't understand why.

That makes no sense. Vanity's house is completely different to Mary's flat in every sense, but there was something…

But she saw nothing that helped her towards an 'aha!' moment. She ducked into the kitchen. Like the sitting room, it was very tidy. A pinboard hung above the toaster, filled with recipes cut neatly from magazines. Saucepans dangled above the sink in order of size, and teacups and were arranged by colour on the kitchen shelves. Kit approved.

Her eyes danced around the tiny kitchen, not knowing what she was looking for, or if there was anything to see.

She knew that Mary wasn't going to be long, so time was of the essence.

Why am I even doing this?

And then she saw it.

It was hidden just behind a recipe for blueberry cheesecake.

With trembling fingers, she reached out to the pinboard, pulled a pin out carefully, and allowed the card to drop into her hand.

It was a business card, decorated with moons, stars and planets. A cheeky robot waved from the corner. Written on it was:

NERD MENTALITY PODCAST
Presented by Owen 'Wolf' Tyler

Underneath was Wolf's Twitter and Threads handle, Facebook address and Instagram account.

Wolf *had* been here. And recently. He'd only had those cards printed within the last year.

"Hello?"

Kit stuffed the card into her pocket and left the kitchen. Mary was sitting at the coffee table with an open suitcase and a full pile of papers and photos. She looked suspiciously at her.

"I was just putting my cup in the sink," said Kit. "I hope that's alright."

"I've got the right suitcase now, look! Sorry about the other one. That was where I keep my potting mix for my house plants."

"Don't you keep it in bags?"

"Do you know dear, that's exactly what a non-gardener would say. Potting soil has to be aerated in a large leather suitcase for at least three months. Any horticulturalist will tell you."

Kit shrugged, sat politely, drank more tea, and nodded appreciatively as Mary pushed one dog-eared theatre programme after another under her nose, but she was desperate to leave. She had Wolf Tyler's card, a key piece of evidence in her pocket, but she had no idea what it meant.

She's lying. But why? Does she have something to do with Owen's death? And what about Patrick Finch? Where does that fit in? Or does any of it fit in?

None of it makes any sense.

After fifteen minutes (she counted the seconds in her head) she got out of her chair and gave her warmest smile: "Okay. Thanks so much, Mary. I think I've taken up enough of your time."

Mary stood up too. "I hope I've been useful to you and your documentary."

"Incredibly useful. I'm so grateful that you took the time to see me. I really mean that."

"Would you like to take something from the pile? A photo of Lily? A theatre programme?"

"Can we just put a pin in that?"

Kit jammed her hands into her pockets and felt the shape of the pin from the pinboard. She rolled it around in her fingers.

"I mean, can I get back to you. I'll have a chat with the people who're making the documentary with me, and if we decide we need something as a visual reference for Lily, then we'll get back to you. Okay?"

"Whatever you like. You can come back anytime, if you give me enough notice. It's all here waiting for you."

Kit walked to the door and Mary followed close behind, like an anxious sheepdog.

Kit stopped as something else caught her eye. There was a bureau tucked in beside the front door with a plant on the top and books on the shelves. As it was right next to the doorway it was at the mercy of the elements, and it wasn't quite as pristine as the rest of the house. Kit could see it was coated with a thin film of dust. And in the dust was a small rectangular shape of no-dust, like something had been removed.

"Oh dear. I hope nothing got broken."

Mary stared at her, mystified. Kit pointed.

"Look."

She drew an arrow in the dust, pointing at the shape.

"There's shape in the dust. Looks like a picture frame?"

Mary looked at the arrow, then the shape, then at Kit, then she spluttered with laughter. "Oh, I see what you mean! That… was a photograph… of Kenneth, my dear husband. After he died, I couldn't face him looking at me. So many happy memories in seeing his face, but all in the past."

"I'm sorry."

"Oh, it's fine, it's really fine."

"Was he a teacher too?"

"No, he was a fisherman. Another perilous underpaid profession." She smiled. "He was a very dear man with so many virtues. He was a lifeboat volunteer too. Such a good sense of right and wrong. I only wish…"

She sighed and stared at the top of the bureau.

"Yes?"

"I only wish Kenneth was still with us. Things would be very different if he was."

47

It was only when she got to the bottom of the stairwell of Phoenix Place that Kit finally worked out what had been bugging her about Mary's flat, and why Vanity's house had popped into her head.

Vanity's house was absolutely covered in photos of herself. Far too many photos. Magazine covers, album covers, pictures of her shaking hands with the Duke of Edinburgh at some charity gala, pictures of her covered in brown goo as part of an ad campaign for HP Sauce.

But Mary's place was the other extreme. No photos at all. Not of her, or her family. And the only photo that the flat contained… wasn't there.

Mary's story didn't ring true. So she couldn't bear to look at the photo of her dead husband? But it *had* been put there before, on that table, so she *had* been able to look at his photo at *some* point! And judging by the layer of dust, it had been there very recently. Mary, being the assiduously neat person she obviously was, would have been compelled to dust that table every day, probably twice a day, and therefore that photo must have been removed very recently.

Like just before she arrived?

A thought formed in her head that was so silly it made her laugh. And she was sure Binfire would agree to it in a heartbeat. But that was for later.

She broke into a trot back to the train station. She had been in Phoenix Place longer than she had expected, and she wanted to get back to talk to her fellow investigators. She rang Victor.

"Hi mate."

"How did the filming go today?"

"Oh, brilliant. Really, really good. Vanity has been an absolute star, jollying everyone along. We've got some hilarious footage of Vanity running along the pier chasing Roger in a 'Kiss Me Quick' hat, and Dorothy and Tara holding buckets and spades making sandcastles. This is going to be a great documentary."

"What about Patrick?"

Victor gave a grunt. "I honestly don't think the piece needed him. And you know what? I've looked at his interview and I reckon we can easily use it. Just cut it before he had the meltdown."

"No, Victor, I meant 'what about Patrick?' in the sense 'what about Patrick, the person who just confessed to Lily's death?' Have you seen him?"

"Oh, I see what you mean. No, I don't know. I've been busy, actually, doing all this filming. Wasn't that your job, to track him down?"

"You know, sometimes, Victor, I get the impression you care more about filming this Blu-Ray documentary than finding Wolf's murderer."

"The documentary still has to be done, hasn't it?" Victor was getting testy. "So are you on your way back yet?"

"I'm on my way."

"I meant to ask, have you patched it up with your girlfriend?"

"Not yet."

"Okay, well hurry up. I'm really looking forward to listening through those cassettes. They might hold vital evidence about Patrick."

"Yes, you're right."

"Glad one of us is thinking."

And he hung up.

As she travelled back to Brighton on the train, she felt a pang of guilt.

Victor's right. Perhaps I should at least try to make it up with Jackie? For the sake of the investigation at least. Who knows?

She might even join me and we can be a crime-busting odd couple, like Cagney and Lacey.

I should give it a try. Nothing ventured...

When she alighted at Brighton station she stood for a short while, head cocked like a spaniel in the general direction of the hotel, feeling sorely tempted to go back and hide in the safety of her room. Then she gritted her teeth, pushed her cap to a slightly more rakish angle and forced her legs to take her to the seafront.

She suddenly felt drained. She realised taking the umpteen flights of steps up to Mrs Creehan's flat had really taken it out of her. Not to mention the stress from making small talk with Mary, and the tension she was *already* feeling at the prospect of a difficult conversation with Jackie.

And her backpack was feeling *much* heavier than usual.

It's a mile-and-a-half walk. Can I really cope with going all that way?

She'd just passed the Sea Life aquarium when she noticed Volk's electric train was just pulling into its tiny station. The train was a historical artefact, its chief claim to fame being that, at one hundred and forty years, it was the oldest electric train in the world. At its delicate age it didn't travel very far; it just trundled along the seafront for a mile or so. The only place it *did* go was Black Rock station – which was very near to the marina.

It's a sign. Damnit. It's an actual bloody sign. Okay, let's go and do this.

She bought a ticket, clambered into a pretty red-and-yellow carriage at the rear, and slumped gratefully into one of the padded seats. After a few moments there was a gentle lurch and it trundled out of the station with a single *toot*.

There were a handful of people who had also chosen to take the train. They were all silent, heads bobbing in sympathy at the gentle buffeting they were receiving. Everyone was staring serenely out to sea, listening to the squeaking and rattling of the wheels and enjoying the quaintness of it all, silently appreciating the fact it wasn't some crazy rollercoaster.

Kit had to agree. It was very calming. Dusk was slowly descending and the ripples on the sea were illuminated by the dying sunlight, making ribbons of silver that wriggled across the surface.

The electric train had one other stop, halfway along the route, just by the crazy golf. The stop was imaginatively titled 'halfway point'. It ground slowly to a halt and allowed a few more passengers on board.

Including Patrick Finch.

Kit slumped low in her seat and put her hand in front of her face. It was a pathetic effort at looking incognito, considering she was still wearing her distinctive pink cap, waistcoat, big boots and velvet coat, but Patrick was fully concentrating on avoiding eye contact with everybody else. He was wearing a Panama hat and sunglasses, and when he sat down he suddenly became fascinated by his shoes, dropping his head low.

The train ground into life again. This time it seemed to be going even slower, crawling like an arthritic caterpillar. Kit didn't dare move, or even breathe for the rest of the journey. After several ice-ages it juddered to its final stop with another defiant *toot* and the passengers started to gather their stuff together to leave. Patrick was way ahead of them, leaping to his feet, unlatching the carriage door and briskly striding down the ramp.

When Kit left the station Patrick was already thirty yards down the road, making a beeline to the marina. She followed, keeping a cautious distance between herself and Patrick's retreating back.

48

Whenever Kit visited the marina, she thought it seemed a bold, if rather futile, attempt to create Saint-Tropez on the south coast of England.

It wasn't an easy task, considering the weather in Brighton, and it wasn't helped by the eccentric choice of shops surrounding the marina. Saint-Tropez had Louis Vuitton. Brighton Marina had a Nando's and a big Asda. Without the exotic shops and glorious climate it was little more than a huge car park for floating BMWs. Hardly a magnet for magnates. Nevertheless, it was always chock-full of boats, cruisers and yachts, so it must have been doing something right.

Patrick boarded the wooden jetty and strode past the TGI Fridays, the Wetherspoons and the Pizza Express towards the area where most of the boats were berthed. Occasionally he would stop and consult his phone and Kit would shrink back into the brickwork, crushing her Mandalorian backpack in the process, but it was getting easier to follow him. Dusk was surrendering to night, and the shadows had grown large and easy to hide in.

Finally he stopped by one of the yachts. It wasn't the biggest or the flashiest in the marina, but it was still impressive. It had a white hull, a blue cockpit and stainless-steel railings surrounding the deck. The stern was dominated by a large silver steering wheel and there was a black inflatable dinghy with an outboard motor strapped on the bow.

Patrick grabbed the tiny ladder and hauled himself on board. He slid the hatch open and peered below, looking for something or someone. Then, not finding what he was after, he slid it closed. He checked his watch again and clambered back onto the jetty, turned, and walked back to the shopping and restaurant hub. Kit jumped back into the darkness as he walked past her. Thankfully he was too preoccupied to see the skinny woman in the big floppy hat hiding in the darkness.

Kit was left alone with the boat. She crept forward and inspected it. On the hull, written in an almost impenetrable font, were the words *The Salty Seaman*.

This was Roger Barker's yacht. She knew this because the year he bought it Roger managed to mention his yacht every five minutes on every *Vixens* panel at every convention. The name of his yacht became his go-to annoying punchline, and even now, ten years later, he still managed to crowbar the fact he owned a yacht into casual conversation whenever he could.

And here it was.

Roger's yacht. Patrick's confession. Mary's lie. She was waiting for things to make sense, but even now it was still just a collage of random events.

A mad, dangerous thought struck her.

Perhaps Jackie's feelings about Lily were spot on. Perhaps Lily was still alive? Perhaps she was hiding away, living on the Isle of Wight in disguise, selling souvenirs made out of seashells or something, and this yacht was the way they visited her?

If she could bring Lily back from the dead, Jackie would be so grateful to her and there'd be no need for any difficult conversation. At all.

One half of her brain was telling the other half that this theory was utterly bonkers, but there was always a big part of Kit that would do absolutely anything to avoid any kind of emotional unpleasantness. Her disastrous engagement was testament to that.

Patrick was a dark smudge in the distance. He had walked right up to the end and, judging by the pattern of lights bathing his tiny form, he had just passed Café Rouge and was still walking.

She gripped the sides of the ladder firmly, braced herself, and clambered on board. The moment her boots hit the deck she felt a huge wave of seasickness. Holding on for grim life, she staggered to the hatch, slid it open and clambered inside. Her boots came into contact with another ladder and she slowly descended.

When she hit the floor the lights came on, bathing her in a savage brightness. She yelled in terror before realising the lights had motion-activated sensors and she hadn't just been caught red-handed by an angry sailor with an eye patch and a cutlass.

The hold was dressed up as a survival bunker. There were rolls of sleeping bags stacked on one bunk, a huge thermos and a refrigerated box with a carry handle near her feet, the kind you took on picnics and plugged into the cigarette lighter.

There was a pile of rucksacks on the other bunk, all different shapes and colours. She opened one and found it full of the usual kit used for camping: thick socks, a cagoule stuffed inside a tiny bag, waterproof trousers, plastic plates, plastic cutlery and a torch. It looked like someone had dashed through Mountain Warehouse and bought half the store.

She tried to comprehend what she'd discovered, but her nausea was clouding out her thoughts. She decided to examine every corner of the boat, file everything away in her brain for later, wait until she was on dry land and work out what it all meant.

She opened drawers in the galley but just found ropes and fire extinguishers. There was nothing in the tiny toilet but a toilet brush and toilet rolls. There was a large-ish triangular cupboard recessed into the bow, but that just contained a few lifejackets.

There was nothing that suggested why Patrick had come here. Unless he was planning on a midnight fishing trip with Roger and some mates, but frankly, neither Roger nor Patrick looked the type.

The boat lurched to one side. She panicked and fell to the floor. Someone had just boarded.

Her brain started to melt inside her skull. She flung her head wildly back and forth, looking for places to hide. Under one of the bunk beds? No, too obvious. But there was nowhere else.

The boat lurched again. She could hear voices above her. Low mutters.

Wait! There was a place. The only place. The cupboard with the lifejackets. She flung open the doors and dived inside. It was a squeeze but she just managed it (thank heavens for her obsessive dieting habits!). She struggled out of her backpack, flung it on the lifejackets and rolled flat on her back, listening to her own breathing and the roar of blood in her ears.

Curling her finger under the bottom of the cupboard door, she could open it a crack without letting it swing open. She lay there, shuddering and watching though the gap, like an exhausted fox hiding from a pack of baying hounds.

The cabin door creaked open and a square of light hit the floor in front of her.

"There you go, gents. Make yourself comfortable. There's a flask of coffee in the corner, and sandwiches in the box."

Then the hollow clunk of boots on the metal steps. From her vantage point she could only see the bottom half of a bunch of bodies, all clad in waterproofs, milling around. It was only when they all sat down on the benches that she could see their faces.

She was gobsmacked.

The boat was full of old men. But not ordinary old men. A 'who's who' of British television from the 1970s, 1980s and 1990s. Every one of them was a legend in their own particular field of entertainment.

There was Sir Hugo Treadway, bowtie-wearing ex-head of episodic serials at the BBC, and commissioner of dozens of hit drama series including *Memory Lane* and *Vixens from the Void*.

Next to him was Mick Bunce, Radio One DJ, genial host and quizmaster of the classic daytime quiz show *Lucky Dippers* and presenter of pop music kids' programme *Livin' It Up*.

Facing them both was Buster 'By Gum' McGee, who starred in the incredibly unfunny long-running ITV sitcom *Storm in a D Cup*, set in a bra factory. McGee was clutching his famous trademark – a huge stuffed black pudding.

And sitting next to Buster was Ernie Winkle, children's entertainer and comedy ventriloquist, complete with his famous puppet, Corky the Crocodile, who was perched on his knee.

They were all dressed in waterproofs and wearing life vests. Even Corky the Crocodile was wearing a child's flotation device.

"Well this is a turn-up," said Corky the Crocodile. "All of us here in the same goat."

"Don't do that," snapped Hugo, glaring at Bernie. "If you want to say anything, just say it. Don't use the bloody puppet."

Corky the Crocodile's head swivelled in the direction of Hugo and gave him a hard stare. "All, right, keep your gloody hair on."

They all sat there, hands resting on their knees, staring everywhere but at each other. There was nothing to hear but the lapping of the water and the occasional rusty cough. At one point, Corky glanced in Kit's direction and her heart fluttered with terror, before she remembered that his eyes were made of rubber.

"Nice night for it," said Mick Bunce, at last.

"As the actress said to the bishop," said Buster automatically.

Nobody laughed.

The hatch thunked open again, and another set of legs arrived. Kit could tell from the expensive slacks that it was Patrick Finch. He perched uneasily on the steps leading up to the hatch.

"Lovely of you to join us," said Hugo. "You're a bit bloody late."

"I actually came early, but there was no one here, so I went back for a coffee."

"You could have waited."

"I could have, but I didn't."

"He's a man of the the-atre," cackled Buster. "He can't come into a room without an audience being there. Would you like a big hand on your entrance?"

The floor vibrated as the boat's engine roared into life. Kit instinctively pressed herself into the hull.

Mick looked up at the hatch. "I thought Ted Proud was going to join us?"

Ted Proud, thought Kit. *I know that name. That was the weatherman from* Eye on the North, *1982 to 1994*.

"I didn't hear that," said Hugo.

"Me neither," said Ernie.

"I'm sure there's a lot of them who cry off at the last minute," Buster shrugged.

"Ted probably knows something we don't about the weather tonight," said Mick gloomily. He was pushing his hand against the hull to steady himself, wincing at each swell of the tide.

Buster gave a dirty nicotine-flavoured laugh. "Ted probably got lucky with some bird, I should wager. One whiff of a fanny and he'd be up there like a rat up a drainpipe. Of course, that was before the booze turned his rat into a dormouse."

"What is that smell?" said Hugo Treadway.

"Fish," said Mick Bunce.

"It's not fish. I know what fish smells like," retorted Hugo.

"So how does this work?" Patrick asked.

"Just make yourself comfortable," said Mick Bunce. "We'll be on our way soon. You must be in a fair bit of trouble. Big name like you slumming it with the rest of us."

"I am in a spot of bother," said Patrick.

"We're all in spot of bother, mate," said Buster McGee. "Just like you. The only difference is I won't have to send back my OBE."

"I haven't got my OBE yet."

"Well, you won't get it now. The only jewellery they'll let you wear if they catch you is an ankle bracelet."

"That's definitely not fish," said Hugo. "It's really sour. Like stale piss."

Corky the Crocodile's head rotated slowly until it faced his owner. Its mouth dropped open, revealing jagged plastic teeth. "Are you going to tell him or shall I, Ernie?"

"Don't make trouble, Corky," said Ernie.

Corky's head swivelled until it eyeballed Hugo. "You really want to know the truth, guddy?"

"That's enough Corky."

"When Ernie got paid after each telly series, he used to go out on the lash, come home stinking of gooze, open up the lid of my gox and urinate on yours truly, calling me a gloody soul-sucking parasite and saying he was so rich now he'd never to stick his hand up my evil green gottom ever again."

Hugo was mesmerised and not a little unnerved by Corky's story. He was staring, hypnotised, at the puppet's clacking jaws.

Ernie frowned and struck Corky on the head. "Please, Corky, the nice man doesn't need to know that…"

Corky winked at Hugo. "Awww, he won't glab to anyone, will you Sir Hugo? So guess what? Then the old gastard would soger up and realise he'd spent all his cash on gottles of geer and we'd have to go and do more telly. That's what you can smell, Hugo, my piss-soaked gody. Take a good sniff, Sir Hugo, this is what an alcoholic's puppet smells like. It's the smell of gitterness. Gracing, ain't it?"

"Well, off we go then," said Hugo, nervously. "What are everyone's plans?"

"I'd rather not say," said Mick Bunce.

Buster grinned. "From the papers, I'd say his plans involve a local school, some lollypops and a rusty Transit van."

"Why don't you just shut the fuck up, Buster?"

"Fine, I can take the hint. Jesus, tough crowd."

Meanwhile, Kit was in some trouble. Her stomach was lurching and the digestive biscuit she had eaten in Mary's flat was threatening to make a reappearance. She stretched her arms above her head, trying to reach her backpack and retrieve the sick bag she always kept in the front pocket. She felt a strap and pulled.

It wasn't attached to her backpack; it was attached to an inflatable dinghy. With a deafening roar it swelled to full size, filling the space and pushing her through the door like a cork from a bottle.

"What the fuck?"

Someone – she realised it was Patrick – grabbed her arm and she was dragged none-too-gently in front of the old men.

"We seem to have a stowaway," said Patrick.

"Gollocks…" Ernie's jaw dropped open, as did the jaw of Corky the Crocodile.

"Who the hell is she?" said Hugo.

"I've seen better strippergrams…" quipped Buster.

"Shut up, Buster," Mick snapped. "You'd better answer Sir Hugo's question. Who are you? What are you doing here?"

"I w–w–was… W–w…"

Her stammer had returned. She looked appealingly at Patrick, but Patrick's face was hard and unreadable.

"She's one of those spazzers," said Buster. "She's soft in the head."

"No, Buster, she's just got a stammer," muttered Patrick. "Anyone got a pen and paper?"

"I think we should tell Captain Haddock up on deck," said Ernie.

"I'll go," said Mick. He climbed the ladder and pushed open the hatch. "Sir?" he yelled. "Can we see you down here a minute? Got a little problem."

"It's alright, I've got a notebook," said Patrick, tearing a page out of the book. "Here you go, write down who you are."

Kit gave Patrick an anguished look and scribbled four words on the page.

WHAT SHOULD I WRITE?

Patrick angled his back so he was between Kit and the others. He waited another thirty seconds, took the page off her and turned around.

"She says, 'Hello, my name is Kerry. I was shoplifting in the big Asda and I got chased by security and I hid in your boat and I heard the engine go. I'm sorry I've ruined your fishing trip.'"

He screwed up the note and stuffed it into his pocket before anyone else asked to read it.

The hatch opened and a man who was the living cliché of a sailor, all chunky knitwear and chunky facial hair, clumped down the steps. He hung on to the rail and dropped the last three feet.

"Right, we're in international waters now. We'll be there in…"

He turned and saw Kit.

"What's she doing here?"

"That's what *we* said," said Mick.

"She's a shoplifter," said Patrick.

Buster groaned. "You believe that load of old toot?"

Ernie agreed with Buster. "She's police. I can smell a copper a mile off."

"I can smell *you* a mile off," retorted Hugo. "She says she was here by accident."

"It doesn't matter what she says." The man in the chunky knitwear glared around the group. "You do know we have to get rid of her, don't you?"

"I don't know what you mean." Hugo sounded alarmed.

301

"This is the game you're playing here. You need to play for keeps. Go hard or go home."

Kit clutched her little badge and twisted it madly.

Are they really saying what I think they're saying?

What have I stumbled into?

"I can't go home," Ernie wailed in despair. "I've left a note for my wife!"

"We can drop her at Le Havre," said Hugo.

"Oh, well done, genius." Chunky Knitwear rolled his eyes. "She knows where we've come from and now she knows where we're going. Perhaps you can hand round our phone numbers next?"

"She doesn't know anything, not in the scheme of things, not really." Patrick was keeping his voice slow and steady and authoritative. "Nothing about this situation warrants the taking of a life."

Chunky Knitwear glared at Patrick. "That's not your decision, mate."

Mick nodded at Patrick. "But he's right. She doesn't know who we are."

"Speak for yourself," sniffed Buster. "I've got quite a following in the universities. Apparently I'm an 'ironic pleasure'."

"I'm sure she doesn't know most of you has-been fuckers from her Aunt Fanny," Chunky Knitwear growled. He pointed at Patrick. "But *he's* a fucking household name, so this discussion is moot. I warned the boss not to take him. I said it would be a problem. And here we are. Shit, this is as much of a clusterfuck as when I met that dinghy full of asylum seekers coming the other way."

He grabbed Kit by the arm. "She's going overboard, because that's the only solution."

Kit flailed feebly, but Chunky Knitwear was very big and very strong. He held her arm tightly and bodily hauled her up the steps without her feet touching the rungs. She couldn't help it, but a whimper of pain escaped her lips.

"Get away from her."

The elderly celebrities turned. There was a gun in Patrick Finch's hand, pointed directly at Chunky Knitwear.

"Where did that come from?" erupted Hugo.

"My pocket," snapped Patrick. "It's always good to have insurance, even though it does ruin the shape of my jacket."

Knitwear put his hands up. "Okay, now. Let's be calm about this."

"We can be perfectly calm as long as you do as I say. Turn this boat back to Brighton."

"What?"

"You heard me, Captain Birdseye. We're going back and there's no harm done."

Buster looked indignant. "There's no way I'm going back. I paid a fortune for this. Who died and made you leader?"

Patrick swung the gun in Buster's direction. "You did, if you're not careful."

When the barrel of the gun moved away from Chunky Knitwear, he lowered his arms slightly, as if getting ready to rush Patrick.

Patrick swung it back again. "Don't you try it. You and I are going up on deck to turn us around. These chaps are staying down here for the—"

Then Ernie Winkle saw his chance.

"You gastard!"

He went for Patrick the only way he knew how – with Corky the Crocodile leading the attack. The hand puppet lunged at Patrick's arm, sending him off balance.

"I'm so sorry," said Ernie. "Corky doesn't like guns. Do you, Corky?"

Corky didn't respond because now he had his jaws fixed around Patrick's neck.

"Gerroff!" screamed Patrick.

Patrick fell onto his knees and sank to the floor. Buster 'By Gum' McGee rushed forward, wielding his stuffed black pudding. He whacked it on the back of Patrick's neck. The last thing Patrick heard before darkness closed over his head were Buster's words:

"Hey! His gun's plastic! It's a fucking prop!"

49

Patrick opened his eyes and tried to focus.

"Hello," said Kit, who was tied up on the other side of the hold.

"Fuck," groaned Patrick. He realised he was tied up, too.

"Fuck," he groaned again.

"Are you alright?"

"Not really. Ow. Ow. Ow. What happened? Why didn't they throw us both overboard?"

"I don't know. They radioed someone and they said something about a change of plan. Then they smashed the radio. I think they took the little boat that was on the top of our big boat and they all went away on that one. At least, I think they did. I heard a little boat engine. It's been quiet ever since."

"You mean we're alone?"

"I think so."

"How long have I been out?"

"Not long. About half an hour."

"Damn it. Where's my hat?"

"I think Buster kept it."

"That little bastard. That was my MCC member's hat."

Patrick rolled over onto his front and wriggled towards the steps. Kit watched him try to get up on his knees. His legs were tied together and it wasn't easy. He made several attempts.

"That was Sir Hugo Treadway, wasn't it?" said Kit. "The man in the bow tie? He was the man who commissioned *Vixens from the Void*. Shame he's gone. I'd like to have shaken him by his hand."

"That was a lucky escape for you. Considering where his hands have allegedly been."

"I know. I'm just babbling. I know that. I think my dissociative disorder is kicking in."

"They just left us here? Alive? That doesn't make sense."

"What doesn't make sense?"

"Oh bugger it. You're going to need that disorder. Can you see over by the stern?"

There were about a dozen holes in the hull. Water was gurgling into the hold. The dinghy that had pushed Kit out of her hiding place had also been punctured. It was lying sadly on the floor like a brightly coloured tarpaulin.

"Yes, I know. The sailor had a gun. My ears are still singing."

"Those bastards. They've scuttled the boat. That's why they left us here. We need to get up top."

He grunted and tried to use the bottom of the steps to loosen his bonds. It didn't work.

"They chucked our phones overboard."

"Of course they would."

"I had all my notes on my phone. I recorded interviews on it. Everything was in there."

"You'll cope."

"No, I won't."

"Is there anything we can use to get out of these ropes?"

"I do have a sonic screwdriver—"

"Is that meant to be a joke?"

"If you'll let me finish, I do have a sonic screwdriver that happens to have a torch in one end and a penknife in the other."

Patrick raised his eyebrows and started wriggling over to her. "That's bloody great. Can you get it out?"

"As the actress said to the bishop."

"Ye gods. Don't even go there. It's bad enough Buster McGee giving me this splitting headache. Please don't do his jokes."

"Yes, to answer your question, I think I can get it out."

She tucked her chin into her neck and nosed her way inside

her coat. She resurfaced with it protruding from her mouth like a futuristic cigar.

"Go'hi."

"Okay, so you can…"

"I'oh wh' I' ooing!"

She leaned forward and delicately put it on the bunk bed, rolling it with her nose until a small ridge was on the top. Then she closed her mouth on it and used her teeth to pluck the knife blade out of the slot. It took several goes, but finally a tiny blade emerged.

"Excellent work, Kit," said Patrick softly.

Kit was unusually pleased to have got praise from the star of ITV's *Wistful*.

She kept nudging it with her nose. It was at a sixty-degree angle, then seventy, then ninety degrees… She didn't stop until it was a full one-hundred-and-eighty degrees from the screwdriver.

"There. Now we have a knife."

"Brilliant."

She turned her back on the knife and her fingers scrabbled for the sonic screwdriver. She pushed the blade into the nearest bit of rope on her wrist and started sawing.

"Who were those people?" asked Kit. "I mean, yes, I know who those people *are*, but… You know what I mean. They're all being investigated by Operation Mulberry, I know that. But what are they doing here on this boat?"

"Political asylum."

"What?"

"Well, not quite. They're avoiding the clutches of the Met by fleeing to France. France is a country where, how can I put it… they're a bit more *flexible* about relations between men and young girls. The age of consent is only fifteen over there."

"But the French government won't give them political asylum, will they?"

"No, but they're gambling they won't look too hard for them if they disappear into the countryside, find a villa and live like characters in a French novel."

"Ta-da!"

Kit brought her hands up, free of their ropes.

"Brilliant. Now do me."

"As the actress said to the bishop."

"Stop saying that."

"I like it. I think it'll be my next catchphrase."

She undid her ankles, dashed over to Patrick and started vigorously sawing at his ropes until they gave way. He brought his hands together, rubbing his wrists.

"Thanks."

"You're welcome."

"Now it's all hands on deck."

He put his foot on the bottom rung of the ladder, but Kit staggered to the stern.

"What the hell do you think you're doing?"

"I've just got to check something."

"Don't be an idiot. We need to get up on deck."

"I won't be long."

She sloshed through the rapidly expanding puddle, scrabbled over the inflatable dinghy, opened the door of her hiding place and felt inside. A grin spread across her face as she touched something familiar. "They didn't get it."

"Get what?"

"My Mandalorian backpack."

She dragged it out and hugged it.

"Are you serious!"

"This is going to be a collector's item in years to come."

"Come on, you little fool!"

50

They clambered onto the deck. The night air was perishingly cold and the water was still and black.

The Salty Seaman was starting to list now. The deck they were standing on was slanting towards the water and Kit had to hold on to the rails to walk up and down.

She peered into the inky gloom. "How far are we from land?"

"Captain Crunch said we were in international waters. That means we're at least twelve nautical miles out from the coast."

"Is a nautical mile really short? I bet it's really short. Is it longer or shorter than a normal mile?"

"Longer."

"Shitarola."

"Yep. We're more like thirteen miles out."

"Too far to swim, then."

"Just about."

He let out a sigh and sat heavily on the railing, his hands resting on his knees. His handkerchief fluttered in the breeze, attempting to escape from his top pocket.

He eyed her suspiciously. "Do you mind me asking what *you're* doing hiding on this boat?"

"I followed you."

"Me?"

"Yes."

"Why?"

"Because you just did an interview with me and started yelling about killing a girl?"

"I was acting."

"Really."

"Yes!"

"So you won't mind me asking what you're doing on this boat? Are you one of them?"

"Absolutely not. I'm definitely not one of them."

"They seemed to think you were part of their group."

"That was part of my plan." Patrick looked up into the sky. The moon was nearly full, and they were both bathed in an eerie soft light.

Kit persisted. "You behaved like you had a nasty secret during our interview this morning."

"Like I said. That's called acting. I was acting."

"Like in the Greek restaurant when you laughed at me."

"Yes. I'm sorry about that. And I'm sorry about shouting at you today. It was a means to an end."

"That's alright. You can apologise by explaining why we're both here on this sinking boat."

Patrick smiled grimly. "Well, there's not much else we can do but drown or die of hypothermia, so I might as well.

"It all started two weeks before you cornered me in that Greek restaurant. I got a blackmail note through the post. You'll have to take my word for it, because I seem to have lost it."

"You mean this?" She pulled the envelope from her pocket and waved it under his nose.

He leaned over and snatched it off her indignantly. "Did you steal it off me?"

"Of course not! I found it on the floor of the dressing room."

"Hellfire. I must have dropped it while I was trying to lever that bloody helmet off my head."

He slipped it into his pocket.

"Anyway, as I'm sure you saw when you read it, I was being blackmailed. There was another sheet attached, with details of this Blu-Ray documentary thing. I was being forced to take part."

"Oh. And then I came along and asked you to do the Blu-Ray thing."

"You did."

"Gosh. I must have looked pretty suspicious. Like I was the blackmailer."

"Yes."

"Do you think I'm blackmailing you?"

"Well, I don't think that *now*…" He gestured around at the listing boat. "You must be a pretty crap blackmailer if you ended up here with me."

He patted the pocket where he'd inserted the envelope. "So, I had to come to Brighton, but I also wanted to find out who sent this. I got no other contact from these mysterious bastards, so I've spent two days watching everyone around me to see if they would give themselves away." He gave a sour grin. "I strongly hinted to Roger that I was prepared to blackmail *him* in retaliation – and he didn't take the bait. So he's not the one behind it."

"He could have been acting."

"He's not that good at acting. I soon realised I had no way of finding out who sent it, so I upped my game. Taking the premise that there was *someone* in that room that sent the letter or knew who did, I tried an old copper's trick: throw out a bit of red meat. If I pretended there was an actual *real* story to be had, it would knock these blackmailers off-balance. It was Tara Miles who gave me the idea, the way she said she felt responsible for Lily's death. So I contrived an outburst about killing Lily Sparkes. Maybe these mysterious types would panic and try to cover their tracks. Or contact me to try and persuade me not to go to the police. Either way I could try to trap them…"

"So you waited for me to ask about Lily in the interview, then pretended you had something to do with her death."

"Yes. I took my cue and went bananas. I'm really sorry I shouted at you…"

"It's okay."

"Well, I'm sorry about it anyway."

They stared into the water.

"You still haven't told me how you ended up on this boat. I know why *I* did. I followed you, but how did *you*…"

"Hah! That's interesting. I stormed out of the Pavilion, but I didn't go to the police station, obviously. I drove around Brighton, making myself scarce. Eventually I went back to my room, and someone had pushed a note under my door. It had the address of the marina on it, the number of the berth where this boat was moored and a time for disembarkation. Just that. I come over to the marina and all of a sudden I'm surrounded by that bunch of jokers getting ready to flee the country."

"Wow," said Kit. "I wonder who left the note?"

Patrick shrugged.

"I bet we can work who's behind it all if we put our minds to it."

"I think, at the rate we're sinking, it's all academic now."

As if to reinforce his point, the boat lurched.

"Is there anything we can do?" Kit felt strangely calm about the situation. Her dissociative disorder had definitely kicked in.

"Without our mobile phones I can't see anything we *can* do. There's nothing we've got that helps us. We've literally just got the clothes we're standing up in."

Another lurch, that made them both stumble. "Though we won't be standing up much longer."

Kit was aching and tired. The day had got too much for her at about the time of Patrick's outburst, and it just got stranger and more dangerous with every passing hour.

Her backpack was *so heavy*.

She put it down on the deck and it landed with a *clonk*. Which was odd. There were only folders in there. She'd put her laptop in her room safe.

She opened it up, looked, reached inside… and a lot of things made sense to her. So that's what Binfire meant when he said she 'shouldn't go in unarmed', and she needed to look like she 'meant business'…

"You know you said we had nothing here that could help us…"

"No."

"That might not be true."

She pulled an object out of her bag. A fat metal tube attached to a handle.

"Would a flare gun do?"

"Bloody hell!"

Patrick lunged forward and examined the gun in her hands.

"Do you normally carry a flare gun around in your bag?"

"Actually, this is the first time."

"That's amazing! Just amazing…" He shook his head and laughed. "It's also an incredibly cruel joke. The visibility on these things is about four miles. Five miles tops. We're over twelve miles out from land."

"Oh drat."

"Unless a passing boat sees it, it's not going to help. Sorry."

Kit's wave of excitement crashed onto the rocks and receded with the tide. She looked at the gun in her hands with dead eyes, as if it was a present she'd found from an old lover.

"That's… deeply, deeply cruel."

"You can say that again."

"Can I set it off anyway?"

"Be my guest. Nothing ventured, nothing gained."

Kit clambered to the edge of the bow, where the yacht was highest in the water. She composed herself, nestling the gun between her fingers, looking down on it as if meditating, 'doing a Tara'. She breathed deeply, in and out. In. And out. Finally, she raised her head and said:

"This is for you, Wolf. I know we didn't see eye to eye, but I'm truly sorry you're dead, and I'm very glad I started on this journey to find your killer."

She ignored Patrick's quizzical look.

"I hope you're happy with what we've done so far, and if you're watching now, from an alternate dimension somewhere in the multiverse where you're not dead, I hope you're smiling down on me, and I hope you can see fit to get me out of this pickle I've got myself in and help me finish this investigation."

She raised the flare gun.

"To Wolf Tyler, a comrade and friend, Whovian and Trekker, Thronie and Jedi. A Hoopy Frood who really knew where his towel was."

She fired. A ball of light erupted from the barrel of the gun and streaked across the sky. It burned with a dangerous intensity, then it plunged to the horizon and glowed gently on the surface of the water.

Then, all too soon, it died.

Just like Wolf.

51

Kit stared until there was no more glow to see and then said, "That's it."

"I rather think it is," sighed Patrick.

Kit tapped the rail, a pattern that resolved itself into a tune. Anyone au fait with 1980s chart hits would have recognised The Human League's 'Don't You Want Me'.

"You haven't actually told me the most important thing of all," she said quietly.

"What's that?"

"The blackmail note. What exactly are you being blackmailed for? And why are you trying so hard to find the blackmailers? Does that mean they know something? Did you do something with Lily?"

Patrick's voice was sharp. "That's none of your business."

"Why?"

"It just isn't."

"I have made a copy of that note, you know. I could take it to the police."

"You're welcome to. Knock yourself out. In the very unlikely event that we do get out of here. And I don't fancy our chances, do you?"

Kit stared into the waters. "It's funny. Of all the ways I thought I was going to die, drowning in the English Channel was not on my radar."

Patrick emitted a hollow chuckle. "We're not on anyone's radar. That's the problem."

She thought about all the people who would miss her when she was dead and was shocked by how short the list was: her parents;

Binfire; her little dog Milo. Milo would definitely pine a *lot*, but he was safe with Mrs Lilywhite. He'd forget her eventually.

When she'd walked to the marina she must have passed so close to Jackie's flat. If she'd just gone that way instead of following Patrick… So many alternative futures opened up before her. Her head was buzzing with so many lost possibilities, so many lives now closed off to her.

And then she realised her head wasn't buzzing.

"There's a noise. Do you hear it?"

There *was* a tiny buzz, warbling in the wind like an exhausted gnat.

"Where's it coming from?"

"Look! Over there!"

The buzz was getting louder and was accompanied by a tiny red light.

"What is that?"

The light got bigger. The buzz got louder. And louder. Patrick steadied himself, clutched the rail with one hand, reached up with the other and snatched the thing out of the sky.

The drone had a note attached to it.

In big messy handwriting it said:

What the FROKK are you doing out here?

52

About five minutes later, they heard the dull throb of an engine. Slowly an object took shape in the blackness, throwing ripples of dark water out before it. A motorised dinghy. Binfire was standing at the front, one foot on the bow like George Washington crossing the Delaware. He was waving the remote control of his drone excitedly.

"We frokking found you!" yelled Binfire. "We did it! We saw the flare!"

Manning the engine was a large man with short blond hair, wearing a black tailcoat, wing collar, plum waistcoat and cravat. A carnation was sprouting out of his buttonhole.

The dinghy bumped into *The Salty Seaman* and Binfire held his arms out. "Drone first," he said. "It's expensive."

Patrick tossed Binfire the drone. Binfire passed it to the man in the tailcoat, who stowed it by his knees.

"Come on then," shouted Binfire. "Get on board!"

Patrick slipped through the railing, dangled himself over the edge, and half leapt, half dropped into the dinghy.

We must be such an odd picture, both of us, thought Kit madly. *Clinging to the wreckage, Patrick in his jacket and cravat and with my long velvet coat and waistcoat. We must look like a couple of first-class passengers being rescued from the* Titanic.

Kit clambered over the railing, her coat flapping madly in the breeze. She looked down, saw Binfire beckoning madly, and closed her eyes.

Thank you, Wolf. You might have been a bit of a shit, but you came through for us.

She gripped the rail tightly, shoulders hunched, like she was preparing to climb into the carriage of a roller-coaster with a single name like 'Swarm' or 'Nightmare'. Then she flung herself into darkness and body-flopped into the dinghy.

Hands immediately grabbed her by the shoulders and hauled her upright.

"This is Greg," said Binfire, jerking a thumb at the man in formal dress steering the boat.

Greg didn't take his right hand off the tiller, but he waved and smiled.

"Greg is dressed like a mad penguin because he's best man at a wedding today."

"I thought I recognised you!" said Kit. "I rescued your groom from Vanity."

"Yeah, that's right. You okay?"

"I'm fine, considering."

"Good. Glad we rescued you."

"Can I ask what you're doing here?"

"Well, I went up to this guy…" – he indicated Binfire – "…in the hotel this morning after breakfast and said, 'Your friend saved my bacon last night. I would have been in such deep shit if we'd lost Tony.' I gave him my card and told him if there's anything I can do to repay the favour, let me know."

He gave a big shrug. "I had literally just finished my best man's speech when my phone goes and it's him asking me if I know how to steer a boat."

"Well, I'm glad you know how to steer a boat."

"I do a lot of parasailing."

Kit turned to Binfire. "Well that's Greg's story. What the hell are you doing here? Not that I'm not insanely glad to see you."

"Well, yeah, confession time." He looked slightly embarrassed. "I put the 'Life360' app on your phone today…"

"What? How many times to I have to tell you not to do that?!"

"It's a good thing I did, isn't it? I watched you go to frokking Crawley! What's that all about?"

Kit waved her hand as if to say *tell you later*.

"Then I saw you go to the marina. Then the little location pin jumped out to sea! I thought you were being kidnapped! Then when your signal went dead, I thought your ex must have been *seriously* pissed off with you and done you in. So I ran down to the marina, hired a dinghy and pulled matey-boy there out of his wedding to help me on a rescue mission."

Kit turned to Greg. "Sorry about putting you to so much trouble."

"No worries," said Greg. His eyes were fixed intently on the horizon. "I only missed the karaoke. I hate karaoke. I wouldn't have missed this escapade for all the tea in China."

"I'm sorry to interrupt, but do either of you guys have a mobile phone?" asked Patrick. "I have to make a really urgent call."

"There's mine," said Binfire, waving the phone in his hand. "But we're using Google Maps to get back, so can you be quick?"

"Thanks, I won't be long." He jabbed at the phone.

Binfire nodded in Patrick's direction. "Does the star of ITV's *Wistful* not have a phone?"

"His phone ended up in the same place as mine. They both got thrown overboard by a people smuggler."

Kit looked at Binfire's puzzled expression and made a helpless face. "I'll explain everything later. I promise."

They watched Patrick gabble urgently into the phone. He ended the call and passed it back to Binfire.

"Just called the police," he explained. "They're going to alert the port authorities at Le Havre and wait for our friends to arrive."

"Wouldn't they have got there by now?"

"I don't think so. They're using a dinghy with an outboard motor, like this one. This little thing is fine for us to get back to Brighton, but it's over eighty miles to France. They were either going to have to turn back, which I don't think they'd do, or carry on and wait to be met by another boat. That's going to take time to organise."

"That's r–r–r…"

It sounded for a moment like Kit's stammer had returned, but it hadn't. Her teeth were chattering. Patrick looked concerned. "Are you okay?"

"I'm f–f–fine."

"You're not, Kit. It's February. You're damp. We're in the English Channel in the middle of the night, and we're not getting back to Brighton for another two hours. We need to warm you up to stop you getting hypothermia."

"You can have my coat," said Greg. "It's wool. Don't worry about getting it wet. It's only rented."

They laid her down in the dinghy and covered her with the tailcoat.

"Comfy?"

"B–better."

"Funny old day this."

"Y–yes. I th–think it's i–rrronic."

"How is it ironic?"

"Well. You and m–me. You're investigating who's b– blackmailed you… And I only asked you down to B–Brighton as p-part of my *own* investigation."

"I don't understand."

She was finding it difficult to form words, so Binfire happily stepped in and explained to Patrick about the death of Wolf Tyler, the link to Lily Sparkes' death, and their plan to round up the suspects under the guise of filming a documentary.

Patrick listened with growing incredulity.

"That's insane!"

Binfire grinned. "Only if you say it out loud."

Patrick actually looked like he was thinking about it. Then he shook his head disbelievingly.

"I *was* only joking in that interview. I never considered for a moment that there was anything about Lily's death that was suspicious." He debated the matter with himself before shaking his head again. "No. Absolutely not. You're both bonkers. She definitely killed herself. She left a note. People saw her jump from the pier. Her friend said she was depressed. It's ridiculous what you're saying. It's completely ridiculous."

Binfire folded his arms. "Ha, as one of the suspects, you *would* say that."

"I'm not a suspect."

"You were very defensive this morning about Lily. I filmed it all."

"I was bloody acting! Tell him Kit! Kit?"

Kit's eyes were fluttering.

"Kit!"

Her eyes opened. "W–why would I t–take your w–w–word f–for it w–w–when you w–w–won't tell me huh–how you were being b–blackmailed?"

"I told you! That's none of your business!"

Kit's eyes closed again.

"Kit! Stay awake! You need to stay awake!"

Kit's eyes stayed closed.

"I think she's too bored to stay awake," said Binfire. "A person like Kit, she needs intellectual stimulus to stay awake. You know, things to go in her brain. *Facts*."

Patrick gave in. He knelt by Kit's head. He moved his mouth close to Kit's ear, so he didn't have to raise his voice, and put his hands over hers to warm them up.

"Okay, stay awake for me, and I'll tell you how I was being blackmailed."

Kit's eyes fluttered open.

"First off, god's truth. I never had a relationship with Lily. Roger slept with her because she was impressed with his star power. He was the big name back then. And she slept with Duggie because he was the charismatic stunt guy who fell out of trees and did backflips. I was a novice actor, a boy. I was just friendly with her."

"F–friendly."

"Yes, and not 'friendly' in the way those sods mean it." He pointed in the general direction of France. "Those old sods in that dinghy. The gropers. The ones who corner make-up girls in their trailers and trap actresses in their hotel rooms when they're on location. The ones who threaten women's careers if they don't play ball. That wasn't me. I didn't do anything to her."

"S–so w–why not just ignore the b–blackmail letter?"

"You know I used to be a policeman."

"I kn–kn–know you used to be a policeman."

"Yes, but that's not the whole truth. I wasn't just a plod on the beat who left the force. I was an undercover copper in the mid-1980s. From 1985 until… erm… Yes. Until 1990."

Kit wrinkled her face in confusion.

"You may have heard about undercover officers deployed to go undercover to spy on political movements in the 1980s and 1990s. CND and the Socialist Workers Party. Groups like that."

"Y-yes."

"Well, during the 1980s there was a strong belief that certain TV industry figures were politically dangerous. It was the time when there was a lot of what you might call 'subversive' political programming. *Boys from the Blackstuff*, *Threads* and the like. And there were documentaries about the IRA which, in the government's opinion, skated near to sympathising with the terrorists. The government didn't trust the BBC and they trusted Channel 4 even less. The Met deployed me to pretend to be a jobbing extra, to infiltrate my way into the world of television production, and find out what I could about left-wing producers, writers and actors who flirted with activists and anarchists."

He gave a bitter laugh. "Of course, I never realised that I would make so *much* of a success of acting! Not really what I wanted to happen, but when I became famous I couldn't go back to the force. It was impossible. So I was quietly let go in the early 1990s, and from then on I was stuck, trapped in a career I never had the slightest interest in." He broke off. "You're smiling."

"S–s–sorry."

"I am telling the truth, you know."

"I b–believe you. I was just s–s–smiling at the notion – you're n–not an actor. You're just acting the part of an actor. That's funny."

"I suppose it is."

"That makes sss–sense. N–no offence. But I always thought you laid the th–thespian stuff on a bit too th–th–thick."

Patrick laughed. "In the 1980s I was practically subtle. By the time everyone stopped wearing the cravats and polo-necks I was too far into the part to change. So... It was the second *Vixens* shoot, we're down in Brighton, it's the night before we start filming, and everyone had got to the hotel. I'd got into a conversation with one of the lighting guys and he'd told me something about a director he'd worked with being pally with the PLO. The details aren't important, but the upshot of it was I wanted to call in and tell my handler what I'd heard. I made my excuses and went to bed early. I got to my room and made a call."

He shook his head at his own stupidity. "I shouldn't have done that. I should have used the telephone box on the corner, but I used the hotel phone. I'd got cocky. They'd given me a big room, with a bedroom, a bathroom and a little sitting room nearest the door, and my handler and I had a conversation in which it was pretty obvious to anyone eavesdropping who I really was. I ended the call, walked through to the sitting room, and Lily was standing there. She had brought in new pillows because I was allergic to feathers, and she'd let herself in."

"Ssh–she didn't knock?"

"No."

"That s–seems unprofessional. Hotel staff sh–should always knock."

You must have had a VERY CLOSE friendship with her, thought Kit. *She wouldn't have been confident enough to walk into your room without knocking otherwise.*

"Anyway, she made it clear she heard what I said, and she was quite upset about it. She didn't like the idea of me pretending to be someone I wasn't, and I don't think she liked being lied to."

An image of Jackie's face swam unbidden into Kit's mind.

"I didn't talk to her again. I didn't dare to have that conversation with her in case my worst fears were confirmed and she'd gone to our producer, or worse, the tabloids. Every time I was near her, I felt awkward. I was tense for the rest of the shoot, waiting for the other shoe to drop, but then…"

"Then you heard she'd committed sss-suicide."

"Yes." He looked troubled. "And I won't deny I did feel slightly relieved, for my own sake, but mostly I felt very sad. She was a very lovely girl. I really liked her. It sounds suspiciously convenient, I know, but I didn't have anything to do with her death. I didn't tell my superiors about my fuck-up. If you've got a picture in your head of me as some ruthless professional spy, some Jason Bourne character, snapping necks and throwing people out of windows, then forget it. If you knew me at the time… Well, I was just a scared kid, and the only option that was in my mind was to keep quiet and hope I hadn't fucked up."

Kit was quiet. "Okay. I b–b–believe you."

"Good. Great."

"But I c–could be s–s–saying that because I don't want you to s–s–snap *my* neck."

Patrick said, "Haha, very funny," took his own jacket off and laid it over Greg's coat.

"So the blackmail note was about that. I could see it in the wording, that stuff about my name being put next to the word 'police' in a newspaper headline. Somehow, someone else had found out about my undercover work. Can you imagine if everyone found out I'd lied to them all these years? Producers I'd worked with? Agents? Fellow actors? That I'd only become an actor on a mission of betrayal, to find dirt on them and their kind? I would be a pariah. I'd never work again. You see my problem?"

She nodded sleepily, fighting to keep her eyelids open. Wondering if Patrick's story about being an undercover copper was remotely true or he had just spun her a fantastical story to take her mind off the fact she couldn't feel her fingers and toes.

53

The journey back to Brighton passed without incident, and two hours later they were bathed in the electric glow of the lights of the marina. The dinghy chugged into port and ended up bobbing against a pontoon.

Binfire and Greg sailed the dinghy back to the rental place, while Patrick half escorted, half carried Kit over to the restaurants. He found a late-night café-bar where he plied Kit with hot coffee, soup and a chocolate cake.

Look at these calories! I can't even begin to estimate the calories!

"I can't eat this stuff, Patrick."

"You will," said Patrick. "Don't argue or I'll make a funnel and pour it down your throat."

After three bowls of soup and two helpings of chocolate cake, she began to feel herself again.

While she was slurping the cream of mushroom, Patrick disappeared to make a call from the payphone in the corner. When he came back, he was smiling.

"I just made a call. I do still have a few contacts in the force, even if they're the sons and daughters and nephews and nieces of the mates I once served with. Anyway, they got the fuckers. They found them marooned off the coast of Dieppe. They were lost. Haha! Captain Haddock wasn't the sailor he was cracked up to be."

"Never be fooled by chunky knitwear."

"They're being grilled as we speak. I don't think it will take long for one of them to talk."

"I think Corky the Crocodile will blab first. He has a big mouth."

"Ha. Yes. So… Are you're going to continue with this investigation of yours?" The scepticism in Patrick's voice was obvious.

"I'm pretty committed. You might doubt if Lily was murdered, and maybe she wasn't, but Wolf Tyler *definitely* was."

Kit told Patrick about her visit to Crawley, and Mary's lie about having met Wolf. Patrick seemed less doubtful when she finished.

"So there is definitely something going on," she said.

"Hm. There could be something dodgy. She might just be absent-minded. Could be nothing…"

"But if it's not?"

"As an old copper, I really should advise you to go to the police with everything you know."

"And your advice as an old actor?"

"As an aged actor, darling, I would always give you Olivier's words: 'What is lying but acting, and what is good lying but convincing lying?'"

Kit raised her eyebrows as if to say '*and?*'.

"I'm saying that you are surrounded by liars. And at least one liar is lying to you extremely well. Because someone as perspicacious as you would *know* if they're being lied to."

"Thank you."

She felt pleased.

I'm getting better at taking compliments.

"Speaking of being lied to – you know you said that you didn't think Roger had anything to do with all this?"

"No. I don't. Why do you bring it up?"

"You know that boat we were just on…"

He looked at her, mystified. "What?"

"You do *know* it was Roger's boat, don't you?"

Patrick's eyes bulged in disbelief. "What? I didn't know that!"

"I guess you wouldn't know that, because you don't go to conventions, but *The Salty Seaman* is Roger's yacht. He always mentions it at great length when he's on panels."

"Holy hell. That slippery old bastard! Maybe he is behind everything, after all. Come on, let's get back to the hotel, pronto."

Patrick asked the waitress to call for a taxi, so Kit could go from a warm café into a warm car, and then straight into a warm hotel lobby.

They walked through into the bar, but there was no one about. It was as quiet as Kit had ever seen it.

"Right." Patrick's face was grim. "You can go to bed. I'll deal with him."

"No, I'd like to come with you."

"I'm not going to argue with you. Just go to bed!"

"Kit!"

Someone hissed her name from above. A woman's voice. Kit looked up. At first glance it looked like there was just a disembodied face hanging in mid-air, a face with wide eyes and a chalk-white complexion, but as Kit's eyes adjusted to the gloom she could see that the figure was wearing black clothes that had been rendered invisible by the shadows.

It was Freya.

"Roger Barker is dead!" she whispered.

"What?"

"He's killed himself!"

54

Freya was standing outside Roger's room, twisting her fingers together. She had been crying. Her eyeshadow had run all the way down her cheeks and collided with her lips.

"He's just lying there!" she sobbed.

The door was ajar and Patrick pushed into the room, Kit following behind.

Roger was lying face-down on the bed, still in his clothes. His eyes were half open and there was a thin line of drool connecting his lips to the pillow. There was an empty hypodermic needle on the floor.

"Damn," said Patrick. "Don't touch anything."

"Have you *called* anyone?" Kit asked Freya.

Freya didn't respond. She stayed in the doorway, eyes fixed on Roger.

"I just came to deliver the revised schedules. Victor made up new ones in case Patrick didn't turn up tomorrow."

Freya glanced quickly at Patrick, wary of offending him, but Patrick wasn't listening. They both watched Patrick as he knelt down and touched Roger's cheek.

"And when I pushed the schedule under the door, the door just opened, and there he was, lying there, and then I just ran out of the room, and I saw you downstairs, and then I said, 'Kit,' and you came up here!"

"Have you called anyone?" Kit repeated.

"No," she said. "Oh my god, should I have done? Is that what you're supposed to do?"

"We should at least let the hotel know. Patrick?"

"I think we should leave it for the moment," he said calmly.

"But shouldn't we—"

"He's not dead," said Patrick.

"He's not?" sniffed Freya.

"He's not dead, he's unconscious," Patrick repeated. He gave Roger a vigorous shake and Roger let out a low groan. Freya jumped and gave a little squeak, as if Patrick had reanimated a corpse.

Patrick tugged at Roger's eyelid and stared into his eyes. "He's drugged."

"Oh my god…" gasped Freya. "I'm sooo relieved. Thanks be to the Earth Mother."

Patrick took a tissue from the box by the bed, bent down and retrieved the syringe from the floor. He sniffed it and frowned.

"What's in it?" Kit wanted to know.

"Nothing. Absolutely nothing. Look."

He proffered it to her to take a look. Kit saw it was just a syringe. There was nothing inside. "It's a clean syringe, fresh out of the packet."

Roger gave another groan. Patrick ran back to him and tried to roll him onto his back.

"Do you want a hand?" asked Kit.

"Yes. If you're up to it."

"I feel fine."

Freya didn't say anything. She was rooted to the spot.

"Freya, I think you should go and get Victor," said Kit gently.

She nodded her head dumbly. "Yes, yes, I should sooo go and get Victor."

She wandered out of the doorway and down the corridor, like someone in a dream.

Kit walked over to Roger's prone form and tried to work out which particular part of him was easiest to grab onto.

Patrick frowned. "I don't think you should have sent her to get help. We shouldn't involve more people than we need to. Particularly if old Rog here has an addiction problem."

"I was just trying to get her out of here."

"Count of three?"

Kit nodded.

"One, two, three!" They grappled with his dead weight, struggling and grunting, until his nose faced the ceiling. Then they grabbed his shoulders and pushed until he was sitting upright on the bed.

Roger went, "Whuur?"

Patrick kept hold of Roger's shoulder and dashed round until he was looking Roger in the eyes.

"Roger! ROGER! Wake up!"

"Whhrr? Whrr y'doin'?"

"What have you taken? What drugs have you taken?"

This seemed to sober Roger up. His eyelids snapped fully open. "I haven' taken' any drugzz!"

"Yes, you have."

"Nuhh, I haven'… Cross ma' har…"

Roger struggled free of Patrick, pushing him away. He lurched off the bed and crawled along the floor. His hand came into contact with the desk chair and he tried to use it as a climbing frame to get upright, cursing as it swivelled out of his grasp. He finally steadied it and gingerly clambered aboard like a man trying to sit on a horse for the first time. His head weaved back and forth, trying to focus on them.

"Wha' are you talkin' about?"

Patrick ran into the bathroom. Kit could hear the *sploosh* of water from the tap, then he emerged holding a glass of water, which he gave to Roger.

"Drink this. All of it."

Roger slumped into the chair and drank messily until the glass was empty. "Okay," he spluttered, gasping with relief. "What are you talking 'bout?"

"We found you lying on your bed, dead to the world," said Kit.

"So what? A man ca' lie on his bed now?" He frowned at Patrick. "Wha' was all that bollocks you were saying about you killing Lily? Did you kill her?"

"I was acting."

"Acting?" Roger said the word as if he'd never heard it before.

"Never mind about that. We found this on your floor." Patrick showed Roger the hypodermic syringe.

Roger looked glassily at the needle.

"I've never seen that before. It's not mine. I don't know wha' you're talking about."

"If you haven't taken anything, Roger, then someone drugged you. What did you do this evening?"

"What?" Roger felt his head tenderly as if checking it wouldn't drop off his shoulders. "Christ. Well… What did we do? We had dinner, and then we a few drinks, as usual. The thin guy…" His brow furrowed. "Victor… He invited the girls over to the hotel, the ones who are goin' to be extras tomorrow. You know, as a treat for them, buy them a round of drinks… get charmed by yours truly."

He gave a woozy smile.

"They were veeeery nice. Nice girls. Just like back in th' ole days. Giggling and laughing, they were. Wearing those little tops in February… I mean, I wasn't complainin' but they'll all catch their death… Shame you ran off, Pat. Cos all the lads there were either gay, or… like Dorothy, so there was no competition. I wa' the only manly guy in the room."

Patrick was growing impatient. "And then what happened?"

"Then nothing. I felt a bit, you know, smashed, and I made my apologies and left. I can't unnerstand how wasted I felt, I only ha' a few pints."

He scratched the crook of his arm.

"What a wasted opper-opportunity. All that fresh meat and me and my chopper went to beddy-byes."

"Is everything okay?"

Victor was at the door. He had bed hair and looked almost as groggy as Roger. He had hurriedly thrown on a T-shirt and a pair of sweatpants. Freya was hovering behind him, looking over his shoulder.

"I heard Roger was ill."

"He's fine," said Patrick. "Roger's a bit worse for wear, that's all."

"I heard something about a needle on the floor?"

"Yes," Kit said. "That's the problem. He forgot to take his insulin, so he's a bit woozy."

"Oh," said Victor, nodding. "Insulin. Of course." He shot Freya a why-did-you-wake-me look. "As long as he's okay."

"He'll be fine," said Kit.

"Okay." Victor leaned on the edge of the open door, his arms folded behind him. "Right. Okay. Are you sure he doesn't need us to do anything? Send for a doctor?"

"I'll b'fine," repeated Roger. He looked irritated. His arm was causing him some trouble. He kept scratching it.

"Okay, as long as everything's fine… Um… Is everything okay with you, Patrick?"

"Of course it is," snapped Patrick. "Why shouldn't it be?"

"Well…" He cleared his throat. "You… did kind of say you murdered someone this morning. And you said you were going to the police station to give yourself up? I just wondered… um… how that was going?"

"Oh."

It was obvious the events of the morning had completely slipped Patrick's mind. Once again, Kit stepped in to rescue the situation.

"He was a bit distraught," said Kit. "He's been on these painkillers for his back, and he's been feeling a bit screwy."

"My back. Screwy. Yes."

Kit continued, improvising madly. "Patrick was suddenly reminded of Lily's sad demise by my probing interview, and his drug-addled brain became sick with guilt that he didn't do more at the time to stop her killing herself. He was convinced he was responsible for Lily taking her own life."

"Yes." Patrick nodded vigorously. "That's right. I don't know what came over me."

Victor looked relieved. "Okay mate, good, as long as we're all friends again. Shall I tell everyone else you're okay now?"

Patrick smiled. "That sounds like a great idea. Just let everyone know I've had a mini-breakdown but I'm fine now. They'll understand. They've all worked in television."

"Great."

Freya put her hand up. "Perhaps we can print an unrevised schedule, and add a footnote to say that Patrick's okay now?"

"Good thinking, Freya. Let's go and do that."

Victor gave a thumbs-up to Roger. "Okay, we're good. Roger, make sure you *take* your medicine, mate. Patrick, make sure you *stop* taking your medicine. Great."

Victor backed out of the room, still with his thumbs aloft. Freya gave them all a feeble grin and followed Victor.

"I thought they'd never go," muttered Roger.

"Are you sure you're fine?" Patrick asked Roger.

"Yes, I'm fine!"

"You've got a mark on the arm of your shirt," said Kit.

Roger frowned and looked at his shirt. Sure enough, there was a little round dot at the elbow, where Roger had been scratching. It was blood red.

"Shit, this is a Jasper Littman, my best shirt." He undid his cuffs and pulled up his sleeve. There was a little red dot of blood in the crook of his elbow – exactly where a nurse would insert a hypodermic needle.

Patrick grabbed Roger's arm and examined it. Roger was too surprised to resist.

"I haven't a clue how that got there," Roger spluttered. "I

swear, I'm not one of those druggy types. My worst vice is a bottle of scotch."

"I believe you."

"It's nothing. It's probably just a mosquito." He wriggled free from Patrick's grasp. "As I was saying. Time to stay goodnight."

"We're not going anywhere," snapped Patrick, reattaching himself to Roger's arm and pushing him backwards. Roger stumbled and sank back on the chair. Kit shut the door.

"What d'you think you're doing?"

"We have more things to talk about."

"What? Go'way!"

"We've just had a very interesting evening, haven't we Kit?"

"Very interesting."

Roger stared woozily, first at Patrick, then at Kit.

"Get out. Just fuck off…"

"We've been on a cruise, on a boat called *The Salty Seaman*, with a group of people. Who were they, Kit?"

"Sir Hugo Treadway, Mick Bunce, Buster 'By Gum' McGee, Ernie Winkle and Corky the Crocodile."

Roger's face grew slack with fear.

"The bastards tried to kill us, Roger. They tried to kill us, and they scuttled your boat. It's at the bottom of the Channel. They've been arrested in France."

"My yacht? It's gone? Shit! Not my yacht! Not *The Salty Seaman*!"

"Didn't you hear us, Roger? That's the least of your problems. Your boat was used for criminal purposes! People smuggling! And – I might have mentioned this – they tried to ruddy *kill* us! Is this your doing?"

"Shit. Look…" He struggled to sit upright. "Oh no. No no no. This isn't my fault. This isn't down to me."

"Who's it down to?"

"Not me. I was contacted…"

"By who?"

"Dunno. Just after all the 'me too' started. I got a letter."

"A blackmail letter?"

"Yes… No! Not really. No, no…" He shook his head vigorously, causing his blond-grey hair to flap across his forehead. "No. Quite the opposite. The letter said they'd sort out any problems I might have… you know… with girls coming out the woodwork. They said they'd buy them off, sort out everything for me. And they did! Not a peep. There was one actress I'd been a bit heavy-handed with one time during filming, and at the time it got a bit ugly. I thought she might try and jump on the bandwagon, get her pound of flesh… But she got paid off and signed an NDA."

"She signed an NDA? So there were lawyers involved? What lawyers?"

"I've got their business card somewhere, but don't bother to ask who hired them. No point. They made it very clear they were not at liberty to reveal who was employing them."

Patrick was getting angry. His fingers curled around Roger's collar. "So you had this fairy godmother – or godfather – doing everything for you, and he or she didn't ask for anything in return? Nothing? Are you expecting me to believe that?"

"Not nothing, no." He shrugged. "They asked for the use of my yacht. I wasn't using the bloody thing, so I thought fine. Use it. Knock yourselves out. Shit…" He looked forlornly up at them both. "I'm in trouble, aren't I?"

"You are an accessory to a major people-smuggling operation, sunshine," snapped Patrick.

"But I didn't know that!"

"Ignorance is your only defence. Look. You need to get ahead of this. We have to go to the police *now* and report your yacht stolen, and pray that those jokers in France didn't know it was your yacht, either."

Roger nodded dumbly.

"Get some clean clothes on and I'll meet you in the lobby in ten minutes."

They left Roger scrabbling in his wardrobe and pulled the door shut.

They wandered away from Roger's room and over to the balustrade, wary of being overheard.

"You go to bed," said Patrick wearily. "I'm only going to make sure he keeps his story straight. You don't have to come with us."

"What happens if the police find out we were on the boat? They might say something."

Patrick shook his head. "No. Those idiots think they killed us when they scuttled the boat. They're not going to be volunteering that information in a hurry. If they tell anyone about us, they'll think they'd be admitting to a murder charge."

"Of course. Obvious." She frowned. "What was that on Roger's arm?"

"A hypodermic needle mark."

"I thought it was. But it wasn't him who did it, was it?"

Patrick looked at her with a quizzical expression. "Why not?"

"I've seen those shows on 5USA. I've even got some of the box sets. If he was a 'habitual user', as they say, there'd be more holes up and down his arm."

Patrick raised his eyebrows, and then nodded.

"Also, his reaction when he saw it. He was genuinely surprised."

"He could have been acting."

"As you've said, he's not that good an actor."

Patrick chuckled. "So I did."

"So someone used a hypodermic on him."

"Yes. Not this one." He brought out the hypodermic in his pocket, still wrapped in the tissue. "But someone definitely used one."

"To drug him."

"No, not to drug him."

"No?"

"Think sequentially, Kit. Follow the logic."

Kit thought. "Oh. Of course. Stupid of me. You couldn't use a hypodermic on him, not without him knowing, unless he's a very sound sleeper, and that would be incredibly risky… You drug him, so *then* you can use a hypodermic needle on him."

"Exactly. Well done."

"So, the injection was for what? To put *more* drugs in him?"

"No idea. Why drug a drugged man? Doesn't make sense."

Kit sighed. She leaned face-down on the rail and allowed her head to rest on her hands. "That's it. I'm done. This day is officially over. I'm off to bed. Good luck with the police."

Patrick nodded. "Goodnight Kit."

"Goodnight Patrick."

Kit trudged slowly towards her room. Patrick turned and walked in the other direction. After a few seconds Kit spun round and said, in a loud stage whisper:

"Unless…"

"What?"

"It wasn't to put something *into* his body. It was to take something *out*. Night night, Patrick."

55

WEDNESDAY

9 a.m. Vanity Mycroft, Roger Barker, Patrick Finch, Joan Peverin, Tara Miles and Dorothy Fletcher to meet at hotel reception. Transport to take guests to Royal Pavilion.

9.30 a.m. Costume and make-up.

11 a.m. Recording of 'CORONATION' episode. Scene 2.

12-1 p.m. LUNCH.

1 p.m. Recording of 'CORONATION' episode. Scene 6.

4 p.m. Wrap.

* * *

Kit opened her eyes and allowed herself a tiny 'eek'.

The previous night felt like a dream. The only evidence of her crazy escapade across the Channel and her death-defying escape from a watery grave was the pile of extremely bedraggled clothes on the chair, the smell of salt in her hair and the queasy feeling in her stomach from eating too much mushroom soup.

She was able to do something about the clothes, as she had identical copies of each garment in the wardrobe. The hair, however, was trickier. She staggered, arms outstretched like a zombie, to the bathroom and looked in the mirror with some trepidation. The sea water had caused everything to frizz until her head had ballooned to twice its normal size. She thought about washing it, looked at her watch, saw how late it was getting, and settled on beating it into submission with industrial amounts of hair gel.

By the time she got downstairs everyone was assembling in the lobby. She noted with some irritation that Patrick and Roger were showing no ill-effects of the previous night. They were chatting and laughing. Roger was particularly perky as the two actors were surrounded by six Vixos warrior guards, still in their regulation knee-boots, crop-tops and denim skirts.

Most of them were clustered around Patrick – the TV star – but there wasn't room for everybody, and Roger was happily working his schtick on the stragglers. He was talking to Sandra, who towered over him.

"Of course, the trick about television acting is to do less with your face," he boomed. "Bring your face down really close to me and I'll tell you how much you can do with it…"

Sandra threw back her head, cackled and slapped Roger on the shoulder, nearly sending him flying.

Patrick gave Kit a brief smile and the briefest of nods, and that was all the time they had. Binfire was at the doorway, urging everyone onto the bus. Kit noticed with a jaded eye that even though Vanity had gone to get her car, Roger and Patrick had decided to join the half-dozen giggling teenagers on the minibus.

I can't think why.

The prospect of taking part in location filming was always fun, and everyone was laughing and making jokes. The atmosphere was jolly, like a coach trip to the seaside. The good vibes didn't stop when they arrived. Vanity was at the entrance, and she even gave them a cheery wave as they left the minibus.

Victor, Robbie and Freya were drinking coffee, sitting around one of the tables in the garden café. Robbie was now dressed in black, like Victor. With Robbie and Victor in their director's outfits and Freya in her goth costume, they looked like a bunch of crows waiting for the bird table to get restocked.

No. Not a bunch. What's the name for a bunch of crows? Oh yes. A murder *of crows.*

Right from the start, Victor and Robbie had agreed to split the directing chores. Victor was to do the interviews. Robbie insisted on taking charge of the reconstructions of the classic *Vixens* scenes. It was his first day as director and he was looking incredibly nervous.

"Are you sure we've got filming permission?" he asked Victor.

Victor rolled his eyes. "Of course we've got permission, mate! I'd hardly get everyone to turn up here today if I hadn't! To call that embarrassing would be an understatement."

Kit and Binfire joined them.

"Hi."

"Hi mate," said Victor. He glanced over at Roger. "Is Roger okay this morning?"

"He seems fine," said Kit. "He was in good spirits on the journey over."

"Oh, Roger's more than fine," grinned Binfire. "Just look at him."

Roger now had his hand implanted firmly around Sandra's bare midriff.

Victor slurped on his cappuccino. "And Patrick? Has he recovered from his mini-breakdown?"

"Oh yes," replied Kit. "A different person. No more of those pills."

Robbie pouted. "Hello? I'm okay *too* by the way, thanks for asking. I'm coping perfectly well with what is likely to be the biggest day of my entire *life*!"

"Aww, you're gonna knock it out of the park," said Binfire. "I mean, what's the worst that could happen?"

"It could be a disaster," wailed Robbie.

"Oh yeah," grinned Binfire. "That could happen."

"You're going to be marvellous, Robbie," cooed Freya.

Robbie stared up in awe at the Pavilion. "No matter how many times I see this place, I can't help but be humbled by the history of it."

When Robbie said "history", Kit suspected he wasn't talking about 1787, George the Fourth and Maria Fitzherbert and all that jazz. And, just like most things she suspected, she was absolutely right.

"The eighteenth of September, 1986," Robbie continued. "I remember sitting watching the television with my little brother, listening to the BBC announcer introduce this brand-new television show. I didn't know what to expect, and there was that brilliant shuttle crash, and then the establishing shot of Vixos, those domes, set against that shocking pink sky."

"Coloured with Quantel Paintbox," said Kit.

"Yes, I *know* that," snapped Robbie. "We *all* know that. Don't interrupt me when I'm eulogising, please. Where was I? Oh yes, that shocking pink sky… And the next shot, right over there, of Vanity and Tara running around in the gardens with their big guns. I was hooked from the start. I was a fan from day one."

"Too early for me," said Victor cheerily. "I wasn't going to be born for another five months."

Robbie glared at him. Their age difference was an open wound, but Victor could never resist picking at it.

Victor continued. "Though I do remember Mum putting it on the television to show me when I was very small. She'd recorded episodes off the telly."

"She sounds like an amazing woman," said Robbie acidly. "I must meet her sometime, you know, us being in a *relationship* and everything. You've met my mum, of course. We should organise a visit. Have some tea…"

Victor shook his head. "Alas, mine is no more. And my dad isn't on the scene."

"Poor darling," said Robbie. "And also: wow! You've actually shared an *actual fact* about your past life with me. Perhaps we should announce the wedding date now?"

The conversation subsided, as it always did when Robbie started to brew up an argument with his boyfriend.

"The first time I saw *Vixens* was from an old BBC video I found in a charity shop," said Freya abruptly. "The first three episodes all edited together on one hour-and-a-half tape."

Robbie looked over at Freya with obvious pity. "Oh my god, I forgot about those video atrocities. Absolute butchery. I'm surprised that you even became a fan watching those abominations."

Kit was tired of Robbie's insufferable attitude and felt like pricking his pomposity "Actually, those edited versions are much better in many ways. They cut a lot of the fat out."

The expression on Robbie's face suggested that Kit had committed blasphemy, but there was no time for an excommunication.

Kit looked over to the refreshments kiosk and saw the familiar shape of Graham Goldingay pacing around the shrubs, eating an ice cream.

"Graham's back, I see. Weren't you going to have a word with him?"

Victor nodded. "I've had a word. And we've sorted out our differences. We've reached a compromise."

"Compromise? That's a word that isn't in Graham Goldingay's dictionary."

"It is now. We are using the new costumes for the principal actors, and the 'classic' old-style costumes for the Vixos guards. Simples."

"How did you get him to agree to that?"

"It's called psychology, mate. If he doesn't compromise, he knows that we'll just carry on, filming *Vixens from the Void* scenes with none of his costumes. He's so obsessed with the show he couldn't *bear* that." He gave a dry chuckle. "You can just imagine his pudgy fingers sliding the Blu-Ray into the machine and watching our documentary *without* the classic *Vixens* costumes in the background? He'd *see* that and he'd *know* he had the chance to have them included, and he blew it. It would drive him mad. So, I offered him the compromise and he nearly bit my hand off." He tapped the side of his head. "Psychology."

Robbie touched Victor's arm tenderly. "You're a genius, Victor."

"I know I am."

"Perhaps you can use your amazing psychology to stop making me feel like a piece of dogshit in our relationship?"

"Maybe," Victor said. He turned, shrugging off Robbie's touch, and walked into the Pavilion.

* * *

Once the preparation started, the atmosphere became joyous to the point of hysteria, more like a student end-of-term revue. The two girls who'd been cast as the Vixos warrior guards in scene two, Bethany and Sandra, were shrieking and cackling at ear-splitting volume with the excitement of it all, but no one seemed to mind. After the tension of yesterday, the girlish glee they brought with them was infectious, and everyone was playing the fool and bursting into song.

Kit felt a little bit lost in all the hubbub. Technically, her job on the documentary was done, so she had nothing to do today. *But my job as detective never ends*, she thought. *So I will sit quietly and keep my eyes open*.

The rack of costumes was still hanging along the back wall of the Adelaide room. Kit had offered to help wheel them out of shot when filming started so she grabbed a cup of coffee from the machine and sat in the corner, trying to make herself invisible.

Sandra and Bethany clumped up to Joan, who was pulling costumes off the rack and issuing them to the cast.

"Wotcha," said Bethany. "We're fearless bitch warriors, and we'd like some costumes please."

Joan gave her warmest smile. "Oh yes, one moment."

She reached into the rack, pulled out two suit bags and handed them to the girls.

"There you go."

"Brilliant," said Bethany.

"Which one's which?" said Sandra.

"It doesn't matter, dear."

The two girls looked at each other.

"But we're different shapes," said Bethany.

"Yeah," added Sandra.

Bethany prodded her ample cleavage. "Cos I've got 'em."

"She's got 'em. She's got a lot of 'em."

"I have a *lot*." She jerked a thumb at Sandra. "And she hasn't got any."

"I haven't got any."

"She's got nothing but hat pegs."

"Itty bitty titties."

"But she's tall, so Kevin – that's her boyfriend – he don't care."

"He loves me as I am."

Joan smiled beatifically. "It doesn't matter, girls, because this is Spandex. Stretch Lycra. One size fits all." She unzipped the bag, pushed her fingers inside to take a handful of the material and gave it a tug to demonstrate. The two girls watched in awe.

Joan put her spectacles on her nose and made a show of appraising the girls from top to bottom. "Yes, they'll be fine for you."

"Brilliant!"

"Your boots are another matter, of course. No one size fits all there! You'll find them in that box, your names are on the labels."

Joan gave another saintly smile and pointed to the door. "Ladies' dressing room is just next door."

Bethany and Sandra collected their boots and scuttled off to the changing room. Kit decided to follow them. She wondered what would happen when they burst into the dressing room, and Vanity realised she'd been asked to share her space with a bunch of teenagers.

As it happened, Kit was disappointed – or was that pleased? Bethany and Sandra were greeted with open arms by the principals. They charged in with a huge whoop like they were sneaking up on a prospective bride on her hen night, but instead of a frosty silence, everybody whooped back. Tara did a little dance and Dorothy waved from her corner. Vanity was hunched over a mirror putting on her make-up, and even she gave them a cheery wave with an eyebrow pencil.

"Come on in, darlings," Vanity boomed. "It's a bit cramped but we can budge up. All girls together."

And so, everything was set.

56

A small area in the Pavilion gardens had been cordoned off, so that Arkadia and Medula could act out their hunt for the gruntark in their re-enactment of scene two of episode one, 'Coronation'. An audience had braved the chilly weather to watch behind the rope, eating sandwiches on the grass and treating it like it was a Punch and Judy show.

When Arkadia and Medula stepped out on the grass, the audience gave a round of applause.

Sensing the carnival atmosphere, Vanity and Tara decided to work the crowd. Vanity waved her phallic gun (original prop courtesy of Graham Goldingay) suggestively in the air and got a big cheer, and Tara (now in her severe black Cleopatra-style wig, also courtesy of Mr G. Goldingay) snarled at the crowd and threw her cloak contemptuously over her shoulder to boos and hisses.

When Robbie shouted, "Rolling," Vanity and Tara started acting, poking around in the bushes with their huge guns. Part of the crowd kept shouting, "He's behind you!" Tara and Vanity didn't acknowledge those pantomime calls and carried on with their gruntark hunt. They knew the 'alien jungle atmosphere' would be dubbed on later, so none of the catcalls would end up on the final version.

The crowd wasn't prepared for the giant purple armadillo when it lumbered out of the Pavilion, and they erupted with a huge laugh. Dorothy took the head off and waved her claws to her audience. She even kept her armadillo head off for the rehearsal, and when she and Vanity practised the Arkadia-gruntark fight they hammed it up, throwing big girlie bitch-slaps at each other, getting more huge laughs.

When the big blue crash mat was dragged out by Freya and Victor and placed at the bottom of the tree, there was a hum of expectation. Dorothy nipped into the Pavilion to change, and when she emerged in her full Arkadia outfit she bowed low, flourishing her cloak like an acrobat about to try a high-wire act. When she started to climb the tree, the crowd obliged with a long and trepidatious, "Woooaaah".

The tension hit fever pitch when Dorothy reached the top of the tree. The crowd fell into a hush. And when she pitched herself off the top and landed dead centre on the crash mat, arms and legs outstretched, they erupted with a standing ovation which lasted for several minutes.

That was when the trouble started. Vanity, who had been waiting for her next bit, was getting bored. She was also feeling rather overshadowed by Dorothy's scene-stealing performance. So when the time came for Roger and his two Vixos warrior guards to emerge and deliver the bad news of the royal shuttle crash, Vanity ensured that the recording slowed to a crawl.

"Well, I don't see how this scene works, darling," said Vanity.

Robbie, who had been silently screaming inside this roller-coaster of an argument for several minutes, dragged his fingers over his bald head.

"But it *did* work. I saw it when it went out. It was on television and people watched it, and I watched it, and it worked."

"But does it work now, darling? For a modern audience? Here I am with Tara, and Roger comes in with the news that our beloved mother may have been killed, and we just stand there and do nothing."

"You don't do *nothing*. You react."

"React? I just say, 'Mother,' and, 'Oh my gods!' That's hardly reacting, darling. Meanwhile, Vizor here goes on about 'losing contact' and 'having no communications with the shuttle' and 'we live in dark times'. I mean, he's just the messenger boy, for god's sake. He's got all the emotional lines and we're standing there scratching our arses."

Roger and Tara, who knew Vanity of old, exchanged glances and rolled their eyes.

"I mean, is that satisfactory, is it even drama? I think the answer is staring us in the face, darling."

Robbie was sinking slowly into the mire. "But this is a re-enactment for a Blu-Ray documentary. We're meant to be re-enacting a scene from 1986. That's the point. We can't really change the script."

"Why not?"

"Because it's meant to be a faithful re-enactment."

"You've changed our costumes, why can't you change our lines?"

Robbie looked stunned. He had no answer for that.

"Yeah, Robbie," yelled Binfire cheerfully. He was leaning on the camera and watching the argument with obvious enjoyment. "You've changed the costumes, why can't you change the frokking lines?"

Robbie's eyes rolled around in their sockets, and he started chewing invisible gum. A sure sign he was losing it.

Tara put her hand on Vanity's arm. "Vanity dear, be gentle with him. He's not a creative like us. He can't see how uncaging our talent can make a positive difference."

Vanity gave Tara a comradely pat. "Darling. You know it, don't you?"

"I know it. Let me have a chat and see if I can show him our potential."

Without waiting for an answer from Vanity, Tara steered Robbie to the other side of the tree. She made several grand gestures with her arms towards Vanity, as if outlining a scene, while talking in a low voice.

"Look, she's going to do what she wants to do, so just let her improvise."

"But we need to stick to the script."

"And you will, Robbie. You're forgetting. It's you who has the power."

"What power? That's Vanity bloody Mycroft!"

"*The power!* The power of the edit button. As long as you get the lines you want out of her, she can emote all she likes and it can all end up on the cutting room floor."

A look of understanding seeped onto Robbie's face. He nodded, strode back to the camera, and said, "Okay, I'm convinced. Shall we go from Roger's line ending with 'we have had no communications with the shuttle since that moment'. Vanity, you say your 'oh my gods line' and then after that… well, you just go where the muse takes you."

Robbie went and stood by the camera. "And Sandra and Bethany? You're doing great, but can you smile a little less? You are meant to be assisting Vizor in his task of bearing terrible news. So look stern and sad, okay?"

Bethany gave a thumbs-up. "Righto."

Sandra and Bethany adopted very severe expressions that were almost comical, wrinkling their foreheads and popping their bottom lips out.

"Okay," shouted Robbie. "Rolling."

Roger put a mournful expression on his face and said, "We lost contact moments before impact. We have had no communications with the shuttle since that moment…"

Vanity looked aghast.

"Oh my gods…" She gave a long, strange scream that chilled the blood, a protracted howl that sounded a cross between a foghorn and a distressed sperm whale. Binfire flinched and pulled his earphones off his head.

Then she said, "Oh my gods! Oh– my gods! Why? Why WHY?"

She threw herself to her knees in front of Roger, much to Roger's obvious discomfort.

"Why do the gods do this? Why do they play with us for their sport so? Mother was a good woman, a fine woman, who held this noble empire together with guts and guile and sheer determination. To be lost on a tiny rock on the infinite blackness of space, why it's so wrong, wrong, WRONG!"

She pounded the ground in front of her, embedding her gloved hand in the grass, then she raised her eyes and her arms to the heavens.

"Why, 'tis almost cruel that such a bright flame be extinguished in the cold hell of space! A rich jest that mocks us all! We cannot let those vengeful gods win."

She struggled to her feet.

"We must fly, like angels to their rest, and rescue her, and bring her back from her dusty death. Out, out, we must go to that undiscovered asteroid where no traveller returns. And bring her back home, home to her loving family and let her sleep... no more..."

She stood up and bowed, and the crowd went wild.

* * *

Kit was watching from the balcony, safely out of shot. She was greatly amused by the drama unfolding in front of her, but she couldn't help but feel that she had *already* missed an important clue today.

She decided to pop into the boys' dressing room to see a proper detective. Patrick was on his own. He was in full costume, and he was applying make-up ready for his after-lunch scene.

"Hi."

"Hi. Close the door."

Kit did as she was told.

"How was the police station?"

"It was fine," he chuckled. "As I anticipated, they were so starstruck by having 'Inspector Wistful' turn up, they treated Roger and me like royalty. Cups of tea, coffee, a lot of selfies..."

"Haha!"

"They took all the details of Roger's yacht and promised they'd keep an eye out for it."

"They don't know it's at the bottom of the English Channel?"

"Not yet. Different department. I guess Operation Mulberry will deign to tell them eventually... Roger thinks he's free and clear. He's very happy today, as you can tell from the way he's flirting like his life depends on it."

"Any word from our celebrity nonces?"

"I've had a call from a nephew of an old colleague, whom I last saw when he was in nappies." He dabbed his chin with a sponge. "He said he would keep me appraised."

"Great."

He turned to her, his face stern. "I'm just going to say this now, Kit. I cannot emphasise this enough. I don't want you to tell *anyone* about what happened last night."

"Ohh-kay…"

"I shouldn't really have to say, do I, that telling anyone about my… my extra-theatrical career would be very bad for me?"

"Of course."

"Promise?"

Kit didn't reply.

Keeping information from Victor? It felt like she was betraying the investigation.

"Promise?" Patrick repeated himself.

"Promise."

She could only cross her fingers and hope that the events of last night didn't have any bearing on the identity of Wolf's and Lily's murderers.

"And your mad chum with the shaved head and the khakis?"

"You can rely on Binfire, too. I'll make sure of that."

"Thanks. I trust you." He turned back to the mirror.

"I've had a thought about Roger," she said.

"What about him?"

"If someone drugged him last night, they must have done it in his drink, right?"

"Most probably."

"So it must have been a date rape drug like Rohypnol."

"Could be."

"Or ketamine?"

"Maybe."

"That was the same drug Wolf Tyler's murderer used to drug him, so they could…"

"Huh. Nice try, Kit, but ketamine's a very common drug. Just because it was used one time somewhere, doesn't mean to say the same person used it somewhere else."

"Hum."

"You should go to the police, Kit. That business card you found in that lady's kitchen, that could be material evidence. The least they would do is look into it."

Kit sighed. "I have a feeling I got lucky with Mary Creehan that one time. Other than leaving Wolf's card pinned up, I think she's been coached to keep a secret. I think if a couple of coppers showed up at her flat, she'd run rings around them."

"Go to the police, Kit. It's all you can do."

Patrick's phone rang and he answered it.

"Okay. Right. Oh. Okay. Thanks for ringing, Si. Give my love to your mum."

He ended the call and sighed.

"Well, they've interviewed the old fuckers, they've been telling the cops everything they know. They're just frightened old men, aren't they?"

"They weren't always frightened old men."

"No. Once upon a time they were nasty pieces of work who thought they could do what they liked. Shitty bastards. Anyway, they can't shut them up. But, they don't know who's behind the smuggling either. This… person… has been very careful, whoever it is. Perhaps those lawyers Roger mentioned will be more forthcoming."

"Oh, I know who's behind it," said Kit.

"What?"

"It's obvious. I thought you knew too."

"No, I don't!"

Freya opened the door and popped her head round.

"Lunch everyone!"

She closed the door.

Patrick glared at Kit. "Well, don't keep me in suspense. Who's behind it all?"

Kit told him who it was, and how she knew.

"Shit. *Shit!* How bloody obvious is that? What an idiot!"

He started jabbing buttons on his phone again.

Feeling rather pleased with herself, Kit walked happily from the dressing room to the Adelaide Suite and sat in the corner.

Roger and Vanity were up first and were tucking into the buffet.

"A good morning's work, I think," said Roger.

"Yes, it was," agreed Vanity.

"You do know all that throwing-yourself-on-the-ground shit is going to end up on the cutting room floor. You know that, don't you?"

"I know, darling, but that's not the point. One has to occasionally remind the director that there is a human being standing in front of him." She held her hand out and made a fist.

"A human being who, while the cameras are rolling at least, still has his balls in her hand…"

* * *

Thankfully, the afternoon went off without a hitch. Tara and Patrick recreated their scene on the balcony flawlessly, to Robbie's great relief.

Kit even noted with some amusement that, on his exit, Patrick shot a flirty look at Sandra, the Vixos warrior guard standing on the right-hand side of the door. The same look he gave to Lily Sparkes thirty-five years before.

What a professional.

Robbie collapsed into his director's chair at the end of the day, oozing puddles of sweat.

Freya scuttled up to him. "Well done, Robbie, it was really good."

"And what, pray, was good about any of it? We lost the light, the new costumes are too dull on camera, and we couldn't get the drone shot of Dorothy climbing up the tree because, according to Binfire, the drone is waterlogged! I mean, we haven't had any rain for a week, how can a drone get waterlogged?"

"I'm drying it out with a hairdryer," yelled Binfire. "It'll be fine tomorrow."

"Yes, but I wanted it *today*!" screeched Robbie. "Christ, I hope we have better luck tomorrow."

Robbie and Freya disappeared inside the Pavilion, leaving Binfire to pack up the equipment. After a while he realised that their audience was still lounging on the grass, watching him fold up the lights. He rolled up a magazine and used it as a megaphone.

"That's it guys, we're all done here. Haven't you got homes to go to?"

The crowd applauded politely and started to leave.

* * *

Kit was in the Adelaide Suite, tidying up the plates and mugs while the cast were hoovering up the last of the sandwiches. Victor appeared in the doorway, looking expectantly at Kit. He weaved his way through the crowd and came up to her.

"Well?" he hissed. "Haven't you got something to tell me?"

He's heard about our nautical adventures last night. Binfire must have said something.

Kit panicked. "Well, it's a bit awkward. I can't say anything."

"Don't play silly games, Kit. What did she say?"

"She?"

"Lily's friend." He flapped his hands. "Your… Jackie. You *must* have talked to her by now? Did she give you the cassettes?"

"I… no."

"Why not?"

"I… went to her flat but she was out."

Victor grabbed her arm, escorted her over to the balcony and pointed down to the garden.

"Well, here's an opportunity," he whispered. "She's right there, mate!"

Kit looked in the direction of Victor's pointed finger. The crowd had drained away, but one person remained. Jackie. She was lying on a tartan rug, munching on a triangular sandwich, propped up on one elbow. Despite her casual posture and the fact she wasn't even looking in their direction, Kit could sense the waves of hatred emanating towards her.

"Go on, then," said Victor. "Ask her!"

* * *

As she walked through the garden, aiming for the spot where Jackie lay, Kit faltered. She felt tempted to keep walking past her and down to the seafront, but she could sense Victor was still standing on the balcony, making sure she completed her mission. She could feel his eyes burning into the back of her head.

She stood over Jackie.

"Hello."

"Well, well. If it isn't the intrepid detective."

"Can I sit down?"

"It's a free country."

Kit sat down awkwardly, holding the tails of her coat so they didn't come into contact with the grass.

"I enjoyed your filming. Did you set all this up to investigate Lily's 'murder'?"

She put down the sandwich and did the quote marks.

"Well, if you put it like that… Yes."

"And all those actors? All those celebrities? They're all in on it? They're all helping you?"

"Well… No."

"Hah. Thought so." She struggled to her feet and started marching to the Pavilion. "Perhaps I should let them know why they're *really* here. It would be the *honest* thing to do."

Alarmed, Kit grabbed her arm. "Please don't."

"Don't you touch me!" Jackie yelled.

Eyes turned in their direction. A tramp looked up from his bin investigation. Kit cringed at the attention. Jackie stopped and turned, her a face a mask of pain and resentment, her eyes darting everywhere but directly at Kit.

"Yeah, you're right. I don't have to do it here, do I? I can just slip a note under their doors at the hotel."

"If I can just talk to you about this, then you'll understand."

"Oh, you gonna mansplain me? Or dykesplain me?"

"No."

"God, I was such an idiot talking to you. All my instincts said no, but you seemed so sweet on the phone, and when I saw you in reception, I thought, *that looks like a nice person*. More fool me."

"I am a nice person."

"Nice people don't lie and cheat just to rake up bullshit."

"I'm not doing all this to cause trouble."

"So you say. From where I'm sitting, you're no different from those reporters. I mean, I gotta give it to you. This is impressive. A journo did once pretend to be from some charity, telling me they were gonna set up a Lily Foundation in her honour, just to get their foot in my door, but this is something else."

Kit waved her arms in what she hoped was a conciliatory fashion. "I didn't just wake up one morning and decide to investigate Lily because of some urge to do some muckraking. I'm here because a friend of *mine* actually got murdered."

"What friend?"

Kit told her all about the death of Wolf Tyler. Up until now Jackie had been refusing to meet her gaze, but now her eyes travelled to Kit's face. Her expression was less hostile, but her mouth was still a thin stubborn line.

"I'm sorry, for the loss of your friend," she said at last. "Truly I am. And I get it. You want to find out who did him in. But whatever he claimed about Lily being murdered... he was full of shit. So's your friend Victor. Either your mate Wolf made it up, or your other mate is lying. Lily took her own life. I know she did. End of story."

"You can't be certain. You said yourself you thought she might be alive."

"No, dear. I didn't think she might still be alive – I *fantasised* that she might be alive! But that's only because they never found her. I *fantasised* that she might have jumped off the pier, survived, somehow got to dry land and she just... ran away, like before."

Kit pointed to the Pavilion gardens café. "Can I buy you a tea and a cake?"

"I don't want anything from you. I don't even know why I came here. Just to look you in the eye, and ask why, I guess."

"So now you know."

"I guess I do."

Jackie turned to collect her rug and her bag.

"I talked to Lily's drama teacher. Mrs Creehan"

Jackie turned, shocked. "You actually *went* to see her?"

"Yes."

"How is she?"

"She seems fine. She speaks very highly of Lily."

"She always did." Her eyes widened. "You didn't tell her you thought Lily was murdered, did you?"

"No, of course not."

"Oh right. You just did to her what you did to me. Pretended you were doing 'research'."

"Um. Yes."

"Figures."

"But I did mention Wolf Tyler. I asked her if Wolf paid her a visit. She said no."

"Well?"

"But then I found this in her kitchen."

Kit produced Wolf's business card from her pocket and handed it to Jackie. She wrinkled her nose and examined it.

"And what? What does this prove? Do you think Mrs Creehan killed her?"

"No, but this proves she lied. Wolf came to her to ask about Lily, and she lied about seeing him. Don't you think that means something?"

Jackie shoved the card aggressively back into Kit's hand. "If you want me to be honest, no. Perhaps she forgot? Perhaps she just didn't want to talk about your stupid friend? Sorry to speak ill of the dead and all that, but your mate just sounds like a fucking troublemaker."

Kit was growing frustrated. "Why are you so certain that Lily killed herself? Why are you so certain she just committed suicide?"

Jackie sighed. "There's a very good reason why I think that. She rang me. Just before she went to throw herself off the pier, she called me."

"She… what?"

"She called me from a phone box, dear. She told me what she was going to do. I was at home when I got the call. I was too far away to stop her."

"Oh. That's new information…"

"Did you never stop and think *why* the police were so *certain* it was a suicide, even when they *didn't* find a body and they'd already had to deal with her running away just a year before?" Jackie was getting angry again now. Her voice was getting louder. "Do you think she would have *lied* to her best friend about something like that? Do you think she would have *lied*?"

"But… But I read all the newspaper articles. There was nothing in the newspapers about a phone call."

"There's a bloody good reason for that. When they didn't find Lily's body in the water, well, a lot of vultures turned up. I told you about the shit-stirrers." She looked pointedly at Kit. "There were quite a few other scumbags over the years – mainly girls ringing up pretending they were Lily and telling the police they had just run off to Hollywood again. For a *laugh*. The police kept the information back so they could weed out the timewasters, you know, they could ask the question: 'what was the last thing you did before jumping off the pier?' If they couldn't answer with 'ringing my best friend Jackie from a phone box', then the police knew they were bullshitters."

"Oh. I see."

"That's why I know she's dead."

"I see your point." A thought occurred to Kit. "You haven't got a recording of that phone call, have you?"

"What? *No!* Do you think I sit by my phone recording every call I get, even ones I get in the middle of the night? Of course not! Who do you think I am? The police checked and they confirmed there was a call to my house from the phone box on the pier, that night. They believed me. Do you think I'm a liar?"

"No."

"So just let it go, Kit. Let it go. Leave it. I'm sorry about your mate, but you're not gonna find his murderer here."

She stuffed her rug angrily into her bag. "Don't try and talk to me again. The only words I want to hear from you are, 'I'm checking out now.'"

And she left.

* * *

Kit walked sadly into the Pavilion, up the garish staircase and into the Adelaide Suite. Victor was waiting expectantly.

"Well? Is she giving you the tapes?"

"No."

"What? Why the hell not?"

"Because she thinks we're a bunch of irresponsible shits who are playing detective and making trouble for the sake of it."

"You told her about—"

"Yes. I told her everything! I told her about Wolf, and she told me that Lily had called her from a telephone box on the pier, just before her *suicide*, and told her exactly what she was planning to do."

"What?"

"You heard me. That's what she said."

"Shit."

"This is over for me, Victor. I feel really bad about this."

"About what?"

"The whole thing. The investigation. We're going nowhere, and it's upsetting people. It's not worth it. Whatever Wolf told you – and I'm sure he was very convincing at the time – I'm really doubting he's telling the truth."

Victor slumped into a chair and pushed his head into his hands. "I get it. I get you, mate. I see where you're coming from. A phone call, right?"

"A phone call. From Lily, to Jackie, saying she was going to jump off the pier."

"Shit. It does seem pretty conclusive. So what was Wolf's deal? Why did he say those things to me?"

"Either he got the wrong end of the stick, or he was just making stuff up to get a rise out of you. And let's face it, that's exactly the kind of thing he would do."

"Yes, that's exactly the kind of thing he would do. Shit. What shall we do now?"

"What can we do?"

"Well mate... I guess we finish the documentary and leave it at that."

"I guess that's all we can do."

57

Jackie let herself into her flat, unpeeled her Puffa jacket from her shoulders and hung it on the coat hook by the door, just under the 'Live Laugh Love' sign. She relaxed as she smelled the familiar calming odour of her plug-in air freshener. Spring meadow with a hint of lavender. Her favourite.

She had walked home along the seafront. The sound of the ocean and the twinkling lights of the marina had burned off her anger, and now she'd calmed down she felt some sympathy for Kit. She knew what it was like to try and make sense of the death of a friend.

She was already regretting her harsh words. She'd certainly gone too far! She prided herself on her even temper, dealing with the most crazed hotel guests with a gentle voice and a beatific smile.

I'm sorry the waves are too loud, sir, but we can't turn the ocean down...

The hotel can't take responsibility for your pregnancy, miss, you must have had taken some part in what's occurred...

She knew she didn't mean what she'd said to Kit, about not wanting to talk to her again. That was particularly silly stuff on her part.

Perhaps I should ring her, we could go out for a proper drink tonight? Maybe help her investigate who really murdered her friend?

She had her mobile phone in her hand, ready to dial Kit's number, when the doorbell rang.

Kit?

Her heart spasmed with excitement and she rushed to open the door. No one there. There were jokers around the area who sometimes rang bells and ran away, but they only came out during Hallowe'en.

She walked into the night. And that was when the Special Mystery Guest struck. All she saw were three pale circles, bits of face poking through a black balaclava like a toddler's jigsaw puzzle, and then the arm slid round her neck and dragged her into the flat.

She put up quite a good fight, before the Special Mystery Guest pinned her to the floor and held her arms down with their knees. There was sharp pain in her shoulder, then the ketamine surged through her veins and relaxed her far more than a plug-in air freshener ever could.

58

That evening, Kit ended up slumped on a barstool in the hotel, the traditional place reserved for the lonely, jaded and miserable. She looked up forlornly every time a hotel staff member glided past, but it was never who she hoped it would be. Jackie was nowhere to be seen.

It was late, and the bar was full of ageing actors. Roger, Patrick, Vanity, Tara and Dorothy were slumped on the sofas, managing the post-filming adrenalin crash with various flavours of alcohol. Joan Peverin had swallowed some sleeping pills and turned in early.

"It was fun today. Wasn't it?" said Roger.

"Yes, it was," agreed Patrick. "It was indeed."

"Just like the old times," Roger raised the glass of whisky in his hand.

"It was fun," said Tara. "But it wasn't like the old times at all."

"No?" Roger sipped his beer.

"The old times were terrible. A sexist, misogynistic nightmare."

"They weren't that bad."

"For you, maybe," said Dorothy.

"Oh, you're oppressed now, Dorothy?" laughed Roger. "I seem to remember you took a lot of advantage of sexism when you called yourself Duggie."

Dorothy put her tongue out and gave him the finger.

"Proper men like me, we're out of fashion now. It's a bit off I wasn't asked to have a part in the new series. Not that I would have said yes, I mean, because it's not the same show, is it? It's all got a bit, well, let's say the word. 'Woke.' There, I've said it.

That's the reason I don't get telly work anymore. I'm a white heterosexual male actor of a certain age."

Vanity sniffed. "It's not that easy being a female actor of a certain age either, darling."

"You can talk. At least you got on the new series."

"One day's filming, darling, so far, and I was utterly unrecognisable. I was made to look fifty years older."

"Oh, you were wearing make-up, were you? I couldn't tell."

Vanity also gave Roger the finger.

He blathered on. "But you got on it, didn't you? You were asked, I wasn't. It proves my point. White men are surplus to requirements these days."

"Come on, Roger," said Patrick. "Let's go for a drink. Us poor misunderstood white heterosexual males that are surplus to requirements have to stick together."

"Good idea." Roger slapped the arms of his chair. "I think I owe you one after last night."

"Quiet pubs only," said Patrick. "If anyone asks me for an autograph, I'm bailing out."

"Deal," said Roger. "Anyone else? Ladies?"

No one responded.

"Fair enough. Your loss. Don't wait up." He gave a Cub Scout salute and staggered in the direction of the lobby. Patrick waved to the group, then followed him.

"Well, darlings," Vanity's eyes lit up. "I hope we're going to outdo the gentleman in the debauchery stakes tonight."

"Sorry, Vanity." Tara stood up and stretched. "I can't believe I'm saying this, but I've really enjoyed my time with you, and I'm really tempted to go on a night out. It's been a lot of fun, weirdly. But this is my last day of filming, and I want to get packed ready for an early start tomorrow."

Vanity waved a graceful hand.

"Ditto," said Dorothy. "I'm not needed tomorrow either,

and I'd like to get off sharpish."

Tara smiled. "Would you like to share a train carriage back to London?"

Dorothy stopped, thought about it, and then smiled back. "I would like that very much."

"Oh well," Vanity sighed, also smiling. "To quote a certain washed-up actor, 'your loss'." She got to her feet and tottered up the stairs. "Last chance to empty my minibar…"

59

Tara, Vanity and Dorothy had reached the top of the stairwell when there was a crash. A door slammed. Then a rhythmic *thud-thud-thud*. Back and forth. Back and forth.

Kit stood up and looked to see what was going on up there. She saw a monstrous shape lumbering along the gallery.

Graham Goldingay. He was agitated, moving faster than she'd ever seen him. Pacing. Slapping the balustrade with his big meaty hands. He saw the women at the other end of the gallery.

"WHERE IS IT?" he roared, marching towards them.

Kit leapt off her barstool and ran to the other stairwell. She reached the upper landing to find Graham bearing down on the women.

"WHERE IS IT?" he roared again. "TELL ME WHERE IT IS!"

"What the fuck is wrong with you?" yelled Vanity.

"Woah woah woah!" Tara raised her arms, assuming a combative stance. "Stop right there," she boomed. "I do Krav Maga..."

Goldingay scowled at her. "If you lay a finger on me, I will sue."

Kit barely thought about what she was doing. She dashed along the gallery and interposed herself between the women and Graham.

"Graham, you need to stop this now, or you will be in serious trouble."

"It is not me who is in the wrong, it is her." He pointed a massive digit at Dorothy. "The *thief*."

He advanced on Dorothy.

"You stole it."

"I don't know anything about it. I didn't steal anything."

"There is no one else. You took it from my room."

"I didn't. I swear."

"It was in my wardrobe yesterday. It's not there now. If you don't bring it back *now*, I will turn this hotel inside out until it is found."

Dorothy just shook her head slowly.

"Fine. I am going to report you."

He waddled past them and down to the lobby.

"What the actual eff?" said Vanity. "He's mad."

Kit was already on her phone, making a call to Victor. *Shit. Straight to voicemail.*

"Victor, we have a situation here. It's a code Goldingay. Get to the hotel as soon as you can, please."

She ended the call. Then she realised Dorothy was clutching the balustrade for support. She was shaking.

"Are you okay?"

"No."

Kit hugged her. "You need to tell us what's happening."

Tara looked over the shoulder. "Shit. He's talking to the receptionist right now. He's really giving her the third degree…"

"What's going on, Dorothy?" asked Kit.

"It's nothing. It's just nothing… It's…" She stamped a foot. "Jesus Christ! Fuck him!"

"Let's go and hide in my room, darlings," said Vanity. "There's a bit of space in there."

Kit gently took Dorothy's arm and led her away from the edge. They sprinted along the gallery and one flight up to the executive suites. Vanity pulled out her keycard and they all piled inside.

Dorothy threw herself onto one of the sofas, her head sinking low until it almost touched her knees. Tara edged near and put her arm around her. "You know what he's talking about, don't you?"

Dorothy's head moved slowly in the affirmative.

"Dorothy darling," said Vanity. "We can't protect you until we understand what's going on."

She pulled her head out of her lap. "No one can protect me. This is all my fault. I was so stupid." Her eyes prickled with moisture and her eyelashes danced like butterflies.

"Have you stolen something?" asked Kit.

"No! I promise!"

"But you know what he's talking about, don't you?"

Dorothy didn't answer.

"It can't be that bad."

"Fuck it," muttered Vanity. "Who wants a drink?" She got down on her hands and knees, and stuck her head inside the minibar.

"I will say this…" Dorothy pushed out a sigh that made her body shudder. "There were many ways, throughout my life, that I knew I was a woman, but I don't think you can ever truly feel like one until you have the experience of being utterly screwed over by a man."

"Go on, Dorothy. You're among friends here. You know that. It's a bit late to worry about what Graham might do to you. He's in full 'bull elephant' mode now."

Dorothy looked up at the concerned faces of Kit, Tara and Vanity, and realised – with a little jolt of surprise – that she *was* among friends. She screwed up her eyes, punched her knees with her fists and breathed slowly.

In… out. In… out.

"When my wife – when Liz died, I felt I was released from my obligation to her. No more lies. I wanted… Okay, I wanted to… to be *myself* as quickly as I possibly could. I wasn't getting any younger. A few days after the funeral, I made enquiries about reassignment surgery and was told it was going to be at least four years on the waiting list on the NHS. At least. I had to show I could live like a woman for a *year*. Christ. I already *knew* I was a woman, what was the point of that?"

She jerked her head at the door.

"I couldn't afford to go private. It was the NHS or nothing. Then *he* contacted me. I don't know *how* he knew about what I wanted to do…"

"He has ways, believe me," said Kit.

"And he offered to pay for everything. I could go on HRT and be done in a year. He flew me to China and got some top surgeon to see me, and after the hormone treatment we went ahead with the operation."

She bit her lip.

"But Graham didn't mention he had an arrangement with the surgeon. He was well paid. The operation… I don't know if you know the details of a penectomy?"

"No, darling," retorted Vanity, nursing a mini-bottle of whisky. "And I don't want to know."

"Cover your ears, then," snapped Tara.

"Just say it, darling." She held up her bottle. "I'll use this as anaesthetic."

"The operation involves making male parts into female parts. The skin of the scrotum is used to make a labia."

"Jesus." Vanity took a swig.

"The erectile tissue is sliced up and stitched together to make a clitoris."

"Fuck." Vanity glugged the bottle dry.

"But they don't quite use everything that was there before. There is a bit left over…"

Kit's mouth fell open. "Graham kept your penis?"

She nodded. "Yes, he did."

"What?"

"Some of it. The part that's not used for the surgery. Yes. He took it."

Tara clapped her hands to her head. "Fuck. That… That monster!"

Dorothy shuddered. "No argument from me."

"That... *monster!*"

"That's why I had to come here." Dorothy sounded very weary. "Because I didn't have a choice. If I didn't come, he threatened to put it on eBay."

"WHAT?!" Tara was incandescent.

"Or he said he had drawn up plans to put it in a charity auction at one of the big sci-fi conventions."

"THAT... FUCK!" Tara roared.

All her pretence at serenity had vanished. She was now a boiling mass of outrage. She turned and lunged for the handle, wrenched the door open.

And there was Graham Goldingay, filling the door frame.

"WHERE IS MY PENIS?" he bellowed.

The women looked at each other, stunned.

Finally, Vanity said, "It's probably in the place you left it, darling. Granted, with a man of your girth, it's an easy thing to lose."

"You utter monster, Graham," screeched Tara. "You are an abomination. I'm calling the police."

"No! Don't!" said Dorothy.

"I've already asked reception to call the police," he said.

"Bloody hell, darling," snarled Vanity. "You fanboys really know how to treat a woman right, don't you?"

Kit stepped forward. "You're utterly humiliating her, can't you see that? Dorothy has two grown-up sons! She has *grandchildren* for g–god's sake!" She was shaking now. The stammer was starting to awaken. "W–why, Graham? Why? W–what you've done to Dorothy... It's horrible! Inhuman! W–why?"

"She signed the contract. It's not my fault she didn't read the small print."

"Sss... Small print? My g–god! Small print? Why did you even want to keep a–a shrivelled piece of dead flesh in the first p–place?"

Graham looked at Kit with undisguised contempt. "I knew you wouldn't understand. If you were a *real* fan you would

372

understand. That penis is a *priceless* collector's item. It has been inserted in some of the most glamorous cult TV actresses the world has ever known. Vanity Mycroft. Tara Miles. Samantha Carbury. Jane Ferrier. Race Keynes. Victoria Bacon. I could go on…"

He glared defiantly at the wall of hatred surrounding him. He shook his head at their stupidity.

"It's more valuable than a prop, or an autograph. Napoleon's penis sold for four thousand dollars. Rasputin's penis has never been sold at auction, but they estimate it could sell for even more."

There was a timid knock on the doorframe. Mags, the purple-haired girl from reception, was there. She coughed apologetically.

"The police are here… They'd like to speak to you?"

"At last," muttered Graham.

"Oh my Jesus fuck," wailed Vanity. "This is a bloody madhouse."

Tara and Kit instinctively moved to the centre of the room, forming a human shield between the door and Dorothy. Two men appeared behind Mags, one older with a beard, the other young. They had come in their plainclothes attire.

"Graham Goldingay?"

"I am he."

The older man stepped forward. "I'm DI Harrison from the National Crime Agency. This is DS Ford."

"Harrison and Ford?" erupted Graham. "You are Harrison and Ford?"

Harrison and Ford looked at each wearily, as if this was the curse they had to carry every day of their lives.

"You could get a transfer," said Harrison.

"So could you," said Ford.

They turned wearily to Graham.

"Anyway, that's a discussion for another day," said Ford.

"Would you like to come with us, sir?" said Harrison.

Graham looked confused. "I don't have to go anywhere. This is the scene of the crime. My penis is somewhere in this building."

Harrison and Ford looked at each other, exchanged glances and looked back at Graham.

Harrison said, "Graham Goldingay, I am arresting you under section two of the Modern Slavery Act, for the arranging and facilitating the transfer of persons illegally across the English Channel, and for the crime of harbouring, aiding and abetting fugitives with a view to perverting the course of justice. You do not have to say anything, but it may harm your defence if you do not mention when questioned something which you later rely on in court. Anything you do say may be given in evidence."

Ford said, "Can you come with us, sir?"

Graham stared at both men, first at Ford, then at Harrison, then he roared and catapulted himself across the room. Surprised, the two officers lunged at him, and each managed to grab a corner of his jacket, but that only served to slow him down.

Kit was by the door, and she instinctively made a grab for Graham. Graham surged forward, straining for release, trying to struggle free from her clutches, but the effect was to create more momentum – towards the balustrade. Kit tried to let go but she couldn't. Her watch chain had caught on one of the loops on Graham's belt.

Like the boulder from *Raiders of the Lost Ark* (1981), they shot out of the room and hit the balustrade. It splintered and collapsed under the impact.

Graham and Kit teetered on the edge, Graham's arms revolving like the sails of a windmill, then they both toppled over the side with an ear-jarring crash.

60

At that moment Dr Alexandra Loske was checking out of the Hotel De La Mer. By complete coincidence, she was staying in the same hotel. She always used it when working in Brighton as it was the closest to the Pavilion.

She toyed with sharing this fact with the Blu-Ray documentary team, but after a helping of Roger Barker's patter she had decided against it, preferring to stay anonymously in her room.

She heard the cracking sound. She looked up and saw the huge shape of Graham Goldingay crashing into the bar.

Her first thought was: *I knew it. I bloody knew it. A large round object descending from the heavens. My premonitions always come true.*

* * *

Kit lay very still, listening to the faint whining in her ears. After a few seconds she realised she wasn't dead, not even hurt. She was lying on Graham's huge chest. Her vision was swimming, but she could see that Graham had collided with a bar table, crushing it into matchwood. Tiny splinters were fluttering around them like snowflakes.

"Are you alive, Graham?" she whispered.

There was – to her – a very long silence, and then came a low stentorian rumble from beneath her.

"Yes."

"So you blackmailed Dorothy to get her here."

"Yes."

"And you blackmailed Patrick to get *him* here."

"Yes."

"You were lurking around the hotel back in the 1980s and you overheard Lily and Patrick arguing, and you found out about Patrick's job as an undercover policeman."

"I did."

"You are a piece of work, do you know that, Graham?"

Graham's huge stomach rose and fell under her. It felt quite relaxing. Kit hoped she could stay here a while.

"You wouldn't understand, Kit Pelham. All six guests had to be here, or there would be no point to this documentary."

"But your plan changed when I interviewed Patrick yesterday. When he had that outburst."

"Of course it did. He said he killed Lily Sparkes. That changed everything. I could not allow the great Patrick Finch to get arrested. I put a note under his door and gave him a way to escape with my other celebrities and flee to the safety of France."

"Huh. I get it. Not easy to interview people in prison about old television programmes. Much easier to get a camera crew to some château in France where a grateful celebrity would be happy to say a few words on camera for you."

"Exactly, Kit Pelham. I think finally you understand."

Dr Loske got to them first. She leaned over and helped Kit get slowly to her feet, dusting her down.

"Are you okay?"

"I'm fine," said Kit. "A little groggy but I'm absolutely fine."

"You were very lucky."

"I know. Lucky Graham acted like an airbag."

"When I worried about a massive object falling from the ceiling, I never dreamed it would be attached to you."

Kit gave a laugh which collapsed into a coughing fit.

Harrison and Ford ran down the stairs and stood over Graham's mountainous form.

"Don't move, Mr Goldingay," said Harrison. "Wait until the paramedics get here."

"I regret nothing," spluttered Graham. "They are legends of classic television. They should not be put in prison to rot. They should be free to record documentaries about their role in television history."

Harrison sighed, reached into his pocket, pulled out a radio and called for backup.

61

Medical assistance arrived quickly. Fortunately, Graham didn't seem to have broken or ruptured anything serious, but it took eight paramedics to carry Graham to the ambulance, holding him aloft like pallbearers. Harrison and Ford followed solemnly in their wake, the mourners at the ceremony.

Victor dashed into the hotel, flushed and sweating. He gaped as he watched Graham getting carried out. Then he gaped at the wreckage in the middle of the bar, the splintered remains of the table.

"Glad you could join us," said Kit, getting up from her chair at the bar.

"What in the name of Sauron's pointy helmet happened here?"

Kit explained about Graham and the stolen 'item'. Victor looked surprised, but not *that* surprised.

"Huh," said Kit. "You look like you already know what's going on here."

* * *

Inside Vanity's hotel room, the atmosphere was subdued. Graham had gone, and there was palpable relief at his absence, but there was still something hanging in the air, the awful knowledge of what Graham had done.

The paramedics and the policemen finally left, the sirens of the ambulance mingling with the sirens of the police car in an ear-splitting cacophony. Vanity was at her window, glass in hand, watching the blue lights flutter and wink into nothingness.

"You'd think they would have had a chat beforehand, about who was going to make the woo-woo noises," she said in an exhausted voice.

Kit knocked on the door frame.

"Hi everyone."

There was a tired mumble of hellos.

"He's gone. They took him away."

"We heard," said Tara.

"Victor's here. He's got something to tell you, Dorothy."

Dorothy had returned to her upright foetal position. She raised her head in surprise.

Victor walked into the room like he was expecting to be attacked at any moment. "Yeah, um hi. I gather there's been a bit of a fracas about an… object? An object that… sort of belongs to Graham but actually… should belong to you?"

Dorothy's eyebrows inched up into her hairline.

"The thing is… that object? I'm the one who stole it from Graham."

Tara was perched on the edge of the study desk. She pushed her bottom off and took a few steps towards him, her eyes wide.

"You?"

"Yes mate."

"You've got the thing?"

"Yes." He held up a hand. "I've got the thing. Before you say anything, I don't want it. God no. I'm not some crazy collector. Not like that, anyway. I knew Graham had it. In fact…" He glanced apologetically at Kit. "I know why you had to come here, Dorothy. The hold he had over you. And I was mortified."

Kit folded her arms sternly. "But you still let Graham use it to get Dorothy here for the documentary."

"I know, I know…" His voice crackled with nerves. "I felt so bad he forced you to come here. I knew you didn't want to come, and I let him do it anyway. So, by way of assuaging my guilt, I decided to remove his hold over you. I got Binfire to break into his room last night, and we found it and we took it."

He gave a terrified grin. "To be honest, I was expecting Graham to blow up earlier. He obviously hadn't looked in his wardrobe until now."

Victor made a placatory gesture, both arms outstretched. "So. Dorothy. It's yours. With my best wishes. You can do with it what you want. You don't have to worry about it anymore."

Dorothy's hands were shaking. She curled them into fists and held them together in front of her. She looked like she was going to strike Victor. He took a step back and cringed.

"Okay," he whimpered. "Maybe you do want to worry about it?"

"I don't bloody want it. That was the point of everything. To get rid of it!"

"Of course you don't. I'll just…"

"I want to see it. And then I want to get rid of it."

* * *

Victor led them all down to the hotel car park, where the minibus was waiting.

"It's in the luggage compartment, down there," explained Victor. He unclicked the hatch at the bottom and the door slid upwards.

He pulled out a sports bag. "It's in here." As he held it up, they could hear a faint sloshing. "It's in a big glass container."

"Of course," sighed Vanity. "He pickled it like a fucking gherkin. Of course he did."

He put the bag back and slid the door shut.

"So, Dorothy," said Tara. "It's your party. You're in charge. Where are we going now?"

Dorothy looked at them all and grinned. Her face was bathed in the yellow lights of the hotel, giving her a slightly manic look.

"We go to the pier," she said.

62

Victor drove Vanity, Kit, Tara and Dorothy to The Lanes car park. When they alighted he handed Dorothy the bag, holding it out in front of him with the merest hint of ceremony, and got back into the minibus to wait.

He's assuming he would be intruding if he came with us, thought Kit. *It's a good call on his part. Well done, Victor. Maybe you're actually serious about wanting to redeem yourself.*

And off they strode, in their long coats, the big boots of Kit, Vanity and Dorothy clumping on the boardwalk, looking for the world like a gang of mature ladies out on the town. One of the classier hen nights.

They walked along the pier, past the rides, past the shrieking Horror House, until they came to the tiny gap by the Wild River ride, where they could look down at the water. The same place where Kit had ended up that first night. The place where Jackie Hillier had ambushed her with her smile.

I hope Jackie's okay.

They all clustered around and peered down into the dark undulating surface.

"Okay," said Dorothy. "Let's get it over with."

She wrestled the sports bag onto the rail, unzipped and pulled the back down so the top was visible. It was a large cylinder with glass sides, filled with a murky orange liquid. Graham had obviously thought a lot about how it was to be presented. The lid was a pretty rose-gold colour, like an iPhone.

Dorothy grasped the lid with her long fingers.

"Which way does it go?"

"Righty tighty, lefty loosey," said Tara, automatically.

"Here goes nothing." She unscrewed the lid, slowly. When it was free she passed it to Kit. Keeping her eyes half shut, avoiding looking directly at the thing, but wanting to see what she was doing, she tipped it. The orange liquid dribbled into the sea. Kit caught a fleeting glimpse of something no bigger than a slug slithering out of the jar, and then it was gone.

"There she blows," said Dorothy. "Bit of an anticlimax really."

"Should we play the last rites?" drawled Vanity. "I'm sure we can find it on Apple Music."

"Bit late now," sighed Dorothy. She kept peering into the depths. "Goodbye, Liz. Love you." She looked up and laughed. "I never did have a head for heights. But at least a bit of me jumped off the pier."

And she laughed, and so did everyone else.

Their work was done, so they locked arms and started back to the minibus.

"You know," said Dorothy at last. "I'm sure I saw this scene in a British comedy film starring Julie Walters."

They all hooted with laughter.

"If they make this into a movie, I want to play myself," boomed Vanity. "But if they don't let me, I wouldn't mind Julie Walters playing me. Or Frances Barber. I think she'd do a good job."

"I baggsy Emma Thompson," said Tara. "Thompson with the pixie cut, obviously."

"Maxine Peake for me," said Dorothy. "I love her. What about you, Kit?"

"I think I would most likely be played in the movie by a very promising up-and-coming actress, who you would never hear from again."

And they all laughed very hard at that.

I'm with the actual stars of Vixens from the Void, *and they're all laughing at my joke*, thought Kit. *It doesn't get any better than this.*

63

THURSDAY

9 a.m. Vanity Mycroft, Roger Barker, Patrick Finch and Joan Peverin to meet at hotel reception. Transport to take guests to Pulborough chalk pit.

10 a.m. Costume and make-up.

11 a.m. Recording of 'ASSASSINS OF DESTINY' episode 2. Scenes 13, 14.

1–2 p.m. LUNCH.

2–4 p.m. Recording of 'ASSASSINS OF DESTINY' episode 2. Scene 17.

5 p.m. Wrap.

* * *

Tara and Dorothy had gone. But even with the depleted cast, the minibus that morning was utterly packed. It was full of excitable teenagers, gabbling about the kinds of things teenagers talk about.

Vanity, Roger and Patrick took one look at Joan sitting forlornly, trapped in the back of the bus, and decided to forego their cars for one day. They all clambered in to join her. Binfire started the half-hour drive to Pulborough Quarry, the location for Chevron, home planet of the dreaded Styrax.

Roger looked much the worse for wear. He slumped on the back seat and nodded off, allowing his head to fall on the shoulder of the girl sitting next to him, emitting a slow grinding snore. The girl giggled, took a selfie and posted it on Instagram.

"Good night, darling?" said Vanity sweetly to Patrick.

"Hardly," grinned Patrick. "Couple of pints in a few pubs along the seafront, and we got besieged by drunken bastards who recognised me. I knew it was going to happen. I came back early and left Roger to it."

"I guess you heard what happened with Graham?"

"My god, yes! I couldn't believe it! He fell off the balcony? And they arrested him? For what? People trafficking?"

"Apparently."

"That's unbelievable. What a crazy thing."

"I know."

Patrick caught Kit's eye and they gave each other the slightest of satisfied smiles.

Kit was correct in her deduction. Patrick had thrown the gauntlet down in his interview, challenging his mysterious blackmailer to come forward.

Question: But who?

Answer: The only person in that room, apart from Kit, who *didn't* go straight to Brighton seafront for filming. The only person who had time to go to the hotel and slip a note under Patrick's door.

Graham Goldingay.

* * *

Binfire parked outside the entrance to the quarry. He hurried to the luggage compartment, brought out wellies for everyone, then unhitched the gate and led them squelching and sliding up a muddy track, over the brow of a hill and down to where the sand formed a basin.

"My god…" gasped Patrick.

There were three tents erected in a cluster, labelled *Catering*, *Ladies' dressing* and *Gents' dressing*, and two Portaloos. But that wasn't what took Patrick's breath away.

Sitting in the middle of the basin was a spaceship.

It was a squat dart-shaped craft that was about forty feet long and twenty feet wide, with wide sweeping fins and a cockpit that looked like the head of a bird. There was an open door in the hull. A gangway led down from it and onto the sand.

"Yeah, good isn't it?" said Binfire cheerfully. "Graham had all the parts made separately, like a kit, and we hired a couple of guys from the local garage to put them together."

There were some 'oohs' and 'aahs' and 'fuck mes' from the extras as they too reached the top of the rise and saw the craft below them.

Patrick was still gaping. "It looks exactly like the ship in the show, but... That was just a model, wasn't it?"

Vanity was also staring disbelievingly at the craft. "Absolutely right, darling. We only had a door and two flats, and they added the model over the top."

"Yeah," said Binfire. "We were going to do a forced perspective shot just like the original, but Graham insisted he make us a proper ship. He gets quite monomaniacal about these things."

"He certainly doesn't understand the meaning of the word 'no'," said Kit, grimly.

"Your truth to god's ears, darling," trumpeted Vanity. She barged in front of the group and yomped down the hill, her slingbacks dangling from her hand.

"Funny, isn't it?" Binfire smirked at Kit. "Graham went ballistic over costumes, going on about recreating the exact look. But he was completely fine with making a ruddy great prop instead of a model."

"I sort of understand it," said Kit. "He sees the costumes as a creative decision made by the production team that should not be challenged. The spaceship, on the other hand... He sees the model they used in the 1980s as a budgetary cost-saving measure to be remedied."

They started to stumble down the incline.

"Yeah, right," Binfire chuckled. "As if the costumes would have been made from Spandex if Joan had had unlimited cash."

"I didn't say I *agreed* with it. I just said I *understood* it."

"Well, wouldn't it be frokking great if Graham got sent to an authentic prison from the 1980s, with big fat bars on the windows and a bucket in the corner? I'd laugh until I ruptured something."

They stumbled to the bottom of the hill and were greeted by a grim-faced Robbie.

"I take it the drone isn't waterlogged today?"

Binfire glanced at Kit and grinned. "All good. I put it in rice, and on the radiator. It's working fine."

"Good, because when the Styrax appears on the rise of that hill, I want a nice looong sweeping shot, from the spaceship past the heads of the Vixos warrior guards and right into the face of the Styrax."

He pointed to the brow of the hill, to the Styrax. It was standing drunkenly to one side, waiting to be moved into position.

Binfire made a show of tutting and shaking his head. "They didn't have drones in the 1980s, Robbie. Graham will not be pleased about this dynamic camerawork you're planning."

"Well, Graham Goldingay isn't here, and it looks like he won't be here for the next fifteen years. So just do as I say."

Robbie stomped to the costumes tent. Kit was going to follow, but realised it would be full of giggly teenagers, so instead she wandered around the basin, inspecting the spaceship. She went up the ramp and was astonished to find the insides of the ship had been replicated too, even though the interiors were studio-bound sets. The effort made to recreate it was incredible, bordering on crazy.

No, it *was* crazy.

"Sooo… What do you think?" said a voice behind her.

That was Freya's voice.

Kit turned and staggered back in shock, stumbling over a guy rope in the process. Freya had divested herself from her layers of dark clothing and was now in a full Vixos warrior guard outfit. Her make-up, usually derived from a palette of blacks and slightly darker blacks, was completely different, rouge on the cheeks and pink glitter lipstick around the mouth. She had donned a huge red wig which crested over her head and fell in tassels around her shoulders.

She looked absolutely stunning. And she looked exactly like Lily Sparkes.

"Wow."

"I know. I could sooo get used to this."

"And for my next question: why?"

"We're a guard short. The thin blonde girl didn't turn up this morning. Sandra Kettering? So, I agreed to step into the breach! What do you think?"

"You look amazing."

"I thought you'd appreciate it. I know you sooo love the 1980s stuff."

She did a little twirl.

"This is her costume. I'm a bit bigger than her, but it's great that Spandex is so stretchy, isn't it?"

"It certainly is."

Victor was on his way between the tents. He saw Kit, waved, and realised who Kit was talking to. He scrambled over to them, his eyes wide and fixed on Freya.

"Wow."

"That's just what I said," said Kit.

"Mate. You look completely… Well. You do. Completely…"

"Yes, she does."

Freya grinned. "I know. I might even do cosplay. I'm not a cosplay person as a rule, but this outfit feels sooo great."

"It's just… great… just… wow. Just wow." Victor recovered himself – with some difficulty – and said, "This is going to be a great reconstruction. You're going to make all the difference, mate."

With all the pink rouge on her cheeks, it was difficult to know if Freya was blushing, but Kit guessed she was.

"Thanks, both of you." Her smile was now incredibly broad. "I'd better say hello to the other girls and practise my moves."

She turned and ran back to the ladies' dressing-up tent, her cloak flapping in the wind.

"Wow," breathed Victor again. "Just wow."

64

The filming was going very smoothly. Even though the shoot was in a chalk pit and featured a giant spaceship, it was much less technically complicated than day three.

Roger was nursing a hangover, but he was still hitting his marks and saying his lines. The fact that his character was extremely irritated to be on the desolate planet of Chevron mirrored Roger's current state of mind, so his performance was really good and very atypical for Roger.

The dialogue between Vanity, Patrick and Roger was dashed off in no time, and it looked like they were able to start early on the next bit – where Patrick addressed the Vixos troops and Vanity led them over the rise to confront the Styrax.

The first problem happened when Roger finished his lines and he made a dash for the privacy of a tent to call his insurance people about his yacht. He bumped into Freya, who was holding a coffee cup in her hand. It was just a tiny nudge, and the cup was almost empty, but a few drops of coffee slopped onto her top. A handful of dark circles about the size of pennies appeared over her bosom.

"Oh no! Oh no!"

"Sorry about that," said Roger brusquely. "But I really have to make this call. Sorry…"

And off he went. Freya looked down helplessly. Knowing that if she patted them or tried to rub the stains off it would only make things worse.

"Oh no!"

Kit looked around. Robbie and Binfire were setting up the next shot, and Victor was nowhere to be seen. She realised she had to take charge.

"Come on," she said to Freya. "Let's go to the costume tent and see what Joan can do."

* * *

Joan was sitting reading her book and puffing on a cigarette. She looked up quizzically when Kit and Freya entered, and visibly stiffened when she saw the stains on Freya's top. "Oh gracious me! What's happened?"

Freya was near to tears. "I'm sorry. I'm sooo sooo sorry."

"It wasn't her fault," explained Kit. "She was holding a cup of coffee and her arm got nudged."

"No excuse!" she snapped, gripping her cane. "Everyone takes care of their own costumes. That means avoiding potential nudging hazards."

Freya whimpered.

"There's no way we can clean the outfit out here in the middle of nowhere. You'll have to stand at the back. Or not take part at all," she muttered.

But once she'd conducted a close examination of Freya's bosoms, she stopped harrumphing. She even sounded amused.

"Not to worry," she said at last. "As you can see, the coffee stains are all in the same area..." She rooted in her plastic case for something. "I'm sure I have some pasties in here somewhere..."

"Pasties?" Freya was confused.

"Nipple covers, dear. Ah!" She brought out two glittery golden circles, about the size of drinks coasters, and placed them over Freya's nipples.

"There, that completely covers up the marks. Luckily, I bought some more heavy-duty tit-tape which should do it."

She applied the pasties to Freya's bosoms and invited Freya to look in a mirror.

"There," Joan chuckled. "History is repeating itself."

Freya looked alarmed. She looked at Kit and winced. "They're a bit... suggestive?"

Joan sounded miffed. "Well, that's the best I can do. Take it or leave it."

"She'll take it," Kit said. "Thank you so much." She steered her to the edge of the tent.

"I can't wear these." Freya was aghast. "I look sooo like a stripper."

"It's fine," said Kit.

"It's sooo not."

"It really is. Look. You know the scene we're doing? One of the girls was wearing pasties just like those."

"Really?"

"You really haven't noticed it before? Everyone else has."

"Well... No..."

Kit picked up her phone. "Give me a second..." She had turned it off to avoid disturbing the filming, so now she had to endure the faff of putting it back on. Finally, after an age, the Apple logo appeared and the screen resolved itself. Kit googled 'Lily Sparkes' and pressed 'Images' and numerous screen grabs came up. She showed Freya.

"There she is, right at the front."

Freya looked up, surprised. "Oh yes."

"Just like the original. I'm betting if you stand in the exact same place, in the front row, Robbie will be cock-a-hoop."

Freya put on a determined expression. "You're right, Kit. I've got to do this. Our mission is to replicate *Vixens from the Void* exactly as it was, and I know that Wolf will be up there in cult heaven expecting me to do this. I will sooo act like I'm part of a matriarchal society that doesn't care what men think, and my provocative outfits are my business and my business alone. Thanks Kit."

She marched out of the tent and into the scene. The girls had begun to stand in two rows of four, and Freya joined them in the place once occupied by Lily Sparkes.

Kit was too far away to hear the dialogue, but she watched Robbie come over to Freya, put his hands on his hips and examine her with stunned incredulity, and after a brief exchange of words, he gave Freya two vigorous thumbs up, to Freya's obvious delight.

Kit was about to leave the tent when she realised something.

"Oh."

There was something she'd missed, and now the universe had given her a second chance to work out what it was.

"Joan."

"Yes, dear?"

"Can I ask you something?"

"Of course, dear, what can I do for you?"

"When I interviewed you back at the Pavilion, you talked about making repairs to a girl's costume."

"That's right."

"Lily Sparkes' costume."

"If you say so, dear. I'm not good on names. If it was the red-headed girl who joined us on location twice, and jumped off the pier, then yes, it was her."

"When you talked about it, you held your hands out in front of you, like you were saying her bosoms were the source of the problem."

"They were. Her bosoms *were* the problem, and she should have realised they were a potential problem."

"So, call me stupid, but I assumed at the time that the problem was they'd become suddenly *larger* between the two location shoots. But… that wouldn't be a problem, would it? Not with Spandex?"

"Well, of course not dear. Lycra… Spandex is stretchy. That will prove no problem if someone changes shape."

"So if the problem was not the size. Then…"

"That's why I used the golden pasties. Do you know, I think they were the exact same pasties I just used on your friend just now! The girl – Lily – she'd marked the costume with her nipples. Stained it with her milk."

"Her milk?"

"She was lactating, dear. Made a bit of a mess. I told her at the time she should have taken precautions…"

65

Kit stood stock still outside the tent, staring at the filming taking place in front of her. Staring, but not looking. Her gaze was turned inside her head,

She was frozen to the spot, almost terrified to move in case the thought tried to escape.

She'd realised long ago that thoughts are not static things; they plop into people's heads like drops of ink in water, and she knew it was important to allow them to spread. The thought grew larger and fatter in her mind, like the stains on Freya's top, and then that thought gave birth to more thoughts, and those thoughts meshed together to form a scenario in her head.

An Incredible Scenario.

Jackie's tape was still in her backpack. She listened to it again to make sure. With the Incredible Scenario now secure in her head, she noticed all the other things she'd missed, tiny inconsistencies that her brain had skated over and which had now become hugely significant.

She had to talk to Binfire. But he was busy. Perhaps she could leave him a message? She texted him.

Binfire I know what happened to Lily. We need to talk ASAP. As soon as we finish here we need to make a trip. We need the minibus and your drone.

As was customary whenever her phone was in her hand, she checked Twitter to see what everyone was talking about. Fear Of Missing Out was another one of her syndromes.

That was odd. She blinked furiously, unable to believe her eyes.

'Lily Sparkes' was trending.

And 'Jackie Hillier'.

Her fingers trembled over her phone, not knowing what to do, not knowing which name to search for first. She chose Jackie.

There was a string of tweets, all different and all the same, from Sky, the BBC and general Twitter users, all with the identical two-minute video attached. Jackie was sitting in front of a blue background with *Sussex Police* written on the back.

There was a grim-faced policeman sitting to one side of her.

Kit pressed the arrow in the middle of Jackie's forehead and it started playing.

Jackie was obviously in distress but trying to hold it together. She read from a prepared statement in a flat voice, drained of emotion.

"Yesterday evening at about six-thirty, I was taken from my home. My attacker forced me to the ground and injected me with something which rendered me unconscious. When I woke up I found I was blindfolded, tied hand and foot, and held inside the boot of a car. I was kept there for several hours. At one point the boot of the car was opened. My kidnapper disguised his voice and told me that they killed my friend Lily Sparkes, and they had decided to kill again."

Kit's body went completely numb. She had to put the phone on a nearby trestle table because her fingers had been turned to rubber.

"After another hour, the boot opened again. I was made unconscious again. When I woke up, I was untied and lying in what I later realised was part of the East Brighton nature reserve. I managed to find someone to help me and I was driven to the police station. Thank you."

There was a flurry of noise from the assembled journalists and the policeman leaned into the microphone. He opened his mouth to speak and the screen went black, with *Watch again?* over the top.

Kit's mind whirled. She put 'Lily Sparkes' into the search bar and there were thousands of tweets with the same queasy-blue school photo of Lily accompanied by infinite variations of the same basic headline:

LILY SPARKES NOT A SUICIDE? KILLER THREATENS TO KILL AGAIN

She emerged from the tent like she was in a dream.

Everything outside was carrying on as normal. Vanity and the girls were just about to yomp up the rise to see the Styrax for a second time.

The first take was in the can. Binfire had used a handheld camera from the top of the incline (the infamous high-angle boob shot). After they'd finished that take, Victor rushed out with a rake to obliterate the footprints they'd made in the sand.

Now for the second take – the experimental one – using the drone. Binfire had his remote control in his hands and the drone was buzzing about forty feet above his head. Robbie sat in his director's chair, his face a mask of concentration.

"You ready?"

"Yep," said Binfire.

"Rolling!" yelled Robbie.

On cue, Vanity and her squad of Vixens charged along the chalk pit once again, up the steep incline, cloaks flapping behind them. The drone zipped over their heads and hovered high above them, waiting for them to reach the summit.

Vanity got to the top and stopped, puzzled, looking over the rise. The girls were also looking confused.

Robbie looked up at Binfire.

"Was that okay?"

"Nope. Sorry. There's a van. It's driven right up to the top of the quarry. It's in the shot."

Vanity turned and shrugged helplessly at Binfire and Robbie.

"We've got company, darling! I think it's the police!"

The van emerged over the horizon, nudging the Styrax, causing it to overbalance and knocking it down the incline. It performed a graceless pirouette before landing face down on the floor of the pit.

It was indeed a police van. Policemen with guns spilled out of the back and they trained their guns on the spaceship. One of them was holding a megaphone and there was a crackle as he turned it on.

"Roger Barker. You are under arrest for the murder of Sandra Kettering, and for the murder of Lily Sparkes. You have the right to remain silent."

Roger, who was leaning on the spaceship fiddling with his ray gun, didn't seem to process what the policeman was saying. The crackly megaphone didn't help. He wandered towards them, into the centre of the basin to hear better, and the air cracked with the sound of half a dozen rounds being chambered in half a dozen rifles.

The megaphone crackled again.

"Let's not do anything stupid, Roger. Put the gun down. Slowly."

Roger looked dumbly at the ray gun in his hand. Then he looked at the huge prop behind him, as if contemplating using the spaceship to make a getaway. Then he looked at the array of marksmen on the brow of the hill. Then he put the ray gun down on the sand slowly and raised his hands.

66

The filming of the 'Back to Brighton' Blu-Ray documentary was now officially over.

The police took Roger away. And they took Bethany away too, in a separate car. As Sandra's closest friend, she had been invited to the station to be interviewed about Sandra's whereabouts last night. She looked scared and distraught, a little girl not in control of events.

Once the police had gone, they packed up in a daze. Binfire drove them back to the hotel and the air inside the minibus was thick with questions. Patrick was doing his best to answer them. He made phone calls to some 'friends' to find out. No one questioned Patrick's sudden ability to tap into the police information network, but he explained himself anyway.

"I've got some mates who work on *Wistful*. Coppers that ITV hire as consultants. They've got a bit of insight."

He confirmed, as delicately as he could, that Sandra had been murdered last night. To a background noise of sniffs and stifled sobs (Sandra was known to most of the other girls) he explained that she had been stabbed on Brighton beach.

They got to the hotel. The girls dispersed into Brighton to phone families and friends. Vanity, Patrick and Joan went to their rooms to pack. Time to go home.

Binfire, Robbie, Victor and Freya prepared to go back to Pulborough to supervise the dismantling of the spaceship and the tents. Kit was supposed to go with them, but she hid, turning off her phone. She waited until the minibus pulled away before knocking on Patrick's door.

Patrick opened his door. His face was grim.

"Come in."

Suitcases were waiting by the door. He was ready to go.

"So what didn't you tell us?"

"I didn't want to go into detail because the girls were already upset… But, yes, Sandra Kettering was stabbed last night, on the beach, near the marina."

"The marina?"

"Exactly. They're guessing from her conversation with her friend Bethany she had gone there to meet someone. They're assuming it was Roger. She tried to fight her attacker off. There's blood under her fingernails, and they're double checking, but it is Roger's. His DNA is already on file. I won't go into the details of that one."

"What about Jackie?"

"They found her carry-case in the back of Roger's car under a blanket. It was empty. The actual cassettes… They found them in a pile on the beach, not far from where Sandra had been killed. Someone had poured lighter fuel on them and torched them. And there's also evidence that someone was kept and tied up inside the boot of Roger's car."

He wearily ran his fingers through his lustrous grey hair. "Now, I *know* what you're going to say. You're going to say Roger's been framed."

"Of course he's been framed! Everything is just so staged! Why burn the tapes and leave the carry-case to be found? If Roger's blood is under Sandra's fingernails, that explains everything. That explains why someone drugged him and took his blood! The syringe! Remember the syringe!"

"Kit…"

"And that same someone could easily have taken Roger's car keys and locked Jackie in there overnight. He was only using his car to drive to the Pavilion and back. Someone has really made a huge effort to frame him. We've got to do something!"

"Kit—"

"And what? Someone whispered in Jackie's ear that he'd killed Lily thirty-five years ago and he's just *now* decided he was going to kill again? Is any of that *remotely* convincing?"

"I agree with you, and believe it or not, a lot of the coppers I've been talking to think it's all a bit whiffy too. But at the end of the day there's a lot of evidence pointing at Roger and no evidence pointing to anyone else. Unless something else turns up, he's going to be charged."

"You've got to do something."

"What can I do? I'm just a civilian like you!"

"So you're not going to do anything?"

"I have done something. I have told you to go to the police with your suspicions about Lily's teacher. We both agree that something is going on there, but *no one's* going to address it until you tell the police!"

Kit made a big show of thinking. She considered telling Patrick about her Incredible Scenario, but what was the point? She didn't think it would change Patrick's opinion.

Finally she said, "I hear you, Patrick. I hear you loud and clear. You're right. I'll go to the police station in the morning and share my suspicions."

"Good girl. You know it makes sense."

Good girl? I'm nearly thirty!

Oh well. What do you expect? He's just as much of an old sexist dinosaur as Roger.

Kit looked at the suitcases. "What are you going to do next?"

Patrick sighed. "Much as I'd love to hang around and see what's going to happen to our celebrity sailing friends, I've got to get back to London. Rehearsals start for the next season of *Wistful* on Monday."

"I understand."

He held out his hand. "Goodbye Kit. It was nice working with you. I felt quite nostalgic."

Despite her instinctive distaste for skin-to-skin contact, she took his hand and shook it.

"Ditto. I won't say it's been fun, but it has been unforgettable."

67

It was Friday, the day after the end of filming. Early morning. Kit had checked out of the hotel.

Mags the purple-haired girl said, "I hope you enjoyed your stay?"

"It's been… It was pleasant."

"Great."

"I don't suppose… Could I leave a message for Jackie Hillier?"

Mags took a sharp intake of breath. "Well, I don't think she'll be in for a while. Did you see the news?"

"Yes."

"Crazy business. But when she does come in, I'll make sure she gets it. You can use our headed paper."

She brought out a piece of paper and placed it on the counter. Kit looked down at the blank rectangle, empty but for a tiny line drawing of the hotel, and the contact details.

"Actually, it's okay. I'll leave it."

"No worries. Hope to see you again soon. Going anywhere nice from here?"

"Not really. I'm going to Crawley."

* * *

Kit walked to the railway station, her little suitcase grumbling on behind, and her Mandalorian backpack slapping against her shoulders. Parked in the middle of the taxi rank, much to the annoyance of the drivers, was a large white minibus.

Binfire was lying on the roof, a khaki baseball cap covering his face and a cocktail stick dancing around his mouth. Cab drivers were trying to get his attention, hooting and hollering and banging on the roof next to his head. They were rewarded with Binfire's middle finger.

Kit walked up to the minibus and spoke next to Binfire's ear. "Sunbathing in February?"

"I got your text, pilgrim. One minibus. One drone. One driver. As requested."

"Thank you. I think we'd better get going, before our incognito mission causes a riot."

Binfire pulled the cocktail stick out of his mouth. "Riots are a perfect cover for incognito missions."

Another honk, and another screamed profanity.

"But time's a-wasting. This tank has to go back to the rental shop by end of play today."

* * *

As they drove up the A23, Kit explained how she'd worked out that Wolf had visited Crawley, how Jackie had supplied the address of Lily's teacher, her meeting with Mary Creehan, and the discovery of Wolf's calling card attached to the pinboard.

"Sounds like you've stumbled onto something big. That's good little grey cells at work, Poirot. So where does your faithful assistant, Dr Watson, fit in?"

Then she explained her theory.

"Frokk. That's frokking crazy. That's the most insane thing I've ever heard. And I listen to my own thoughts *a lot*."

"You can back out at any time."

"No frokking way. I trust you. You and me are in this together, right to the end."

"It's going to be a bit of a waiting game."

"No problemo. I've brought Dobble."

68

They reached Phoenix Place and parked across the other side of the square, putting the children's playground between them and the tower block. Binfire rummaged in his rucksack and pulled on a strap. A shiny black shape popped out of his bag.

"Got my night-vision binoculars. Don't worry, I've got them switched off."

They waited for hours. After they exhausted the delights of Dobble, out came the Travel Scrabble, then Guess Who?, then back to the Travel Scrabble. And just when morning gave way to afternoon, Binfire spotted a figure leaving the main doors.

"Is that pink furry thing her?"

He passed the binoculars to Kit and she peered through them. "Yes, that's Mary."

"Right. Time to spring into action."

"Okay."

"Just remember whose go it is. And don't look at my letters."

Binfire put the drone on the roof of the minibus, switched it on, and they watched it hum and rise into the air. A couple of the children on the swings watched it as it glided away, but there was very little interest. Drone-flying was more common than kite-flying these days.

Binfire stared intently at the screen on his controller. "I can see a window. I can see lots and lots of windows."

"It's the one on our left at the top, facing the playground. She keeps the blinds open so she can watch the birds."

"I can see a coconut shell hanging outside."

"That's it."

Binfire twitched the paddles and the coconut shell loomed large in the screen of the handset.

"Okay, where now?"

"If you go to the right of the window and angle the drone to the door, you will be able see a little table right beside it. If I'm right, there should be a photograph on the table."

"Here goes nothing. I'm getting good at this. One extreme close-up will be delivered."

The screen wobbled as the drone manoeuvred to one side. There was the little table. A tiny black photo frame on top. But the photo was obscured by the edge of a pot plant.

"Can you make it clearer?"

"Sorry pilgrim. It's not the movies. You can't tap on a keyboard and enhance grid reference pinky-perky bollocks. That's a great big pot plant in the way and that's the way it'll stay."

"Damn." She slumped lower in the passenger seat. "I suppose we'll have to think of something else."

Binfire licked his lips. "I already have, pilgrim. I already have."

Kit looked at the screen. Binfire had moved the drone to the left of the window and was aiming it at the far wall where the theatre posters were. They had been replaced by photos. Photos of a baby. Photos of a child. Photos of a family. Photos of an adult.

"Frokk," said Binfire in a tiny voice. "You were right."

"I am. Criminy with an extra side order of shit."

Binfire brought the drone back to earth. They stared at the film they'd made. They played the last few seconds, as if hoping that the images would miraculously change.

They didn't.

"What do we do now?"

"We confront her, and persuade her to turn him in."

"And if she doesn't? What if the pink furry woman pulls out a shotgun?"

"Then…"

"We need insurance."

"I'll send a text. If anything happens to us then they'll know what we've done."

"You mean they'll avenge our deaths?"

"That's about it."

Then they waited again, this time for Mary's return. They didn't go back to the Travel Scrabble. The magnitude of what they'd witnessed rendered them wordless.

She was back in less than an hour, carrying two bags of shopping. They gave her fifteen minutes to get into her flat before Kit dialled her number.

"Hello?"

"Mrs Creehan?"

"Yes."

"It's Kit Pelham here."

"Yes?"

"I came and interviewed you about Lily Sparkes, the day before yesterday?"

Was it only the day before yesterday? It felt like months. Years even.

"What about it?"

"I was in the area, and I just wondered if I can talk to you again about Lily?"

"Now?"

"As I said, I am in the area right now. I might not come this way for a while…"

"It's not really convenient."

"Oh, but you did say I was welcome to turn up any time and take a few photos and programmes and stuff."

"Oh. I did, didn't I? But it's still not a good time."

"That's a real shame. This tribute to Lily Sparkes is really taking shape and I just need your help, just one more chat, and I can pull it all together. I think it's going to be really moving. I don't think there'll be a dry eye in the house."

There was silence at the other end of the line.

"Okay, just give me ten minutes to run a duster round. The place is a bit of a mess."

She ended the call.

"What can I say?" said Kit softly. "I'm very good at getting interviews."

69

If Mary seemed hostile over the phone, she couldn't have been nicer when she opened her little white door. She ushered them into her spotless flat and gestured to the chairs, inviting them to sit.

"Hello again!" she beamed. "Long time no see!"

"Haha, yes. This is my colleague, Ben Ferry. He's been helping me with my research and he's editing the documentary together."

"Oh really. He sounds like a complete technical wizard, if not a real one. Come in, come in. Would you like some tea?"

"Um…"

"Or maybe coffee?"

"Oh. Coffee? That would be nice."

"Wonderful! And you, Mr Ferry?"

"Coffee's good."

"How do you both take it?"

"Black," said Kit.

"I take it like the Millennium Falcon," said Binfire.

"Flat white, you mean? I must say, Mr Ferry, I love your ear necklace! Very novel!"

They sat around the table while Mary Creehan busied herself in the kitchen. Kit leaned over to Binfire and whispered, "She knows the flat white joke."

"Of course she does."

"Look. Note the family photographs have disappeared from the wall."

"Yes pilgrim. I have noted that the wall has completely transformed from what it was thirty minutes ago. I'm not a complete space cadet."

Mary bustled back with a cafetière and some cups. She had already made herself a cup.

"That one's mine, I'm trying to go decaf. This is a very stressful neighbourhood sometimes. Help yourself to milk and sugar, why don't you? The only biscuits I've got are digestives, I'm afraid. Shall I get my pile of memorabilia out and you can go through it again?"

"Well, not yet. Before we do that, we'd just like to tell you we've discovered something a bit surprising about Lily."

Mary pushed the plunger down, poured two cups of coffee and nudged them along the tray to Kit and Binfire.

"Surprising?"

"And a bit disturbing, actually."

"Oh dear. What about Lily?"

"We believe that shortly before she disappeared to go to Hollywood, Lily discovered she was pregnant. And she had a baby."

Mary looked askance, first at Kit, then at Binfire. "Really? That sounds absurd. I don't think that's the case. You must be mistaken."

"No, I think you'll find we're correct."

"Surely not."

"It's true."

"No. You're wrong."

"No. I'm right."

"Absolutely not."

There was a long pause. Binfire leaned over to Kit again.

"You're meant to show your workings, Poirot. Do your amazing deductions."

"I don't want to do that. That's embarrassing. I'd feel stupid."

"Do it anyway."

"What's the point? I know it, you know it, and she knows it. I don't have to convince her because she knows it already."

Binfire sighed. "I'll frokkin' do it then." He turned to Mary, who was watching them with perplexed indulgence. "Okay. Quick sum up: when Lily 'came back from America'" – he did air quotes – "her breasts had got really big. Cos that happens when you give birth. Agreed? Everyone agrees that happens. Doctors, everybody, blah blah. Lily was clever, though, and she was good at thinking on her feet. Smart cookie. She told her friend Jackie she'd had a boob job. Jackie believed her without question because a boob job is such a Hollywood thing to do."

Binfire picked up one of the digestives and stuffed the whole thing in his mouth.

"Awwywy…" He chewed furiously and swallowed. "Anyway, Lily forgot that her lactating breasts would make a mess of the costume. Joan Peverin was really upset about that. Also, did you notice that I used air quotes when I said Lily 'came back from America'?"

He did air quotes again, this time in Mary's direction. "Did you notice that? Did you notice the air quotes? That's because she didn't actually go to America at all. She stayed in Brighton."

Mary clapped her hands to her face. "Now Mr Ferry, that's silly. She did go to America. Of course she did! She called her parents and her friend Jackie from America and told her! Everyone knows that. If you're going to slander Lily, I'm going to have to *ask you to leave*."

"Tell her, Kit."

Kit sighed. "Come on, Mary, we know. We listened to one of the tapes. She gave herself away so many times."

Binfire held up a finger. "Another summing up. One: Lily said she was going to audition for *The Dukes of Hazzard*. That had been cancelled by 1986. Kit spotted that one, because she's a real telly nerd."

"I just looked it up on Wikipedia. It's not hard."

He held up a second finger. "Second thing. On the tape, when Jackie said she was going to have her breakfast, Lily said *she* was just about to have her breakfast too. What, in LA? With a seven-hour time difference? I don't think so! If it was eight o'clock here it would have been the middle of the night over there. Not breakfast time. Not usually. I think I'm the only one I know who eats breakfast in the middle of the night."

Kit's voice was filled with pity. "It's a ridiculous story, Mary. And you said it yourself, as did Jackie. Lily was a very practical, level-headed girl. A girl like her running off to America to be an actor without any qualifications? And actually managing to get auditions for TV shows? It's nonsense. What about her green card? Did she even have a passport?"

"It just doesn't pass the smell test," added Binfire.

"So she didn't go to America," Kit continued. "But she *did* run away. But realising that her disappearance was causing an absolute circus – a manhunt, items on the local news – she remembered Tara's *terrible* advice about aspiring actors, so she rang her parents and told them she had gone to America. There wasn't a lot they could do with that news. In the days before social media there was no easy way to prove that what she said wasn't true."

Binfire slurped his tea. "Even if her folks did try to go complete Columbo and put a tap on their phone to trace her whereabouts, Lily made a point of calling Jackie instead of them, and Jackie would never have agreed to help track Lily down."

"I don't know what to say," said Mary. "I'm stunned at this revelation. If what you say is true, then where was she all that time?"

"Oh please," sighed Kit. "Are we still going to go through this charade?"

"Charade?"

Binfire stepped in. "She lived with *you*, of course."

"Me? That's absurd."

"Where else? She couldn't stay with the whacko parents." Binfire made a dramatic gesture, sweeping his arm across, but the cup was still in his hand. The coffee slopped onto the table.

"Shit. Sorry."

"Not to worry, I'll get a cloth."

She disappeared and appeared moments later with a kitchen towel.

Binfire stared at her glassily while she cleaned up.

"There. No harm done. Now, where were we?"

Binfire scrunched up his face. "Haven't a clue."

"Y-you were saying she couldn't stay with her loony p-parents," Kit prompted.

"Is your stammer coming back?"

"Course not. I'm not ssstressed." She looked at Mary. "Am I ssstressed?"

"You don't look stressed," Mary said.

"No. I'm not. So on you go."

"Right. Where was I?"

Kit sighed. "You were *saying* she couldn't stay with her parents!"

"Right. Yeah. Can you imagine the reception she would have got if she'd gone back to them and told them she was up the duff?" He frowned. "That's all I was going to say. Doesn't seem worth it now."

Kit added, "But iss a good point. Can you 'magine her p-parents letting Lily raise her child how she wanted?"

Mary said, "Well, there we do agree. They were the most unpleasant people. I would have said that any child in that environment would have had difficulties. Lily was able to testify to that."

"Exactly. And Lil… Lily couldn't move in with, um… Jackie, cos… Um… Jackie, she was still living with her folks." Kit gave her head a shake and blinked. Then she pointed a shaky finger at Mary. "Yuh–You were the only cannidate."

Mary sighed and poured them both another cup of coffee. "Really, you two. Can you hear yourselves? You've been working too hard. You've become obsessed with Lily. You've concocted this mad story out of nothing…"

"Nnno," said Kit, shaking her head violently. "Nno we din't. Nnnot cun-cuncosted out of nothing. Because w-we were assed to vestigate a mmurder."

"Murder?" Mary sounded politely astonished. "A murder? So it's a murder now. When will this ever end? So Lily was murdered now?"

"Nno. Nnot her. Our friend Wolf. Well, his friend Wolf ackshuly…"

She waved a finger at Binfire, who had already started to snore.

Kit looked at Binfire and then slowly back to Mary, smiling sweetly and drinking her coffee. Then Kit frowned, which took a lot of effort because the muscles in her face weren't working. Then she tried to turn her head back to Binfire and found her head wouldn't move.

70

The first thing Kit noticed when she woke up, apart from the drumming in her head, was that her hands were tied behind her.

Not rope. Some kind of plastic. She guessed zip ties. It wasn't a difficult deduction, because Binfire was lying on the sofa facing her, and even though she couldn't see his wrists she could see plastic cables around his ankles.

Binfire was awake and staring at her.

"Finally," he said. "Are you alright?"

"I'm fine." Her voice sounded small, like it was coming from behind the sofa. "How about you?"

"Nothing damaged. How about you?"

"Only my pride. Frokk it. Why did she have to drug the coffee? I could have resisted tea, but fresh coffee?"

"I know. Ditto. Where's Mary?"

Someone came into her line of vision. Someone wearing black cargo pants and a black polo-neck. He sat down on the coffee table and pushed his face close to hers.

"I sent Auntie Mary out to get some shopping," said Victor. "Because we need to talk, mate."

Victor was very calm. Unnaturally so. He lounged on the sofa like it was a lazy weekend at 33 Hanover Parade. He drank from a cup which smelled of fresh coffee.

"Don't worry," he said. "I've made some fresh. That would be embarrassing if I drugged *myself*. That would be *really* embarrassing."

"You crazy frokker," said Binfire.

"Please stop with the silly fake swearwords, Binfire. It's very irritating."

"Frokk you."

Victor didn't address Binfire. He turned instead to Kit. "Tell Binfire to shut up. Tell him to shut up, or I will hurt *you*."

"Binfire…"

"If you frokking hurt her I will slice you open like a tauntaun and use you as a tent."

Victor patted Binfire on the head. Binfire stretched his neck out and tried to bite Victor's fingers.

"Alas, poor Binfire. Falling in love with the only lesbian in the group. How very Binfire. I guess we all have our crosses to bear."

Binfire growled.

"Stay quiet for now, Binfire," said Kit. "Victor obviously has a lot to get off his chest. We should let him talk."

Victor grinned at Kit. "You're talking. No stammer, I see, mate."

"I'm not afraid of you. And I'm not your 'mate'."

"I've killed two people. It's not like you to discard facts so lightly." He took another slurp of coffee. "I bet you're wondering why I'm here waiting for you."

"I'm not."

"Yes you are, Kit. Because I *know* you, mate. Well, I'll tell you why I'm here. You make one visit to Auntie Mary in Crawley, and yeah, I can safely assume we got away with it. But you make a *second* trip, and I have to conclude the game's up."

He laughed. "Ironic. Word to the wise: if you tell a hotel receptionist where you're going, make sure the hotel receptionist is aware that that crucial information is supposed to be secret and not to be freely discussed with other interested parties. I came into the hotel and asked reception if you'd checked out yet, and she told me you were off to Crawley."

He laughed again. "So ironic. Vanity ended her first marriage that way and tried to get my mum fired for *her* mistake. Loose talk is never good. Vanity lost her husband, who knows what you're going to lose by the end of today? So, I came here to intercept you. And here you are."

"Here, as you say, we are."

"I don't blame Auntie Mary. She is so careful. She is truly a diamond. A saint. She took down all my photos before you came last time, got the whole place ready, but she forgot Wolf's card on the board. You know Wolf, he forced it on her, right at the end of the meeting, practically threw it at her, and she just stuck it up there in a tearing hurry and forgot all about it."

He tapped his fingers on his mug.

"Wolf was here. You both know that. When Wolf and I were researching the new book, I dropped Lily into the conversation. Nudged him into thinking about her death. Conjured up a few sensational theories in his head. I thought, maybe he would agree to give her a mention in the book, and people would start asking questions about Lily's death again, maybe work out who was actually responsible?"

He shrugged. "But Wolf… I underestimated the old bastard. He went all in. He did a lot of research…"

"I would, if I was in his place."

"You would. But he's not like you, Kit."

"That's true."

"He was never the kind of person who rings people up and politely asks for an interview. He just turns up and doorsteps them. He loves – *loved* throwing people off balance. He looked up everyone who was mentioned in the articles about my mum's death and found their addresses. The old guy who was the witness, the one with the dog, he was dead, of course. So was the dog. So he turns up at Jackie's flat uninvited. She wasn't at home. She was probably on holiday. I mean, it was high summer. So then Wolf comes straight here, to Auntie Mary's. He surprises her, pushes his way inside…"

He gestured to the wall of photos, now restored to their proper place.

"And he sees the photos of me." He walked to the wall and took one off.

"This is me with Uncle Kenneth."

He brought it across to show them, holding it in front of Kit's face. "We're on a sea-fishing trip. I caught a huge bass that day. It was eight pounds. I swear. We were grinning ear to ear all the way home."

"Very nice."

He held it in front of Binfire.

"Look."

Binfire didn't answer. Victor looked at Kit.

"He's being a bit sulky."

"You told him to shut up or you'd hurt me."

Victor frowned. "So I did."

He put the picture back on the wall.

"Anyway, mate. There we go. Me and Uncle Kenneth. I didn't call him Uncle Kenneth then, of course, I called him 'Dad'. And Auntie Mary was 'Mum'."

He shook his head. "Anyway, Wolf goes and confronts me. You heard the phone message from him. I sent you it."

"I heard it."

"He's telling me he knows, right in that message. 'Baby' this and 'baby' that. Cheeky bastard. So he gets the full story out of me. I admit to him that my mum was Lily Sparkes, and my dad is a *Vixens from the Void* star. This makes me a celebrity by association, and he wants me to 'come out' live as a guest on his podcast. I didn't want to do that. I didn't want to be *that* person, known for just that one thing."

How funny, thought Kit. *He's echoing Dorothy's words. She didn't want to be known as 'just' that trans woman. She wants to be seen as a person.*

And it's true of everybody isn't it? Nobody wants to be known for just one thing. I never wanted to be 'just' a fan. I wanted to be a professional fan, a podcaster, an interviewer, a writer.

Who wants to be 'just' a fan?

Victor bit his lip sadly. "I did *tell* you what happened. Didn't I? When I killed him?"

"Yes."

"I told you, in not so many words."

"You did."

"I agreed to do his podcast, I pretended to be really enthusiastic about it, really up for it. But that was to lull him into a false sense of security. I knew I'd have to drug him and kill him. But the drug did take a bit too long to take effect, and there you have it. A livestreamed murder."

He put down his coffee and stared at Kit. It wasn't a threatening stare. He was just appraising her.

"I bet you worked that all out."

"Most of it."

"The minute you saw my photo on that wall over there you must have worked out who my mum was. And then you worked out it was me with the secret, so it had to be me who killed Wolf."

"Before that."

"Seriously?"

"Oh yes."

"I don't believe you. You're just trying to act clever, like you always do."

"Fine."

"You couldn't have known."

"Victor, why did you think I didn't tell you about our mission to Crawley if I didn't have a pretty good idea who you were? Why would I take Binfire on a secret mission if I trusted you? You were part of our investigative team, after all."

"Hmm."

"See?"

"But I bet you haven't worked out stage two. I bet you haven't worked out *why* we're doing this documentary. Cos it's not to find out who killed Wolf is it? I *know* who killed him. It was me!"

He struck himself on the chest.

"So that wasn't the reason. I bet you haven't worked out why we're doing it, have you?"

"I have, actually."

He pouted. "I don't believe you."

"I have. I've worked it out."

Darkness crept into his voice. "Don't play games with me, mate."

"I'm not playing games. You just have to ask me, and I'll tell you."

"Okay. Fine. Why are we all in Brighton filming this documentary, with all these guests?"

Kit smiled.

"You did all this so you can find out who your father is."

71

Victor pursed his lips.

"You guessed."

"Yes."

"Damn you. You *are* clever, mate."

"I am."

"When did you guess?"

"Yesterday, in the tent with Joan, when I discovered Lily had been pregnant. What if she had a child? He or she would have been around thirty-five now. About your age. Then I remembered you said you were born five months after the first episode aired. That meant you were born nine months after the first location filming of *Vixens from the Void*."

"So I was."

"So going from that hypothetical, that you were Lily's son, I tried to work out what you'd actually been trying to do while we were filming this documentary. I made a list of things that had happened that didn't make sense. Like, for example, that sabotage of the new costumes on the first day. Putting sticky tape inside the helmets? What was all that about? Graham didn't do that. It's ridiculous for you to say he did."

"No, he didn't."

"And Roger getting drugged and having a needle mark on his arm on the second day, what was the point of that? And then your mysterious theft of Graham Goldingay's, erm... phallic merchandise? That was *really* weird of you to steal it. Not in your character at all. None of it made any sense..."

Kit fidgeted a little. Her bonds were getting uncomfortable.

This is the second time I've been tied up in three days, she thought. *Anybody would think I had a fetish.*

"But then I realised what they all had in common. I worked out what you were doing. You were collecting DNA samples."

Victor slapped the arms of his chair and shook his head in amazement.

"You clever bastard. You clever, clever bastard."

Even Binfire emitted a soft, "Frokk," under his breath.

"You weren't investigating six suspects for murder. You were investigating the three men who were at the location filming for both shoots. Three men. Roger. Patrick. Duggie. One of them you knew was *definitely* your father."

"All true."

"You put the sticky tape inside the helmets to pull out some of Patrick's and Roger's hair by the roots, to get DNA. You got Patrick's hair, but Roger never put his helmet on, did he? So you tried something else, a bit more daring. You slipped something in Roger's drink and waited until he went to bed…"

"Ohh…" Binfire finally made a noise.

"Yes Binfire. I used your credit card trick to break into Roger's room earlier in the evening, just after he started drinking, and taped over the latch. I slipped a little something into his drink, and when Roger went to bed he was so out of it he didn't notice his door didn't lock. He just fell onto the bed, dead to the world. I walked in and took some of his blood. So easy. He didn't even stir."

He shook his head and grinned.

"My rotten luck that Freya pushed the schedule under the door just as I'd finished and the door popped open. I hid behind the wardrobe. She saw Roger lying there, screamed and ran. So I dashed out, leaving my spare syringe behind. Rookie mistake. But I *also* left the sticky tape on the latch! Good job Freya called me back into the room, so I could peel it off behind my back while I was blathering on to you and Patrick."

"Then there was one DNA sample left to collect," said Kit. "Dorothy's."

"Possibly the hardest one, but then again, the easiest one," said Victor. "The tricky part was getting Graham to bring the merchandise with him. I persuaded him that it was a good idea, just in case Dorothy decided to walk out on the documentary halfway through. It would show her he meant business if he had it physically with him, and he could photograph it and put it on eBay in front of her, or he could conduct a live Zoom auction."

"You are one sick puppy," said Kit.

"Don't judge me," snarled Victor. "Everything worked out fine, didn't it? You got your heart-warming moment with your girlie gang, and Dorothy is free of Jabba the Hutt. I just took a little piece of her to check her DNA. And no, Dorothy is not my father. I have a department in my hospital that can do very quick and reliable DNA tests. And Patrick isn't my dad either."

"Of course not. Roger's your dad."

"He is. Roger by name and Roger by nature. And after I found that out, I went into phase three…"

He leaned into Kit's face.

"Revenge!"

72

"So you framed Roger for murder. You kidnapped Jackie and you put the fear of God into her, and you killed an innocent girl, Sandra Kettering, and you planted evidence to make your dad into a murderer."

"Yes!" Victor's eyes gleamed. "He killed my mum. He got away with it before, so he should go down for the same crime. A teenage girl is dead, and now he's being held accountable. It's poetic."

"But how?"

"How?"

"Yes, how?"

"I don't understand the question."

"How did he kill your mum?"

"Oh, he didn't push her off Brighton Pier himself, but he killed her."

"I know, but how?"

"How? How can you ask that?"

"Pedantry. I'm good at pedantry. How did he kill her?"

"He got her pregnant and left her, of course."

"Did Roger know he got Lily pregnant?"

Victor didn't want to say the word.

"Did he know?"

"No."

"Did *anyone* know she was pregnant? Because that's the impression I've been getting from those who were there at the time. Patrick, Tara, Dorothy, Roger, Vanity. None of them have even speculated or hinted about the notion of Lily having a baby. None of them had a clue. Apart from Joan. She had the information, but she was so disinterested in those girl extras it didn't even register in her mind as important."

Victor got up, wandered across to the dining table and kicked a chair.

"Fuccck!"

His anger having vented, he sat back down, gathered himself and spoke. "Auntie Mary told me that my mum kept the pregnancy – and the identity of my father – a total secret. She didn't want the slightest chance that her crazy parents would find out about me. She had me on the floor of Auntie Mary's house, in Brighton, and she went back to work a few months later."

A tear emerged from his left eye and struggled down his cheek.

"The only clue she left us about the identity of my father was a few days before her death. She told Auntie Mary that she'd seen my father. She didn't mention his name, but she'd seen him, while on location filming, and she was sad she couldn't go up to him and tell him about me, because she was scared he wouldn't take responsibility for me, and it would all leak out, and her parents would swoop in and ruin my life."

He stared at Kit. "Can't you see? Can't you see how he was responsible?"

"No, I can't," said Kit brutally. "I can see a girl trapped by her own crazy parents. It's their fault more than anything."

"Well, they're dead."

"Exactly. You're not lashing out at them because you can't. Roger didn't kill your mum. The truth is what it always was. She committed suicide."

This stung Victor.

"She was murdered, Kit! If he hadn't got her pregnant, she wouldn't have been so… so…"

"Depressed?" Kit said dismissively. "That's why she did what she did. She killed herself. She was probably suffering from post-natal depression. She felt alone. And she threw herself off Brighton Palace Pier."

"I see." He sneered. "I see what you're saying. You think it's my fault."

"I think that's what *you* think. I think you're utterly twisted with guilt over your mother's death."

Victor stood up again and stared out the window. "I don't know why we're even having this conversation. This is waste of time. I'm not here to justify myself to you. Keep your amateur psychology to yourself, mate."

He went into the kitchen.

"So what do we do?" whispered Binfire.

"We keep him talking."

"But he's sooo boring. You sent the text message, right? When we were in the minibus?"

"Yes."

"Who to?"

"Freya."

"Freya? Why the frokk did you send it to Freya?"

"I couldn't think of anyone else! I don't have Patrick's contact details, and I couldn't very well email his agent! And I can't text Robbie and tell him his boyfriend is a mass murderer. Who else could I text?"

"Okay, what did you tell her?"

"I told her I knew Victor murdered Wolf. I told her why I knew. I told her where we were, and I told her if something happens to us to track down Patrick and tell him."

"But not to *do* anything, like *rescue* us?"

"What's Freya going to do? She can't do anything. She's a goth. What can a goth do? Convince Victor of the hopelessness of life and the futility of existence?"

The bead curtains tinkled as Victor emerged from the kitchen.

"What are you two talking about?" snapped Victor.

"We were just discussing what title music we should have for the 'Back to Brighton' documentary. I was thinking 'Brighton Rock' by Queen, but Binfire thinks it should be 'Drowned' from *Quadrophenia*, or of course we could go full retro and play the *Carry on Girls* theme tune."

"You're so fucking funny, both of you. Right little Laurel and Hardy."

"So what happens now?" said Kit.

"You should turn yourself in," said Binfire. "We rang 999 before we came up. It's only a matter of time before we hear the nee-naws."

"I *told* you!" yelled Victor. He lunged over to Kit and slapped her. Hard. Kit's head rang with a high whistle.

"Get it now?"

Binfire didn't answer.

"Well, if you did call the police, they are taking their own sweet time. Funny that…"

Victor's phone was on the dining table. It rattled across the surface. He looked at the screen and fear crossed his face.

"It's Freya."

He reached out to the phone, then withdrew his hand, then reached out again, tentatively, as if it were hot. Then he snatched it up. "Hello?"

The voice was tiny and squeaky. It sounded agitated.

"No, they're *not* with me," he said. "No, I don't know where Kit and Binfire are. You got a what? That's bollocks! Kit's just gone crazy. No, they're not with me…. What *about* the minibus?"

He looked out the window. Victor's shiny BMW was parked untidily on the pavement. Outside it were Robbie and Freya, looking up at him. Freya was still yelling into the phone. She was also pointing across the square at where Binfire had parked the minibus.

Robbie was screaming up at him, his face pink with the effort. The words were distorted by the acoustics of the square, but Kit and Binfire could just hear the words "please" and "love you".

As Victor stared, he noticed a procession of blue flashing lights on the horizon. He ended the call. His face had become paler than Freya's.

"Fuck," he said. "Fuck," he said again. "Right."

He dipped his hand into a carrier bag on the floor and pulled out Binfire's flare gun. He pressed *speaker* on his phone and the dialling tone erupted from the speaker. It rang only once before Freya's voice was heard:

"Victor, what's—?"

"Shut up. This is what's going to happen, Freya, so listen."

Robbie's voice joined hers.

"Victor, you need to explain yourself—"

"You shut up too, mate."

There was a silence. Then Robbie said, "I love you."

Victor said, "I know. I wish you didn't."

More silence.

"I don't believe that."

Victor was crying now, but his voice was steady. "You believe what you want to believe, Robbie. But I'm telling you, it's all been a lie, mate. My whole life has been a struggle to get out from under my past. I got into *Vixens* because my Auntie played it to me, the only thing she could show me to give me an idea of what my mother was like. I loved it, and then I hated it…"

With a shudder of horror, Kit realised something dreadful.

The story I confessed to Jackie? The one about being born and forcing my parents to miss the final episode of their favourite TV show? It feels incredibly similar to Victor's story. The feeling of letting down a parent. The urge to overcompensate as a result of the guilt…

We're a cliché! Victor only has to say to me the words 'we're very alike, you and I' and I'll literally die of cringe.

Victor was still talking to Robbie on the phone. "…because as I grew up, I realised this was the thing that ruined my mother's life. I've been so sick of it. Every time you open your mouth and say something about Arkadia, or the Styrax, or the planet Vixos, I just want to punch your stupid face in, and keep punching until you never utter another word about it." Victor sighed. "It's not you. It's me."

There was no response.

"Hello?"

"It's me," said Freya. "Robbie's gone for a walk across the park. He's a bit upset."

"I'm sure he is. Look, this is what's going to happen. You're going to go far away, and you're going to tell the police to evacuate this building. I've got Binfire's flare gun, and I've turned on the gas in the kitchen."

Kit sniffed the air. A familiar sickly smell was faint but getting stronger.

She called out, "He's not lying, Freya! I can smell it."

"Kit?"

"Listen to Kit, Freya. She knows what she's talking about. If *anyone* comes knocking on that door, I fire this gun and I take the top off this building."

Victor ended the call with an angry jab, and his face folded in grief. Saliva bubbled on his bottom lip and a rope of drool descended, forming a silver thread between his chin and his mouth.

He slumped on the back of a chair, hanging his head.

"So that was your game plan, Victor. Find your dad, send him to prison for murder, and walk off into the sunset?"

He nodded. "Pretty much."

"No one would even know you were Lily's son. And after a decent interval you would – what? Sell 33 Hanover Parade, leave fandom and Robbie and Freya and Binfire, and forget about *Vixens from the Void* for ever?"

He nodded again. He raised his head.

"And this is plan B? It's quite a plan. Are you going to ask for a helicopter and a billion pounds?"

She started to cough. Even though the window was open, the smell of gas was starting to become very strong.

"I don't know. Maybe. I don't know."

Binfire said, "Bullshit."

Victor pointed at him. "I've warned you, mate."

"You're not going anywhere. You're gonna torch this place whatever happens, aren't you buddy?"

"Shut up."

"Binfire, shush."

"Look at him. I've seen that look on a man's face before. When I saw action in Korea."

"You saw action *figures* in Korea. You made a trip over there to see them being made."

"Yeah, but I saw things out there. I saw this guy, his job was to paint the dots in the eyes of Macho-Man dolls for twelve hours a day. His expression was just like Victor's."

Victor raised the flare gun. "Don't make me fire this, mate."

"You're gonna do it anyway, Vicky-boy. It's a bit late to make threats. In fact, while we're waiting to get fried, I think I'll go for a walk and get some fresh air…"

Before Kit and Victor realised what was going on, Binfire had struggled to his feet and hopped madly towards the door like he was a competitive dad in a school sack race.

Enraged, Victor dashed after him, knocking him to the floor and slamming the butt of the flare gun in his face. Binfire lay there, blood smeared across his lips, cackling hysterically like one of the better Jokers (*The Dark Knight*, 2008). He spat out a tooth and kept on laughing.

"Stop laughing, you idiot!" screamed Victor.

That was when Victor heard the shouts outside from the

spectators far below, but by then it was too late.

There was a clatter and *flumph* behind them, and Kit strained to see the source of the noise.

It was Dorothy. She had climbed in through the window, catching the coconut half-shells with her shoulder as she jumped to the floor. Binfire had seen her at the window and distracted Victor so she could enter undetected.

She landed in a combative crouch and launched herself at Victor, accelerating like a sprinter. Victor barely had time to react before Dorothy's right fist exploded against his jaw.

Victor swung the flare gun wildly, trying to aim, but Dorothy grabbed his arm like the experienced fight choreographer she was. She dropped, twisting his arm so it locked at the elbow, creating enormous pain. Victor let go of the gun with a yelp and it landed with an incredibly loud clatter, as Dorothy pushed him backwards so she had room to land an incredibly well-placed punch between Victor's eyes. He collapsed like a sack of coal.

Dorothy scrambled to the kitchen to turn the gas off and open all the windows. Then she went back into the kitchen and emerged with a wicked-looking carving knife, which she used to saw at Binfire's straps.

Binfire struggled to his feet, feeling his face tenderly.

"Frokk it. Broken nose. I'm gonna look even more beautiful now."

Dorothy attended to Kit, sawing at her bonds.

"Hello," said Kit.

"Hello."

"Can I ask what you're doing here?"

"You texted me."

"I texted you?"

"By mistake. I think you meant to click on 'Freya' but you clicked on 'Fletcher'."

"Oh my god."

"Not to worry. I forwarded it to Freya, but it sounded urgent, so I decided to make my own way here. I was in London and it's only an hour on the train."

The straps gave way and Kit leapt up, rubbing her wrists and jogging on the spot to free her from the pins and needles.

Dorothy slumped on the sofa, struggling not to hyperventilate, waiting for her heart rate to slow.

"Jesus," she said at last. "I don't want to do that again in a hurry."

Kit looked at the window. "Did you just climb all the way up this tower block?"

"Yes," she gasped.

"All the way up, no ropes or anything?"

"Freeclimbing. Yes."

"And you with your vertigo?"

"You're welcome."

Kit sat down alongside Dorothy and put her hand on her knee.

"Oh my god. You're so *brave*."

"Oh piss off," said Dorothy.

But she was smiling.

73

Burly policeman crashed into the flat, shouting and pointing their guns in all directions. They were huge, and looked even bigger because they were encased in helmets and bullet-proof vests.

Once they realised the danger had passed, they calmed down and took Victor's unconscious body downstairs. As Kit was escorted gently into the sunshine, she saw a fleeting glimpse of a pink furry shape in the back of a police car. Auntie Mary had also been picked up.

Kit, Binfire, Freya and Robbie were taken to Brighton police station and statements were taken. Kit was interviewed until she hated the sound of her own voice. The questions were exhausting and repetitive. For the first time ever, Kit truly understood what it felt like to be a star of an old science-fiction show being asked the same questions about the same incidents over and over again.

When she was released, she didn't check in with Binfire or the others, she just ran to the train station. When she got to Tunbridge Wells, she ran home, her suitcase careering crazily behind her, and didn't stop until she was at her front door.

Mrs Lilywhite from the downstairs flat was looking after Milo. Kit knew that she would be looking out for Kit's return, and sure enough, two minutes after she got in the door there was the pitter-patter of paws on the steps outside, the clatter of the dog-flap and Kit was mobbed by a rocket-powered sausage delivering an avalanche of licking and tail-wagging.

She felt safe and loved. She didn't want to think about what had happened, and she *certainly* didn't want to leave the safety of her little flat ever again.

74

One year later

Roger Barker was very quickly released without charge He obviously had nothing to do with the murder of Sandra Kettering, and the police decided not to press charges about his unwitting involvement in Graham Goldingay's people-smuggling. They literally had their 'Mr Big'.

Roger bought another yacht and called it *Nautical but Nice*.

Not only did Roger escape prison, but he also got a few juicy anecdotes for his future sci-fi con appearances. Kit knew that it would be just a matter of time before Roger would be on stage, recounting an incredible story about how he solved Sandra Kettering's murder and thwarted a major celebrity-smuggling ring single-handed.

However, with Graham out of the picture, there was no one to buy off the many girls he'd bothered in his long career. Already there were rumblings that a young actress was considering informing Operation Mulberry about an incident in a hotel room during filming in the Canary Islands.

* * *

As Victor's trial unfolded, it became clear why he had concluded he needed to blow up Phoenix Place. He was protecting his beloved Auntie Mary.

On that fateful night in 1987, when Lily fell to her death, Mary's husband Kenneth followed Lily to the pier. He had seen how depressed she had been over the last few days. He could see Lily had been grappling with so many things, concealing the truth about her 'gap year' in the US, moving back with her parents, and most of all, only being able to see her baby at odd times when her parents were looking the other way. And her parents *never* looked the other way. All that combined with post-natal depression meant Lily was in a dark place.

Kenneth had had little Victor in the back of his car when he saw Lily leave the hotel. He was hoping to cheer her up after she'd finished work by surprising her with a brief reunion.

He saw her go to the pier. He waited for her to emerge. When she didn't, he went inside to look for her and found the note stuck to the railing.

I'm sorry. I just can't cope with it all. I'm going to end it. Sorry. I don't want to live any more.
Lily.

Reeling from what it said, he gazed into the dark waters and tried to see Lily. He saw nothing. Leaving the note where it was, he returned home and told Mary the terrible news. Mary urged Kenneth to go back to the pier and try to help the coastguard to find her. When he returned, the alarm had yet to be raised. It was still quiet.

Kenneth went out in his own boat and managed to find her body. He brought it to shore on a secluded patch of waste ground near the marina and informed his wife.

Mary and Kenneth watched the desperate search for Lily unfold, the coastguards, the helicopters, and knew what it meant for them both. They could not bear the thought of handing Lily's child to anyone, not the authorities, and certainly not Lily's parents. Realising any autopsy would reveal that Lily had recently given birth, and being uncomfortably aware that a baby suddenly appearing in the Creehan household might prompt awkward questions, Kenneth buried Lily where she lay and they made immediate plans to move away from Brighton. They sold up and moved to Crawley, picking the most inaccessible, anonymous address they could find.

When the marina expanded in 1996, Kenneth had no choice but to go back and dig Lily up and bring the remains to their new flat. He was in the process of working out a new location to dispose of them when he died suddenly of a coronary.

Lily's dry and dusty bones were found in a large suitcase on top of Mary's wardrobe. Mary had been intending to tell Victor about their whereabouts for some years, but she felt he already had a lot on his plate, so didn't bother him. Victor was told by his aunt that his mother's remains were in the flat literally minutes before Kit and Binfire turned up.

So Binfire was right. Victor was prepared to blow everything up to spare his Auntie Mary jail time. All this had come out in the trial, but it seemed that Victor's defence team hadn't finished yet.

* * *

Kit was sitting in a soulless room, waiting to be cross-examined by the defence counsel. She had already appeared for the prosecution, where she laid out what she knew, and her part in what happened, in exhaustive detail. She did rather well, she thought. The recapping of facts settled her, and she didn't stammer once. But now she was about to be cross-examined.

The prosecuting counsel, a fussy man with thick glasses, walked back and forth in front of Kit, sighing uneasily. His expensive shoes *tik-tik*ed monotonously across the cold marble as he paced to and fro.

"You're going to be fine."

"I know," said Kit.

"The facts are all established. There's nothing more to be said."

He was saying it to convince himself, rather than Kit.

As she was called to the witness box, she allowed herself a quick look up at the gallery. Robbie was there. He had attended every day of Victor's trial, sitting loyally in the gallery like a labrador waiting for his owner to come home. He had written many letters to Victor, all with no response.

There was Freya, in her usual black clothes, but also wearing a veil, making a point of still mourning her beloved Wolf. And there was Binfire, a splash of colour in a sea of drabness. He made no concessions to formality, aside from leaving his ear necklace at home and replacing it with a garish tie that hung loosely around his neck.

And Jackie was up there too, just like she was that morning. She was smartly dressed in a dark blue trouser suit. Her face was unreadable. She stared straight at Kit, but not smiling, not as a friend, more the gaze of a child looking at a fish in an aquarium.

Kit moved her eyes down from the gallery to Victor, sitting in a glass cubicle at the back, looking bored by proceedings. He was back in his oversized suit and looking like his old self.

Victor caught Kit's eye and gave a sly grin.

Kit felt very small.

The counsel for the defence, as thin and angular as the prosecuting counsel was large and pudgy, took to his feet.

"Ms Pelham, thank you for giving us your account of events this morning. I just want to go over a few details." The counsel for the defence made a quick recap of what Kit had said before lunch, for the benefit of the jury. He said it all in a semi-incredulous tone, as if the facts were in dispute. He was careful to say 'alleged' a lot.

Finally, he said, "It is an incredible story we have heard here today, is it not?"

"Yes. Yes it is."

"A man pretending his mother was murdered as a pretext, in order to assemble his potential fathers together, discover who begat him, and thus inflict revenge through murder of an innocent. An act almost Oedipal, wouldn't you say?"

"I would say it's a bit more like an evil ABBA musical."

That got a titter from the jury. Kit smiled at them.

The counsel did not look amused. "I would say it was a plan so incredible in its execution that it boggles the mind."

"I would agree."

"Yet once you realised who my client's mother was, you worked his plan out with incredible speed."

"Thank you."

"Unbelievable speed. Such a genius."

"Yes."

"That is the aspect that I find so incredible. You were clever enough to work *that* out, but you were *not* clever enough to be aware of what you were doing when you were shooting this documentary."

"I wasn't."

"You had not a clue."

"No. Not a clue."

"Really?"

"As you said yourself, it was an incredible plan. Difficult to work out from the outside looking in."

"You insist on your story, that you thought you were part of some 'murder mystery weekend' to discover the truth of the decades-old demise of Ms Sparkes."

The scorn in his voice was evident.

"Yes. And to find out who killed Wolf Tyler."

"Indeed. But I put it to you, Ms Pelham, that you are much cleverer than that. I put it to you that you knew what was going on from the start, and that you were manipulating my client to perform these acts."

So this is what this is about. Nothing of this is about helping Victor's defence. He just wants to drag me down. Make me an accomplice.

Kit felt a flash of anger.

He knows I'm going to blush. He knows I might start to stammer. I'm going to look so shifty. He could very well put me in a great deal of trouble.

You utter bastard, Victor…

"I really don't see how that can be the case."

"You assembled my client's possible fathers together. You brought them together, interrogated them yourself for possible connections to my client's mother."

"To find out if they were responsible for Lily's death."

"Just so. However, it can be viewed, in my humble opinion, in a completely different light: that you knew you were bringing them together to help find out who my client's father was, and in doing so use this information to spur my client into a rage and goad him into a murderous act."

Kit controlled herself with a mighty effort. "I think we've gone over these facts. Victor was collecting the DNA to find his father, not me."

"Are you telling us you had absolutely no clue?"

"No, I didn't. And Binfire – Mr Ben Ferry – he backed me up, didn't he? He was there in the coffee shop when Victor lied to us. He agreed with me that that was exactly what happened."

"Yes. Mr Binfire. His testimony was interesting… was it not?"

There was another faint titter from the jury.

"I think we might take his very colourful testimony with a grain of salt…"

The prosecuting counsel had had enough. He stood and puffed himself up like a robin trying to attract a mate.

"Your Honour, I humbly object. Ms Pelham is not on trial today. The police have already decided there is nothing in Ms Pelham's actions that reflects badly on her role in this. And we too have listened to the facts of Ms Pelham's involvement in this matter, and my learned friend has not brought any more facts to light with his fishing expedition."

The judge looked down from on high.

"The defendant has a right to a defence, Mr Shaw. The cross-examination will continue." The judge eyeballed the defence

438

counsel. "But please, Mr Levar, less innuendo about Ms Pelham's motives and more direct questions. Questions pertaining to the deaths of Mr Owen Tyler and Miss Sandra Kettering, if you please, which is, after all, the reason why we are here."

The defence counsel had nothing but innuendo about Kit, and he had no intention of asking a string of questions about Wolf or Sandra, all of which would reflect poorly on his client, so he knew it was time to end it.

"I just have one more question for you, Ms Pelham. And may I remind you that you are under oath. You do take the truth very seriously, don't you?"

"I do."

"Then answer me this. When did you *really* become aware of my client's true intentions? Was it on the morning after Ms Kettering's death, as you claim, or was it earlier? Months earlier? Right at the start?"

75

"Thanks for seeing me, mate," said Victor.

The prison visitor's room looked like the saddest canteen in the world. Lots of tiny little tables spaced far apart. Muttered conversations between unshaven men in grey sweatshirts and harassed-looking women.

Victor didn't look haggard, not like the other prisoners. Despite his ugly grey sweatshirt and jeans, he looked good. His chin was shaved and his gaze was clear, as if he hadn't had a single sleepless night since he was arrested.

"You're looking well," she said.

"Thanks mate."

"Very clean-looking."

He grinned in that lazy, arrogant way of his. "Robbie sent me a Loin King deluxe box to keep me fresh. It works just as well on my chin as it does on my scrotum. You can tell him that, if you like. That might make him happy."

"I don't want to be here," Kit snapped, her eyes darting around the room. "This is the last place I want to be. I'm only here for Robbie. You won't reply to his letters and you won't see him when he tries to visit. He's going spare about not seeing you."

Victor looked unmoved.

"You said in your letter that if I came to visit you, you'd consider seeing him."

"'Consider' is the word. I've considered and the answer is 'no'."

"You were never going to say yes."

"Correct."

"Then why am I here?"

"You were my biggest mistake, Kit. I should never have got you involved. I underestimated you. I thought you were just another nerd who would switch off their brain at the prospect of working with their heroes, like Freya and Robbie."

"Thanks for the compliment," said Kit coldly. "Thanks for wasting my time."

She started to get up to leave but Victor grabbed her hand.

"Sit down, mate."

Alarmed, Kit looked around, but the warders weren't looking in her direction. *I can sound the alarm*, she thought. *I can raise my voice, yell at him to let go of my hand, but that would mean everybody would turn to look at me.*

She sat back down.

"I just want you to know that you could have stopped me," he grinned. "Right at the start. You could have stopped me. I knew you suspected right from the start. When we met in the coffee shop."

"That's ridiculous." She sounded uncertain.

"Oh no it's not. I know it's not. When I told you my plan, and you said it was like *Hamlet*, I looked shocked. I couldn't help myself. And you saw I was shocked."

"I don't know what you mean."

But she had. Kit *had* seen the expression on Victor's face.

"Cos, when you said it was like *Hamlet*, I didn't immediately think about 'the play's the thing catching the conscience of the king' stuff. My mind went to the plot, and my brain went to jelly right there and then. Because when all's said and done, what is *Hamlet* about, Kit, mate?"

Kit supplied the answer. "It's about someone taking a long time to get revenge. Taking revenge on behalf of a dead parent."

Victor gave a delighted snort. "I knew you'd get it. I was so shocked when you said '*Hamlet*'. I thought you'd worked it out right from the start. Thank god you hadn't."

He leaned back and put his hands behind his head, a familiar Victor move. "I just wanted to let you know that you had the answer at your fingertips, but you didn't do anything about it, and because of you a woman is dead. I just wanted to put that in your head. Call it payback for putting me and my aunt in jail."

He stood up and made an imperious gesture to the warder.

"Thanks. You can go now. Show this lady out."

76

Nine months later

"When did you *really* become aware of my client's true intentions? Was it on the morning after Ms Kettering's death, as you claim, or was it earlier? Months earlier? Right at the start?"

Kit's pedant monster started to wake up.

It uncoiled itself from its dormant position and started to mutter in her ear.

I think you'll find, Kit, the pedant monster hissed in its usual compelling way, *that we suspected right from the start. The moment you mentioned* Hamlet. *That was the moment, wasn't it? Wasn't it? That was when you thought something was up. You have to tell them that's when you suspected something was off. Just say it. For the record...*

Kit gripped the rail of the witness box tightly. The pedant monster was trying to break free. She could feel it.

"Well? Was it when you claimed, or was it earlier?"

Kit did not blush and she did not stammer.

"As I said before lunch." She spoke very slowly and clearly. "I only worked out what Victor was doing on the morning after that poor girl's death. I tried to make sense of what was happening. God knows I racked my brain until it hurt trying to work it out, but I can honestly and truthfully say that nothing made any sense to me until that moment – the moment I worked out who Victor's mother was."

And that was that.

77

The defence's attempt to throw sand in the eyes of the jury was in vain. Victor was given a minimum term of thirty years. Auntie Mary was given a five-year sentence for assisting her adoptive son.

Robbie plunged into grief after the trial finished, and Freya did everything she could to snap him out of it. Freya didn't see it as odd to console Robbie over the loss of *his* boyfriend for murdering *her* boyfriend. Life was funny like that.

She finally scooped him out of his depression when she and Binfire enlisted his help to set up a sci-fi convention in Brighton. 'Bri-Fi' was set around the Pavilion, with a particular emphasis on dressing up. They held a competition called 'The Lily Sparkes Memorial Cosplay Contest' where everybody dressed up as Lily Sparkes in her Vixos warrior guard guise, and the winner got awarded a 'Lily', an action figure sprayed gold mounted on a wooden plinth.

Joan and Dorothy were two of the guests of honour. The third guest was Mervyn Stone, co-creator of the classic *Vixens from the Void* and showrunner of the new series.

When Kit found out about this, she couldn't resist. She asked Freya, Robbie and Binfire if she could come down to interview him.

Kit hadn't been to Brighton for a year, not since the trial. Her dissociative disorder had kicked in, and she'd put everything out of her head. Kit had only thought of that traumatic week at the Hotel De La Mer once in the last six months, when she'd received a complimentary copy of the Blu-Ray box set in the post.

So, she came down to interview Mervyn Stone. When she arrived, she found Freya and Robbie and Binfire had put together a novel spin on the usual convention. Most of it was held outside, in the grounds, with stalls, autograph tables and a live *Nerd Mentality* podcast hosted by a local comedian who was almost, but not quite, as offensive as Wolf Tyler. The interviews were held in the Pavilion, but as large numbers of people were forbidden to traipse into the building because of the priceless historical artifacts, big screens were erected in the gardens for the attendees to watch while lying on the grass.

She interviewed Mervyn Stone in the music room. It was a very odd experience. There was only her and Mervyn, and Binfire training a camera on the both of them.

She knew the first question she was going to ask.

"So why did you decide on a continuation of *Vixens from the Void*, and not a reboot?"

Mervyn was always slightly overweight, but success had made him distinctly tubby. His bizarre shock of grey hair, which used to look like it was searching for ways to escape his head, was now controlled with expensive hair products. Someone had had words with him and told him if he was going to appear on behind-the-scenes documentaries, he had to look a bit more presentable.

"Well, I'm not a fan of reboots, really," said Mervyn. "You spend time and effort creating all those characters, people get to know them and love them, and then you suddenly announce to the world, 'no, they're not good enough, I'm going to keep the names, which are irrelevant anyway, and then you recast them and change them completely so they might as well be new characters anyway.' I know others will disagree but I find it a little insulting."

"But there are advantages," Kit said. "You can wipe the slate clean, avoid all that baggage."

"But you can do that anyway, by starting the story a little further down the line. And the best bit about doing a continuation, like our new series, is that you can have one or two of the 'classic' characters turn up from time to time, and they can interact with your new characters, and that gives you more opportunities for drama, don't you think?"

"Oh absolutely. I loved Vanity turning up out of the blue and interacting with the new main cast. It makes it feel the same, but also fresh."

"And to be honest, the idea of having to create a new world from scratch... As a writer, even the thought of it sounds utterly knackering."

Kit laughed.

"Take it from me, Kit," he said. "Never waste a character. Never make them a one-off when you can make them a continuing presence in the show. The audience appreciates it, and there's never the tiresome process of having to work out what the next character's backstory is."

The interview continued, and Kit asked the standard questions. *How did you feel when you were told* Vixens *was coming back? Did you ever think about handing it over, like George Lucas did with* Star Wars? *Did the big budget feel daunting?* But just as during the interviews she conducted two years ago in the same location, her mind was buzzing with other things.

The interview concluded to muffled applause from outside. She thanked Mervyn profusely and left the convention without a backwards glance. Binfire watched her leave. He didn't shout out to her or call her back. He knew her too well not to notice that she was going on another mission.

The marina was a long walk, but Kit didn't mind. She was enjoying the sunshine and enjoying rolling Mervyn's words around her head.

Take it from me, Kit. Never waste a character. Never make them a one-off when you can make them a continuing presence in the show. The audience appreciates it, and there's never the tiresome process of having to work out what the next character's backstory is.

Kit rang the bell, and the door opened before she took her finger off the button.

"So the wanderer returns," said Jackie.

"I'm sorry for what I put you through," said Kit. "I didn't realise I was helping the man who kidnapped you."

"Huh."

"I assumed Lily was murdered, when of course the truth was simpler. That's how reality works. Just post-natal depression. I was seduced by a fantastical story, and I should have been more critical from the start. And if I'd talked to you earlier, I might have realised that."

"That sounds like a prepared statement." Jackie's face was grim.

"It is a bit. It is a lot, actually."

"I got put through hell two years ago."

"I know."

She sighed. "But then, when everything came out, I heard you were put through hell too."

"That's true."

"We both suffered a bit of trauma."

"I guess we did."

"I suppose we owe it to each other, to help each other through our traumas."

"That sounds logical."

Jackie reached out and grabbed Kit's waistcoat. She popped open the top button with a long thumbnail.

"Let's see if we can get rid of that thundershirt for a start."

"Criminy," said Kit.

78

When Kit's shaking fingers undid her shirt buttons and peeled away the white cotton, Jackie's tattoo was revealed in all its glory. It was a dragon that looped past her breast and down to her elbow. With its cruel face and huge talons, it would not have looked out of place in the Brighton Pavilion.

As Kit moved her lips over Jackie's shoulder, she felt tiny ridges where the dragon's scales were, running down the length of its body. She realised that the dragon was there to hide physical scars from an old injury. Jackie must have been sensitive about the imperfections, because she lifted Kit's lips from her shoulder, kissing her deeply on the mouth and taking her by the hand.

"Through here," she said.

Jackie's bedroom held an innocence, a capsule of happy times in the past. Of someone never quite ready to leave childish things behind. All the classic teenage obsessions – ponies, ballet, pop stars – were still on display. Teddies and rag dolls lay limply on the bed, piled high like bodies waiting to be thrown into a plague pit. Jackie swept them onto the floor and pulled Kit by the pockets of her waistcoat and swung her onto the bed. Then they fell upon each other, holding each other tightly.

* * *

Later, they spooned. Kit lay under an eggshell-blue duvet cocooned by Jackie's body, big meaty arms surrounding her and holding her fast. Kit felt completely secure for the first time in ages, longer than she could remember, and she dozed contentedly, eyes half closed, gazing at the bottom of a windowsill and the corner of a white bedside table.

There was a photo of Jackie and Lily on the table, two young girls in school uniforms standing with their arms around each other laughing at the world.

The table had a tiny drawer covered with stickers: Rick Astley, Bananarama and the Bangles. The drawer contained pens and a diary and a vibrator. And one more C90 cassette. This one had no writing on the side because it wasn't supposed to exist.

"Slow down, Lily. I don't understand what you're saying."

"It's not hard to understand, Jax. I'll say it slower. I'm leaving."

"Again? But you only just got back from Hollywood."

"I never went to Hollywood."

"You never went to Hollywood?"

"Yeah, I was hiding in Brighton."

"What the fuck?"

"It's a long story, and I don't have time to explain. Because I'm going tonight."

"They won't let you. Your folks won't. They'll find you and stop you."

"I don't care. I'm done with Brighton. I'm going to fake my own death."

"You're going to... what?"

"Meet me on the pier tonight. I want to say goodbye to you."

But Kit didn't know what was in the drawer, and what she didn't know couldn't worry her, so she drifted off into a glorious harmonious sleep, filled with dreams of spaceships and planets and stars and cheap-looking robots and beautiful women dressed in tight Spandex.

Jackie dreamed too, but her dreams were more troubled. They were filled with darkness, and cold. There was someone in front of her, someone she loved, shouting wordlessly over the blare of distorted songs, the howl of fairground rides and the distant rush of the sea.

"I've written a suicide note and I've stuck it here. They'll find it, and maybe they'll believe I've thrown myself over and maybe they won't, but even if they don't, I have to hope they'll give up looking for us eventually."

"Us? What do you mean... us? You and me?"

A surge of hope. They would go together! *It was just as she dreamed for so long!*

"No, me and my baby. I got pregnant."

"What?"

"It'll take too long to explain, and I really haven't got time. I've got to get him away from this fucking place, so we can have a good life far away. I'm just here to tell you goodbye, Jax. I'm sorry, but I don't think we'll see each other again..."

They hugged. They hugged for a long time. And when Lily tried to disengage, she found she couldn't. Jackie wouldn't let her go.

"Take me with you. Please."

"I can't. It wouldn't work."

"It would work."

"Be serious. They'll find you gone, and know we've run off together. You've got to stay behind."

"But I love you."

"And I love you too, but not the way you want. You know that."

Jax started to cry. The tears were hot and full of rage. "First you run away, and then you lie to me for a year, and now you tell me you've got a baby, and now you suddenly say goodbye to me again and you can't even be fucking bothered to tell me where you're going?"

"Jax, I haven't got time for this."

"What kind of friend are you?" Her voice was a scream, lost in the screams of many others, hurtling around helplessly on their fairground rides. Round and round. "It's been a whole year and all you've done is hurt me and lie to me! Well fuck you, Lily Sparkes! You're not going anywhere, because I'm going to tell your folks everything! Fuck you and fuck your baby!"

She turned and Lily grabbed her arm.

"Don't you fucking dare."

"Fuck you, you bitch."

"Don't you get between me and my fucking baby, or you will be sorry, Jackie Hillier."

And then there was pushing and screaming and fingernails being raked across the neck and the face. And Jackie was screaming and crying and Lily was screaming and crying. And Jackie was gripping so tightly and ramming Lily against the railing of the pier, gripping Lily's coat and sobbing with a white-hot fury.

And when the rage cleared, there was only one girl left at the end of the pier, lying on the floor and sobbing and sitting beside a railing upon which a sad little note was stuck, sheathed in plastic and fluttering like a wounded bird trying to escape.

And Jackie stumbled away and staggered home.

* * *

Jackie gave a little start and awoke, and she saw that she was back in the present. And she felt Kit's fragile birdlike body beneath her and she felt content. She was home and happy, and she had someone in her arms to love. She had found her new Lily Sparkes.

Jackie drifted away, her breathing grew thick and shallow, and soon she was asleep again. This time the dreams were calm and serene and there was no screaming and no crying.

And Kit slept on, happy, unconcerned. Because she knew nothing. Which was just as well, because after all, it was possible for a fan to know *too* much.

ACKNOWLEDGEMENTS

I would like to thank a few people who were responsible for giving this load of nonsense a ring of authenticity, notably Chris Chapman for his help and advice on the nuts and bolts of producing a Blu-Ray documentary, Dr Alexandra Loske for taking the time to show me around the Royal Pavilion and giving me a few juicy insights into the history of the building, and Ashleigh Lamb for chatting to me about the Brighton branch of Forbidden Planet.

I would also like to give huge thanks to Eliza Clara Hemming and Stacey Smith? for giving me a tiny insight into the Trans experience.

Massive thanks to all at Titan books, particularly George Sandison and Rufus Purdy. Props also to my cheerfully urbane agent Piers Blofeld, and Kim Newman for inviting me to his birthday party and starting the whole ball of wax moving. Thanks also to John Lawton and Jonathan Morris for their consistent metaphorical thumbs-up.

And last, but not least by any yardstick, an appreciative nod to Nicola Bryant for her help, insight and all-round wonderfulness.

ABOUT THE AUTHOR

Nev Fountain is an award-winning comedy writer and journalist for *Private Eye*, chiefly known for his work on the radio and television show *Dead Ringers*. He has also contributed to programmes such as *Have I Got News For You*, *2DTV* and the children's sitcom *Scoop*. A huge *Doctor Who* fan, Nev has written several audio plays based on the series, and occasionally appears as a host or MC at *Doctor Who* conventions. His three Mervyn Stone Mysteries novels – *Geek Tragedy*, *DVD Extras Include: Murder* and *First Among Sequels* – follow the exploits of an ex-*Vixens from the Void* script editor as he investigates crimes. He is also the author of the thriller *Painkiller*. Follow him on Twitter/X at @Nevfountain.

DEATH AT THE DRESS REHEARSAL: A LOWE AND LE BRETON MYSTERY

Stuart Douglas

"The best cosy crime novel since *The Appeal*."
George Mann, author of the Newbury & Hobbes series

In 1970, while on a location shoot in Shropshire for BBC sitcom *Floggit and Leggit*, ageing actor Edward Lowe stumbles across the body of a young woman, apparently the victim of a tragic drowning accident. But there's something about her death that rings the faintest of bells in his head and, convinced the woman has been murdered, he enlists the help of his laid-back, upper-class co-star John Le Breton, a man for whom raising a wry eyebrow is a bit too much of an effort, to investigate further.

Crossing the country and back again during gaps in filming, the two elderly thespians make use of their wildly contrasting personalities and skillsets to uncover a series of murders. But, as the body count mounts and a pattern to the killings begins to emerge, can Lowe and Le Breton put their differences aside to save the innocent victims of a serial killer and still be ready for when the cameras start rolling?

THE MURDER OF MR. MA

John Shen Yen Nee and SJ Rozan

"*The Murder of Mr. Ma* is a joy, with this Chinese Sherlock Holmes and his Watson bringing a thrilling, complex, and thought-provoking new take on 1920s London."
Laurie R. King, bestselling author of *The Lantern's Dance*

London, 1924. When shy academic Lao She meets larger-than-life Judge Dee Ren Jie, his life abruptly turns from books and lectures to daring chases and narrow escapes. Dee has come to London to investigate the murder of a man he'd known during World War I when serving with the Chinese Labour Corps. No sooner has Dee interviewed the grieving widow than another dead body turns up. Then another. All stabbed to death with a butterfly sword. Will Dee and Lao be able to connect the threads of the murders – or are they next in line as victims?

John Shen Yen Nee and SJ Rozan's groundbreaking collaboration blends traditional gong'an crime fiction and the most iconic aspects of the Sherlock Holmes canon. Dee and Lao encounter the aristocracy and the street-child telegraph, churchmen and thieves in this clever, cinematic mystery that's as thrilling and visual as an action film, as imaginative and transporting as a timeless classic.

THE VINYL DETECTIVE: NOISE FLOOR

Andrew Cartmel

"One of the most innovative concepts in crime fiction
for many years. Once you are hooked into the world
of the Vinyl Detective it is very difficult to leave."
Nev Fountain, author of *The Fan Who Knew Too Much*

The Vinyl Detective enters the fraught and frenzied realm of electronic dance music.

Lambert Ramkin aka Imperium Dart, techno trickster and ambient music wizard of the 1990s, has gone walkabout, disappearing from his palatial home in Kent. This isn't the first time he's pulled a vanishing act, but he's never been gone so long before and his wife – wives, actually; it's complicated – are worried and hire the Vinyl Detective to find the old rascal.

But does Lambert, a man known for his love of outlandish and elaborate pranks, really want to be found? And are the increasingly strange scenarios that the Vinyl Detective and his friends keep finding themselves in due to his trickery or something far more sinister?

THE PAPERBACK SLEUTH: ASHRAM ASSASSIN

Andrew Cartmel

"An intriguing mystery with an amoral protagonist. Who knew the world of paperback books could be so deadly?"
Ben Aaronovitch, author of the Rivers of London series

"Packed with Andrew Cartmel's customary wit and cleverness, the Paperback Sleuth novels make a splendid successor to the Vinyl Detective."
Stuart Douglas, author of *Death at the Dress Rehearsal*

When a collection of rare and valuable volumes is stolen from a West London yoga ashram, its leaders turn to Cordelia, the Paperback Sleuth, to recover them – a request that's a little awkward, as they've previously booted her out for dealing weed to the other students.

But once Cordelia takes the job, she finds her quest for the missing paperbacks turning into a murder hunt as those associated with the ashram can't seem to avoid violent death – whether bludgeoned with a whisky bottle or poisoned by an admittedly delicious curry. Can she work out who the killer is and bring them to justice before she ends up as the next victim?

For more fantastic fiction, author events,
exclusive excerpts, competitions, limited editions and more

VISIT OUR WEBSITE
titanbooks.com

LIKE US ON FACEBOOK
facebook.com/titanbooks

FOLLOW US ON TWITTER AND INSTAGRAM
@TitanBooks

EMAIL US
readerfeedback@titanemail.com